CORRUPT PRACTICES

CORRUPT PRACTICES

A Parker Stern Novel

ROBERT ROTSTEIN

SEVENTH
STREET
BOOKS™

59 John Glenn Drive
Amherst, New York 14228–2119

Published 2013 by Seventh Street Books™, an imprint of Prometheus Books

Cover design by Jacqueline Nasso Cooke
Cover images © Media Bakery

Inquiries should be addressed to
Seventh Street Books
59 John Glenn Drive
Amherst, New York 14228–2119
VOICE: 716–691–0133
FAX: 716–691–0137
WWW.PROMETHEUSBOOKS.COM
17 16 15 14 13   5 4 3 2 1

Library of Congress Cataloging-in-Publication Data

Rotstein, Robert, 1951-
    Corrupt practices : a Parker Stern novel / by Robert Rotstein.
        pages cm
    ISBN 978-1-61614-791-4 (pbk.) • ISBN 978-1-61614-792-1 (ebook)
    1. Legal stories. I. Title.

PS3618.O8688C67 2013
813'.6—dc23

2013002602

Printed in the United States of America

To my family

PROLOGUE
April 27, 2010

He'd told his wife that he'd bought the Glock 22 for protection. Now, the barrel of the gun was lodged between his teeth. His heartbeat was normal, his breathing steady. His body wasn't trembling. He'd conquered the legal profession—which to him meant that he'd conquered the world—by mastering the art of calm.

Even now he was thinking, not about his family, but about his law firm. The firm had always come before everything else. It bore his name and appealed to his paternal pride. It gratified his desires. Only during the last two weeks had he realized how poorly he'd served it.

One of his favorite aphorisms was "hubris kills more legal careers than greed and stupidity combined." He'd drummed it into the young lawyers, but hadn't heeded his own words. He'd infused the firm with a virus, believing that he could control its spread. His mistake was unforgivable.

When he heard the *click*, he tried not to gag on metal and fear. There was no longer any point in resisting. This morning's news had reported that the Malibu surf would be particularly dangerous today, bringing powerful riptides that could sweep the strongest swimmer out to sea. The last sound ever to penetrate his consciousness was the crash of an all-consuming wave.

CHAPTER 1

I haven't set foot in a courtroom for eighteen months. I've altered my lifestyle, I tell everyone. I've decided to get out of the pressure cooker of trial work and start over before I turn forty. Only my two closest friends know the truth.

On this afternoon, as on most, I'm sitting alone at a back table at The Barrista Coffee House in West Hollywood sipping a macchiato and reading a book about the law. This one is a biography called *Defender of the Damned*, about famed LA trial lawyer Gladys Towles Root. Root represented mostly murderers and sexual predators because during the forties and fifties no one else would hire a woman. A flamboyant dresser, she was such a skilled advocate that the convicts composed a ditty about her: *Root de toot. Root de toot. Here's to Gladys Towles Root. Her dresses are purple, her hats are wide, she'll get you one instead of five.*

Lawyers truly can become legends.

Deanna Poulos comes out from the back and bops over to my table. She owns The Barrista, so named because she was a lawyer herself, one of my partners at Macklin & Cherry. Not so long ago, she wore pinstripe suits with pencil skirts to work. Now she dresses in black tee shirts and jeggings, and her left arm is half-covered with tattoos. When the firm fell apart, she quit the practice of law and opened her store on Melrose. Everyone told her she was making a huge mistake. But the shop has thrived despite the bleak economy and the cutthroat competition from the chains. I admire her bravery; I envy her freedom; I think she's gone crazy.

"Waz up, Parker?" When she speaks, a silver tongue bar is visible. She touches my cheek, and then playfully pats me on the shoulder in a way that makes the gesture seem less intimate. She glances around as if she doesn't want anyone to overhear, although there's no one around. I think I know what's coming—a story about an ex-colleague's upcoming divorce or latest affair or professional misstep.

"Rich Baxter's in jail," she whispers.

Just because Deanna says it doesn't make it so. This kind of slander flares up all the time, the spontaneous combustion of volatile nouns and verbs.

"Where did you hear this?"

"From him. He called me from the jail."

I was going to take a sip of coffee, but my arm freezes in midair. I set the cup back down on the table so I don't spill.

"The FBI arrested him five days ago," she says. "They're holding him for money laundering and fraud. The Church of the Sanctified Assembly has accused him of embezzlement."

"Rich wouldn't rip off a client, much less his own church. Hell, that guy wouldn't overstay his welcome at a parking meter."

She hesitates. "He actually called me because he wants to hire you as his lawyer. He didn't think you'd take his call."

"Is this your idea of a joke?"

She shakes her head.

"We haven't spoken in years. Why would he possibly want me? "

"Because you're the best."

"Once, maybe. Not anymore."

"If you'd just . . . Wouldn't you enjoy taking on the Assembly?"

"No one enjoys fighting the Assembly. They always make you pay for it."

"It's time for you to get back in the game. To show some guts."

"It's not about courage."

"So you say."

Her words sting. Before I can reply, she gets up and goes back into her office. With her short bottle-black hair, slender body, and swaggering gait, from the back she resembles a rebellious adolescent boy.

This is how it started: I was down at the old Van Nuys courthouse on a simple discovery dispute over a confidential e-mail. Moments before the judge was to take the bench, my cell phone buzzed. I still don't know why I answered the call. It was my partner, Manny Mason. He sucked in air, almost a gasp. "Harmon Cherry's dead. There's an emergency partnership meeting at five thirty. Parker, Harmon shot himself." He started sobbing.

I tried to speak—to ask how it happened, to swear at him, to call him a liar, anything—but I couldn't find words. Then the door leading from the judge's chambers swung open, and the judge walked into the courtroom. I hung up on Manny without saying goodbye.

When the clerk called my case, I stood up, determined to muddle through the hearing despite the odd detachment I was feeling. Harmon used to preach that sometimes the ability to muddle through is a lawyer's greatest asset.

The opposing counsel entered her appearance. When I tried to enter mine—all I had to say was "Parker Stern for the defendant"— my voice caught and my vocal cords felt raw and swollen. The courtroom walls elongated, and the judge's bench became a shimmering mirage. Then my cheeks flushed hot and my stomach leapt up and pressed against my throat. I croaked, "Sorry, Judge" and sprinted out of the courtroom and down the hall to the men's room, where I found an empty stall and vomited. When I finished, I went to the sink and rinsed my mouth out with cold water. Thank God the episode was over. Embarrassing, but the embarrassment would go away as soon as I won my motion. "Victory is the strongest palliative," Harmon would say.

When I returned to the courtroom, the judge was waiting for me. She told me to proceed with my argument, but when I tried to speak, the nausea returned. And then I heard a high-pitched whirr, like a child's humming top. My knees buckled. I groped at the lectern for support, but my flailing arm pulled it down with me, and I tumbled to the floor.

The shrinks call it *situational glossophobia*, a fancy name for stage fright. I've tried everything—psychotherapy, yoga, meditation, biofeedback, Valium, Xanax. Nothing works. Deanna wouldn't think of telling someone with a bum knee to suck it up and start running, or of admonishing an addict to show some willpower, but now she's called me a coward.

One of the baristas brings me a fresh macchiato, even though I didn't order one. I really am a fixture in this place.

A little while later, Deanna comes back to my table. "Listen to me, Parker. Rich needs a lawyer. If nothing else, you should do it out of loyalty."

"Loyalty? Where's his loyalty? He bailed on his partners only weeks after Harmon died, took the firm's biggest client with him, and stood by while rest of us split apart. Meanwhile, he's made millions off the Assembly. As much as I hate that damn cult, the legal fees could have kept the firm afloat. Not to mention that if he did commit this crime, he betrayed his family and client and church."

"All the more reason why you should help him. Remember what Harmon used to tell us? Loyalty is most meaningful when its object has betrayed you."

"That's bullshit."

"Maybe so. But it's what Harmon believed."

"You're not playing fair."

She turns and glances at me over her shoulder, her smile knowing and flirtatious, her dark brown eyes dancing like they always do when she knows she's won an argument. "When you see Rich, tell him I said to keep fighting."

CHAPTER 2

I park at the lot on the corner of Temple and Alameda and walk toward the Metropolitan Detention Center, a nondescript high rise located near the federal courthouse and Union Station. For the first time in over a year, I'm wearing a suit. It's mid-October. The downtown air is fresh for once, the sky a pristine aqua. The sun gleams off the polished walls of the skyscrapers. Even the maple leaves, which usually turn from green to a brittle brown without bothering with the fiery in-between colors, are a vibrant yellow. All in all, it's much too nice a morning to be visiting a jail.

I pass through the rigorous security check and take a chair on my side of the Plexiglas barrier, waiting for the guard to bring Rich Baxter into the attorney meeting room. In here, the government respects the attorney-client privilege, meaning the marshals can only watch, not listen—or so say the regulations.

We were part of Macklin & Cherry's vaunted class of 1999—*Harmon's Army*. Deanna Poulos and I were The Gunslingers, litigators anxious to take depositions and get into a courtroom ASAP. Manny Mason was The Intellectual, the thoughtful lawyer who loved the law's logic. Rich Baxter was The Dealmaker, intent on negotiating eight-figure financial arrangements for powerful individuals and huge companies. And there was mercurial Grace Trimble, The Genius—the brightest of us all, but also the most fragile.

My friendship with Rich ended five years ago. He oversaw the Church of the Sanctified Assembly's day-to-day representation. I thought it was just business until he announced one day that he'd become an Assembly member. I tried to talk him out of it, insisting that the group was a dangerous cult that only wanted his money.

Things degenerated from there. He accused me of blasphemy and said I didn't believe in anything except winning cases and making money and getting laid by a different woman every week. I shot back that he'd joined the Assembly because it was the only way he could finally get some pussy—I was talking about Monica, who would later become his wife. After that, he would have nothing to do with me. When Harmon died, Rich left the law firm and took the Assembly's legal work with him, a move that not only made him wealthy, but also led to the firm's collapse. I haven't seen him since.

Last night, I pulled the indictment off PACER, the federal court website. The charges are more serious than I imagined. The government claims that a confidential source notified the Internal Revenue Service about unusual banking transactions involving the Church of the Sanctified Assembly. Rich allegedly controlled the Assembly's bank accounts. The IRS monitors identified a series of large withdrawals, followed by deposits into shell accounts in European and offshore banks. What knocks me off-balance is the amount they say he stole— the indictment details numerous transactions between May 2010 and May 2011 that total approximately seventeen million dollars. The last alleged illegal transaction alone is for six million dollars, supposedly a transfer of laundered Assembly money into a British West Indies shell company called The Emery Group, which Rich set up and controlled.

It's hard to see how the accusations could get worse, but they do. A couple of weeks ago, there was a flurry of activity in the bank accounts. Believing that Rich was about to flee the country, the FBI arrested him at an apartment in the Silver Lake district of Los Angeles. In the course of the search, the agents found a false passport bearing the name and social security number of one Alan Thomas Markowitz alongside Rich's picture. The real Alan Markowitz is a used car dealer in the valley who has no apparent relationship with The Church of the Sanctified Assembly. The agents also discovered a large quantity of methamphet- amine, along with $428,000 in cash, hidden in the casing of a Gateway desktop computer. Rich faces up to twenty years in prison for each count of mail fraud, up to ten years in prison for each count of money laundering, and more time added on for the drug and passport charges.

The Rich I knew wasn't capable of any of this. His idea of bending the rules was leaving work early to catch a Dodgers game or hitting the bar across the street after work for a good scotch.

The door on the other side of the barrier opens. He's been jailed for less than a week, so despite his bleak situation, I still expect to find the person whom I worked with, the pudgy, avuncular man with the rosy complexion and blond hair styled so perfectly that we'd tease him about using a can of hair spray daily. When he walks in, I recoil. He's sickly thin with gaunt cheeks, as though he's suffering from a serious illness. His hair is tangled, more gray than blond. His once-bright eyes are deep-set and dull. Jail alone couldn't have done this to him. On the face of it, he's lived conservatively. The Assembly's promotional materials emphasize family values, stable marriages, physical fitness, and disdain for Western medicine. Christian fundamentalism meets New Age doctrine; the Pentecostals meet Scientology. As far as I know, he's adhered to the tenets of his faith. And yet, something insidious has eaten away at him. Maybe he *has* been using hardcore drugs.

He takes a seat at the counter, picks up the handset, and forces a smile. "Long time, Parker."

"Tell me what happened, Rich."

"What happened is they locked me up without bail for no reason. Josh is turning two in a couple of weeks. I have to get out of here so I can be at his birthday party. You'll make that happen, right?"

He hasn't changed—he always believes everything will turn out fine. His unchecked optimism is one of the reasons his clients like him so much.

"Why are you in here?" I ask.

He reveals his teeth, although I wouldn't call the way he's parted his lips a smile. "Attorney-client privilege?"

"It's too soon for us to—"

"If you're not going to agree to represent me up front, then you might as well leave. I'm only going to talk to my attorney."

"I . . . Sure, Rich. I'm your lawyer." My words send a current of exhilaration through me. It's the first time that I've felt like an attorney since Harmon died. At the same time, I feel as if I've jumped into battle wounded and unarmed.

"I'm innocent. I've always been loyal to the Assembly, both as an adherent and as an attorney. The charges are bogus. I've been set up."

"By who?"

"I don't know."

"Why would anyone do something like that?"

"Because I learned something." He takes the handset away from his ear, and for a moment I think he's going to hang up. He slowly raises the handset again and covers the mouthpiece with his free hand. "Someone inside's been stealing from the Assembly. I'm getting the blame, but it's someone on the inside. And . . . and I also think they murdered Harmon."

"Harmon fell into a depression and killed himself."

"Whoever killed him made it look like suicide. Harmon had information."

"Which was?"

"I don't know. I was looking for a workout agreement I drafted a few years ago and stumbled on these notes that Harmon wrote. They were on a DVD of scanned documents that the firm sent over when I left."

"What did they say?"

"It was hard to understand. You know how Harmon wrote in riddles. But they talked about how someone was diverting funds from the Assembly. There were some initials, but no detail. It was like a code or something. I couldn't . . ."

"Where's the DVD now? Did the cops—?"

"That's the thing, I . . . someone stole it from me."

"Who?"

"I don't know."

"Can you remember anything else in the notes?"

"It's all so fuzzy, I . . ." He shrugs his shoulders in defeat.

"Focus, Rich."

He pushes the heels of his hands hard against his temples, as if by compressing his brain he could squeeze the lost information to the surface. "Something about a financial crime. There was all this code that I couldn't understand, and all these numbers, bank accounts, initials. I'm sorry, it's all so foggy. I just can't . . ."

"Any chance the original document is still in storage?"

"No. I took all the original Assembly files with me when I left the firm. The client directed me not to leave anything behind. Not even copies." He mumbles something, an incomprehensible hum, and then perks up. "Talk to Layla Cherry. Maybe she still has some of Harmon's old documents. You remember how Harmon was a packrat. When I left the firm, we found some Assembly documents at his house. Talk to Layla."

"What have you told the authorities?"

"You know I wouldn't speak to anyone without an attorney present."

"The indictment alleges that you received the illegal payment from a company called The Emery Group."

"It's a lie."

"What's The Emery Group?"

"That's confidential."

"I just told you I'm your lawyer."

"No. I mean the Assembly's privilege. The hierarchy has given me strict orders not to—"

"You're really going to protect the people who got you thrown in here?"

He sets his jaw. "Attorney-client privilege."

"Can you at least tell me if the company's legit?"

"Everything the Assembly does is legit."

"What about the false passport? And that apartment you rented? You used a false name. Alan Thomas Markowitz."

He just shrugs in response. As he does the next two times I ask the question.

"Jesus, Rich," I say. "How do you expect me to help you?"

"You'll find a way."

Fifteen minutes later, I've almost run out of questions. For someone who's acted as the Assembly's lawyer for so long, he knows precious little—or so he wants me to believe. "I have to ask this, Rich. The FBI found drugs. Why? And what about gambling? Or women?"

"Those were your vices, not mine."

"We're done."

"Parker, wait. I'm sorry. It's just all this . . ." He sweeps his free arm in the air helplessly.

I want nothing more than to hang up the phone and walk out, but instead I say, "If this is going to work, you have to cooperate with me."

"There were no women. I don't take drugs. And I haven't gambled since I joined the Assembly. This is a frame-up."

"Anything else you want to tell me? The false passport?"

"There's . . ." He stops and takes an audible breath.

I can almost feel his discomfort refracting through the glass barrier. "There's what?"

He puffs himself up. "There's nothing more to tell."

"Whatever you say." I take a deep breath. "What does Monica know about this?"

"Absolutely nothing. And don't you dare try to contact her. You're not my wife's favorite person, you know. And anyway, she's being guided by the Fount."

The "Fount" is short for The Celestial Fountain of All That Is, adapted from a line in the Book of Common Prayer—"Almighty God, the fountain of all wisdom." It's never been clear to me whether The Celestial Fount is supposed to be a prophet or God or a combination of both or a bastardization of the Christian concept of the Holy Trinity or a magic wormhole into some parallel universe where the sanctified members of the Assembly know everything.

"So I can't talk to Monica. Who can I talk to at the Assembly?"

"No one. You're an outsider. Worse. You're known for your antagonism toward the Assembly."

"I've never tried to hide that."

"I bet you're thinking *I told you so*."

"I just didn't want you to get hurt."

"The Assembly hasn't hurt me. Somebody else."

"But you don't know who."

He shakes his head.

I'm about to wrap the interview up when he says, "You should know that no matter what's happened, I still believe in the Fount's truth."

"Really. Then why in God's name would you want *me* to represent you? My feelings about your church haven't changed."

His eyes turn stony. "You do know that if you get involved in this, you'll become a target. Just like Harmon. Just like me."

"I'm well aware that the Assembly does whatever's necessary to silence its critics. What does that have to do with my question?"

"Harmon and I have families who've been hurt by what's happened to us. All the other lawyers I'd consider hiring have families or people they're close to. You're the only good lawyer I know who doesn't really have anyone in your life."

"That's not true. I have—"

"Don't tell me about Deanna and Manny. In the end they're just work friends. It's not the same, as you and I proved. So if something happens to you, no one else will care, Parker. No one else will get hurt. That's why I want you. To avoid collateral damage."

"I'll get back to you, Rich." I hang up the phone and walk out, not waiting for the guard to take him back to his cell.

CHAPTER 3

I leave the detention center and walk the three blocks to the old federal courthouse, built in 1940 as part of a Depression-era stimulus program. The main lobby has a musty odor of yellowed parchment and imperfect justice. I always make sure to breathe deeply when I enter the building. I love that smell, just as a boxer might love the sweaty smell of an old gymnasium.

I take the escalator to the second floor, where my friend and former partner Manfred Mason is arguing a pro bono case on behalf of some gang members. Manny is now associate dean at St. Thomas More School of Law. He's convinced me to teach a course in trial advocacy. The only person other than Deanna who knows about my stage fright, he views the teaching gig as the first step in my getting back into the courtroom. He doesn't realize that teaching isn't trial work.

My first class begins at three o'clock this afternoon. Yesterday, he called and said he had to talk to me before the class started, so I agreed to meet him at the courthouse. I'm not wild about the idea of walking into a courtroom, but I'm curious—I've never seen Manny argue a case. He's a corporate finance and tax lawyer, not a litigator. He certainly doesn't have the typical attributes of a trial lawyer. Most of us are outgoing, combative. Manny's humble, so reserved that people mistake his shyness for arrogance. In the past, his career suffered for it. At the law firm, he didn't bring in much business. When the firm broke up, he became a law professor, a job that suits him perfectly. Finally, he's on the fast track.

As soon as I enter the courtroom, my heart skitters. I find a back corner seat, close to the exit. I recite a silent mantra—*no reason for stage fright because I'm not on stage.* My heart just beats faster. I touch my fingers to my carotid artery so I can measure my pulse, but lower my hand when I see the judge's clerk looking at me.

Manny is at the podium, asking the judge to dissolve an injunction against members of the Etiwanda Lazers street gang. The Lazers control the illicit drug trade in the north San Fernando Valley. Although Manny could use his considerable height to his advantage—courtroom presence is as much physical as intellectual—he hunches over, as if trying to hide his six-foot-four-inch frame behind the small lectern. He speaks in a scholarly monotone, his argument fraught with legalisms. *Void for vagueness. Arbitrary deprivation of liberty interests. No* mens rea *requirement.* He should be trying to humanize his dangerous clients, but he can't muster any passion. After speaking for another five minutes, he raises an index finger, leafs through his notes, and sits down. So much for ending on a high note.

"The case is submitted," the judge says. "Until I rule, the temporary restraining order will remain in effect."

As soon as she leaves the bench, my adrenaline levels off. I approach Manny.

"I'm glad that's over," he says. "At least I've survived another day before this judge lowers the boom."

"From what I saw, Harmon should have assigned you to the trial department." We both know it's a lie.

He raises his hands in mock horror. "I'm a business lawyer and a teacher. These pro bono matters are just my way of giving back to the community. And, of course, the constitutional issues are fascinating. But I'm not a litigator. I'll tell you what. If one of my cases ever gets to the Supreme Court, you can argue it."

"Right now, I couldn't argue a fender bender in small claims court."

"That will pass."

"Sure it will." There's an uncomfortable silence. "Come on," he says. "Let me introduce you to my client." He gestures toward the back of the room.

I thought the courtroom was empty. I didn't notice the man still sitting in the back row, on the opposite side of the room from where

I'd been sitting. He appears to be in his mid- to late-twenties, wearing a conservative gray suit and white shirt without a tie—a well-dressed spectator. Only when he stands and swaggers toward us does he resemble a gang member. Though he's no more than five foot nine, he must weigh 190 pounds, all weight-trained muscle. He has a buzz cut, a dark brown moustache, and a soul patch. Up close, I can see the tattoos on his knuckles.

"Parker, I want you to meet Victor Galdamez. Victor, this is Parker Stern. He was my law partner. And one of the best trial lawyers in the city. Starting today, he's teaching a class at the law school."

We shake hands. Though his grip is weak, it's typical of powerful men who don't want to hurt anyone. He smiles warmly. "Dean Mason did a great job, today, huh?" I expected to hear at least a hint of the barrio in his speech, but there isn't any.

"I was just telling him that," I say.

"Not many people are brave enough to take our side, even when we're right. We don't have the money to pay lawyers, and Dean Mason has been very generous with his time."

We chat for a while about constitutional law and the merits of the Lazers' legal position—fortunately, Manny doesn't hold out false hope—and then Galdamez excuses himself.

"He doesn't sound like your typical gang member," I say when we're alone.

"What's typical?"

"Look, I wasn't saying—"

He waves his hand dismissively. "That's the problem. Even someone like you makes assumptions. Victor's a junior at Whittier Poly. Prelaw. We hope to have him with us at St. Thomas More in a couple of years. He's a former member who got out and wants to better himself and his community. He serves as a liaison. He's the perfect client representative." He checks his watch. "Let's go down to the cafeteria and talk. I have an administrators' meeting over at UCLA in an hour."

The courthouse cafeteria hasn't been renovated since just after World War II ended. I suspect the food is of the same vintage. I buy a granola bar; at least it's wrapped. Manny orders two hot dogs, the casings of which have a greenish tinge. When I point that out, he says it's just the lighting. We find a table in the corner and he gives a mini-lecture about how to teach a law school course—assume the students know nothing, but don't talk down to them; teach only what you're interested in; don't let them walk all over you, but don't be a tyrant. Platitudes.

"We've gone over all of this before," I say. "What's the real reason you made me come down here?"

He takes a drink of Coke. "You'll be performing in front of an audience in a few hours. I just want to make sure that—"

"It's a classroom, not a courtroom. It only happens in courtrooms."

"Still."

"How many students are enrolled?"

"I haven't checked lately. Usually there are twelve, fifteen people in these practice courses. You'll get the enrollment sheet from the registrar's office."

"I can handle a dozen law students."

He raises his arm and gives me a desultory fist bump. "I know you can."

"There's something I want to talk to *you* about. Rich Baxter's in jail."

"For what?"

"A federal rap. They say he embezzled money from the Assembly."

He shakes his head slowly and scratches his scalp with a bony index finger. "I'm shocked, but not surprised."

"You're not surprised?"

"I know it's an odd thing to say. But you know how he struggles with the technical aspects of the law."

"He got by at the firm."

"At the firm, he had help. As a solo practitioner he's been left to his own devices. And the problems that arise in representing the Church of the Sanctified Assembly are labyrinthine. I'm one of the legal ethics teachers at the law school. Studying that area from an academic standpoint has been very illuminating. Didn't Harmon used to say that incompetence breeds wrongdoing? He was right. Most attorney defalcations start with malpractice, and I fear that for our friend Rich, the malpractice part was only a matter of time."

"You actually think he could've ripped off his own church and only client? We're talking about Rich."

"I don't know anything, of course. It's just that I've worried about him since the firm split up, feared he was adrift."

"Rich wants me to represent him. I just met with him at the federal detention center."

"Whoa. Back up. You saw him?"

I nod.

"You're not serious." He shuts his eyes for a moment, as if trying to choose just the right words. "Listen to me, Parker. Given all you've been through this last year and a half, you're not making sense. You said it yourself. You can't handle a simple procedural hearing."

"I can at least look into the charges. I owe him that after what happened between us."

"You don't owe him anything. And as far as your career is concerned, you've got to take things a step at a time. See how you do teaching this class over the next few months, and maybe after that—"

"Deanna thinks—"

"Deanna's reckless, and she wants everyone around her to be reckless. The last thing you should do right now is to jump into a major criminal case. Especially a case where you'd be adverse to the Church of the Sanctified Assembly. Under normal circumstances, there'd be no one better, but these aren't normal circumstances, are they, Parker?" He sounds like a parent gingerly trying to dissuade a child of limited talent from pursuing a pipe dream.

"You're patronizing me, Manny. Don't patronize me."

"I'm just being a caring friend."

"You know, as *your* good friend, I could give you some helpful pointers about how to present an effective oral argument. Like telling the judge a story rather than speaking in legalese. Or having a conversation rather than reading from your notes. Or changing your facial expressions so you look like you give a shit about your case."

He smiles thinly, but his eyes are cold and hard. "You might be suffering from stage fright, Stern, but you're still a contentious son of a bitch. Insult me if you must. I'm not going to change my mind about your representing Rich. But the next time I have a pro bono court appearance, I'll definitely have you tutor me." He looks at his wristwatch. "I've got to head out to the Westside. But keep this in mind. If you were to take this case on, you'd be jeopardizing Rich's freedom. That cannot happen."

We stand and face each other, the tension still palpable. After a moment, he smiles again, this time more broadly. "Look, Parker, I know how much you love trying cases, how much you miss it. But slow down. Your time will come again. And knock 'em dead in class this afternoon." He squeezes my shoulder with his large hand.

I force a smile. As a star trial lawyer with a growing number of accolades, I was once more important than Manny. I made more money and had more power. Our relative positions at the firm even distorted my visual perception of him. Back then I never thought of him as physically imposing, though he's at least six inches taller than I. Now, he towers over me.

CHAPTER 4

The windowless seminar room at St. Thomas More School of Law, like all the other rooms in the school, has a crucifix hanging from the wall. I'm not Catholic, but focusing on it lessens the humiliation of having only three people enrolled in my trial advocacy class, not the twelve or fifteen that Manny predicted.

The low turnout proves what I've long suspected—this so-called job is nothing but Manny's act of charity. Though I'm no expert in law school administration, I do know that even small seminars are canceled if only three people sign up for them.

I wait for my trio of students to boot up their computers. The two women and one man sit at the long rectangular conference table and stare at me with bored yet insolent looks signaling that they're not easily impressed, that no matter how good my credentials might be, my classroom performance is all that matters. When I was a law student thirteen years ago, I used to give the new professors that same look.

"My name is Parker Stern," I say. "For twelve years, I worked at the law firm of Macklin & Cherry, where I practiced both civil and criminal law, mostly white collar. I've tried about thirty-five cases, ranging from personal injury to defense of a racketeering prosecution. I've also handled a number of *pro bono* matters, including one on behalf of a class of federal prisoners. Now, why don't you introduce yourselves and tell me what you plan to do after law school." I gesture toward a blonde woman. She has a model's high cheekbones and the curvy body of a Texas homecoming queen. "You are . . . ?"

"Lovely. Lovely Diamond."

Giving a false name to the new professor is an old law school prank. "Very funny," I say. "But it doesn't show much originality. When I was in law school, my classmate Dennis Beryl told our torts professor that his first name was *Trash*. Now do you mind sharing your real name?"

The man in the class snorts and covers his mouth with his hand. The other woman blushes. The blonde shakes her head. She reaches into her backpack, takes out her wallet, and retrieves something, which she slides across the table as though she's playing arcade air hockey.

It's her driver's license. Her name is, indeed, Lovely Diamond. No middle name. An address on Westmoreland Avenue, a dicey area, but increasingly BoHo. Height: five feet five inches. Weight: 118 pounds. Hair: blonde. Eyes: green. The picture doesn't do her justice. And her eyes are more gray than green. DOB: June 8, 1982, which makes her twenty-nine—older than I thought.

"My mistake, Ms. Diamond."

"Didn't you check out your class roster?" she says, her tone rife with censure, as if she's the teacher.

The truth is, I didn't bother to study the roster. When I saw that my twelve students had dwindled to three, I didn't see the point. "Let's move on. Tell us something about yourself."

She sighs in exasperation. "I'm a third year. I worked in the entertainment field for a couple of years before going to college. After that, I was a paralegal for three years and then went to law school. I'm interested in constitutional law, particularly the First Amendment."

I point to the man sitting next to her, a wiry, red-haired kid wearing a University of Arizona sweatshirt. He has fair skin and a wispy goatee, which he probably grew so he could look older, but which, when combined with his slight build, makes him look like a ninth-grader.

"I'm Jonathan Borzo. Also a 3L. I have a degree in computer sciences. I'm interested in Internet law. So, I think the studios and record companies are a threat to our individual freedom." This kid apparently believes that the ability to watch stolen copies of *Spiderman* on the Internet is more important than global warming or ending world hunger.

"Welcome, Mr. Borzo."

As soon as I focus on the woman sitting next to Jonathan, her neck turns splotchy. "Well, my name is Kathleen. Williams. I guess . . . I'm also a 3L." She has limp brown hair, a round face, and a pudgy body. She's as plain as Lovely is striking. "I went to Cal State Reseda and got a BA in English. I don't know what kind of lawyer I want to be yet."

"Good to have you with us, Ms. Williams. Now let's talk about what we're going to do this semester. We're going to pick a case, and—"

"Before you go on, I have a question," Lovely says.

"Absolutely, Ms. Diamond." I try to sound enthusiastic—an olive branch.

"Is it true you're Parky Gerald?"

And with those words, Lovely Diamond has intentionally or unwittingly exacted revenge for my thinking her name a joke. I begin drumming my fingers on the table bottom, which is tacky with what I pray is nothing worse than used chewing gum.

"I did go by that name when I was a kid," I say, or rather, confess. I've spent my adulthood trying to hide it.

Kathleen considers me with a look I haven't seen in years—celebrity worship. "Oh my god, that was you, professor?"

"Who's Parky Gerald?" Jonathan asks.

"A child actor," Kathleen says. "He starred in that movie *Alien Parents*. And *Alien Parents 2*. And then a soccer movie, I forget what it's called."

"I remember that guy," Jonathan says. "You don't look anything like him."

Of course I don't. I'm thirty-seven years old, not ten. And I have dark brown hair and a swarthy complexion and a stocky build. Back then, they wanted their child star blond and fair and rosy-cheeked and rail thin. They bleached my hair platinum and layered on the pancake makeup so I'd look pale. And there was the rouge and the eye shadow to make my eyes look big and the constant dieting to keep me skinny. The only good thing about that part of my past is the Screen Actors Guild residuals.

Kathleen continues to gawk at me like an obsessed fan. "Wow. When I was nine, I watched your movies on the VCR over and over.

You were so cute. Then you were gone. Wasn't there . . . some lawsuit or scandal or . . . ?"

She looks at Lovely, who shrugs. I bet this Diamond woman thinks she knows exactly what happened to Parky Gerald.

"Let's leave my checkered acting career for some other time," I say. "And I know it's a lot to ask, but I'd appreciate it if you wouldn't mention it to anyone else. It's not something I want people to know." I'm sure that my request is hopeless—law students love gossip.

I summarize what I want to accomplish during the semester. They'll each be responsible for monitoring a lawsuit so they can get some real-life experience. They'll work with me and the outside attorney of record. I ask them to come to our next class with a proposed case to handle. I pass out a list of possibilities that I got from an ex-colleague who works at Legal Aid—mostly credit card fraud and slumlord cases for impoverished clients, unexciting but worthy causes that can give them valuable experience. I spend the rest of the session describing the nuts and bolts of a legal case from complaint to trial, something I was never taught in law school. I let them go twenty minutes early. As they're leaving, Jonathan nods, and Kathleen grins at me like a moonstruck schoolgirl. Lovely walks past me without a gesture of goodbye.

CHAPTER 5

During law school, I'd planned to go to work for a large international law firm. And then I got the phone call from superstar lawyer Harmon Cherry. He told me that the firm was still only a few years old and that I could get in on the ground floor if I joined him. I came in for an interview, and when it was over, he offered me a job. I still don't know whether my impulsiveness was a sign of wisdom or immaturity, but I took his offer on the spot because he made me feel like he was bestowing a great honor upon me, but also like I'd be honoring him if I accepted. Within a few weeks, he also hired Deanna, Rich, Manny, and Grace Trimble.

Five months into my tenure, Rich Baxter came into my office and gleefully announced that Harmon had brought the Church of the Sanctified Assembly in as a client. It was a major coup for a small firm. I bolted out of my chair, barged into Harmon's office, and told him I quit.

He leaned back in his chair and waited.

I hadn't shared my secret with anyone, but now I blurted it out. "I used to be known as Parky Gerald. I sued for emancipation from my mother when I was fifteen years old after I found out she'd taken every penny that I'd earned as an actor. That was public knowledge. What no one knows is that she gave my money to the Church of the Sanctified Assembly. I can't work at a place that represents that group."

He looked up at the ceiling, reached across his desk, picked up an unlit meerschaum pipe, and began chewing on the stem. "I get it. But don't be hasty. You've got a bright future here." He thought for a moment. "How about this? You stay at the firm and I guarantee that you won't have to come within a hundred miles of the Assembly. You'll work on other things. There's plenty to do around here. We'll set up an ethical wall between you and them."

"I don't think so."

"Think it over. And then say yes. We'll revisit all of it in six months."

I gave him my decision two days later. I'd stay at the firm on his terms with an added condition—my compensation would be calculated as if the Assembly wasn't a client. It would mean leaving a lot of money on the table, but even as a young associate, I refused to profit from the Assembly's legal work.

He kept his promise. I never had to work on an Assembly matter. And as far as I know, he never revealed my identity to anyone. I haven't trusted many people in my life, but I trusted Harmon Cherry. And then he killed himself.

Harmon ran our law firm as democratically as you can operate a multimillion dollar business. His wife, Layla, however, considered herself Queen Consort. When she called Harmon, she always demanded that his assistant interrupt him no matter how important his meeting and how trivial her need. A half-dozen times a year, she would order one of the paralegals to ghost write her twin daughters' school projects. Once, she threatened to have the office custodian fired when he refused to break into a vending machine so she could have soft drinks for her girls' upcoming birthday party. The few who had the courage to refuse her demands would receive a visit from Harmon, who'd give a defeated shrug, apologize profusely, and tell the naysayer to do what Layla wanted. As far as I know, she was his only blind spot, but she was a big one.

She still lives in their sprawling Hacienda-style house in Hancock Park, an old, upscale Los Angeles neighborhood. Once residents of Beverly Hills, she and Harmon bought the house just so their daughters could live close to their all-girls private school. Deanna hears that Layla has fallen on hard times. I don't believe it. I'll bet Layla still buys couture.

I stop to admire the magnificent pueblo door to the courtyard. At a firm party a few years ago, Layla told us about it—knotty pine with a mesquite finish, hand-carved rosette design, bronze clavos costing seventy-five dollars apiece. "That's for each nail, not for the whole set," she said. I push the door open. To my surprise, it's sagging on its hinges, so much so that the bottom scrapes the concrete and makes a sound that jangles my nerve endings. I step into the patio. The trees need trimming, the lawn needs mowing, and a juniper bush is overgrown and half strangled by ivy. It looks like the gardener comes every three weeks rather than twice a week, as when Harmon was alive. Maybe Deanna's right about Layla's money woes.

Layla opens the door before I can ring the bell, a broad smile on her face. She's wearing a chestnut sleeveless blouse and baggy black bloomers. It's a balmy day, and she's an attractive woman, but she's also forty-two years old and dressed like one of her seventeen-year-old daughters.

"Parker." She puts her hands on my shoulders and gives me three audible air kisses, alternating cheeks. "It's been too long." She leads me into the living room, sits down on the sofa, and gestures for me to sit next to her.

"How've you been, Layla?"

She takes the question literally, launching into a long narrative about how, since Harmon's death, her life has been in perpetual crisis. When one of her daughters developed a drug and alcohol problem, Layla had to send her to an expensive boarding school in Montana for troubled teens. She can't pay her housekeeping staff. She had to sell Harmon's Lamborghini—she calls it his "Lambo"—and some treasured artwork. She's in a bitter dispute with the company that issued one of Harmon's life insurance policies. She's put their Malibu beach house up for sale for a paltry $8,250,000. And on and on. Throughout her monologue, she flutters her hands and occasionally reaches out and touches me on the knee or arm.

"The Malibu house is a bargain," she says. "But not a single offer. My broker keeps talking about the bad economy, wants me to lower the price again, but I'm holding out. It's not the economy that's keeping the house from selling. It's because the broker has to disclose what happened there. And no one wants a house where . . ." She doesn't have to finish her sentence—no one wants a house in which its prior owner shot himself in the mouth. "So if you know anyone looking to live by the beach . . . You live by the ocean, don't you?"

"Marina Del Rey."

"Well, if you know of someone . . ." She seems to lose her train of thought. Her eyes flood with tears. "God, I miss him so much."

"I do, too. Everyone does."

"Really?"

"Of course. Why would you think—?"

"He pushed everyone at the firm so hard. Especially your class. Sometimes I wondered whether you resented him."

"We all loved him."

She stares at me with a forlorn look that makes me think she expects a hug or a comforting touch. I wonder what else she wants from me. My cynicism makes me a good lawyer but often a hard-boiled human being.

She forces a smile. "I'm sorry. I get . . . you said you wanted to talk to me about Rich Baxter."

"He's in jail."

"Oh my god, what for?"

"Embezzling from the Church of the Sanctified Assembly."

Her eyes narrow into slits. "*Those* people. You know, they even tried to convert our girls? When I asked Harmon why he kept them on as a client, he said they didn't just put the bread on our table, they provided the whole meal."

"I'm looking for some documents. I know it's unlikely, but I was wondering if you kept any of Harmon's work files."

"The firm took everything, which was fine with me. The firm and the Assembly. In fact, when Rich went out on his own he insisted I let his people search Harmon's office. He was kind of an asshole about it. I'm a widow for six weeks, and all he cared about was files. Nowadays, the girls use the office as kind of a rec room to hang out with their friends. Anyway, there's nothing here."

I feel a strange combination of disappointment and relief, the way I felt as a kid when I'd lose out on a movie role only to get to stay in school and feel normal for a while longer. "Thanks for your time, Layla. I hope things get better for you soon."

"That's it?"

"I told you it wouldn't take long."

She grabs my shirt cuff. "Could you stay a minute, Parker? There's something I want to ask you."

Reluctantly, I sit back down.

"My fight with the life insurance company. They won't pay on a five million dollar policy. There was a suicide exclusion. Harmon didn't kill himself."

I know Layla has never accepted the fact of Harmon's suicide, but I didn't realize that her incredulity has a pecuniary component.

"Someone killed him," she continues. "There's no way he would've . . . We need that insurance money to survive. Harmon used to say that you were the best young trial lawyer in the firm. We need an aggressive attorney to handle a lawsuit against the insurance company. I can't pay an hourly rate, but maybe if you took it on a contingency you could—"

"I don't practice law anymore, Layla."

"But you're representing Rich Baxter."

"Just doing him a favor by talking to you. Besides, it's been what, a year and a half since Harmon died? You must've talked to other attorneys about suing the carrier."

She lowers her eyes. "I've talked to a few others."

"And what did they say?"

"They . . . none of them wants to take the case on a contingency. They say the police investigation and the medical examiner's report are conclusive. They're wrong. I have a report that proves Harmon was murdered."

"You have—?"

"I hired a private investigator to look into Harmon's . . . what happened to Harmon. He says it was murder. So the insurance company has to pay, right?"

She keeps focusing on the insurance issue and not on the fact that if Harmon really was murdered, his killer is still at large. It doesn't matter. She's sucked me in.

"Can I see the report?"

She hurries into another room and returns in all of ten seconds. She prepared for this. She hands me a sheaf of paper about two inches thick.

"I can't read all of this right now."

"You don't have to. There's a, what do you call it? Executive summary. It tells you all you need to know."

When I see that the author is a man named Ray Guglielmi, *that's* all I need to know. Guglielmi is a notorious conspiracy theorist who thrives on tabloid publicity and manufactured controversies. He once had his own reality TV show. Six months ago, he was convicted of illegally wiretapping his own clients, sentenced to prison, and stripped of his private investigator's license.

"Layla, Guglielmi is a fraud. Publicity hungry. He's in prison. He has no credibility at all." I try to give the report back to her, but she jerks her hand away as if I've tried to prod her with a branding iron.

"That's what Andrew and the other lawyers said. I don't believe any of them. I thought maybe you'd be more open-minded." "Andrew" is Andrew Macklin, the other named partner in our old firm.

"Andrew read this report?"

"He was the executor of Harmon's estate, so he helped me with probate after Harmon died. I asked him to read it."

"If he told you there's no case, then there's no case."

"Please just keep an open mind and read the summary. Please."

I take a deep breath, flip to the executive summary, and start reading. Layla keeps her eyes fixed on me the whole time. The report lists the reasons Guglielmi believes that Harmon was murdered: there was no suicide note; one of Harmon's credit cards was missing and never recovered; a week before his death, Harmon told Layla that he feared for his life and that he'd bought a gun to protect himself; apart from the single bullet to Harmon's head, the gun was fully loaded, more consistent with protection than suicide; although the medical examiner's report claimed that Harmon was barricaded in his room at the beach house the night he died, there was no evidence of that; Harmon had prescriptions for a number of powerful antidepressants and pain killers, easily potent enough to kill him in a much less violent manner than a gunshot; the shell casing from the gun was found to the right of his body, even though the gun itself was found on his left; there were two sets of latent fingerprints on the gun, neither of them legible, leading to the conclusion that someone wiped the gun clean; Harmon's eyeglasses had been found thirteen feet from his body behind a planter, too far to have been propelled by the force of the gunshot; the gunpowder residue on Harmon's hands could have been caused by a postmortem placement of the gun in his hand and the firing of a second bullet; Harmon's calendar was full for the next four months and included extensive travel plans, behavior inconsistent with suicidal thoughts.

Guglielmi raises some interesting question if his facts are accurate—and that remains a big *if.* Had Rich not told me he believed that Harmon was murdered, I would dismiss the report out of hand. But Rich added something vitally important—a motive. Still, I'm not about to take on a hopeless contingency case against an insurance company with an unlimited legal budget. And I'm not about to get entangled with Layla. I set the report down on the coffee table. "Sorry, but I agree with the others. There's no civil case. Have you talked to the cops about reopening the criminal investigation?"

"Many times, and they won't. They think I'm just a distraught widow. But I know in my heart that someone took my husband's life." She laughs bitterly. "Ironic, isn't it? None of you who worked at the law firm will help me. Harmon always said the firm was a family."

The firm *was* a family. She just wasn't part of it.

"I should be going," I say.

She grabs my wrist. Her eyes wobble nystagmically. "Are you seeing anyone? Because you and I should go out sometime. Maybe have coffee at Deanna Poulos's place? You have my number, right? Of course you do, or you wouldn't be here." Desperate people emit a peculiar kind of energy, animating and crude. She glows with it.

"I'm flattered, Layla. But I don't think it would be a good idea."

"Oh, wow. OK." She primps her hair to show she doesn't care. "Thanks for at least listening. No one listens to me anymore."

She once occupied a lofty station in life, but now she's a commoner. I know the feeling.

An hour later, I'm sitting in the Century City office of Andrew Macklin, the other titular head of our law firm. In his late sixties, Macklin is short, round, and bald, with a grizzled beard. People at the law firm used to call him "Papa Smurf" behind his back.

He was Harmon's equal in name only. Harmon brought in all the clients and wielded all the power. The clients that Macklin brought in were unsavory—a meat packing plant in trouble with the FDA, a small union pension fund with ties to local mobsters, a sleazy Russian entrepreneur. But Harmon had a soft spot for Macklin. They'd left a large downtown law firm together and started Macklin & Cherry in the late eighties. So Harmon protected him, even though a lot of the younger partners resented Macklin for not carrying his weight.

"What can I do for you?" he says in a gruff voice that has never lost its Chicago twang. "Like I told you over the phone, I don't have much time." I'm sure it's posturing—I suspect he has nothing to do.

I tell him about Rich's arrest and my meeting with Layla and their belief that Harmon was murdered.

"You can't trust anything that either of them tells you," he says. "Layla is a delusional narcissist and always has been. As for Richard Baxter, he worked for me on some Assembly transactions. I had to bail him out of malpractice over and over. He couldn't draft his way out of a paper bag. He's a salesman, not a lawyer. His assessment of a situation is worthless." He's not quite telling the truth—*he* worked for *Rich* on Assembly matters, not the other way around. Harmon insisted on it because Macklin didn't have anything else to do. It must have been the low point of his career.

"What about this resurrected idea that Harmon was murdered?" I ask. "Layla has a private investigator's report showing that—"

"That Guglielmi report? Pure fiction. When Layla first sent it to me, I showed it to an ex-detective friend of mine from the Ventura PD. He laughed out loud when he saw who wrote it and laughed even louder when he got down reading it. The thing is full of holes." He rattles off the flaws in the Guglielmi report as if he just spoke with his detective friend an hour ago: Not all suicides leave a note. One of Harmon's daughters likely used his credit card, probably with her father's permission—he was always buying them things if they promised not to tell their mother. Harmon might have told Layla that his life was in danger, but that's not inconsistent with suicide. He probably shot himself because he believed it a more manly way to die. He had gun residue on his hands. There was only one shell casing found at the scene, so there couldn't have been two shots as Guglielmi suggests.

Then he says something that shocks me. "Harmon Cherry was a selfish son of a bitch. And a traitor. He abandoned his wife and children by committing the most horrendous act you can imagine. He didn't even have the decency to secure their future. In the end, he thought the firm belonged to him alone, the rest of us be damned. It didn't belong just to him. I started the place with him, nurtured it, but he forgot that. As we grew, the other partners, guys like you, helped build it, and he forgot that, too. The only thing that Harmon did alone was destroy the place and damage his family beyond repair." He stares at me, his eyes glistening, his lips curled in a half snarl.

I look back at him, speechless. Andrew Macklin was bitter about a lot of things, but never about Harmon Cherry.

"Do yourself a favor," he says. "Avoid Layla Cherry and Richard Baxter like the Ebola virus. Let them hire other attorneys to handle their problems, attorneys who aren't tainted by Harmon's insanity. Harmon is dead. The law firm is dead. Put it all behind you."

CHAPTER 6

I spend the rest of the day on the balcony of my condo studying the criminal charges against Rich. I read through documents and conduct computer searches until the sun goes down and the ocean wind picks up and forces me inside. Just after nine o'clock, my security bell rings. It's Deanna. As soon as I open the door she rushes in and wraps her arms around me.

"I need you tonight, Parker," she whispers.

Since our early days at the law firm, we've had sporadic trysts like this, except when one of us was seriously involved with someone else. We've mutually agreed that these sessions aren't romantic, but rather expressions of friendship, acts of generosity. All my other relationships with women have been brief, born out of lust and interred by boredom. Intimacy means revealing my past, which I want to bury forever. As for Deanna, she claims to have three kinds of lovers—feral men with big cocks who fuck her hard, pixyish women with soft lips and a tender touch, and me.

"You're the only man I've been with who eats pussy as well as a woman," is how she describes my presence in the mix.

When we began dating during our first year at the firm, I thought that I could fall in love with this strong, ambitious, irreverent woman with eyes so dark they could spin your insides around. But then I found out that she was also sleeping with the woman who worked at the lobby gift shop. When I ended our relationship, Deanna was truly baffled.

"I didn't think women counted," she said in all seriousness, and despite myself I burst out laughing.

Improbably, we remained friends. I could manage it only because Deanna seemed to be completely without malice. And then, six months after our breakup, we were working late and ended up going home together. The same thing happened several months later, and the pattern has continued to this day.

She remains an unsolvable puzzle. Her devout Greek Orthodox parents disowned her when she came out, yet she travels to Greece every other year and meets up with them on neutral territory, hallowed ground. She's a militant supporter of gay rights, yet had no qualms about representing the openly homophobic Sanctified Assembly ("That's what lawyers do in an adversary system, Parker!") She got more pleasure out of back-alley discovery fights than any attorney I've ever met, yet gave up the profession to open a coffee shop. She spent her legal career representing the powerful, yet decried injustice against the weak. She shows equal disdain for laws criminalizing recreational drugs and laws funding welfare for the employable and able-bodied. I once saw her drop ecstasy at an all-night rave party and then show up in court the next morning clear-headed and articulate.

We undress and lie on the couch. I inhale her familiar scent of verbena and coriander, now leavened with the aroma of roasted coffee. I trace little circles on her ribcage and breasts and thighs with my fingertips. When I've gone down on her long enough to bring her to the edge, she pulls my head away with both hands and makes sure to kiss me deeply, and then I slide into her. Afterwards, we lie in silence, arms and legs entwined, bodies pressed together spoon-like. I find myself measuring her evolution from lithe young woman of twenty-five; to restless thirty-year-old who'd just gotten her first tattoo, a scarlet hummingbird on her lower back where she could hide it under her business suits; to neo-punk entrepreneur whose body is pigmented with colorful swirls, whose thighs and ass are dimpling. I wonder if she, too, feels the leaden solitude that I've lately begun to feel after these encounters.

She rouses herself and sits up. "I didn't ask about your meeting with Rich."

I go over the charges against him and tell her about the drugs and the cash.

"Rich doesn't do drugs."

"He sure looks like he does."

We're quiet for a while.

"Rich thinks Harmon was murdered," I say. "I also met with Layla Cherry. She thinks the same thing."

She looks at me strangely. "You're not taking them seriously, are you?"

"I don't know."

"Representing Rich is one thing, but if you're going to believe some crazy theory—"

"I'm not sure I am going to represent him. Manny thinks it's too soon."

"Manny's a wimp. It's like he's from our parents' generation."

"If I do it, I'll need your help."

"Of course."

"I mean I'll need your legal assistance."

"As a lawyer? No. I run a coffee house."

"You're still an active member of the bar."

"Yeah, but—"

"Do it out of loyalty. Remember what Harmon said about loyalty."

She shakes her head in disbelief. "God damn you, Parker."

CHAPTER 7

In its most idealistic formulation, the law exists to defend life and liberty by substituting common forces for individual action. But the architect who designed the campus of the St. Thomas More School of Law apparently took a more militaristic view, having built the campus to resemble a contemporary version of a medieval fortress. The buildings all have irregular walls and turrets and parapets. Inside, there are nooks and crannies that serve no utilitarian function, and two staircases that lead nowhere, as if to confuse invading armies. I'm surprised there isn't a moat around the place.

I didn't really expect my students to keep my past as a child actor a secret, especially Lovely Diamond. But maybe they stayed quiet. No one on campus has come up to ask me if I'm Parky Gerald. Of course, it could be that people know but just don't care.

When I walk into classroom, Jonathan and Kathleen are dressed casually, but Lovely is wearing a business suit.

"Job interview, Ms. Diamond?"

"No. Job."

Despite her curt tone, I'm not ready to give up on trying to establish a rapport with her. We have an entire school year ahead of us. "It's admirable that you're working and going to school at the same time." During my years in law school I did nothing but study, living off guild residuals and savings from my acting career. "Mind if I ask where you work?"

"The Louis Frantz Law Office."

"As a law clerk?"

"Paralegal."

"Very impressive."

Landing a job—even as a paralegal—with Lou Frantz's law firm is a major accomplishment. He's one of the top trial lawyers in the country, specializing in any case that might generate a sizeable fee. Not only does he own a share of a pro football franchise, but he also set up a seven-figure endowment for this law school. One of the buildings on campus bears his name.

A few days ago, I asked Manny about Lovely. He called her a loner. He also called her one of the brightest students to come around in years. She'd be ranked number one in her class, except that last year she got into an argument with her prolife constitutional law professor over abortion rights. The debate got so heated that two of her fellow students had to restrain her from going after the guy. She took an *F* in the class rather than sitting for the final exam.

"Let's get started," I say to the class. "Your assignment was to find a pro bono case to work on. Where are you on that?"

Jonathan says that he's going to represent an eighteen-year-old Ukrainian named Dmitri Samoiloff, who's being sued by some videogame companies for copyright infringement. Kathleen is going to work on a case involving a battered woman seeking sole custody of her children. Both are acceptable. I turn to Lovely. "OK. Ms. Diamond, what do you have?"

"I want to represent a website called The Wild Cavalier Erotic Story Site. The site owner is being hassled by the morality cops who say it's obscene. But Tyler—that's the website owner—writes stories. So it's pure speech and absolutely protected by the First Amendment."

"Jurisdiction?"

"The client lives in the Mojave Desert. Riverside County. So, the Central District. No charges filed yet."

"Is there a lawyer involved who'll mentor you on the court appearances and meetings?"

"Tyler can't afford a lawyer, and none of the First Amendment groups have gotten involved."

"So the answer is no?"

"The answer is no. But I thought you could mentor me for now, Professor."

This could be a chance to start over with her. And if it doesn't work out, I won't be stuck helping her. At some point, a public interest group will get wind of the case and want to replace me. "We'll try that, Ms. Diamond. It sounds like a very cool matter."

When she smiles, her eyes beam with a childlike luminescence.

"A final announcement," I say. "There's going to be an optional case for you all to work on."

Since there are only three of them, none of them groans out loud, but there's a collective slump of shoulders. They obviously don't take the word *optional* seriously.

"It's a criminal case. The defense of a man named Richard Baxter against allegations that he embezzled money from the Church of the Sanctified Assembly." To represent Rich adequately, I'll need more than a reluctant Deanna Poulos for backup.

"What would we be doing?" Jonathan asks.

"Research. Fact-gathering. Strategizing. Attending court hearings or meetings or depositions where appropriate."

Kathleen raises a limp hand. "I read . . . I mean, there are rumors that this Sanctified Assembly group is some cult and that . . ."

"Say it, Ms. Williams."

"That it abuses its members. Commits violence against its critics."

"The Sanctified Assembly *is* a cult," I say. "My old firm represented the Assembly, so I know them well. I don't like them. I refused to work on their cases. But we're not up against the Assembly. We're defending Richard Baxter against the US government. That being said, if anyone is uncomfortable about becoming involved, you don't have to work on the case. I promise it won't affect your grade. So if you want to say no, please tell me."

No one speaks up. I take their silence as assent. It's not really fair, but I don't have a choice. I can't properly defend Rich unless my three law students serve as proxies for the nonexistent Law Offices of Parker Stern. It's certainly not the curriculum that Manny Mason had in mind when he asked me to teach this class. I just hope I'm right about the Assembly not being our adversary.

CHAPTER 8

I last appeared in court a week after Harmon Cherry died. I was representing Lake Knolls, the acclaimed film star who's now a member of the US House of Representatives. A victory was crucial to the survival of the law firm, because it would mean that Knolls would stay on as a client at the firm despite Harmon's death. And if a high-profile client like Knolls stayed, so would lesser lights.

Not long before his successful run for Congress, Knolls starred in a movie called *Repulsion*, portraying an aging rapist and serial killer. His performance was riveting, but after women's groups and victims' support organizations attacked the movie, he donated all his earnings from the picture to a shelter for abused women and exhorted his fans to boycott his own film, a move that dashed any hope of an Oscar nomination. Knolls didn't care—he had higher aspirations. To everyone's shock, he decided to give up his acting career to run for a congressional seat (a senate run was out of the question because he belonged to the incumbent's party). He won the election hands-down. Of course, the House is a mere stepping-stone to higher office.

The producers sued Knolls for fifty million dollars. I thought of a way to get rid of the case early by arguing that the producers were using the lawsuit as a way to censor Knolls's First Amendment rights. It was a novel legal theory, but I'd won eight consecutive jury trials, two in supposedly unwinnable cases. Six weeks earlier, *National Lawyer Magazine* had named me one of its top five attorneys under forty. I felt invincible.

I lost. Worse, I didn't put up a fight. The Knolls hearing took place a week after I'd collapsed in court after learning of Harmon's death. I'd kept telling myself that the incident was a one-time thing, an understandable reaction to the trauma of losing Harmon. But as soon as I walked into the courtroom for the Knolls hearing, the same debilitating fear overwhelmed me. Though the only way I could win was to plead my case—oral advocacy had always been my most potent weapon—I submitted on the papers, telling the judge in a barely audible voice that I had nothing to add to what I'd already said in writing. I could've shredded my opponent in less than five minutes, but I sat mute while she took pot shots at me, couldn't get up from my chair to speak even after the judge urged me to. Knolls fired the firm the next day.

After that, I postponed as many court appearances as I could, and if I couldn't get a postponement I invented a conflict and persuaded a colleague to cover for me. But I couldn't hide in my office forever, not with major hearings and jury trials approaching. I lived in dread of the humiliation.

And then, six weeks to the day after Harmon shot himself, the law firm imploded. Although there were fifteen lawyers still at the firm, Harmon was responsible for generating something like 75 percent of the firm's revenue. His clients found other lawyers within a matter of weeks. Rich Baxter could have kept the firm afloat with his representation of the Sanctified Assembly, but he announced he was leaving to open up his own office, a one-person operation with a single client.

The rest of us couldn't afford to pay the rent, much less the firm's considerable operating expenses. The last thing I wanted was to shutter the doors, but when it happened, I felt the way a criminal must feel when an unforeseen catastrophe obliterates the evidence of his crime.

United States v. Richard Baxter is the only matter on the judge's calendar this afternoon. Although I asked my students to help on the case, I didn't tell them about the hearing, couldn't tell them. I hope they haven't found out about it. If they were to show up and watch me perform, they'd drop my class immediately.

The instant I walk into the courtroom, the muscles in the back of my neck tighten. My shoulders roll forward, giving me a slight hunchback. My feet turn cold and numb. My gut twists. I put my hands behind my back and interlace my fingers so no one will see them trembling. The odor of disinfectant and mildew constricts my breathing. My woolen suit weighs me down like armor, but unlike armor, offers no protection from my enemy. Worst of all is the flop sweat. I can more or less hide the other symptoms, but I can't hide the flop sweat. I find a seat at the defense table, reach into my pocket, grope around for some tissue, and dab at my brow. At least I'm not feeling nauseated. Not yet, anyway.

I've met with Rich several times to prepare him for his arraignment hearing. He'll enter a plea of not guilty to the charges against him, and the judge will set a trial date. Because of the phony passport and the cash stashed in his computer, there's no chance of bail. During our meetings, I've tried repeatedly to get him to admit to a drug problem. He won't, although on my third visit he finally owned up to knowing about the crystal meth.

"There are reasons," was all he said. "I'm not an addict. Not a user."

"What reasons?"

"That's personal and confidential. They have nothing to do with this." No matter how much I plead or cajole or point out that he *looks* like a drug user, he won't budge.

I glance around the courtroom. To my dismay, it's filling up. The Church of the Sanctified Assembly has been so high profile recently—only last month it ensnared a Hall of Fame ex-NBA player and a Grammy-winning songwriter in its ever-widening net—that the news media is interested in anything it does. Deanna, the only person I do want to see, hasn't arrived yet.

United States Attorney Neil Latham and his young assistant walk into the courtroom and take their places at the counsel table. Latham is powerful, pompous, and on the fastest of career tracks—Princeton undergrad, Harvard Law School, editor of the Law Review, president of the National Black Law Students Association, a top partner in a large international firm before becoming US Attorney. At forty, he's one of the youngest US Attorneys in the country. He'll be a federal judge someday, but his aspirations go much higher than just the district court.

I can hear the courtroom filling up, can actually *feel* the spectators approach like the advance guard of an invading army. Where's Deanna? I don't dare look back. When fear is rational—in the heat of war or in the throes of a natural disaster—the presence of others is comforting, a way to diffuse the cruel force of uncertainty. But with a phobia like mine—an irrational fear of something with no true inherent threat— the presence of others is incendiary.

The hearing was set to start at 1:30, and it's already ten minutes after that. The marshals should have brought Rich into the courtroom twenty minutes ago. Maybe there's a holdup over clothing. Neither of us wanted him to come into court in a jail jumpsuit, so I arranged to have a suit and tie delivered to the detention center. Proper attire has always been important to Rich. He insisted on a charcoal blue suit and a blue tie. He says a blue tie signifies honesty.

I feel a hand on my shoulder.

"Sorry I'm late," Deanna says.

She's dressed in her black T-shirt and pants and still has the piercings in place. The tattoos on her arms are visible. I didn't expect her to wear a business suit, but this is unacceptable. Only when I see her expression of remorse for her tardiness do I understand—no matter what I've told her about my stage fright, she doesn't get it. She still thinks it'll be like before, that I'm still me, that all she'll have to do is stay quiet and enjoy my performance. She sits down directly behind me on a long bench where young associates and paralegals usually sit so they can whisper in lead counsel's ear.

"Where's Rich?" she says.

"They haven't brought him in. Probably just a glitch in logistics."

"All rise," the clerk cries out, and I stand up herky-jerky on shaky legs.

Our judge, the Honorable Cyrus Walker Harvey, is a crusty old-timer. He's in his late seventies, but with his bald dome, pasty skin mottled with liver spots, and triple-chin, he looks older. He's a loose cannon who's been known to shout down lawyers he doesn't like. He could have gone senior years ago—meaning a reduced workload at full salary—but he stubbornly remains on active status with a full slate of cases. The good news is that he doesn't trust the US government.

The clerk says, "Criminal Case 2011-455-A, United States of America v. Richard Elton Baxter. Will counsel please note their appearances for the record?"

"Good afternoon, Your Honor. Neil Latham for the United States."

"Parker Stern for the defendant." I can barely hear my own voice.

The judge raises his hand to his ear. "Speak up, counsel."

"Parker Stern for the defendant!" It's a crackly shout. I hear a few titters behind me and feel my cheeks flush. I sense Latham's eyes on me.

The judge raises his eyebrows over his half-size reading glasses. With many other lawyers, Cyrus Harvey's short fuse would have ignited after this misstep, but he's cutting me some slack. "We're here for the arraignment hearing on the indictment. Is the defendant present in court?"

I look at Latham, who looks at me. I want to tell the judge that I don't know where my client is, but I'm paralyzed, so I shake my head.

The judge squints at me. "Mr. Stern, does the defendant waive the right to be present?"

"He does not," I say, and then force out the words, "Your Honor." They come out as an afterthought, which makes me sound disrespectful.

The judge scowls at me, and I don't know if it's because he thinks I'm being sarcastic or because he believes that Rich and I are playing some sort of game.

"Where is the defendant?" the judge asks.

It's really a question he should ask the marshal. I feel the perspiration on my chest and underarms seeping through my cotton dress shirt. I stand mute for five, ten, thirty seconds, wanting to tell the judge that I have no idea where Rich is, but the words are irretrievable, mired in mental quicksand.

There's a rustle from behind me, and Deanna says, "Your Honor, we expected our client Mr. Baxter to be here. Is there a way to check on his status at the jail?"

Judge Harvey's eyes expand, twin moons half-covered in fog. "Who are you? And what are you doing in my courtroom looking like that?"

I want to step in and take over, I really do, but the part of my brain that controls the power of speech is frozen.

Deanna straightens up to her full five feet three inches and juts out her jaw. "I'm Deanna Poulos, Your Honor. Cocounsel for defendant Richard Baxter. And I'm respectfully asking the Court to inquire about his whereabouts, unless the US Attorney knows where he is."

The judge frowns. Deanna speaks with so much authority that he accepts her, at least for the moment. "Well, Mr. Latham?" he says.

"I do not know where the defendant is, Your Honor," Latham says.

The judge raises an index finger and then huddles with his clerk, who picks up the telephone and dials a number. The courtroom falls silent as we wait; they should have a law school class that just teaches you how to wait.

While the clerk is still on hold, a marshal bursts into the courtroom. "My apologies, Your Honor." Without waiting for permission, she approaches the bench and whispers something to the judge.

Judge Harvey taps his fingers on the bench three times but otherwise seems impassive. "Ladies and gentlemen, we're going to take a short recess because of a procedural matter. I'll see counsel in the United States v. Baxter case in chambers."

The judge goes through the private door into his office, while Latham and I follow the marshal through another door that leads into a hallway, and then to an anteroom where the judge's secretary sits. She shows us inside. Judge Harvey has already taken off his robe. He sits behind his desk in shirt sleeves. From up-close, his eyes are rheumy and red.

"Sit down, gentlemen," he says.

We sit. He takes out a cloth handkerchief and wipes his brow, which doesn't seem damp, and I wonder if it's a sympathetic reaction to the sweat that's undoubtedly glistening on my own forehead.

"I just received some startling news from the detention center," the judge says, blinking his eyes. "They tell me that the defendant Richard Baxter has committed suicide."

CHAPTER 9

It's been three weeks since Rich died, and I still see his eyes swimming in their hollow sockets, hear him insisting that he was framed and pleading with me to get him out before his son's birthday.

Shortly before he was to be transported to the federal courthouse for the arraignment hearing, he was found hanging in an empty holding cell. The blue silk tie that I'd picked out for him had been fashioned into a noose and looped around a low-hanging fire sprinkler. Jail administrators believe that the pipe held only because of his light weight. They cite Rich's despondency over his drug use and his fall from grace as contributing factors. The other inmates in the vicinity claim to have seen nothing.

I didn't attend his funeral because there wasn't one. The teachings of the Church of the Sanctified Assembly forbid a funeral for a person who commits suicide. The bodies of suicides must be cremated without delay and without memorial. Assembly dogma teaches that the nuclei of cells of a suicide are physically corrupted and that this contamination can be transmitted from person to person like an infectious disease.

Although I have no proof, I have doubts about whether Rich killed himself. First of all, I can't see how he could have looped the tie around that pipe, much less crawled up on the ledge. And then there's the way he talked about his wife and young son. He loved both of them so much that he actually fooled himself into thinking that he could get out on bail in a matter of days in time for his son's birthday, despite the cash and the false passport.

Another question nags at me. If Rich was murdered, would that mean that there was something to his and Layla's belief that Harmon Cherry had been murdered, too? During the past three weeks, I've

talked to federal jail authorities and law enforcement officials, who've
dismissed my concerns.

"Suicides in a federal jail are rare, but staged suicides are unheard-
of," one cop told me. "He was a meth user who just a few weeks earlier
was worth millions. He was going to spend years in prison. The only
mistake was that he should have been on suicide watch."

On this night, Manny, Deanna, and I are sitting at a corner table at
The Barrista. A rowdy crowd is here, but I try to shut out their raucous
laughter and harsh shrieks and focus on my colleagues. It doesn't work.
On an ordinary night, the three of us can seamlessly talk about our lives
and squabble about politics and dissect the strengths and weaknesses of
our favorite sports teams. Tonight, we sit in virtual silence and stare at
each other like strangers.

Finally, Deanna says, "This is bullshit." She stands up and pushes
her way through the crowd toward the kitchen. She quickly returns, her
hand hidden beneath her apron. When she sits down, she leans in confidentially, at the same time pulling out a bottle of Hennessy cognac. "If
anyone reports this to the alcohol beverage control police, I'm fucked."

Manny, the collector of fine wines, leans in and checks the label.
"VSOP. Very nice."

She discreetly pours a generous amount of cognac into each of our
coffee cups and hides the bottle under the table. She holds up her cardboard cup. "To Rich Baxter's memory. May he rest . . . may he rest wherever Sanctified Assembly followers rest."

We touch our cardboard cups together. When I swallow the liquid,
the alcohol singes the back of my tongue; then the heat dissipates, radi-
ating a mellow warmth throughout my body.

Manny takes a sip and makes a face. "Hennessy mixed with tepid
cappuccino. You've defiled an elegant brandy."

Deanna reaches down, takes the bottle, and pours more into his
cup. "Here, Manny. Drown your sorrows." I extend my cup toward her.
She refills it and replenishes her own.

And still, there's an awkward silence.

"Why's it so hard to talk about him?" Deanna says.

"Because it's horrific," Manny says. "So sad. The man was only thirty-eight years old, with a wife and small child. It was such a waste."

"I look at it another way," Deanna says. "I think we can't talk about this because the act of suicide is so accessible, because it's so human. No other species does it. Not really. And there's a perfect logic to it—what better way to end pain? And it works for the atheist and the true believer. For the atheist, the nothingness of death ends pain. For the believer, the afterlife does, unless you believe that suicide's a sin, that there's a hell, which I don't. Sometimes I feel like there's something captivating about the whole idea, like Romeo and Juliet, or Mark Rothko, or—"

Manny visibly shudders. "My God, Deanna. Don't talk like that. We've had enough with . . ."

I don't know whether Deanna is just being provocative or really means it, but I reach out and take her hand, a rare display of affection outside the confines of our sporadic trysts. She rolls her eyes and pulls away.

I take a swig of cognac. "I'm beginning to truly believe he was murdered. I think someone strung him up to a water pipe. Nothing captivating about that."

Deanna and Manny catch each other's eyes. She reaches for the Hennessy bottle and splashes another shot in each of our cups. Eventually, the power of the alcohol and just being in each other's presence impels us to begin sharing stories about Rich, some of them not so kind.

"Remember when I tried to fix him up with that college friend of mine?" Deanna says. "He was so shy with girls she told me he didn't say more than two words at dinner . . . until he started talking about banking law and wouldn't shut up. My poor friend ran an art gallery in Santa Monica. Finance was the last thing she wanted to talk about. They didn't go out again."

"He used to ask me for dating advice," Manny says. "What the hell did I know about dating? I've been married forever." Manny wed his college sweetheart when he was twenty-one, a youthful romance that's worked. Now, at thirty-eight, he has three sons.

"I still say that the weirdest thing was him and Grace lasting so long," Deanna says.

Manny nods his head in agreement. Rich and Grace Trimble, the fifth member of our class, dated for eight months, when we were all third-year associates. Two mismatched souls drawn together by the force of the new millennium. Grace was brilliant, but also disturbed. She was wilder than Deanna—well, not wilder, but far more self-destructive. Every night after work and on weekends, Grace would hit the music clubs, ostensibly to sign talent in her quest to become a music lawyer, but really to dance and pick up men and do drugs. She'd tell outlandish stories about sleeping with rock stars and rappers and fighting off muggers and rapists. Shortly before she left the firm—a few years before Harmon died—she was diagnosed as being bipolar. When she crashed, we all realized that she'd been self-medicating.

"This is mean," Deanna says. "But I was pretty surprised when Rich came to the firm summer party with Monica. She was so hot, and Rich . . ." She half-shrugs. "Well, he was Rich." She takes a drink of cognac and smiles salaciously. "If Rich hadn't been my friend, I would've hit on Monica myself."

Manny grimaces, then takes a long drink, as if to wash away the bad taste of Deanna's comment.

"Monica married him because his so-called church arranged it," I say.

"Jesus, Parker," Deanna says, shaking her head in disapproval.

We sit in silence. And then we start reminiscing again, repeating well-worn stories that have become more fanciful with each telling. Rich's chronic inability to keep his meal off his clothing, so bad that he once walked out of RJ's restaurant with half a chicken wing hanging from his collar. Rich always playing the "fish" in our monthly card games. Rich as a marvelous rainmaker who spent time wining and dining clients at the expense of learning technical legal skills.

"This is another shitty thing to bring up," Deanna says. "But I always worried that he was a walking malpractice suit. When he left the firm, I couldn't see him making it on his own with a demanding client like the Assembly."

Manny glances at me. He said the same thing about Rich. So did Andrew Macklin.

I chug down the last of my cognac. "Maybe that's why he was murdered. The Assembly doesn't tolerate mistakes. Maybe he made an error that cost him his life."

"Come on, Parker," Manny says. "There's absolutely no reason to believe—"

"You know what? Forget what I just said. I don't think Rich was killed because he malpracticed. I think it was because he discovered something about the church that he wasn't supposed to know. Just like he told me at the jail. The Assembly wouldn't hesitate to eliminate him if that happened. Not for a second. And they could arrange a jailhouse hit with the snap of a finger."

Deanna and Manny in tandem take long sips of their drinks. For the next few minutes, they both avoid looking at me. I know they've always found my dislike for the Church of the Sanctified Assembly irrational, that they resented me for refusing to pitch in on Assembly matters. Parker Stern, prima donna.

They don't know my history with the Assembly. I'm sure they'd feel differently if they did.

CHAPTER 10

Over the next few weeks, I teach my law school seminar and spend time at The Barrista and drink coffee. And I read. I learn that Gladys Towles Root, the lawyer who specialized in defending rapists, maintained that there were only two types of rape—the brutal and the invited. Absent a beating or a threat, the woman asked for it. Once, during a trial, Root held up a sheet of paper with a hole in it and defied a male juror to stick a pen in the hole while she moved the paper around. I can't tell from the biography whether this was merely a trial tactic or whether she believed it. I hope she didn't believe it. There are few things more dangerous than a lawyer who's a true believer.

I think about Rich constantly, about how and why he died. And the more I think, the more convinced I am that he was murdered. Deanna and Manny don't want to hear about it anymore. I consider calling his wife, Monica, but I know she won't talk to me. I think about contacting his parents, but what would I say? Would they find comfort in hearing some stranger speculate that their son might have been murdered?

Today, while I'm working in my law school office—a windowless hole in the wall reserved for part-time faculty like me—the autopsy report shows up in my e-mail inbox. Because I was Rich's lawyer at the time of his death, the medical examiner's office agreed to send me a copy. I know what the report will say without looking at it, which doesn't stop me from dropping what I'm doing and opening it immediately. I scroll down the computer screen, trying to decipher the pathologist's hypertechnical language. The cause of death is listed as suicide, of course. Then the techno-language. *Partial suspension; asphyxial death; presence of conjunctival and facial petechiae; hyoid fracture; thyroid cartilage fracture; no injuries of a defensive nature; absence of ligature furrow;*

signs of vital reaction around constriction area ambiguous.

I print the report, hoping that reading the hard copy will make things clearer. Before I can begin rereading, there's a loud knock on the open door. Lovely Diamond stands in the doorway, backpack slung over her shoulder. She's never spoken to me outside the classroom, much less come to my office.

"Got five minutes, Professor?"

Over the past weeks, we've managed to forge a barely peaceful coexistence. One of my strengths is figuring people out, digging beneath the exterior and understanding their motivations and fears and strength and weakness of character. Maybe that's how I became a good actor and a successful trial lawyer. But I'm not close to figuring Lovely out. Around her, I feel as if I'm trying to decipher a frustrating but glorious avant-garde novel, dark and impenetrable and lyrical. She reveals herself in fragments.

She sits down and glances around the office. "I've never been in one of these adjunct professor offices before. Is this the best they can do for you?"

"This is about it."

She crinkles her nose. "It smells like mildew or black mold. You adjuncts should go on strike or something. Or get masks."

"The others never come up here. They all have jobs and offices of their own. It's just me."

"Poor you." She reaches into her backpack and pulls out some sort of energy bar, unwraps it, and takes a small bite without asking if I have any objection to her eating in my office. I don't, but I would have appreciated her asking.

I'm about to ask her what she wants when I remember that Lou Frantz handles a lot of medical malpractice cases. "Ms. Diamond, in your job do you review medical reports?"

"Yeah. A lot, unfortunately."

"I just got the medical examiner's report on Richard Baxter's death. I was wondering if you could—"

"Yeah, I'll take a look. I've read my share of pathology reports. Mostly accidents and botched surgeries, but . . ."

I hand her the report. She attacks it with a palpable intensity. She nibbles at her energy bar until it's gone, leaving a crumb stuck to her upper lip. When she finishes, she looks up at me. "So what do you want to know?"

"You . . . you have some food on your lip."

Without a hint of embarrassment, she circles her tongue over her lips, catching the crumb and pulling it into her mouth. "Gone?"

I nod. "What I want to know . . . can you see anything in the ME's report that would lead you to question the conclusion that Rich committed suicide?"

"Possibly."

It's not the answer I expected to hear, and I have to fend off a morbid rush of excitement at the thought that Rich might have been murdered. "What makes you say that?"

"I'd rather hold off on giving an opinion. I need to do some more research."

"Can't you give at least me a hint?"

"No point." She folds her hands in her lap and gets that stubborn look that I see so often in the classroom.

"But you came to see me," I say. "How can I help you?"

She reaches into her backpack, takes out some paper, and hands it to me. "My client, Tyler, has been indicted." Her voice, usually a steady alto, sounds off-key, like a guitar string wound too tightly by a fraction of a turn. "I guess I'm going to get to defend a real case."

The document charges one Tyler Daniels with three counts of Transportation of Obscene Matters in violation of 18 U.S.C. §1462 of the United States Criminal Code: *Whoever knowingly uses any interactive computer service for carriage in interstate commerce of any obscene, lewd, lascivious, or filthy book, pamphlet, writing, print, or other matter of indecent character shall be fined and imprisoned for not more than five years for any first offense and ten years for each such offense thereafter.*

I flip to the second page and read the specifics of count 1. It's just one paragraph, seven lines, but by the time I finish my teeth are clenched so hard that I can hear a high-pitched whine in my ears.

"Oh, Lovely. Why in God's name didn't you tell me what this was?"

CHAPTER 11

Count I: On or about July 29, 2011, in the Central District of California, Defendant, TYLER DANIELS, did knowingly use an interactive computer service for carriage in interstate commerce of an obscene matter: that is "darlene.txt," a text description of the kidnapping and sexual molestation of ten-year-old Darlene.

Count II: On or about July 29, 2011, in the Central District of California, Defendant, TYLER DANIELS, did knowingly use an interactive computer service for carriage in interstate commerce of an obscene matter: that is "nursery.txt," a text description of the sexual molestation of a five-year-old boy.

Count III: On or about July 29, 2011, in the Central District of California, Defendant, TYLER DANIELS, did knowingly use an interactive computer service for carriage in interstate commerce of an obscene matter: that is "kids.txt," a text description of the sexual molestation of an eight-year-old girl, a nine-year-old boy, and a four-year-old girl.

/s/ Neil Latham, United States Attorney
Assigned to Hon. Cyrus Harvey

Lovely sits with hands folded primly in her lap. I want to be angry with her for not disclosing what she was getting into, but I'm more upset with myself for not asking the right questions. When defending sexual-predator clients, Gladys Towles Root maintained that most children lie about being molested. *A child possesses an imagination rivaling Alfred Hitchcock's, and often just as macabre*, she said. She used her status as a woman and a mother to influence juries. When I read this, I almost hurled the book against the wall. No matter how much you believe in the adversary system, there are some cases you refuse to take. This sleazebag, Tyler Daniels, doesn't deserve a defense.

I slide the indictment back to Lovely. "You're actually OK with this?"

Her cheeks redden. "Of course I'm not OK with stories about abusing kids, if that's what you mean."

"I mean that—"

"They're horrible, disgusting stories. But if you mean defending this client, I'm more than OK with that. I've talked about this with Tyler and checked the court records, and there've never been any arrests or convictions or accusations of wrongful conduct, if that's what you're worried about." She pauses for a moment. "The case is just about words, not pictures or actions, and the First Amendment protects words no matter how despicable. Words are sacred. Besides, Tyler needs me."

I try to reserve judgment. I've only read the indictment, in which the prosecutor always slants the facts. "I assume you've read the actual stories. How bad are they?"

She straightens in her chair. "They're as bad as you can imagine. Worse. It's like I had to shower after I read them. But it doesn't matter. This is a case of free speech. It's like Justice Stewart said: 'Censorship reflects a society's lack of confidence in itself.'"

"He also said he knew obscenity when he saw it." I read through the indictment again, deciding. "I'm sorry, Ms. Diamond, I don't think you can be involved in this. Not under the auspices of the law school. Why don't you see if Lou Frantz will take it pro bono."

"He won't. Will you at least talk to the client first?"

"You haven't been meeting with this Tyler person, have you? That would be dangerous."

"It's not dangerous." She thinks for a moment, and then picks up Rich's autopsy report. "Look. You wanted my help with this Baxter thing, right? In return, I'm just asking that you talk to her before you make a decision."

"Talk to who?"

"What do you mean, who? Tyler, of course. If you'd—"

"You said *her*. Who's *her*?"

"*Her*. The client." She sits back in her chair. "Tyler Daniels is a woman, Professor. I thought you knew."

I flip through the indictment again. There's no reference to the defendant's gender. That Tyler is a woman shouldn't lessen my disgust and trepidation over this case one jot. But it does. "OK, Ms. Diamond. I'll meet with her." My voice is disembodied, as if I'm listening to someone else talk on a cheap speakerphone.

"I'll set up a phone call."

"No. It has to be in person. That's something I should've told the class. Always meet with your client in person before you get in too deep, especially in a dicey case like this. You can't get to know a person over the phone, much less e-mail."

"But I don't know if she'll meet in person. She's—"

"It's not open to debate." I check my calendar. Other than teaching once a week, I have nothing to do. So I try to accommodate her job and school schedule by picking a weekend. "How about Saturday, November nineteenth?"

"I can't do a Saturday. I observe Shabbat."

"You're—?"

"Yeah, I'm Jewish. And don't say I don't look it."

"People don't really say that nowadays."

"Oh, they absolutely do. I'll see if Tyler can meet with us on Sunday the twentieth, if that's OK with you."

"The twentieth will be fine."

At a little before six o'clock, my cell phone rings.

"Is this Parker Stern?"

"Yeah, this is Parker."

"Mr. Stern, you don't know me. My name's Raymond Baxter. Richard Baxter's father. I know you were Richie's attorney before he died. I was wondering if you and I could meet." His voice squeaks in that way of decrepit old men. His speech is labored, a half-breath behind.

After so many weeks, I didn't expect to hear from anyone in Rich's family. "I'm very sorry for your loss."

"Kind of you to say, sir." A forced, perfunctory reply—nothing he wants to linger on.

"Can you tell me what you'd like to meet about?"

"I'd rather we do it in person."

"Of course. I'm free every day except Thursday afternoons, when I teach."

He wheezes a couple of times. "Actually, how about tonight? The Lansing Bar and Grill on Third Street? Eight o'clock?"

"I'll be there."

I spend the next couple of hours trying to frame a gentle way of describing Rich Baxter's last days to his father, to spin a story that will give a grieving parent comfort. I attack it from all angles, but can't come up with anything to blunt the horror surrounding Rich's death. We attorneys so often forget that there really aren't two sides to every story, that some things just can't be lawyered away.

CHAPTER 12

When I walk out of the administration building, it's pouring. This is the first rain we've had in eight months, and it's already early November. Even in a drought year, it's late for the season's first storm. The air smells like fresh-cut grass and pine resin and wet asphalt. The temperature must have dropped fifteen degrees, into the low-fifties. I don't have a jacket. I linger under an awning for a moment, steel my courage, cover my head with the book I've been reading, and sprint across the plaza to the parking lot. By the time I reach cover, I'm drenched and shivering. I get into my Lexus—a status symbol from a different time of my life—start the engine, and turn up the heat. I can't get warm.

I drive out of the parking lot and merge into the inevitable traffic jam. I make a right onto Wilshire Boulevard. Traffic is snarled from downtown to the ocean, the procession of cars like twin serpents of red and white light trying to slither in opposite directions but going nowhere. Honking, oil slicks, potholes, street-floods, signal-outages, gridlock, profanity, road-rage.

When I still practiced law—when I considered myself an important man—traffic jams like this would unravel my nerves and make me pound the steering wheel with the heel of my hand. After all, I had places to go and deadlines to meet. But now I have precisely the opposite reaction. Now, there's something enchanting about the ebbs and flows and fits and starts of the cars and buses. It's as if we're all doing a kind of impromptu dance that has its own peculiar rhythm. Spontaneous environmental art; automotive choreography, with the dilapidated storefronts and harried pedestrians as our audience. Some of us master the steps and some of us falter, but we're all in it together. I don't bother turning on the radio. The city generates its own music, enthralling even on this most dissonant of nights.

After fifty minutes in traffic, I arrive at the Lansing Bar and Grill on Third and La Brea. The place is half-empty. The patrons who have shown up are mostly older men dressed in synthetic suits—veteran insurance executives or stockbrokers with too much time to kill. At thirty-seven, I feel like a kid in this room. I sit in a corner near the window. When the waitress comes, I order a Bass Ale. Though smoking in bars and restaurants has been illegal for years, I could swear I smell stale cigarette smoke emanating from the upholstery. I nurse my beer and look out the window. The headlights from the cars driving down La Brea refract through the raindrops.

In my peripheral vision, I see an older man walking toward me with deliberate steps. He's dressed casually in a khaki windbreaker and brown slacks. Even stooped with age, he's tall, much taller than Rich. The overall impression is gray—gray hair, gray skin, gray stare, gray demeanor. For a fleeting moment, I wonder if Rich was adopted.

"Parker?"

I stand and extend my hand.

"Sorry I'm late. The traffic in the rain is terrible."

He orders a Chivas 18, but has to settle for a Dewar's. We make small talk about the traffic and the weather until the waitress brings him the scotch. He looks like the type of man to toast you automatically, but he doesn't toast me. His hand is shaking. He takes a long drink of the booze and sets his glass down on the table. "You know, when the law firm was still around, Rich would say that you were the best young trial lawyer in the city."

"Rich liked to exaggerate his friends' abilities."

He raises his hand and waves it in a way that makes me embarrassed about my false modesty.

"Richie was great with people, but he struggled with the cerebral part of life. He did well enough in school, but he got by on hard work more than anything. He knew it. He would say that other people at the firm were smart or articulate or crafty, but that you were the only one who had all those skills. That's why he hired you when he got involved in this last scrape with that so-called church of his. He admired you."

No matter how much Rich admired me, I hardly acquitted myself well as his lawyer.

"I never understood why Harmon Cherry took that evil cult on as a client," Baxter says. "A horrible thing for him to do."

"The Assembly deserved representation just like any other client," I say, unable to suppress my compulsion to defend Harmon's memory no matter what the truth. "Besides, Harmon could control them."

"That's bullshit. No one can control them." He takes a quick breath. "I thought Richie was really going to make it until that woman got him involved in that Sanctified Assembly crap." Without warning, he leans in toward me, so close that I can smell the booze on his breath. That, and the sour odor of human decay. "They murdered my son."

I don't know yet where this man is coming from, so I don't reveal my own suspicions. I knit my brow almost imperceptibly and pretend to be perplexed. I'm a still a good actor. "What makes you think that Rich was murdered? I've seen the pathology report, and the medical examiner concluded otherwise." I can't bring myself to use the word *suicide*. Not to his father.

"Because Richie was starting to awaken from the nightmare that is the Sanctified Assembly. He called me from the jail just two days before he died. The first time in years. Did he tell you that?"

"He didn't."

"It was an act of bravery on his part, and God knows Richie wasn't always brave. You know about the Assembly's policy of disengagement? Sounds like they plagiarized it from the Cold War. They ordered him to disengage with us because we were vocal nonbelievers. Said we were toxic, that we would threaten the health of him and his family. And they meant physical health. According to their Fount or whatever, it's other people's attitudes that cause disease, not germs. His mother and I were bacteria to him. That kind of thinking literally killed my wife. He didn't even come to her funeral. She never got to see her grandson."

The dim bar lamps shimmer in the glaze that coats his eyes. "But then Richie called me. He told me he was in jail, that he was being framed by someone, that he had some information about doings at the Assembly that made him rethink everything. He just wanted to get back to his little boy. I never heard him so driven. Suicide? Impossible."

"Did he name names? Give you any evidence?"

He shakes his head. "I asked him. But there is one person I know about. Richie worked with a man named Christopher McCarthy. He's the Assembly's top PR man."

Christopher McCarthy is more than a PR man. He runs the Assembly's Technology Communications Organization—TCO for short—and serves as the Assembly's public face. He's a member of its hierarchy. He was also the main client contact back at the law firm. He'd walk in unannounced looking for Rich or Manny or some other lawyer he knew and demand that they drop whatever they were doing and meet with him. Only Deanna had the guts to blow him off if she was busy on another matter.

"I don't mean to be insensitive," I say. "But Rich was found with a false passport in his possession. That's a crime, and evidence of guilt. The FBI also found a large amount of cash and drugs in his apartment, which, by the way, he rented under an assumed name."

"Richie was frightened of the Assembly, and he had reason to be, as it turned out. Who wouldn't have a contingency plan? I think he was going to go to the authorities, but just in case . . ." His voice trails off. He doesn't mention the drugs. The identity theft and the drugs are the two pieces of evidence that I find impossible to explain away. "What do you think happened to Richie?" he says.

"I don't know."

"Yes, you do. You know they killed him. You have no use for them. Of all the people at the firm, you refused to work for them. Poulos did, and Mason and that Trimble woman. But not you. The firm's biggest client and its rising star, and never the twain met. You don't like them."

"How can I help you, Mr. Baxter?"

"I need a lawyer and I want you. I think the Assembly is going to sue me."

"For what?"

He clenches and opens his fists several times. "I don't know. But I'm the executor of Richie's estate and his sole beneficiary. I expect them to come after me for the money."

"I'm sure his wife Monica is the—"

"Harmon Cherry required all lawyers at the firm to have a will, right?"

I nod. I was the only one who didn't follow Harmon's instructions. I had no one to bequeath my estate to.

"Well, Rich had the will drawn up because of that rule. It was before he joined the Assembly, before he was married. And I know he didn't change it since then."

"How can you be so sure? He got married and had a kid and—"

"You should know why he didn't change it."

It takes me a moment. "OK. I get it. The Assembly doesn't believe in bequeathed wealth. They believe it's a transgression to die with resources. Possessions are supposed to be gifted to the church while the person's alive. So they don't allow wills."

"A scam by those phony bastards to increase their coffers by getting people to give up their money sooner. But I'm sure Richie had money left when he died, and they're going to want it. I'm going to fight them for it."

"What about Monica and the child? Ordinarily—"

"The wife will get half anyway, right? Community property? And if the rest of the money would actually go to the wife and the kid, that would be fine with me. But the Assembly will try to take it all, and I won't let that happen. I'll donate the money to a real charity instead."

Though I can't be sure, he doesn't seem like someone who wants to deprive a widow and child of their inheritance. He really seems to want justice done. But he needs to be realistic. "Mr. Baxter, if the Assembly sues you—and I don't know that they will—it won't be pleasant. In fact, I'd advise you to settle quickly. The Assembly settles cases all the time. On a one-sided basis, sure, but it's better than going to war with them. And that's what a lawsuit would be. They've broken men with far more money and power than you. And as for me being your lawyer, I don't even have a law firm anymore."

"I don't give a goddamn rat's ass about that," he says, his lips contorted in anger. "And you shouldn't either. Don't you get it? You were supposed to be Richie's lawyer, his advocate. You. He died on your watch. Not only did he lose his life, he lost his legacy. If the Assembly comes after the estate, they're going to smear him. He'll be remembered as Richard Baxter the suicide, Richard Baxter the crook, Richard Baxter the drug addict. You owe him a chance to clear his name."

I start to protest, but I don't have it in me. "I'll tell you what. I'll check around."

"It'll take more than checking around. I need legal representation." He shakes his head. "I don't know why I expected anything of you. Apologies." He downs the rest of his drink and makes a move to leave.

I remember that biography of Gladys Towles Root. Whatever I might think of her ethics, she took on controversial, dangerous cases—a rape case in a hostile small Nevada town, the defense of the man who kidnapped Frank Sinatra's son—in the steadfast belief that the law would keep her safe. The only reason I'd refuse to help Raymond Baxter is fear. I'm tired of being afraid.

"Wait." He turns around. "I'll look into it. I'll act as the estate's lawyer for the time being and start preparing a defense in case they do sue. I'll also get the probate process going. We'll see how it goes."

He doesn't respond, just looks at me, his eyes once again lifeless now that his anger has subsided. He reaches into the inside pocket of his windbreaker and takes out a pen and a checkbook. "How much of a retainer will you need?"

"Nothing. But I will need a copy of the will and all the other testamentary papers. The sooner you get them to me the sooner I can start. Send them to me at the St. Thomas More School of Law."

"I'll have them delivered tomorrow." He drops a twenty-dollar bill on the table and shuffles out of the bar more slowly than he did when he came in.

CHAPTER 13

Instead of holding my next trial advocacy class at the law school, I take my three students on a field trip—an inspection of the apartment where Rich Baxter supposedly hid out and committed his illegal acts under the name Alan Markowitz. It's the beginning of the lawyer's chase, which is mostly grunt work: pursuing recalcitrant witnesses who won't cooperate because there's nothing in it for them, sifting through trivia to try to glean one relevant fact, fitting disparate bits of information into a logical pattern.

We drive the short distance from the law school to the Silver Lake district, an area in the hills east of Hollywood known for its modernist architecture and bohemian residents. We talk about Rich Baxter's alleged crimes and about the law. I spend most of the drive telling war stories about my days at the law firm representing celebrities, and the rest of it peeking in the rearview mirror because I notice Jonathan and Kathleen holding hands in the back seat. All the while, I hope Lovely will update me on her analysis of Rich's autopsy report. She doesn't say a word about it.

We arrive at a beige structure backed up against a steep hill. The apartment is constructed in a series of cantilevered terraced rectangles made of glass and wood and stucco. The design gives the illusion of a single family dwelling, but actually there are nine units. A nice place for Rich to hide out.

We meet the building manager, a man named Dale Garner. Anywhere between forty-five and sixty years old, he stands well over six feet and has the girth of a professional wrestler. But unlike a wrestler, there's not a hint of muscle in his body. From the moment we walk in, his eyes fix on Lovely and rarely look elsewhere.

To establish our right to enter Rich's apartment, I show him the document appointing Raymond Baxter executor of Rich's estate, along with a letter from Raymond identifying me as the estate's lawyer. Garner examines them meticulously. "How do I know you're who you say you are?" He speaks in a reedy voice that doesn't match his girth.

"I can show you my ID. And you can call my client. He's standing by."

"And how will I know he's really your client?"

Garner's clearly one of those petty people who likes to exert whatever scintilla of power he possesses. There's only one way to handle guys like him.

"If you don't let us in right now," I say, "I'll go directly to court and file a wrongful eviction suit citing your lack of cooperation. Today. I'm sure you know that the lease has an attorney's fees clause. And you're on notice, Mr. Garner—I'm expensive."

He tries to stare me down, and when I don't look away, he frowns and grudgingly hands me the key to Rich's unit.

"OK if I ask you a few questions before we look at the apartment?" I say.

"I don't know what you'd ask me. I don't know anything."

Jonathan raises his hand. "How about if Kathleen and I start looking through the apartment?"

I give him the key, and they leave.

"I don't know how I can help you," Garner repeats. "Everything I had to say I told the cops."

"What kind of tenant was Baxter?" I ask. "How often was he here, who did he see? Anything unusual?"

"I just told you I gave all of this to the cops. You say you were his lawyer. Didn't you read the report?"

"I never saw it. My client died before the US Attorney had to turn it over."

"Well, isn't that too bad for you and your client."

"We know you're a busy man, Mr. Garner," Lovely says with a broad smile. "We don't want to waste your time. But we'd like to hear it directly from you, if that's OK. You know how the cops are. You can't always trust what's in a police report, am I right?" I expected her just to listen, to act like the student she's supposed to be. When I was at the firm I always handled interviews myself.

"You are right," he says, as if her words have jumpstarted his heart. "And call me Dale."

"And you can call me Lovely."

"That's your name?"

"My real name."

He smiles at her. "Well, it fits."

"Why, thank you, sir." She tilts her head and actually blushes. Her eyes glimmer. It's as good as any performance I saw from the actresses I worked with as a kid.

"So what can you tell us about Richard Baxter?" she says.

Garner acts as if I'm not in the room. "Well, you call him Baxter, and that was his name I guess, but I knew him as Alan Markowitz. He signed a year lease. He had what looked like a valid ID, passed a credit check with flying colors, said he was a car dealer, seemed like a straight arrow. He sure put one over on me. In fact, he almost cost me my job."

"He was a problem?" she asks.

"Yes and no. He kept to himself, didn't annoy anyone, but that wasn't the issue. He wasn't here much, only a few nights a week. It became pretty clear why when those women started showing up."

"What women?" she asks.

He folds his arms across his chest, making a show of moral indignation. "I'm embarrassed to say this around a nice young lady like yourself, but those women of his were obviously whores. The expensive kind. What do they call themselves these days? Escorts? They were well-dressed, you know, high class. But still whores. He probably got them over the Internet like that ex-governor of New York, what's his name? I didn't approve and didn't appreciate that kind of behavior in my building. We operate a very respectable apartment complex, not a brothel."

"Can you describe these women?" she asks.

"There were three of them. One was a sorority-girl type, satiny dresses, wholesome looking in a way. The one with the black hair was, what do they call it nowadays, Gothic? Dressed in black leather, freaky makeup, piercings, like some kind of S&M dominatrix. She looked like a character out of one of those vampire shows. The other one was just plain trashy—short skirts, spiky heels, that kind of thing."

My body tenses. "The woman who dressed like a Goth. Did she have tattoos?"

Because I've spoken, he goes back into that place where recalcitrant witnesses go—on his guard, resentful and distant. "Can't say one way or another."

Lovely waits for me to follow up. When I don't, she says, "You're sure they were escorts?"

"Oh yes. By the way they walked and the way they dressed."

"How old?" she says.

"I only saw them at night. Twenties or thirties, probably."

"Just a couple of more questions, Dale," she says. "Did you speak to any of these women?"

"I tried once. The night the cops came and raided the place and Markowitz . . . I mean Baxter . . . was arrested. Two hours later, I saw the sorority girl going up to his apartment. Don't know what she was doing there. Maybe she didn't know that he was in jail. Anyway, I was out in the driveway doing something when she came back outside. I said hello, tried to make conversation. I wanted to find out once and for all what Markowitz was really up to. Do you know that she kicked at me with those pointy heels and took off running before I could do anything about it?" He shakes his head. "All I wanted to do was talk to her."

"You said that she was leaving his apartment," Lovely says. "How did she get in?"

"Beats me. I assume she had a key."

We shoot more questions at him for the next five minutes, but he doesn't have anything else useful to say.

"You've been very helpful, Dale." Lovely says. "Is there anything else that you can think of that's relevant? Anything at all?"

"There might . . ." He hesitates. He's fighting himself, torn between his inclination to stay uninvolved and his desire to please Lovely. "You know, I wanted Markowitz out of here for breaching the lease. Using his apartment unit for illicit purposes. But I had no proof. So I took some pictures. Of the women."

Lovely and I glance at each other. I don't say anything. This is now her show.

"Do you still have them, Dale?"

He hesitates again, and then nods. "They're not very clear. I took them with my cell phone camera in the dark and uploaded them to my computer."

"Can we see?"

He leads us into his bedroom, where the computer sits on a scratched-up pine desk covered with stacks of papers organized in discrete piles. He launches three thumbnail photos.

To say that the quality is poor is an understatement. It's not just that they were taken at night. The women were obviously on the move, blurring the pictures. You can make out the hair color and the outlines of their bodies, along with the clothing—they look just as he described them—but their facial features are indistinct. They're all petite. I ask Garner to switch the photos to full screen. The larger images are so pixilated that the women's features have been obliterated. Unless we find something when we enhance them, these pictures are worthless, no more informative than construction-paper silhouettes.

"Is it OK if we get a copy of these images, Dale?" Lovely says. She reaches into her backpack and hands him a portable flash drive. "If you just put that in your USB port, you can copy them onto this."

"Help yourself, Lovely." He moves aside and pulls the chair out for her with a flourish.

After she's made the copies, we leave his apartment, but not before he asks Lovely to have dinner or lunch or coffee with him, offers she deftly rebuffs.

"Good job," I say when we're out of earshot.

"The guy's pathetic."

"You got him to give up those photos. They're a great find if we can enhance them and get a look at those women's faces."

"Did you notice why their faces are blurred, Professor?"

"Garner said he took the pictures at night when they were moving."

Lovely shakes her head. "That might be part of it. But the creep wasn't interested in their faces. He was trying to get a picture of each woman's ass."

CHAPTER 14

Lovely walks into The Barrista a little after seven o'clock, comes over to my table, and says, "I want to talk to you about the Baxter autopsy. I'll be right back."

"Ms. Diamond, wait."

But she's already halfway to the coffee bar.

She returns five minutes later carrying some sort of syrupy drink topped with a huge mound of whipped cream. She sits down across from me, sips the drink through a straw, and says, "Dean Mason told me where to find you. He didn't want to, but when I told him the reason, he gave in. He said this is where you always hang out."

I hate that I've become so predictable.

"This place is awesome," she says. "The coffee's great. Much better than the chains."

"Thank you," Deanna says from somewhere behind me. She pulls up a chair and situates herself between Lovely and me. She extends her hand. "I'm Deanna. The owner."

"This is Ms. Diamond," I say. "One of my law students."

"My name's Lovely. I'm in Professor Stern's trial advocacy class."

"Good meeting you," Deanna says with a look so solemn that it's clear she's trying not to laugh at Lovely's name and at the idea that anyone would call me *Professor* Stern.

"The autopsy report," I say.

"I finished my analysis. I wanted to debrief you on it."

"Whoa," Deanna says. "Serious stuff. You know, Parker here has the crazy idea that Rich might've been murdered."

"I think the professor is right," Lovely says.

Deanna and I sway back in our seats and move forward again at exactly the same time, as though we're performing a bizarre dance.

"Are you saying someone strung poor Rich up into a noose?" Deanna asks her.

"Unlikely. Murder by hanging is almost unheard of. It's almost impossible for one person to overpower another and hang him, even when there's a big difference in size and strength. At least, not without other signs of violence or a beating, which don't exist here."

"Then how—?"

"Let Ms. Diamond finish," I say.

Deanna frowns and rolls her eyes. She's on her best behavior, because ordinarily, she'd flip me off.

"First I checked some resources at work," Lovely says. "And then this guy I know at the USC Medical School did me a favor. My firm has used him as an expert pathologist, and he and I dated for a couple of months, so . . . He says that people who've been murdered by strangulation usually have a mark on their neck where the cord cut in. It's called a ligature furrow. It takes a lot of strength to strangle someone, and the application of force results in the mark. People who commit suicide usually don't have a ligature furrow, especially if they use a soft material to hang themselves. Like Rich Baxter's silk necktie."

"The coroner found no evidence of a ligature furrow," I say. "Wouldn't that support his conclusion of suicide?"

Lovely nods.

"Then how—?"

"There are ways—arm bars, specialized holds—where Rich could have been murdered without the killer leaving a ligature furrow. A professional hit man or martial arts expert or military special forces veteran could easily do it."

"So the absence of a ligature furrow isn't proof of suicide," I say. "But that doesn't mean it was homicide."

"But there was a fracture of the hyoid bone." She straightens her neck and rubs it at a place just under her chin. "Right here. A fractured hyoid bone—and a fractured thyroid cartilage, which Baxter also had—usually come from manual strangulation, not from hanging.

After forty, the likelihood of a hyoid fracture from a suicidal hanging increases because old bones are more brittle, but Rich Baxter was only thirty-eight. If it was really suicide, he shouldn't have had a fractured hyoid. There was also some hemorrhaging at the spot, which would indicate homicide. And there was a wound on the back of his head. The ME's report concludes that the head injury was caused when the marshals pushed the door of the cell open to get inside, but someone could have hit him."

"So why the conclusion that Rich killed himself?" I ask. "Was the pathologist negligent or corrupt or—?"

"My friend says it's still a judgment call," Lovely says. "But in his opinion, when someone has a fractured hyoid bone like Baxter did, he thinks the presumption should be murder unless proven otherwise. The problem is that while the feds don't like suicides in their jail, they like homicides even less. Baxter faced a long sentence and the disgrace of being branded a criminal and a drug addict. And a traitor to the Assembly. It was easy for the coroner to conclude that he killed himself to escape all that."

"In other words, the ME took the easy way out," I say.

Lovely nods.

"I can't believe Rich was really murdered," Deanna whispers.

"Probably murdered," Lovely says. "I wish I could be more definite."

Lovely begins walking us through the autopsy report in more detail, explaining the technical terms as best she can. Deanna slides her chair close, puts her hand on Lovely's shoulder, and leaves it there for a long time. I'd take the gesture as innocuous if I hadn't seen Deanna put the moves on women before. Lovely doesn't shrink from the contact. Eventually, the glances and the smiles flow only between them. It's as if I'm on the wrong side of a sheet of Plexiglas. Nothing makes you feel lonelier than being with people who are paying attention to each other and ignoring you. Worse, it's not Deanna's attention I crave, but Lovely's.

CHAPTER 15

Last week, I assigned Kathleen Williams the task of researching and reporting on the origins and beliefs of the Church of the Sanctified Assembly. If my students are going to help me investigate the Assembly, they need to know what it stands for. Now, she's so nervous that she restarts her presentation three times. With each misstep she takes, I want to flee the room, as though I'm the one melting into a shapeless puddle of embarrassment. All the while, I nod sympathetically and dole out bits of wisdom about how lawyers can learn to manage stage fright, how it's natural to feel anxious before speaking in public, and how adrenaline, if harnessed, can help you succeed. I wish it were true.

As she scans her notes, she twists her stringy brown hair around her left index finger. Red splotches appear on her plump cheeks and then dissipate almost as quickly. "OK," she says. She fumbles with her pages and takes three short breaths. "The Church of the Sanctified Assembly was founded . . . was founded maybe twenty . . . I guess twenty-five years ago, in around 1987 or '88, by the late Bradley Kelly." She speaks in a monotone, almost as if her voice were computer-generated. "Kelly was a former actor who experienced a spiritual transformation during what he described as a state of pure celestial ecstasy. In 1978, during the darkest time of his life, he found a crease in the universe that had opened up to him. By passing his soul through that crease or tear, whatever, in the time–space continuum, he was able to converse with the Celestial Fountain of All That Is, or the Fount, which transmitted the Celestial Laws to him, like Moses and the burning bush. He described his experience as almost like making love with God. He wrote a best-selling book about all this stuff, which really kick-started the religion." She scans her notes, momentarily lost. When she gets back on track, she summarizes the Assembly's basic tenets, not only those packaged for public consumption—mostly benign platitudes plagiarized from other religions—but also the extortionate tithing policy, the intense brainwashing palmed off as "self-criticism" sessions, the church-sanctioned homophobia, the contempt for the mentally ill.

"Anyway, in 1995, Kelly died in a boating accident. He was sailing with some friends in a yacht off the coast of California and was thrown off the boat in rough seas. The death kind of deified him. The Assembly says that Kelly didn't really die, but instead was translated through that crease in the universe in a fiery chariot just like Elijah the Prophet from the Old Testament. His death—Kelly's, not Elijah's—sent the sale of his book through the roof, and Assembly membership as of 2011 has increased to six million people worldwide since his death. The Sanctified Assembly is banned as an illegal cult in some countries. You know, countries that don't have a First Amendment protection for freedom of religion like we do. Anyway, that's all." She collapses into her chair.

"Nice job," I say. "Very thorough."

She mumbles a "thank you," but doesn't believe my praise for a minute.

I glance at the clock. I'm about to end the class when Lovely says, "I just checked the Internet Movie Database. It says here you appeared in a movie with Bradley Kelly when you were a kid?"

Kathleen and Jonathan snap to attention.

"You know I don't like talking about my acting career, Ms. Diamond."

"This isn't about that," she says. "It's about the founder of the Church of the Sanctified Assembly." She simply will not give up, on this or anything else.

"OK. We were in one silly movie together. Doheny Beach Vacation or something like that."

Lovely checks her computer screen. "*Doheny Beach Holiday,* 1986. He costarred with you. Played your stepfather."

"*Erica Hatfield* was the costar," I say in a tone more emphatic than I intend. I feel my face flush.

Lovely shifts in her chair and gives me a puzzled look, which I pretend to ignore.

"Erica was a superb actress. She played my mother."

"Who's this Erica Hatfield?" Jonathan asks.

"She was big in the eighties," I say.

Lovely types into her keyboard. "A lot of TV and movies, and then nothing after 1989."

"What happened?" Jonathan asks.

"She got sick of the industry bullshit and moved on with her life."

"What's she doing now?" Lovely says.

"I lost track of her twenty years ago."

"What was Kelly like?" she says.

"I really didn't know him. I do know that he wasn't much of an actor. In hindsight, he probably didn't care much about acting. He started out in the sixties as a pretty-boy type. He was Hollywood slick, if that means anything to you. I certainly didn't see anything indicating he was the Messiah. But what did I know? I was just a kid." I cross my arms. "That's all for today. See you next week."

CHAPTER 16

Christopher McCarthy's assistant leads me into a large corner office where McCarthy sits behind a beveled glass and chrome desk that has only one piece of paper on it. Though we're indoors, McCarthy's wearing sunglasses with tinted blue lenses. He's dressed in an expensive brown silk suit, monogrammed pink dress shirt with a white collar and cuffs, and pink tie. In this era of sunscreen and skin cancer, he has a deep tan.

He gives me the once-over, and I know why—I'm wearing a polo shirt and blue jeans. Back when my law firm still existed, the Assembly insisted that its lawyers wear suits to meetings. He stands, and when we shake hands I smell his spicy cologne, perfumy and cloying.

"Have a seat," he says in the stentorian, mocking tone of a talk-radio host. His voice scrapes at my nervous system, just as it did back at the law firm when he'd walk into the lobby and assault the receptionist with a loud, "Hello there, Kay, I'll show myself back."

I sit across from him in a sleek chair with a hard, uncomfortable back.

"One moment," he says. He picks up his phone and buzzes his secretary. "If Jillian Jackson calls, put her through." It's his way of letting me know that he won't interrupt his day for someone as insignificant as I am. He replaces the handset in the cradle. "It's been a long time. I'm always interested in my former lawyers."

"I was never your lawyer. Though God knows you asked Harmon to assign me to your cases often enough."

He's always had this peculiar tightening of the right corner of his mouth that at first looks like a smirk. Only when it repeats do you realize that it's a nervous tic. Now, his lips twitch twice in succession.

"So you're here to talk about that unfortunate Rich Baxter, huh?"

"The Assembly accused him of stealing and had him thrown in jail. Then he died. He didn't steal and he didn't kill himself."

"What's your interest in this?"

I can't tell him that Raymond Baxter has hired me to defend the estate against a future Assembly lawsuit. If he knew that, he wouldn't tell me anything. "After Rich was arrested, he hired me as his lawyer. I want to clear his name. He was my friend."

"From what I hear, you and he were hardly friends."

"He was my friend," I repeat. "I thought you might be interested in helping me find the people who're really ripping off your organization. And who murdered Rich."

"Rich Baxter was diseased. He was offered the cure—faith in the Fount and in its teachings—but he flouted it. He embezzled from the Assembly. A tremendous amount of money that had been earmarked for good works, and he stole it. He consorted with prostitutes. He was a drug abuser. The Assembly offers salvation. Baxter had every opportunity to save himself, but he fell. He let his church and his family down. Of course, misguided, empty people like you and his father—Raymond Baxter's your client, right?—can't accept the truth of that."

"How do you . . . ?"

"How do we know what?" he says, taunting me. "You mean that Raymond Baxter hired you?"

I don't respond, though I'd very much like to know how the Assembly learned this confidential information.

"Do you think secrets really exist, Stern? Belief in secrets is a superstition, a figment of the imagination of those who don't accept the Fount, who can't see beyond their own limited reality. People like you and Raymond Baxter. Only the ignorant believe in secrets, because secrets seem to explain away their lack of enlightenment. There's only one true secret—the mystery of the Fount."

"I suppose that's why everyone knows that the TCO is a shill for the Assembly even though you try to keep that secret?"

He doesn't react to my lame attempt at a counterpunch. I feel as though he's gripped my spine and twisted it violently. I *have* built my life on secrets. But this is how they manipulate you, how they lure you into the fold or frighten you into silence—by pretending to possess some extrasensory power that lets them see inside you. Like all false prophets and petty grifters, they have no power unless their target believes. I refuse to believe.

"Rich was murdered," I say. "He discovered something incriminating about your church or someone in it and he was killed for it."

"If you and Baxter so much as wink at the news media about a false accusation like that, you'll be hit with a lawsuit so large that in the end you'll be working for the Assembly for the rest of your lives. However long those lives are."

"I thrive on lawsuits, remember? That's what I do. And I assume you're not making a physical threat with that last remark."

He's not smiling anymore. His lips are pressed together, drained of color.

And at that moment, I'm sure that Raymond Baxter is right—the Assembly intends to come after Rich's estate. They're just biding their time while they build a case. That's how the Assembly approaches a lawsuit—like a well-coordinated military campaign. "How about some cooperation," I say. "To our mutual benefit."

"Why would we need your help with anything?"

"Because I'm better than you at getting to the truth."

He crosses his arms and leans back in his chair. "You are an arrogant man. You always were, with your self-righteous refusal to work on our matters as if you were superior to us, when you were the one dwelling in the darkness." With his shaded eyes and his impeccable tan and his perfect hair, he's machinelike. "You're to stay away from us."

I get up to leave.

"Wait." He points a finger at me and jabs it in the air. "You and your client must stop harassing Monica Baxter. No matter how contaminated her husband was, she's still a grieving widow, and she doesn't deserve such treatment."

"I don't know what you're talking about."

"I'll spell it out for you. Mrs. Baxter has gotten anonymous e-mails claiming that her husband was murdered." He shakes his head in disgust. "Harassing a widow while she's in mourning. I would have thought as a protégé of Harmon Cherry these tactics would be beneath you. That's something he never would have tolerated. Stop the e-mails. If you don't, there will be consequences. The Assembly protects its own."

"That's the second time you've threatened me. And your second grave mistake."

The side of his mouth begins to twitch almost nonstop. Without saying another word, I walk out.

CHAPTER 17

The ninety-minute drive to the Mojave Desert takes Lovely and me through some of the most desolate terrain in Southern California. Because it's early on a Sunday, there's not much traffic. She's dressed down—blue jeans, a red Nike T-shirt, and a navy blue hoodie, hair pulled back in a ponytail, no makeup. It doesn't matter. Her voice is electric, and her smoky gray eyes continually draw me in, so much so that I often find myself looking at her instead of the road.

We talk about our search for the women we've come to refer to as "Rich Baxter's hookers," about how Rich could have been murdered in a crowded jail, about the constitutional defenses to obscenity prosecutions. I talk about my days at Macklin & Cherry. She reveals that after law school, she's going to join Lou Frantz's firm—nothing short of remarkable, because he never hires directly out of law school, preferring lawyers with at least five years of trial experience.

There's a long stretch of quiet, as exciting as standing water. The radio is tuned to a jazz station. I wrack my brain for something clever to say. When Joe Pass's rendition of "Night and Day" comes on, I ask her if she knows the late guitarist's work. She's never heard of him. I bring up basketball, but she has no interest in sports. She mentions a couple of recent movies that I haven't seen. We have absolutely nothing in common, except that we both agree on how wonderful Deanna is, a fact that gives me a twinge.

After escaping the smog of the suburban Inland Empire, we hit the desert and drive another hour on a highway that's empty except for an occasional tumbleweed. For the first twenty minutes, the desert scenery, dotted with Joshua trees and brittlebush, seems exotic. After that, tedium sets in again, and the landscape resembles overdone meatloaf.

When we near our destination, I grip the steering wheel hard. "Ms. Diamond, I have to read the stories."

"Oh my God, you're doing this now? When we're just about to get to her house?"

"I've asked you for them before, and you haven't—"

"I hope you're not suggesting that I read them out loud while you're driving."

"What I'm suggesting is that we stop at a McDonald's, get a cup of coffee, and I'll read them. They're Internet postings. It couldn't take longer than what, fifteen, twenty minutes? We're early anyway."

"But why now?"

"Because it's time I started treating you like my student and not my peer. I'm your professor. I'm responsible for you. I should've read those so-called stories a long time ago." I check my speed. I've drifted up to eighty-five, a sure ticket if the highway patrol is lurking.

"They're stories, not *so-called* stories." She pouts for a moment, and then reaches out and puts her hand on my shoulder, her fingers charged with a faith healer's energy, and I try to remember whether this is the first time we've touched. "OK. I'll show them to you. But please promise me something. Don't decide what to do until you talk to her. Because ... because if you read those stories before meeting her, you'll turn this car around and never want to get within a hundred miles of her again."

"They're really that bad?" I say, less to her than to myself. "Jesus."

After more silence and empty desert, I exit the highway and head south. We find a place just off the main drag called the Perth Café. Googie architecture from the 1950s: a large red neon sign, flying-wedge roof, and plate glass walls. As we wait for a table, people look at us with a combination of curiosity and hostility. Some of the male customers leer at Lovely.

After our server takes our order, I lean over the table and whisper, "Let me see them."

She hesitates before digging into her backpack and pulling out a half-inch sheaf of papers. I reach for them. She looks like she's going to pull them back, but thinks better of it.

By the time I finish the second paragraph my hands are shaking.

Several times, I restrain myself from crumpling up the pages. The stories recount in gruesome detail the sexual corruption, torture, and rape of children, not only by strangers but also by their own parents. And this isn't overblown Gothic pornography that at least allows you to suspend belief. These stories are written in a detached, reportorial style that leaves you with the sense that they actually happened.

The waitress brings our breakfast, but I don't realize it until the odor of eggs and oatmeal and coffee almost makes me gag.

When I finish a story in which a sexually aroused mother jabs knitting needles into her four-year-old daughter's buttocks while exhorting her husband to sodomize the screaming child, I slam the stack of paper face down on the table. I shut my eyes, but the vile words hover in the darkness like retinal imprints.

I open my eyes. Lovely's using her spoon to toy with her oatmeal, none of which she's eaten. I know how much working on this case means to her, so I choose my words carefully. "Look, it's noble of you to want to represent this person. I know she can't afford a lawyer. But—"

"You promised you'd meet her."

"That was before I read these stories. If I'd known what—"

Before I can finish my sentence, there's a hard jolt. Lovely gasps. The table feels as if it's about to buckle to the floor. Dishes clatter. Ice water and coffee slosh onto Tyler's stories. I look up to see a wiry man glowering down at me. There's a large Buck knife sheathed in a holster attached to his belt. Only then do I realize that he's pounded on the table with his fist.

"What the hell was that about?" I say, standing and facing off with him. Lovely, too, begins to stand, but I motion for her to sit down.

He shoves me against the back wall so hard that I stumble, knocking down a stand containing a pot of hot coffee that crashes to the floor, splashes over my shoe, and scalds my shin. Lovely stands and gropes for him, but he shakes her off without effort, and she falls back into the booth. I regain my balance and use my superior weight to shove him back, and at first it's one of those silly brawls where we both try to exchange punches but can't land a blow because we're so tangled up, until I free my left hand and land a clear shot just above his right ear. He doesn't go down, his knees don't buckle. His hand reaches for his knife.

A crowd of men descends upon us, and I lose track of my attacker and his knife, I've made a mistake, I've mixed it up with a local, these guys are intervening on behalf of a friend and neighbor, they'll welcome the opportunity to beat on an outsider who drives a fancy car and travels with a beautiful blonde, and no cop around here will believe or care that the other guy started it.

"Philistine!" my attacker hisses. He breaks free and makes a dash for an emergency exit I didn't know was there, setting off an alarm that sounds like an annoying schoolyard bell. A few of the men make a half-hearted effort at giving chase, but the guy is long gone.

"Turn that fucking thing off," one of the men says to the busboy.

"Are you OK?" I ask Lovely.

"Yeah. Fine." She's trembling. I reach out, take her hand, and squeeze it to comfort her. She squeezes back.

The busboy comes over with a stack of towels to clean off the table and a mop to wipe the floor. The man in charge approaches us. "I'm sorry about this," he says. "I'm the manager. Are you two OK?"

"Fine," Lovely says, barely looking at him.

I check out the burn on my leg. It's painful, but not blistering yet.

The manager shakes his head. "Do you know that guy?"

"No idea who he is," I say. "You?"

"Never seen him before. But we got a big-time crime problem out this way. You'd think it was the big city. Drug dealers, gangsters, coyotes smuggling illegal aliens through the desert. You know, trash. Maybe he saw your nice car or and the pretty lady here and decided to give you grief. Anyway, let me know if there's anything else I can do."

When he's out of earshot, Lovely whispers, "You really don't know what that guy was about?"

"Probably just like the manager said. Some nut who didn't like the way we look." What I don't say is that the man was a messenger from the Sanctified Assembly. He called me a "Philistine," which is pure Assembly-speak. After we had our falling out, Rich Baxter would call me a Philistine behind my back.

CHAPTER 18

We leave the diner and hurry to the car. I put the key in the ignition, but before I can start the car, Lovely grabs my arm. "We had an agreement. You're going to honor it, right?"

I inhale deeply. I should turn the car around, but I say, "Tell me how to get there."

We drive another five miles south. I keep checking the rearview mirror. Luckily, the landscape is so flat and desolate that we can see for miles around us. Several of the turnoffs are unmarked, so we guess at direction. Isolated homes pop out of the barren landscape, aluminum-siding oases. We pass trucker cafés that couldn't possibly stay in business but apparently do. We finally come upon a small, square, one-story house made of adobe and white stucco that has baked gray in the sun.

"This is it," Lovely says.

"We're in the crystal meth capital of the world."

She frowns at me, ever protective of her client.

There's no curb or sidewalk. I park halfway off the road so a passing vehicle won't sideswipe me. The air is warm and dry. A few imported trees that must need constant watering set the house off from the vacant desert. Some persistent blades of dried-out grass grow on what passes for a front lawn. There's an old-fashioned mailbox out on the curb, but it's rusted and looks as though it hasn't been used for years. While Lovely retrieves her backpack from the back seat, I scan the terrain. I see only uninhabited desert and the distant San Gabriel Mountains.

We look for a doorbell, but there isn't one. Lovely tries to open the screen door, but it's locked, so she knocks on the frame. I don't know whether to expect a victim or a monster. Maybe both. We wait thirty seconds, forty seconds, a minute, but no one answers. Lovely pounds on the screen door with her fist this time. There's a rumbling inside, and the door cracks from behind the screen.

The woman opens the door. I know from the court records that she's thirty-six, a year younger than me, but she carries herself like someone thirty years older. Her drab housecoat can't hide her pear-shaped body. She dyes her short frizzy hair an orangey-red. Her face is puffy, and her chin droops and doubles in on itself. This woman seems so straight and dowdy that I can't believe that she knows anything about the Internet, much less that she maintains her own website devoted to child pornography.

Lovely smiles broadly. "Tyler? I'm Lovely Diamond, and this is Professor Parker Stern."

She motions for us to come in.

The house is tiny—a cramped living room and a small kitchen with a stove and refrigerator jammed into a tiny space. There's a rancid smell, as if last week's garbage was left inside the house too long. The furniture, consisting of a mismatched green cloth sofa, two blue Naugahyde armchairs, and a scratched up walnut coffee table, looks like it came from a thrift shop. Although Tyler lives in the desert, all the drapes are drawn. The brightest thing in the room is her clownish red hair.

"Sit wherever you like," she says. She speaks with a slight southwestern drawl—Missouri or Oklahoma, I'd guess.

Lovely and I sit down on the sofa. Tyler maneuvers herself into an armchair across from us.

"Anyway," she continues. "I'm hoping this will all be behind me soon. Do you think that can happen? By next month or so?"

"There's only one way to do that," I say. "Negotiate a plea bargain." Lovely frowns at me. "Tyler wants to fight this."

"Is that right?" I ask Tyler.

She nods. "I did not do anything wrong. I will not plead guilty."

Lovely takes out her notes and launches into what should be an interview, but that instead turns out to be a virtual monologue that treads over what I'm sure is old ground—the government's claims, our legal defenses, the case law pro and con. Like so many inexperienced lawyers—and all too many veterans—Lovely thinks that the more she talks the more she accomplishes. All this time, Tyler doesn't say more than a few words at a time. On the rare occasions when Lovely does ask a question, it's leading, requiring only a one-word answer. The questions should be open-ended so that Tyler has to do the talking. Only then can we truly tease out all the facts and evaluate what kind of witness she'll make.

"I have some questions," I say when Lovely finishes.

Tyler looks at me and immediately begins kneading her hands.

"Why don't you tell me about your background."

She looks confused for a moment, but then starts speaking in a halting voice. She's been itinerant for most of her life, living in Oklahoma, Colorado, Utah, Oregon, and Nevada before coming to California. She's had various jobs, all of them menial—supermarket checker, pharmacy clerk, waitress, telephone psychic. She lives off state disability payments, the result of social anxiety disorder and a bad back from a slip-and-fall at Wal-Mart. She has no known living relatives and no close friends. She had one semester of community college and then dropped out. This last fact is the most puzzling, because in a strange, horrible way, her stories show literary talent that seems far beyond her range.

When she finishes, I say, "How many members of your website were there? At its peak?"

"There were twenty-six."

"Twenty-six hundred?" Lovely asks. "Or twenty-six thousand?" That she doesn't know this already is another reminder that she's still just a law student.

"No. Twenty-six people in all. That was about a year ago. Then about ten dropped off, so maybe sixteen when the FBI came in and seized the computer."

"Why would the US Attorney sue over twenty-six members?" Lovely says. "There's so much crap on the Internet that's just as bad. Worse. Stuff that goes to tens of millions of people. Why bring charges over this? Neil Latham's a liberal, right?"

"He's a liberal except when it comes to issues of what he considers personal morality. He's a devout Christian, a rare right-to-life Democrat. Fighting obscenity is one of his causes. He's dead serious about this case. On top of that, he'll welcome the publicity. Mr. Latham has higher aspirations."

"But this is a progressive administration," Lovely says. "Is the Justice Department really going to just let him go forward with this?"

"This case might not be to the administration's taste, but they're not going to shut it down. Not in this political climate."

Tyler follows this exchange like an observer at a tennis match who doesn't quite understand the rules. But there's one thing she does understand. "There can't be any publicity. Please. There just can't be."

"There will be," I say.

She interlaces her fingers and squeezes them together hard. "Can't you just ask the judge to close the court? I've seen on *Law & Order* that they can close the court."

"There's no basis for closing the courtroom. We have freedom of the press in this country. The First Amendment doesn't apply only to you."

Tyler doesn't seem to get the sarcasm, but Lovely glares at me and says, "It wouldn't hurt to ask."

"Yes, it would. We'd antagonize the judge and look like buffoons."

"Maybe I could just talk to the judge in private," Tyler says. "I'm sure I could straighten this whole thing out." She's behaving so naïvely that I find myself wondering if it's an act.

"We can't do it that way. Courtrooms are open. And the other side gets to be present for every court hearing."

"Why don't we move on to something else?" Lovely says.

"Sure. I want Tyler to tell me why she wrote those stories." I look at Tyler. "The US Attorney claims you did it for the money. That's one of the reasons they've come after you."

"Oh, no, sir. I don't write my stories to make money."

"Then why did you charge a fee for the website?"

"Because I wanted to keep the children away. They shouldn't be reading these kinds of things. I never want them to read my stories. I figured out that if I required a credit card, the kids'd keep out."

"Why did you write the stories if it wasn't for money?" I say.

Tyler twists her fingers with so much force that I can hear her knuckles pop in a sickening arpeggio. She sighs. "I told this to Ms. Diamond already, sir. Over the phone."

"Tell it to me."

"Well. I guess my stories are a way to deal with an eternal dread, a heavy darkness that never leaves me. My dreams and days are full of scary beasts. My stories let me create a place where the demons can't harm me." She shrugs and looks down at the sofa, arms crossed.

"There's a question I've never asked you before," Lovely says. "I should have. It's hard for me to say. But it's very important for your defense. Were you abused as a child? I mean, sexually?"

"I wish I knew," Tyler says.

"That doesn't make any sense," I say. "Either you know something like that or you don't."

"No, sir. The truth is, I have no memory of my life before I was nine years old. I don't know what happened in the blank period. I just know that there are monsters all around me, and I felt powerless to fight them until I started writing my stories."

"Are you protecting somebody?" I ask. "Are you covering up for the person who really wrote those stories? Someone who's abusing you now? Because if that's what's happening, if you're being hurt—"

Tyler shakes her head vigorously. "Oh, no sir. I'm not protecting anybody. The stories are all my own."

"Husband? Boyfriend? Brother?"

"No, sir. I wrote them stories!" It's the first time this morning that she's used poor grammar.

"She's the author, Professor," Lovely says. "Now, let's move on. Please."

I've alienated Tyler already, though that doesn't bother me much. And I still think she's hiding something. But if I press any harder, we'll both lose her trust, and I don't want to do that to Lovely. So I ask some innocuous questions just to button down the facts. The bad odor I smelled when I walked in seems to be getting worse. As we're about to leave, I say, "Your arraignment is in a few weeks. January . . . ?"

"January eleventh," Lovely says.

"January eleventh. You'll have to come to court. Do you have transportation to LA? Because we can arrange—"

"Oh, no. I can't go to Los Angeles. I'm a homebody. I don't leave the house much."

"But, it's a requirement that you—"

"I'm sorry. I'd like to help you but I can't. I like to stay at home. I'm safe here in my house."

"You need to help yourself," I say. "You could go to jail. Your freedom is at stake."

Lovely gives me a withering stare. "Let's drop it."

I shrug. "If that's what you want. It's your case to try."

"Yes it is." She reaches over and puts her hand on Tyler's wrist. "Everything will be OK. We'll be in touch." She gets up to leave, but then stops. "I have to ask you something, Tyler. Before we drove out here, Professor Stern and I stopped at the Perth Café in town. Some guy attacked us."

"Why, that's terrible! Are y'all OK?"

"We're fine," Lovely says. "The man was short, skinny, about forty, brown hair. Not a very good description, but does he sound like anyone you know around town?"

"No ma'am. I don't know very many people. And I would never go to that diner. Too crowded." She shakes her head in dismay. "It's just like I said. The world is full of scary beasts. They're everywhere."

CHAPTER 19

"How could you do that to her?" Lovely says as soon as we're back on the road. "She's fragile, and she's our client."

"She's *your* client and she's not so fragile. A lot of it's an act. And I babied her compared to what Neil Latham will do to her if she ever testifies, what the media will do when they get wind of this. Someone has to drum some sense into her so we can at least try to get her ready to testify."

"She won't ever have to testify. We'll get the case thrown out on a motion."

"I hope so. But we've talked about how hard that's going to be with Harvey as the judge."

"I think we're going to win."

Neither of us says much else until we reach the highway. I keep checking my rearview mirror to make sure we're not being followed. I don't let my guard down until we drive onto the highway onramp.

She lets out a musical sigh. "This has been an exciting morning."

Her cheeriness suddenly makes me out of sorts, wired, suspicious. "How did you find out who I was?"

"How did I—?"

"How did you know I was Parky Gerald?"

"What made you ask that now?"

"Because I want to know now."

"OK," she says in a measured tone. "My father told me."

"How did he know?"

"He's . . . he was in the movie business. He worked with you a couple of times when you were a kid."

Over the past months, her ability to discover my secret has taken on a mythic quality. I've speculated about her unmatched intelligence, her underground sources, her preternatural capacity for reading my memories. It's never occurred to me that she had a relative in the business.

"Did he use a stage name? Because I don't remember working with anyone named *Diamond*. Except this one guy, Ed, who turned out to be . . ." I catch myself. Too late.

"Shane Edmonds, the film director."

I try my best to look at the road and not at her. During the seventies and eighties, Shane Edmonds was the foremost director of adult films, known for making highbrow porn. He was a kind of bizarre legend in the entertainment industry. In the mid-nineties, there was a critically acclaimed mainstream movie about the porn industry; the director character was based on Edmonds. He insisted he was an artist and not a pornographer. His films had complex plots and impressionistic lighting and sophisticated dialogue and competent actors and classical musical scores. With the emergence of home video, his career flagged. Few, if any, porn producers would finance the high production costs that an Edmonds film required, especially when consumers would pay high prices for a few non-plotted sex scenes shot with a handheld video camera.

I remember Ed Diamond as an irascible son of a bitch, bitter and condescending and foul-mouthed. Back then, everyone in the industry knew that he yearned to go legit. On my films, he took a monotonous and low-paying job as a production accountant—he'd started out as a CPA—just so he could direct some second unit work. People joked that he approached his mundane second unit job as if he were a combination David Lean and Federico Fellini. Those who worked with him said that he was, indeed, supremely talented, that you could tell from the way he filmed stock settings at the beach or close-ups of inanimate objects. He made almost no money—not compared to what he made directing porn—but hoped his willingness to do grunt work using his real name would cleanse his reputation and allow him to become a mainstream director. It didn't happen. Studio executives wouldn't touch him.

"So, how did Ed know about me?"

"My father never forgets anything. We were talking about my classes and professors like we do. When I told him your name, he remembered that the kid actor's full name was Parker Gerald Stern. The first day of class when I asked you about it was a shot in the dark." She hesitates for a moment. "Now I have a question for you. Why did you stop acting?"

My hands tighten on the steering wheel. I reach over and power off the stereo. "What makes you so interested in my past?"

Her cheeks turn scarlet. I'm not sure whether she's angry or embarrassed. I glare at her for all too long, and when I turn forward again, I realize that we've hit a stretch of heavy traffic, and I have to slam on the brakes to avoid rear-ending an SUV.

"Shit," she says. "Be careful."

"I still want to know. Why the great interest in my past?"

"Oh my God, why do you think? Because you're my teacher. Because we've sort of become friends, or so I thought."

I glance over. Her eyes have narrowed, the irises darkening to a turbulent gray. Her question wasn't simply idle curiosity or something more nefarious, but a kind of test to see if I would reveal myself to her the way she'd just revealed herself to me. She props her right leg on the dashboard, the sole of her boot threatening to scuff the vinyl, a pose that tells me that she doesn't care what I think. At the moment, I want nothing more than to break through that, because I do care what she thinks.

"It's complicated," I say. "It started . . . my mother was only nineteen when I was born. I never knew my father. It was 1974, and she was this hippie flower child. When I came along, her life changed. She'd wanted to be an actress, but there was no way. So she started taking me on auditions when I was just three years old. She got caught up in the whole Hollywood thing. It was fine when I was a little kid doing bit parts, but then I got pretty successful and my career became her main focus in life." It's an understatement. My career became her obsession. When she watched dailies and rough cuts of my movies, she would silently mouth my dialogue. At every close-up of me, her coruscating eyes seemed to emit a peculiar cinematic light of their own.

"There were a lot men in my mother's life," I continue. "When I was eleven or twelve, she got involved with a jerk who claimed he could manage my finances. He convinced her to give him access to my money."

"I thought the Coogan law made it impossible for a parent to rip off her kid."

"He found a loophole. He took what he called salaries and commissions and pension distributions and investments for my future. Anyway, by the time I turned fifteen, I'd figured out what was going on." I stop and take a breath. "I've only told this to one other person in my adult life. My mother and her boyfriend took almost everything I'd earned and gave it to the Church of the Sanctified Assembly. The church wasn't much in those days, but . . ."

"And that's why you feel the way you do about them."

"I sued to become an emancipated minor. What the public never knew was that I entered into a settlement with the Assembly prelitigation. The terms are confidential to this day, so that's a major reason why I can't talk about it. All I can tell you is that afterward, I was on my own."

"You were so young. It must have been really hard."

"The best thing that ever happened to me. Anyway, after that, I didn't want the acting anymore. It just didn't seem important."

"What made you become a lawyer?"

"My own case got me interested in the law. And you know what? It's much more gratifying than being an actor. Trials are real, far more important than the fantasy world of movies and plays and reality TV. I actually did a little stage work during summers. My mother thought it would hone my skills. And the first day of trial feels like opening night of a stage play, except that if you make a mistake at trial, people get hurt and there isn't a repeat performance the next day."

She takes her foot off the dashboard, and places her hand on my upper arm.

We make good time the rest of the way. Just as I approach the law school to drop her off, I have an idea. It's far-fetched, but worth a try.

"What's your father doing these days?"

"You mean is he still directing porn?"

"God no, I mean . . ." I relax when I see her playful smile. "I was wondering if Ed's maybe retired."

"He's got a lot of time on his hands. Why?"

"This is crazy, but you know we have all those financial documents that we got from Rich Baxter's computer. I don't have the background to understand them. Neither does Deanna. Dean Mason took a quick look at them and didn't find anything, but he's too busy to really dig deep. Both of the forensic accounting firms I worked with at Macklin & Cherry have a conflict, or so they say. I think they're afraid to oppose the Assembly. And I'd rather not go to a stranger. I'd pay your father for his time."

She laughs. "My father hated being an accountant. He's a film-maker. And he doesn't need money."

"I told you it was off-the-wall."

"But, if I ask him, he'll do it for me."

CHAPTER 20

Christopher McCarthy warned me away from Monica Baxter—which is exactly why I want to speak with her. And I have to do it before the Assembly sues Rich Baxter's estate, because after that, there will be no chance. The Assembly will spin the lawsuit as the only way to protect a grieving widow against a vindictive and avaricious father-in-law. It's ironic—as heir to half of Rich's fortune under the community property laws, an attack on his estate is an attack on her interests, which means she really should take Raymond's side in any lawsuit. But she'd never do that—logic means nothing to an Assembly zealot like her.

I can't just telephone her. The Assembly is undoubtedly monitoring her calls. Worse, when Rich and I argued about his joining the church, I'd implied that she'd used sex to entice him into the fold. I'm sure she knows every gory detail of our quarrel. He wasn't the kind of man who'd keep a secret from the woman he loved.

Manny Mason might be able to arrange a meeting, though. He and Rich stayed in contact after the firm split up. Unlike Deanna and me, he's family oriented, the kind of outsider whom Monica could tolerate. So I phone him and ask him to set up a meeting with Monica. I expect him to put up a fight, but he says, "I'm not teaching today. Be at my house in an hour. And dress for hoops."

"Does that mean you'll—?"

The line goes dead.

I throw on a faded Lakers jersey and a sweatshirt and some old shorts I've had since college and make the forty-minute drive to Moraga Canyon, a neighborhood of lush hillsides and mansions and winding roads and venture capitalists and spotty cell phone reception and reality TV stars and guys like Manny Mason who are lucky enough to have married a woman from a moneyed Argentinean family. As soon as I park in the driveway, Manny's wife, Elena, comes out the front door. I haven't seen her since Harmon's funeral. She's nearly six feet tall with a coltish prettiness, a good physical match for Manny. When she sees me, she hurries over and gives me a hug. "It's been too long, Parker."

"How are you, Elena?"

"Good. Good. I'm just running over to the boys' school to give a tour. I'm a proud parent volunteer." Though she came to this country when she was eleven, her speech has a vague Spanish lilt. "Now, why haven't you come by to see us?"

"You know how busy we attorneys get."

"I certainly do." Her look of pity leaves no doubt that Manny told her about my stage fright. She kisses me on the cheek. "Manny is in the back waiting for you. We'll have you over for dinner soon."

I walk around to the backyard, where Manny's shooting baskets on a regulation size court. He's come a long way from sweltering Lodi, California. His family owned a vineyard planted to zinfandel and petite sirah, which they sold for cheap bulk labels like Gallo and Charles Shaw. They didn't own nearly enough acreage to compete with the huge agricultural conglomerates. His parents declared bankruptcy when he was ten and were wiped out again as a result of the 1992 phylloxera infestation. His older brother is a high school dropout who works in an auto body shop. His sister was pregnant and married at seventeen. Manny tells us he escaped their fate because of his 3.87 high school GPA, his facility for shooting a basketball, and his good fortune in meeting Elena in a sociology class.

He sinks a shot from just beyond the three-point arc and jogs over.

"So, about Monica Baxter," I say.

"Later. Now we're going to play one-on-one. First to eleven by ones."

"I don't know what you're trying to do, but—"

"Humor me."

"You can't be serious. You're a former division one ballplayer, and

I'm an out-of-shape lawyer. Too many of Deanna's pastries. Not to mention the six-inch height advantage."

"You're a good ballplayer. Quicker than I am and a better ball handler. Let's go. First to eleven. You have to win by two baskets. Then we'll talk. What's the downside?"

Aside from the humiliation of getting crushed, the downside is that physicality is part of his game. He's typical of a lot of even-tempered men who excel athletically—the basketball court is the one place where he's combative. I remember one Lawyers' League game, six or seven years ago, when some jerk intentionally low-bridged me on a fast break, a real cheap shot. I flipped over him and hit my lower back on the floor. The guy could've killed me. When I managed to get up, he and I got into a shoving match, but Manny played peacemaker. I actually resented him for stopping the fight—until five minutes later, when he came down with a rebound and in the process smashed the guy's nose with a sharp elbow. Since then I've always felt that Manny and I have each other's backs. Still, I don't relish guarding him even in a friendly game.

"This is BS, Manny. Just tell me if you'll talk to Monica."

"After the game." He stares at me impassively, the ball cradled in the crook of his arm.

I grab the ball away. "OK, OK. But I get first outs."

I spend five minutes warming up and then take the ball out. I hit two mid-range jump shots from the baseline and make three layups, Manny offering only token defense. After I score my fifth point, I say, "What're you doing?

"You want me to try hard?"

"I want you to tell me what's going on."

"Just take the ball out. It's getting cold. I don't want to pull a muscle."

I dribble the ball to the right of the key and rise for a jump shot. My ability to elevate isn't what it used to be. Manny blocks the shot, snatches the ball out of the air, and drives in for a layup. In the next two minutes, he sinks four more baskets, and the score is tied. I don't have a chance.

"This is a fucking joke," I say.

"Just play."

The next time he drives in for a layup, I try to block it, fouling him hard. "Your ball," I say.

"Why?"

"Because I fouled you."

"Clean block, Parker. Take the ball out."

"I don't want any more charity."

"My court, my rules."

I take the ball out and score. For the next twenty minutes, we jostle and bump and exchange buckets. He does a much better job of disguising the fact that he's letting me keep it close. I convince myself that a couple of my baskets—a Hail Mary reverse layup and a turnaround jumper—are legitimate. Sweat pours down my face and stings my eyes. I didn't think to bring a headband. At least I'm getting a good workout.

Eventually, I go ahead, 10-9, a basket away from a win. I take the ball out, dribble hard to the left elbow, and fake a drive. I stop suddenly, and Manny flies by. I've created space and now have the first open shot I've clearly earned on my own. I shoot the ball with a smooth rotation. From the moment it leaves my hand, I know it's in. No matter that Manny let me stay in the game. A win is a win.

Manny's long arm swoops high above me and swats the ball away. We both lunge for it, but he out-muscles me. After that, he quickly scores two layups, and for good measure hits a long jumper to win the game, 12-10.

We bump fists and sit down at a picnic table by the side of the court.

"I'm not going to contact Monica Baxter for you," he says.

"And if I'd have won?"

"I still wouldn't have done it."

"Even if it means helping me find her husband's killer?"

"You know, you can tell a lot about a person by the way he plays basketball. If a guy repeatedly travels but always disputes the call, he's probably going to cheat someone in a business deal. Another man always goes ballistic at a referee and gets into fights and you know he wants to hit his wife or girlfriend."

"So you've always said."

"Then there's you, Parker. You never give up. Even when you're down twenty points with a minute to go. That's admirable most of the time. But not always. You knew that I was letting you stay close, yet you actually convinced yourself that you could win. Am I right?"

I glare at him. The cold wind against my sweaty skin sends a shiver through my body.

"You never had a chance. Just like you don't have a chance with this so-called Baxter investigation. You're deceiving yourself into thinking you can win. There's nothing to win."

"That's bullshit."

"Is it? No pulling punches, Parker. I'm concerned about you. You're spending your time tilting at windmills on some case where the conclusive evidence is that Rich killed himself."

"Not tilting at windmills. Looking into a possible murder and a trumped-up autopsy report, and—"

"And you know that the pathology report is phony because Lovely Diamond told you? My God, man, she's a third-year law student, not a pathologist. What are you doing to yourself?"

"I'm representing a client."

"I don't think you're representing anyone at all. There's no case. You're crazy obsessed with the Sanctified Assembly. You always have been. They're not your law firm's client anymore, so you can't claim you're acting on principle. You should've left it behind a long time ago. But instead you're getting worse, and I think it's because you're clinically depressed. It all fits. You can't work, you can't even walk into a courtroom. You were pallid as death when you came to court to see *me* argue a case. Until I got you the teaching job, all you did was sit around Deanna's place and drink coffee. You need professional help. I have some names of people who could—"

"This was what the so-called basketball game was about?"

"I'm sorry. I couldn't think of any other way to get through to you. I just want to get through to you."

I don't know what I expected from him, but certainly not some ridiculous object lesson and a lecture about my mental health. "The only kind of help I need is for you to set up a meeting with Monica Baxter," I say.

He shuts his eyes for a moment and exhales through his teeth, obviously trying to keep his composure. "Let it go, Parker. Take care of yourself and let it go."

CHAPTER 21

Even at two thirty in the afternoon, The Barrista is teeming with customers, mostly young working professionals who order prodigious cups of coffee to go so they can stay awake during the afternoon doldrums. I'm hoping that Deanna will do what Manny won't—convince Monica Baxter to meet with me. For it to happen, Deanna will have to call in a debt on my behalf. Monica owes her.

Rich and Monica met when she was working as a bookkeeper in the Assembly's accounting department. One of her jobs was to liaison with outside counsel. Six years ago, a company called Elkin Printing sued the Assembly for refusing to pay for some promotional brochures. The amount in controversy was a pittance, maybe twelve thousand dollars, far less than the cost of defense. The case should have been settled, but Rich wanted to impress Monica, so he decided to handle the lawsuit himself even though he'd probably never seen the inside of a courtroom.

He filed a motion, taking the position that the brochures were defective. His exhibits included the purchase order and some invoices. But when Monica gathered the documents, she inadvertently included a top-secret mailing list of the Assembly's Southern California members. An oblivious Rich filed the mailing list with the court. Only when he sent Monica a file-stamped copy of the motion did she catch the mistake. Monica would have been fired for the blunder, maybe even excommunicated, and the law firm would've never worked on an Assembly matter again.

A panicked Rich sought out Deanna. The first thing she did was telephone Elkin Printing's attorney and demand that he return the membership roster without reading it or keeping a copy. She said that if she didn't have the list in her possession within the hour, she'd report him to the state bar. She claims that was all she said, but I'm not so sure she didn't threaten to come over with some of her biker friends and kick the guy's ass. The roster was back in our office in forty-five minutes. Deanna shredded it herself.

Retrieving the roster from opposing counsel was the easy part, but the document was in the court file and now belonged to the public. Stringers from the news media loiter around the courthouse and troll for newsworthy pleadings. Everyone from the shady blogger to the mainstream press would want to see a membership list of the enigmatic Sanctified Assembly. Deanna pulled an all-nighter, doing research and drafting legal papers. The next morning, she camped out on the court-house steps until the doors opened. Somehow, she convinced a judge to take the unprecedented step of sealing the court record. Judges just don't remove publicly available documents from the court file. To this day, I think the order is illegal. Neither the news media nor the Assembly found out. In fact, Deanna didn't tell anyone about the inci-dent herself until she revealed it to me during a vulnerable moment after a night of lovemaking.

Now, I corral a frenzied Deanna and ask her to set up the meeting. She narrows her eyes and takes a half-step back, as though I'm about to make her the butt of some practical joke. When she realizes I'm serious, she bursts out laughing. "Monica Baxter hates your guts."

"I have to find out what she knows."

"I don't want any part of it. Go ask Manny to set it up."

"I did. He was an asshole. He told me to stop obsessing about the case and see a shrink."

"He's right."

"Come on, Deanna."

"It would be awkward."

"She owes you, right? Elkin Printing?"

"I should never have told you that story. I don't want to call in a favor that she'll never do anyway because it involves helping you."

We stare each other down in silence. With her crossed arms and squinched eyes and tattoos and nose rings, she looks like a petulant tween gone punk. I can't stifle a laugh.

"You find me disarming, huh Parker?"

"Not a bit."

She grins impishly. "Dude, did I ever tell you the story of my thank-you dinner with the Baxters?"

I shake my head.

"Remember that woman I was seeing back then? Roseanne?"

"The tiny girl with the buzz cut and the peach fuzz moustache?"

"Rosie didn't . . . Yeah, her. That girl was outrageous. After three or four glasses of wine, she leaned over to me and whispered that she wanted to see how a couple of homophobic Assembly devotees would react to a couple of dykes making out in the middle La Serre."

"You didn't."

"With tongue."

"And you think I disrespect the church."

"Monica was livid. Kept looking from side to side. Remember how Rich would get these red splotches all over his cheeks and neck when he got embarrassed? He looked like a neon sign on the Sunset Strip. They would've walked out for sure if I hadn't saved both their butts. The rest of the dinner was more than a little tense, though."

"Sounds to me like Monica still owes you a favor."

"Parker, no. She won't do it. I can't help you."

We banter back and forth like the litigators we were, but she holds firm, finally ending the debate by pleading work duties. I sit at my usual table in the corner and read for a while, but I can't concentrate. I take out my computer and surf the Internet as a diversion, looking for something inspirational, or at least something to give me a bit of psychic energy, because the three cups of espresso sure haven't done it. I search the names of famous lawyers—Bailey, Belli, Darrow, Root, Kunstler, Thurgood Marshall. I seize on a quotation from Clarence Darrow: "lost causes are the only ones worth fighting for." The old-fashioned sentiment recharges my enthusiasm for continuing the Baxter investigation. Then I search further and find that Darrow never said that at all, that the quote came from a Depression-era crime novel by a British writer named Ethel Lina White and then was ripped off by Frank Capra in the movie *Mr. Smith Goes to Washington*, and I see the quotation for what it is, Hollywood fluff, and it doesn't mean anything to me anymore. I consider looking through some of the financial documents that the IRS seized from Rich's apartment but don't see the point because I can't really follow them. I shut down my computer in disgust and order a fourth cup of coffee and watch the patrons wander in and out of The Barrista.

Around five o'clock, the shop empties out and Deanna comes over to my table. She smiles a smile that's self-consciously feminine. She usually sits across from me, but now she brings the chair right next to me. She rests her head on my shoulder and says in her sultriest voice, "I'll come by your place tonight after work."

We've never refused each other, not in the years since we started this dance—one of the many peculiar traditions that develop in relationships like ours. And yet I say, "Not tonight. I just want to be alone tonight."

She lifts her head from my shoulder and slides her chair away from me. "You're not serious."

I nod my head.

"And this is because I won't try to set up a meeting with Monica Baxter?"

"That's not why."

"Bullshit."

"It's got nothing to do with the Baxter case."

She studies me for a moment, as if searching for an answer. When she finds it, she says, "I can't sit around all day shooting the shit with you. I have to do some work."

"Deanna, I—"

She abruptly stands and walks over to a table of three women, and in a remarkable transformation smiles broadly and says something to them. They all laugh, charmed. I take a last sip of coffee and leave.

I drive back home to the Marina. The coffee has kicked in, and I'm jittery and hot, so I down a beer and then another, which just leaves me jittery and buzzed. I go out on the balcony and try to read, but I have no patience, so I turn on ESPN and pay half attention to a college basketball game. When I lose interest in that, I shut off the television and lie on the bed and listen on my iPod to the self-referential male alternative rock music that I loved when I was in school—REM, Pearl Jam, Counting Crows. Dinnertime passes, but I have no appetite, so I keep the ear buds in while I grab another beer. I walk around from room to room, aimless. The alcohol doesn't relax me, and I realize that I'm restless because this place feels less like home than The Barrista does.

I drink a fourth bottle of beer—it's unusual for me to have more than one—and when the caffeine high subsides, I crash on the living room couch. The doorbell awakens me. I glance at the clock—11:30 p.m. I can't believe I've slept that long. Still fully clothed, I lurch off the sofa, and my arm gets tangled in the wires from my ear buds, sending the iPod to the floor. Without retrieving it, I go to the door and look through the peephole.

When I see Deanna, I deflate. The last thing I want is a heart-to-heart, or worse, some sort of faux-lover's quarrel. But I can't bring myself to ignore her, so I open the door.

She's not someone who embarrasses easily, but when she sees me, she blushes. "I'm sorry to disturb you. I just came by—"

"The last thing I want to do is hurt you."

"I know. I get it." She glances down at her shoes for a moment, then whispers, "She's beautiful."

"It's not like even like that. She's my student and . . ."

She looks at me for a long time before speaking. "When I said I couldn't help you connect with Monica Baxter, I wasn't telling you the truth. I can't lie, Parker. I can help you."

CHAPTER 22

When Deanna visited my apartment two nights ago, she confessed that a few weeks after Rich died, Monica Baxter showed up at The Barrista on a Thursday afternoon at three o'clock—the precise time when my trial advocacy class starts. It wasn't a coincidence. Monica told Deanna that she knows that I hang out at the shop and that she timed her appearance so I wouldn't be there.

"The very first time she showed up, I told her how sorry I was about Rich," Deanna said. "She didn't react. It was like Rich hadn't died or she didn't know him or he didn't matter to her. She talked about her toddler and the Assembly."

"They always talk about their precious Assembly."

"Most of the time she was smiling with that condescending look they all get, like they're in the hands of a higher power and you're not. But when she left she asked if she could stop by the shop the next week. As if she needs my permission to buy a cup of coffee. Then, when she was about to leave, her expression changed and she said, 'Please don't tell Parker Stern I was here.' She's afraid of you, Parker. Like, really terrified."

"Why would—?"

"Just let me finish. She's getting these harassing e-mails from someone claiming they knew Rich. She thinks you're sending them. She also blames you for Rich's death."

"She thinks I murdered Rich? You're not serious."

"No, she thinks . . . I don't know what she thinks. Something about your getting him in over his head. I told her she was full of shit. The weird thing is, she keeps coming back. Every Thursday at three. Like she wants to hang out with me all of a sudden, which doesn't make sense given the way the Assembly views gays and lesbians. But I think things have been different for her since Rich died. I think she's been ostracized because of how the Assembly feels about suicide. You know, the way some people used to feel about HIV, still do, shunning not only the victim, but the victim's family? So she comes in and nurses her cup of coffee and I keep her company. Like I said, I doubt she'll talk to you, but if you want to come around Thursday at three . . ."

So I canceled today's law school class and now sit hiding in a dark corner of The Barrista, lying in wait like an alley thug and hoping that when Monica sees me, she won't spit in my face.

She walks into the shop at precisely three o'clock, pushing a stroller. Rich told me the child's name—Josh. Two years old, now. The next few minutes play out like a silent movie. She orders coffee and a scone and a cup of milk, finds a table, and lifts the wriggling child into an industrial highchair. She fills a yellow plastic cup with the milk and hands it to him. He shakes it a bit, then drinks, dribbling milk on his chin. After wiping his mouth, she tears off a piece of the scone and feeds it to him—a surprise, because the Assembly's dietary guidelines forbid the consumption of refined sugar, especially for young children. Deanna walks over to the table and sits down. The women chat for a while, Deanna smiling often and Monica mostly stone-faced, smiling only when attending to her son. At one point, she reaches into her bag and hands him a velvet-green stuffed turtle, which the boy takes with obvious delight. Deanna talks to the toddler and makes him smile. She leans forward and places her hand on Monica's wrist, whispering something. Monica purses her lips in a tight frown and scans the coffee shop. When she sees me, her face darkens with a mixture of anger and fear. She tries to stand, but Deanna keeps a hand on her wrist. From where I sit, it looks like Deanna is physically restraining her.

Back at the law firm, Deanna pled her cases like an evangelist. Now, she's talking nonstop. Monica keeps shaking her head and glancing over at me and turning away and half-standing, only to sit down again when Deanna leans in closer and says, I can't imagine what.

Deanna releases Monica's wrist and gestures for me to come over. I stand up, walk across the room on wobbly legs, and sit opposite Monica. She won't meet my eyes. She's still attractive, but the muscles of her face and neck are taut. She has uneven circles under her eyes from crying or lack of sleep or grief.

The child, well-behaved for a two-year-old, seems engrossed in his toy turtle. He looks like his father—blond hair, green eyes, pudgy cheeks, and a ruddy complexion. Deanna stands up and takes the boy out of the highchair.

"Come on, Joshy," she says. "Let's go see where we make all the coffee and hot chocolate. And where we keep the cookies."

"Mommy, no!"

"Mommy will be right here, sweetie," Monica says, her voice quavering. "Deanna won't take you far." She points to the pastry counter. "Right over there. Mommy will be sitting right here, and you'll be able to see me all the time. And Deanna will give you one cookie. But only one."

This pacifies him. Deanna takes him over to the counter. He keeps looking our way to make sure his mother is still there. Why shouldn't he fear letting her out of his sight? His father left one day and never came back. But maybe all two-year-olds act this way. How would I know?

"It's been a long time," I say. "I'm so sorry about Rich."

Her cheeks are flushed. "They say you and his father just want Rich's money. I don't know why I'm doing this."

"Why are you, then?"

"Because of what Deanna said. She told me you found something in the autopsy report that shows that someone . . . that Rich didn't kill himself. If that's true, Joshy and I . . ." Her voice trails off, but I now understand why she agreed to speak with me. If Rich didn't commit suicide, then under Assembly dogma, he wasn't diseased after all, and neither she nor her son could be contaminated with the same illness. She's hoping I can offer absolution.

"Did you send those horrible e-mails?" she asks.

"Absolutely not."

"Then Rich's father."

I shake my head. "I realize that you don't know him very well, but there's no way."

"I don't know him at all. I only know that he hates me."

Each time I try to make the slightest eye contact, she looks away. I see no sign of the Monica I expected—the calculating femme fatale, no better than a temple prostitute who lured an innocent like Rich Baxter into a nefarious cult. This person just seems frightened and grief-stricken.

"I'd like to ask you a few questions," I say.

"Of course you would. You're a lawyer."

"What do the e-mails say?"

"They're so scary. Written by a defective. They say that the person who stole the Assembly's money also killed Rich. And Harmon Cherry. They say that Joshy's life and mine are in danger. That I should go to the police; that I should hide; that whatever I do there's no escape. That I shouldn't trust the Assembly elders. That I shouldn't trust anyone. That the Assembly's involved in a worldwide conspiracy . . . and on and on and on."

"Whatever would make you think I sent those?"

She finally looks me in the eye, and I feel as if she's slapped my face. "Because you have contempt for our beliefs. Because you dislike me, even though you don't know anything about me. Because you got involved in this with Rich, and I don't understand why."

Now I'm the one who looks away.

Her words come quickly now. "Because Rich said he was working with an outsider. He wouldn't say who it was. It was too dangerous for him to tell, he said. But when he hired you as his attorney I figured it must be you. It was you, right? You're the one who got him into that stupid investigation about embezzlement and Harmon Cherry, the reason he got arrested, and then . . ." Her eyes fill with tears, and I think she's going cry, but instead she smiles broadly, an act so eerie that I feel as if an icy finger is tracing curlicues down my spine. Then I realize that she's forcing the smile for Josh, who's waving to her. She waves back.

"I don't know what you're talking about," I say. "The first time I spoke with Rich was when I met with him at the jail. What did Rich tell you about this . . . this outsider?"

"He discovered financial irregularities and he needed help in analyzing them. That kind of work wasn't his strength. I offered to help—I worked in accounting, you know—but he said it was too risky, that he had to keep me out of it. I wanted him to go to Chris McCarthy, but he said he had to work with someone outside the Assembly, because he thought the embezzler was inside. I didn't believe him, but he insisted. That's when he rented the place in Silver Lake, because he said what he was doing was dangerous, that he couldn't have an outsider coming to our house. He was always talking about how good a lawyer you were, so I assumed . . ."

"You knew about the Silver Lake apartment?"

"I knew he had a safe house. I didn't know where until after."

"Do you know that . . . that the FBI and the building landlord say . . . you must know that they say he was bringing women there. And that he was found with drugs."

"You're rude to bring up those lies."

"If I'm going to get to the truth, I can't sugarcoat my questions."

She shakes her head so hard that her straight brown hair swishes back and forth across her shoulders. "Rich wouldn't go with prostitutes. He was always faithful to me. And he wouldn't take drugs. The Assembly forbids drug use, and so he wouldn't. He's—he was—a good husband and a devoted father. He was using the apartment to meet with the outsider and investigate the financial irregularities."

I've always assumed that on her side, the marriage was one of expediency, not love, and that the Assembly arranged the marriage. Did I have it wrong? Or did she learn to love him? Whatever the truth, I'm not going to try to convince her that her husband consorted with whores.

"Where did the drugs come from? And the false passport?"

"They must've been planted. Maybe he thought that the murderer . . . I don't know. But there has to be an explanation." Now she sounds just like her estranged father-in-law.

I pose a few follow-up questions, but she can't tell me anything more. When I ask to see the anonymous e-mails, she balks. I'm sure that Christopher McCarthy or one of his subordinates instructed her to have nothing to do with me. But after some prodding, she agrees to leave copies of the e-mails with Deanna.

"I have to get my son home," she says. "I really shouldn't have talked to you. Just know that nobody from my church would harm Rich. We're devoted to peace and curing the defects in man that lead to war and violence and disease and unhappiness." Monica nods at Deanna, who walks Josh back over.

"He's such a good boy," Deanna says.

"He's a wonderful boy," Monica says, straightening his clothing. "So are all the children of the Fount." She places him in the stroller.

"There's something else I have to ask you," I say. "It'd be helpful to know everyone Rich was close to. Friends. People who worked with him. Secretaries, staff, anyone."

"Now you're trying to intrude on the lives of others?"

"No. I'm just trying to find witnesses who—"

"Everyone you call a *witness* is devoted to the Assembly. All our friends, all of the people who worked with Rich—who mainly work for Chris McCarthy, too, by the way. No one will talk to you. If you try to contact them, Josh and I will be the ones who suffer."

"If there were even a couple of them who might—"

She shuts her eyes in frustration. "I knew this was a mistake."

"You didn't make a mistake. I won't cause trouble for you. I promise you that."

She says a terse goodbye and leaves.

As soon as Monica's out the door, Deanna sits down across from me.

"So you promised I could bring her redemption, huh?" I say. My tone is sarcastic, but the truth is, I have become responsible for the future of her and her child.

"All I can say is that it's a good thing the kid was here. She would've bolted if she'd been alone. What did she tell you?"

"She told me that he was using the apartment as some kind of office and working with someone she calls an 'outsider'. She thought it was me. That's why she blamed me for his death. She insists that he would never sleep with prostitutes, didn't take drugs, that there must be some mistake with the phony passport. Is she really that gullible? I mean, I saw the pictures of those women, and there's no doubt that . . ."

I sit back in my chair. Harmon used to say that assumptions are the archenemies of truth. He was right.

CHAPTER 23

Although it's been a warm day, an ocean fog rolls in as soon as the sun goes down. Water droplets hover in midair, glimmer under the stadium-style lamps that illuminate the law school campus. Dressed only in a T-shirt and jeans, I jog across the plaza, not sure whether I'm shivering from the cold or in anticipation of discovering something that will crack the Baxter case open. I fling open the door to my classroom, expecting only Jonathan Borzo. Kathleen and Lovely are there with him.

Lovely is wearing date clothes—a candy-apple red blouse over a shiny black dress that falls to mid-thigh, and sexy tan peep-toe heels that accentuate her creamy-smooth legs. *She'll get a chill dressed like that*, I think. Unless she's wrapped in the arms of some powerful partner from her law firm, or a hunky fellow law student, or Deanna, who announced as I was walking out of The Barrista that she was leaving early even though she never leaves early.

"Did you tell them why we're here?" I ask Jonathan.

He grins slyly and strokes his sparse goatee like a cheesy cartoon character. He seems to enjoy riddles.

"We're going to take another look at the photographs of the women who visited Rich Baxter's apartment," I say.

Lovely sighs in disappointment. We've already spent hours examining those photos, blowing them up, shrinking them to thumbnails, sharpening them, cropping them.

"We've gotten some professional help," I say.

"Professor Stern asked me to contact my copyright client," Jonathan says. "You know, Dmitri, the dude who hacks video games. To see if he could do a better job enhancing the photos of Baxter's hookers. Dmitri e-mailed me some stuff."

Jonathan projects the photograph of the Sorority Chick on the large monitor at the front of the classroom. Just as Dale Garner said, she gives off a college girl vibe—satiny blue dress, bare shoulders, small waist, slender legs, looking as if she's about to go clubbing on Sunset Boulevard. Although Dmitri has enhanced the photograph, I see only disconnected pixels, taunting electronic speckles that suggest a face but aren't a face.

"Let's see the next one," I say.

It's a picture of the woman we call the Streetwalker. She's wearing a skimpy form-fitting dress—Lovely calls it a bandage dress—but to me it looks like she used a spray gun to cover her naked body and ran out of paint before she could finish. She's the shapeliest of the three women, her breasts round and pushed up so that her cleavage is visible. But no face.

"Next."

The Goth Girl. A calculated S&M look—hair styled in a Cleopatra cut and dyed black; a tight leather blouse that leaves her midriff bare; a leather miniskirt. But again, her face is unrecognizable.

"Sorry I wasted your evening," I say.

"Wait!" Lovely says. She stands, smooths her dress with her palms, and goes to the computer screen. She points to a small blotch on the woman's left ankle. It wasn't visible on the photos we enhanced ourselves.

"Is that what I think it is?" she says.

Kathleen gets up from her chair and walks toward the screen. "What do you think it is?"

"Jonathan, can you zoom in?" I say.

He zooms in on the blotch. The woman has a tattoo on her ankle. Although the image is mildly pixilated, the resolution is good enough for me to recognize a picture of a woman who resembles a Greek or Roman goddess petting a lion. The figure has a kind of halo over her head that looks like a horizontal figure eight—the infinity sign.

"Does anyone know what that's a picture of?" I ask.

Lovely shrugs, but Kathleen says in a half-whisper, "It's . . . it's a tarot symbol. Strength. It symbolizes discipline. Inner strength."

I smile at her with approval, and she smiles back, grateful for the smallest bit of affirmation.

"I don't get it," Kathleen asks. "Why is her ankle visible but her face still blurry?"

"Because that perv Garner wasn't aiming at her face," Lovely says. "He was aiming at her legs and ass. In fact . . . oh my God, could we see those other women again? The same kind of close-up?"

Jonathan clicks the mouse, and the sorority girl pops up on the screen.

"Right there," Lovely says, pointing.

This woman also has a tattoo on her ankle, in the identical spot. The image isn't as clear as the one on Goth Girl, but it's the same tattoo, the strength tarot. Jonathan quickly brings the photo of the third woman up on the screen. She, too, has the tattoo.

"So there aren't three women," Lovely says. "There's only one."

"It looks that way," I say. "But, there's one thing I . . . the blonde and Goth Girl have pretty much the same build, but the Streetwalker has a different body. Shapelier."

Lovely and Kathleen both laugh. Lovely says, "There are bras out there that will push up anything, Professor. Or nothing. That's the same body. The same person."

I study the photos for a while longer. "You're right. This is the same person."

"So, is this some kind of dress-up game?" Jonathan asks. "A weird sexual fantasy?"

I shake my head. "This woman isn't a prostitute. She's the person Monica Baxter was talking about. The one she calls the outsider."

CHAPTER 24

Judge Harvey won't let female lawyers wear pants in his courtroom. Lovely took my advice and dressed in a dark suit jacket and skirt and a plain white cotton blouse, but I worry that the skirt is a bit too short, falling an inch above the knee. We have bigger problems than Lovely's skirt length, however. Once Judge Harvey reads Tyler Daniels's stories, he'll loathe our client.

During the drive to the courthouse, I try to visualize my best moments in court—a closing argument in a copyright case in which I mocked the plaintiff's legal position so effectively that the jurors laughed out loud; my appearance before the California Supreme Court on behalf of prisoners who were denied access to a computer; my cross-examination of a racketeer who sued my magazine client for libel. I conceive of these triumphs as indestructible threads that I can weave together into a protective cloak that will ward off the terror.

I park in a lot across from Olvera Street, the tourist area that bills itself as the birthplace of Los Angeles, though LA natives don't go there unless they have children, and even then, usually just once. As soon as we exit the car, a stagnant heat envelops me, and I worry that it's not the weather—it's still January, after all—but the first signs of the stage fright. With each step toward the courthouse, the confidence that I thought I'd built up on the drive over leaks out of my pores like an inert gas. I can no longer picture my courtroom successes. Now all I can remember are the times after Harmon's death when my knees gave out and my vocal cords seized up like rusted machinery.

Lovely's belt buckle sets off the magnetometer. A marshal pulls her aside and sweeps her with one of those metal-detecting wands, moving the instrument close over her entire body. During the process, Lovely has to keep her hands raised in the air. As the man maneuvers around her, she keeps her eyes fixed forward with a look of detachment. The marshal is only doing his job, but I want to throttle him. By the time we clear security, she's so wired that she races toward the escalator, although we're early.

"Slow down," I say. "If you walk that fast you won't have any energy left to argue the case."

She glances over her shoulder, but doesn't slow down. When I began practicing law, I too had that kind of enthusiasm for the court-room. It's intoxicating, but like any intoxicant, destructive. She'll have to learn to stay calm before a court appearance, or she'll burn out within five years.

I hold open the door to the courtroom while Lovely wheels the litigation bag inside. While she exudes self-assurance, I have to psych myself up to follow her. I tell myself that this is only a pro forma arraignment hearing, that Lovely is poised for a law student, that all I'll have to do is sit silently at counsel table and use yellow Post-its to pass notes.

"Sit in the second row," I whisper. It's superstition. I never sit in the front row, because I don't want to draw the judge's attention until I stand up to argue my case. But I want to stay close enough to the podium so that I can get there quickly if I feel the need to speak first.

We take our seats, and about a minute later Neil Latham walks in, balancing a large stack of files in his arms. He goes directly to the government's table next to the jury box. So much for winning the race to the podium. After he gets settled in, he approaches us and extends his hand to me.

"Haven't seen you since that unfortunate Baxter case, counselor," he says. "The worst experience of my career." He nods at Lovely. "And I'll wager this is your law student."

"This is Ms. Diamond," I say. "Lovely, this is Neil Latham."

She stands, and they shake hands.

"Welcome, Ms. Diamond," he says. "Do not feel intimidated by this room or the judge or me. Especially me. We're all sworn to do justice no matter which side we're on." He winks, and then goes back to his table.

"That was nice of him," I say.

"Lou Frantz says that your enemy is never nice."

"Harmon Cherry impressed upon us from the day we started at the law firm that most lawyers want to serve justice. Like Latham said."

Before she can reply, the clerk announces the judge's arrival. We stand and remain standing while Judge Harvey dodders to the bench and struggles into his chair. The clerk calls our case first. I hold the swinging gate open for Lovely, who takes a tentative step forward and looks at me questioningly.

"Take the first chair," I whisper. "The one nearest the lectern."

She places her files down on the table and sits in the first chair. I sit next to her. The perspiration has soaked through my shirt. I can feel the sweat on my forehead coalescing in larger droplets. I reach into my pocket, take out a wad of Kleenex, and dab at my brow and upper lip. I know I must be disgusting to anyone watching me, but it's better than raining perspiration all over the table. I glance at Lovely, who's so engrossed in reviewing her notes that she doesn't seem to notice.

Judge Harvey puts on his reading glasses and squints at some papers on his desk. "Now, who's appearing for the defendant, this Daniel Tyler?"

Lovely stands and walks to the lectern. "I am, Your Honor. Lovely Diamond. And, just for the record, Your Honor, it's *Tyler Daniels*, not *Daniel Tyler*."

I cringe. Although Lovely spoke with deference, you don't correct a judge like Cyrus Harvey unless he's about to commit an error that will send your client to prison.

"You're not an attorney admitted to practice before this court, are you Miss Diamond?"

"No, Your Honor. I'm a third-year law student at St. Thomas More certified under Local Rule 83-4.2 to represent the defendant. We've filed the client's written consent, and I have the required certification from my law school dean, and that's been filed, too."

"Where's the defendant's real lawyer? I want to talk to the defendant's real lawyer."

As soon as I stand up, a current of fear shoots through my body, so powerful that I don't think I'll be able to say my own name. The judge gives me a temporary reprieve.

"Good morning, Mr. Stern."

I nod.

"This is a serious, complicated First Amendment case," the judge says. "The defendant is charged with a felony. This isn't a good case for a training run."

"She's . . . she's one of our top students. I will supervise. She . . . she . . . she . . . Ms. Diamond, you know, has trial experience as a paralegal." I sound as if English isn't my first language. "The Frantz law firm. For Louis Frantz. For the man himself. Very capable." I take a breath, but it sounds like a gasp. I fix my eyes on Judge Harvey, not daring to look at Lovely or I'll melt down. Out of my peripheral vision, I see Latham. He's pretending to flip through some file folders so he doesn't have to look at me. Even he's embarrassed by my performance.

Judge Harvey shades his eyes with his hands, as though he's trying to pick someone out of a crowd on a bright day. He shakes his head slightly. "All right, counsel. We'll try it, although I don't know how long I'll be comfortable with it. I'm not going to jeopardize the defendant's civil and constitutional rights for a school project. You may proceed, Miss Diamond." He pauses. "Where's the defendant?"

Lovely straightens up and folds her hands on the lectern. "Your Honor, under Rule 10(b), the defendant has waived her right to appear at this arraignment. She was charged by an indictment, and we've previously filed her written waiver affirming that she received a copy of the indictment and that her plea is not guilty."

"Mr. Latham," the Judge says. "Does the government have any problem with the defendant's waiver of appearance?"

Latham half-rises. "No objection, Your Honor."

The judge thinks for a moment. "You know, a defendant's absence at a felony arraignment is unusual, Miss Diamond. This court wants to be sure that the defendant understands her constitutional rights, and that's why she should be here in court today."

"She's waived under Rule 10," Lovely says.

"You already told me that. But if you've read Rule 10, you also know that I have discretion under subsection (b)(3) not to accept the waiver."

"Yes, Your Honor, but—"

"But what, Miss Diamond?"

"Excuse me, Your Honor, I meant to say—"

"Miss Diamond, tell me why I shouldn't reject the waiver, continue this proceeding, and order the defendant to appear in person. It's a felony arraignment." Such an order would be disastrous. Since our meeting in the desert, Lovely and I have tried many times to persuade Tyler to show up in court, but she refuses.

"My client suffers from social anxiety disorder," Lovely says. "It's difficult, if not impossible, for her to leave her home." Outwardly, Lovely doesn't seem flustered, but her voice is unusually soft. Like anyone making her first real court appearance, she's petrified.

"Do you have a psychiatric report, Miss Diamond?"

She brushes a lock of hair from her forehead. "Not yet, Your Honor. We intend to get one for our client if necessary." She should stop there, but she breaks a rule that I've consistently tried to drum into my students—when speaking to a judge, don't say more than is absolutely necessary. "I should add, Your Honor, that we don't think the defendant will ever have to appear in court, because you must dismiss this indictment under Criminal Rule 12 as unconstitutional under the First Amendment."

The regulars in the courtroom rustle and murmur with anticipation, the way animals scurry and fret just before the first jolt of an earthquake.

"Wait just a minute, young lady," the judge says, his lips twisted in disdain. "Did you say I *must* dismiss this case? I *must*? I don't have to do anything, and if someone doesn't like it, they can convene sixty-seven US Senators and impeach me. I'm a federal judge, and no lawyer—and certainly no wet-behind-the-ears law student—tells me I *must* do anything."

"Excuse me, Your Honor, I didn't mean to imply—"

"You said I must dismiss this case, did you not?"

"I meant—"

"Answer my question, Miss Diamond. You did say that I *must* dismiss?"

"Yeah, but—"

"Yes or no, Miss Diamond. Stop ignoring my question."

"But I'm not ignoring—"

"Yes or no. I order you to answer!" Judge Harvey's voice reverberates off the walls. He's mastered the acoustics of his courtroom the way a billiards player masters the angles of a pool table.

"Yes," Lovely says. When the word comes out as a puff of breath, I know she's defeated.

The judge leans back in his chair and crosses his arms, his thin colorless lips curled up in a self-satisfied smirk. "See, Miss Diamond? That wasn't so hard, was it?"

"No, Your Honor."

"Now, what did you want to say about a motion to dismiss?"

She purses her lips and shuts her eyes in the tragic way of a woman fighting back tears. I'm supposed to be her mentor, but I can't protect her.

For a lawyer, silence means opportunity, and now Neil Latham jumps up take it. "Your Honor, the government—"

In the early eighties, the Dodgers had this second baseman named Steve Sax—a former Rookie of the Year who inexplicably lost his ability to make the simplest throw to first base. It got so bad that the reporters coined a term for it—Steve Sax Syndrome. The strange thing was that Sax could make the more difficult *bang-bang* throws that depended on reflex and left no time for conscious reflection. I've never understood until now how that was possible.

"Pardon me, Your Honor," I say, rising to my feet. "The government's indictment is unconstitutional because it abridges my client's free speech right by seeking to criminalize purely textual material."

"Your Honor," Latham says. "I ask that I be heard."

My voice gets stronger. "Something that's written down on paper in words with no images is pure thought, and the US government can't be the Thought Police. Under the law—"

"I was speaking," Latham says. "The Supreme Court in *Kaplan v. California*—"

"Mr. Latham interrupted Ms. Diamond," I say. "So we should have a right to finish our argument before he speaks. Now, Mr. Latham did mention *Kaplan v. California*, but since that case was decided in 1973—"

"Enough, counsel," Judge Harvey says. "This is just an arraignment. Save the argument for your motion to dismiss."

Latham raises his hand. "Your Honor, I—"

"We're done, Mr. Latham. I'll accept the waiver and enter the defendant's not guilty plea." He gestures toward his clerk. "Call the next case."

Lovely's still standing at the lectern, looking like a bewildered child.

"Let's go," I whisper.

She nods. But just before we reach the exit doors, Judge Harvey calls after us. "Miss Diamond, your skirt is much too short. Next time you appear in my court, dress appropriately. Do a better job of teaching your student professional decorum, Mr. Stern."

"Very well, Your Honor," I reply in a flat tone, because that's what the hierarchal difference between a federal judge and a mere lawyer requires me to say.

Lovely's jaw is clenched with such force that the cords in her neck are visible. I fear that she's about to lose control and talk back to the judge. I take her arm and lead her out of the courtroom as quickly as I can. We find a private corner at the end of the hall. Only then does the fact that I spoke in open court overwhelm me, but instead of feeling triumphant, I'm shaken, like someone who's just realized that he nearly tumbled off the ledge of an eighty-story building. My hands begin to shake, and I become so queasy that I want to run to the men's room and throw up. But I fight it, because I can't let Lovely see my weakness.

She crosses her arms and turns her back on me, and for a moment I think that she's going to burst into tears.

"Are you OK?" I ask.

She doesn't respond.

I take a step forward and make a move to put my hand on her shoulder, but stop myself. "Listen. Cyrus Harvey is a son of a bitch."

She spins around and faces me. Clouds of fury roil in her eyes, but to my surprise, I see no sign of tears.

"Never again," she says.

"This was your first court appearance before a difficult judge. You can't let one irrational judge dissuade you from trial work."

She straightens her body and clenches her fists. "Never again will I let anyone walk all over me like that. I don't care if it's a federal judge or whatever. I'd rather be thrown in jail for contempt than take that kind of shit."

I want to throw my arms around her. "That's good. That's exactly how you should feel. I'm . . . I'm proud of you. But there are ways to defuse the situation without losing your temper. We'll devote one of our class sessions to learning how to handle asshole judges. I should've done that before I let you appear before that old jerk."

She smiles despite herself. "When you got up to argue . . . It was weird. At first you were so nervous, I wondered if . . . But then when you shut down Latham you were so wonderful."

"It was just an arraignment, and I talked for all of thirty seconds."

"No. It's the way you talked. I've seen Lou Frantz argue so many times, and he's great, but you sounded . . . I hope this doesn't upset you because of how you feel about what you did as a kid, but you sounded like some great actor on stage."

"How could praise like that upset me?"

She smiles, averting her eyes. So Lovely Diamond can be shy. She checks her Blackberry.

"I got a message from my father," she says. "He's done reviewing the financials in the Baxter matter."

"Did he find anything?"

"My father doesn't like to put things in writing. He wants to meet with you. So if you could come to his house Friday at around three thirty—I don't have classes Friday afternoon—afterward I can make the three of us dinner. If you're up for it."

"Absolutely."

We start toward the exit, but I abruptly drag her into an alcove. "That guy going down the escalator," I say. "His name's Brandon Placek. He's a reporter for the *Times*. An obnoxious little weasel. Let's wait until he's gone."

CHAPTER 25

Ed Diamond lives in Little Holmby Hills, a tree-lined upper-class neighborhood not far from the UCLA campus and only a few blocks away from the Playboy Mansion. Whatever else he might have been, he was a shrewd businessman. There was a lot of money in porn before the Internet made so much of it free. Lovely didn't grow up poor.

I pull up to an elegant two-story Tudor-style house, the pitched cedar-shake roof and half-timbered second story signaling Southern California wealth. Lovely's beaten-up copper Honda Accord is parked in the driveway, a relief, because it means I won't have to spend time alone with her father. The moment I ring the bell, he answers the door.

"Well, well. Parky Fucking Gerald." He makes a show of checking his watch. "You're late, Parky. It's 3:40." His mouth is twisted in a half-scowl, but from what I remember, that was tantamount to a smile for him. After all these years, his voice remains familiar—the nasal intonation of the intelligent New York artist à la Kubrick or Scorsese, men whom he probably both admires and resents.

I start to tell him that he should call me Parker, but he knows that. When we worked together, the only trace of a sense of humor came when he needled people, often mercilessly. He called me Parky to see if he could get a rise out of me. I say, "It's been a long time. Do I call you Shane or Ed?"

The near scowl becomes a full-fledged snarl. "What do you think?"

Physically, he hasn't changed much. Time has ratcheted up his most distinctive features. When he worked as a cost accountant on the *Alien Parents* movies, he always looked as if he'd just tasted something bitter. Now, he looks as if he's swallowed a rancid meal whole. He still pulls his hair back in a ponytail, but he's gone gray and bald, so the only hair he has is the ponytail. His blue work shirt, jeans, and boots, which used to seem cool and arty, now make him look like a geriatric hippie.

"Jesus, you have dark hair," he says. "And a couple of gray ones. And you're tan and got muscle on your bones. You don't look anything like that scrawny kid."

"Thank God for small favors."

"Follow me."

I step into the entry hall. Lovely has never mentioned her mother, but the interior design must be her handiwork. In contrast to Diamond's dark personality, the place is warm and bright—light hardwood tongue-and-groove floors, yellow and white enamel walls, vibrant colorist oil paintings, and French doors that open into a large backyard and pool area, calculated to capture the maximum amount of sunlight. A portrait of a beautiful woman hangs over the fireplace—without a doubt, Lovely's mother.

I follow him back onto a covered outdoor patio. Lovely, dressed in a maroon sweatshirt and tight cutoff jeans, is sitting at a circular glass and wrought-iron lawn table, typing on a laptop computer. When she sees me, she closes the cover. "Hey, Professor."

"Hello, Ms. Diamond."

"*Professor?*" Ed says. "*Ms. Diamond?* Holy shit. Who the fuck would've thought I'd hear my own daughter and little Parky Gerald talking that way to each other?"

"Dad, call him Parker."

"What difference does it make what I call him?"

I sit next to her. Ed picks up a stack of papers from a chair, sits across from us, and says, "Let's get this over with. I hate this accounting crap."

"Thanks for helping me out on this," I say.

"I'm helping my daughter out." He reaches into a manila envelope and takes out a huge spreadsheet, the old fashioned printed kind you rarely see in this computer age.

"Here's the deal," he says. "I think there are some idiosyncratic facts here that you'll find interesting."

"What about this Emery Group that the IRS says—?"

"Do not interrupt me, Parky. Let me tell this goddamn story my way. If you still have questions when I'm done, ask them then, but do not interrupt me."

Lovely gives an embarrassed half shrug. "Dad's a storyteller. He doesn't like anything to break the flow."

I close my eyes so that the Diamonds don't see me rolling them. As much as Ed would like to believe otherwise, I doubt that plot was the strong point of his adult films.

"Please continue, Ed."

"Whoever set this up was a devious motherfucker. It's hard to tell with certainty what your friend Rich Baxter did and what he didn't do. One thing that's clear is that he had access to all the accounts for the Church of the Sanctified Assembly's businesses, not-for-profit foundations, and political action committees. This is difficult to analyze, because the Assembly has its hands in such diverse business. Drug rehab centers, battered women's shelters, thrift shops—it's very easy to launder money through thrift shops. Hundreds of millions of dollars were funneled through those entities each year. Mind-boggling, the amount of money those pompous assholes have at their disposal. It makes it easy to skim, easy to set up phony accounts or create false invoices or forged checks." He pauses to take a breath. "You know what the Technology Communications Organization is?"

"The TCO. It's their propaganda wing. Headed up Christopher McCarthy, a man I know all too well."

Ed tilts his head forward and rubs the back of his neck, as if talking for even this short time has made him weary. "Well, a lot of the money flowed in and out of that TCO entity. They charge them off as consulting fees—public relations, legal and related expenses. Richard Baxter, on behalf of the TCO, set up an offshore bank account through a Pakistani contact who once worked for a European bank based in the Netherlands. Then the Pakistani opened up an account at that bank in the name of Octagon, LLC. Money flowed out of that account and into a Vienna account in the same bank. The account holder is something called Pentagon Investments, LLC."

My head begins to spin. "Whoa. Can you slow down?"

"Jesus Christ, do I really have to repeat myself?"

"You absolutely do," I say. "This financial stuff isn't my strength. But I know one thing, unfortunately. From the names of those companies you mentioned, they could definitely have been set up by Rich."

"How do you know that?" Lovely asks.

"Because naming a company after a geometric shape was consistent with our law firm's MO. Use vanilla names for a corporation. I don't know why, I wasn't in the corporate department and never thought to ask."

"The names don't mean Rich embezzled, though," Lovely says. "Or even that he set all of them up."

"Of course not."

Ed lifts his eyebrows in annoyance. "Will the two of you please let me continue?" A gust of wind riffles his spreadsheet, and he has to shield it with his body so it won't blow away. It's late in the afternoon in January, and as pleasant as the day has been, it's still winter.

For the next half hour, he leads us through a convoluted series of transactions involving limited liability companies with the names Triangle, Hexagon, Heptagon, Trapezoid, Isosceles, and Rhombus, each of which opened various offshore bank accounts through which the Sanctified Assembly's hundreds of millions of dollars flowed. He describes the mechanics of electronic funds transfers and the difference between cash receipts schemes and disbursement schemes and the three stages of money laundering: *placement, layering,* and *integration.* He details a series of financial transactions as tangled as old computer wire, and then he unwinds them seamlessly. I now fully understand why the feds arrested Rich—many of the transactions are traceable only to Rich and involve accounts that he controlled. And now the Assembly says that the transactions weren't authorized.

"And with all that, there's nothing conclusive," Ed says. "The evidence is like a fucking shoeprint that might have come from Baxter's Bruno Magli—or from someone else's." Despite his gruffness, he sounds like a top-notch forensic accountant who would make an effective expert witness at trial, and for the moment it doesn't seem possible that he's famous for filming well-endowed men and busty women having sex, the hardcore scenes invariably shot in tasteful soft focus and accompanied by a stirring classical music score.

He puts down the spreadsheet and looks directly at me. "At the end of the money trail, millions were wired from Heptagon, Octagon, and Rhombus into a British West Indies account in the name of a company called The Emery Group LLC. That's a shell set up specifically for these kinds of transfers. And then the money went out again to some anonymous recipient. End of the line." He punctuates his sentence by pounding his fist on the stack of papers.

"But we need to know who The Emery Group paid the money to. You found nothing?"

"I didn't say that."

"Then, what—?"

"This goes no further than us three?"

"Of course."

He exchanges looks with Lovely. "You know what I did for a living."

"Yeah. I've known since I was ten years old. What does that have to do with my case?"

"You don't survive as long as I did in that business without reaching accommodation with a certain class of people. At least, not if you started when I did. There were mutual exchanges of favors. On this Baxter thing, I called in a favor. Because we needed someone who, shall we say, could gather more information than you can find on the Internet or in the documents you gave me."

"You're saying that you asked the . . . some Mafioso to get this information? You're not serious."

"I wouldn't use that word, exactly, but . . ." He shrugs.

"If you used illegal means to get information, I don't want it."

"A rather holier-than-thou attitude, don't you think, Parky?"

"I'm a disciple of Harmon Cherry. I honor his legacy by following the rule of law."

He waves his hand dismissively. "I'm not sure that your vaunted Harmon Cherry didn't set this all in motion. His name appears in some of these documents, you know."

"Harmon wouldn't do anything illegal. But I don't care if he did or didn't. I care about what *I* do."

"*You* didn't do anything. So stop worrying. You've been given a gift. Accept it graciously."

"It's not that easy. The Assembly is the criminal organization. We're supposed to be the ones who respect the law. And there's something I don't understand. If what you're telling me is true, you've used up some goodwill with some very dangerous people. Why would you do that for me?"

"I wouldn't."

"I . . . I asked him to do it," Lovely says. "I know how important this investigation is to you. I knew you wouldn't like it, but I thought . . ." Her voice falters and she lowers her eyes, a rare time when she seems truly embarrassed. Only from her would I accept the fruit of a tainted tree.

"What did your source—what did you learn?" I ask.

He takes a couple of deep breaths and then leans in close, as though we're sitting in a crowded diner rather than an ultraprivate, walled-in backyard. "There were two payments that my sources could trace. One was small . . . well, small by comparison. A transfer in the amount of about five hundred thousand to a US account in the name of Delwyn Bennett."

"I don't know that name," I say.

"Jesus Christ. Don't you follow politics? You should know what's going on in your world. Del Bennett is chief of staff to Congressman Lake Knolls."

"There's no way that the Assembly bribed Knolls. He's one of their biggest critics."

"Do we know it's a bribe?" Lovely asks. "Maybe Bennett's scamming his boss."

"I have no answers," Ed says. "It's for you to figure out. But on the same day as the payment to Bennett, The Emery Group transferred out approximately six million dollars to a person or persons unknown. That's money your friend Rich supposedly took from the Assembly, right?"

"Yeah. The feds say he diverted Assembly funds. But they can't really prove the money went to Rich."

"I can tell you this. The six million was transferred out of Emery and deposited into another offshore account in the name of a company called Nonagon Investments, LLC."

"Who controls that?"

"I have no idea. Maybe Rich Baxter, maybe someone else."

I deflate. Another shell company with invisible owners. "Not even your connected buddies could find that out, huh, Ed?"

"But I'll tell you what they did find out," he says, ignoring the jibe. "The person who was the authorized signatory for The Emery Group's account was none other than Christopher McCarthy of the TCO. Which means that he or someone acting on his behalf would have had to authorize that six million payment. Doesn't that float your boat?"

CHAPTER 26

After Ed finishes his report, he pushes back his chair with authority and stands up. "I've done my fucking job. You two legal eagles can take it from here." He walks quickly into the house, as if he's fleeing a crime scene.

For the next forty-five minutes, Lovely and I sit in the yard and debate the meaning of her father's revelations. While Lake Knolls's involvement with the Assembly is the more startling piece of evidence, I know how I'm going to deal with it. I have a history with Knolls. But Christopher McCarthy will never own up to having his name on that account, and I can't confront him with information that was obtained illegally.

And what, if anything, does McCarthy know about the seventeen million in diverted funds? As signatory on The Emery Group's account, did he give Rich permission to transfer the money, and if so, why? Did he take the money himself and frame Rich? Is he covering up for someone else in the Assembly?

Lovely raises another possibility, one that I won't consider. What if Rich stole the money after all? Maybe McCarthy and the Assembly truly are the victims. I still can't explain the drugs and the false passport that the cops seized when they raided Rich's apartment.

Lovely checks her watch. "It's 5:20. Almost sundown. Let's go inside."

She summons her father, and he and I sit down at a dining room table that could easily accommodate twelve people. The table is set with a white tablecloth, fine china, crystal wine glasses, a bottle of cabernet sauvignon, and a large unsliced loaf of bread with a twisty brown crust.

"My mother was a challah baker," Lovely says. "I can never bake it like she did, but I try."

At Lovely's mention of her mother, Ed looks sad, but that passes as quickly as the shadow of a scudding cloud, and he just appears irascible again. I remember an old piece of show biz lore about him—despite his sleazy occupation and the temptation all around him, he supposedly adored his wife, to the exclusion of any other woman. *No wonder*, I think. She looked like her daughter.

Not long after Lovely goes into the kitchen, I hear a wicked sizzling—the sound of oil splashing into an over-heated saucepan. The aroma of scorched garlic wafts in, and the smoke alarm begins screeching.

"Shit!" Lovely says from the other room.

I start to get up to help her, but the noise stops.

"My daughter in the kitchen is like a Chicago hog butcher performing brain surgery," Ed says. "I'm glad she's going to law school."

"She's going to be a terrific lawyer."

He glances at the kitchen door for a moment and says in an irritated whisper, "Speaking of which, why in the hell did you permit Lovely to take on that obscenity case for the whacko woman from the desert? That case is poison. Isn't one of your jobs to teach good judgment? Because you both showed bad judgment."

"I assumed she took the case because of you. Weren't you convicted on obscenity charges in the early seventies? Badly beaten in an Atlanta jail, from what I read on the Internet? You should understand about someone like Tyler, who—"

"Do not go there, goddamnit," he says through clenched teeth. "That Daniels woman and I are nothing alike. I made films that exalt human intimacy and passion, that exposed the hypocrisy of this country's sexual repression. That Daniels woman is a purveyor of filth."

"This is an important First Amendment case that could make law," I say, paraphrasing the very argument that Lovely makes to me when I question our decision to handle the case. "Tyler Daniels is entitled to a vigorous defense."

"Not from my daughter, she's not." There's a clanging of pots and plates in the kitchen, like a warning bell. His face lights up with a forced cheeriness. "So Parky. How's that mother of yours?" He's left out the obvious adjective, but it's implied by his tone: How's that *crazy* mother of yours?

"I have no idea. I haven't seen or spoken with her in years."

"I can fully understand why the two of you don't have contact."

"Then why did you ask me about her?"

"Because even when things go bad between kids and parents, time heals."

"I'm surprised that someone as streetwise as you would use that cliché. We both know it's bullshit."

"It certainly is not. Believe me, I know from personal experience." He sighs. "Parky, back when you were a kid, everyone working on the production was concerned about you. We worried that Harriet . . ."

"What? Worried that she let the director work me to exhaustion despite the child labor laws? Or that she was using my earnings to support her coke habit? Or that she was sleeping with any man who she thought could advance my career and a lot of men who couldn't? What worried all you grownups, Ed?"

"I'm sorry I brought it up."

Lovely walks in through the kitchen door. "Sorry you brought what up?"

Ed glances at me, and I think he's going to pursue this thing about my mother just because he likes to jab with the point of the knife, but he says, "We were just continuing our debate about my tactics in conducting financial investigations."

"No more talking about work," she says. "It's the Sabbath."

That will be a problem for me because work is all I have to talk about. Even politics and religion now seem like subsets of my job.

"OK," Lovely says. "I'm going to light the candles."

"Wait a minute," Ed says, placing his elbows on the table and leaning toward me confidentially. "So, Parky, you're a Jew, right?"

"Father!" Lovely says.

"It's a legitimate question. I mean, you're about to say a prayer, to go through the candle-lighting business, so . . ." He spreads his arm in mock apology. "I only assumed you were because Stern's a Jewish name."

"If you're talking about religion, I'm not Jewish, and Stern isn't necessarily a Jewish name. And if you're talking about ethnicity, the answer is, I don't know."

"What do you mean, you don't know?"

Lovely places her hand on her forehead and shuts her eyes, the gesture of an adult child who can't control an incorrigible parent. I can refuse to answer, and she'll understand. But I want her to know.

"My mother never talked about our background. I grew up without knowing who my father was. I still don't. Maybe she never knew herself. When I was little, she'd make up stories. She told me that he was a war hero who died in a plane crash. Later, she flip-flopped and said he was a revolutionary who was in the Weather Underground. Of course, I was six years old, so I didn't understand what a revolutionary was, much less know of the Weather Underground. Another time she claimed he was a famous actor who'd come and live with us someday. When I kept pressing for the truth, she got angry and told me that my father's identity was none of my concern." I try to make a joke of this, but neither Ed nor Lovely hints at a smile.

"The stories she told about herself were equally outlandish," I say. "She said she'd worked as a chorus girl on Broadway. Another time, she claimed that she grew up dirt poor on a farm in Ohio, earned a college scholarship, but had to give it up when she got pregnant with me. Once, she said she was the child of former Vaudevillians, which was chronologically impossible because she wasn't old enough to have parents in Vaudeville. Anyway, when I got old enough to recognize these tall tales for what they were, I stopped asking. I told myself she was like one of those mothers who refuse to share her special tuna casserole recipe with her kids. Finally, when I was twelve, in a rare moment of candor—at least I think she was being candid—she admitted that she grew up in Sherman Oaks. A Valley girl. She said her parents—my grandparents— were both dead. She claimed her maiden name was Stern, that I have her name, but who knows?"

"Have you tried to find them?" Ed asks. "Or maybe there are other relatives?"

"After I started law school, I did a lot of research, but there was nobody. So that's why I don't know what my religion is supposed to be or what my ethnic background is. It's fine with me. There's something liberating about it. I've always felt that I can fit in anywhere or be anyone. Maybe that's why I did OK as an actor. And as a lawyer." The wind blows through the white sycamores that frame the yard, and for a moment I want to smile, because the rustling of the leaves sounds like applause.

"We'll honor Shabbat," Lovely says softly. She takes a book of matches and lights the candles. "We light two candles because there are two references to Shabbat in the Torah, one in Exodus and one in Deuteronomy. The words are a little different. 'Remember' the Sabbath and 'Observe' the Sabbath. I think this means that rote observation without knowledge of its significance is meaningless and that you can't understand it without following its rituals."

She covers her eyes with her hands, like a young child playing peek-a-boo, but paradoxically it's the action of a mature woman. She says a blessing in Hebrew and removes her hand from her eyes. "I covered my eyes during the prayer so I could focus without distraction on the blessing and reflect on whether during the past week I followed a righteous path. I connect with the Torah and the eternal harmony that it brings us. When I uncover my eyes and see the flame, I can truly experience the light, both figuratively and literally—the light from the candles and the light of God."

Ed glances at his daughter and smirks. "Do you know why women conduct the Friday candle lighting ceremony, Parker? Because women were responsible for dimming the world's light when Eve gave in to temptation in the Garden of Eden. The slut."

"Stop, Dad," Lovely says.

"What's the problem?" Ed says. "The great scholar Rashi said so."

"I hate when you say stuff like that." She clenches and unclenches her jaw, like she does when she gets angry in class. Ed raises his palms in reconciliation.

She says blessings over the bread and the wine, and then brings out dinner—salad and some kind of pasta with tomato sauce.

"Linguini puttanesca," she says. "Olives, capers, tomatoes. Vege-tarian. I didn't know if you eat meat, so . . ."

We pass her our plates, and she piles a large helping of linguini on them. She takes a smaller portion for herself. When we've all been served, I take a forkful. The burnt garlic has given the food a charred, bitter taste, and the pasta is so gloppy I have to wash it down with the wine. Fortunately, the salad is edible and the egg bread is quite good, so I eat those first and force down as much of the pasta as I can before pleading fullness. Ed eats his linguini without enthusiasm. At least she chose a good wine.

With work topics off-limits, I learn that like me, Ed is an avid bas-ketball fan. Father and daughter get into a heated debate about the merits of a Coen Brothers movie that I haven't seen, so I just sit and let them entertain me with their fervor. Ed hasn't been this animated since I arrived. It becomes clear that he truly knows cinema and that Lovely's passion for debate will make her an excellent trial lawyer.

I finish a second glass of cabernet, and during a lull in the conver-sation surprise myself by saying, "What do you get out of honoring the Sabbath, Lovely?"

"First you have to promise that your question doesn't have anything to do with your investigation into the Sanctified Assembly. Because if it does, it's work, and I won't discuss it now."

"No, I just . . . when you were saying those prayers, you looked so . . . joyful? I've just never understood how people feel that way about prayer. I've tried, but I can't."

"There are a lot of answers to that question, but none will satisfy you."

"Try."

"All right. How about poetry? It's said that on the Sabbath eve, you greet God as the bridegroom and the Sabbath as the bride, and by observing the Sabbath you honor the bride and groom. Or pragma-tism. It's important for your mental and physical health to take a day off from work. And there's loyalty. Lighting the Shabbat candles meant so much to my mother." She glances at her father. "Momma was Norwe-gian. She converted to Judaism when she decided to marry my dad. Not for expediency, but because she truly believed it was the right choice for her. Her family basically disowned her after she married my father."

Ed looks down and squirms in his chair.

"My mom died when I was seventeen. Prayer is a way to hold her close."

The only loss in my life that comes close to equaling hers was the death of Harmon Cherry. I try to honor him by practicing law the way he taught me, not through useless superstition or ritual.

She studies me, as if reading my thoughts. "I told you that my answers wouldn't satisfy you."

I shrug in apology.

"Well, try this. Religion can be very similar to an embrace. And you can't really explain an embrace. But there are people who comfort me with just a hug." Grinning slightly, she tilts her head toward her father. "If that same person hugged you, you'd probably recoil in disgust. But the trick, with both people and faith, is to find what will comfort you. We all need a divine embrace."

I nod as if I understand, but I don't. Oh, I comprehend the meaning of the words, but I don't believe in mysticism.

At around nine thirty, I say goodbye. As I walk to my car, I feel relaxed, and it isn't just the wine. I truly haven't thought about the Baxter investigation for the past couple of hours.

This changes as soon I power on my Blackberry. There's a message from a frantic Raymond Baxter. Several news reporters have called him about a rumor that early next week the Church of the Sanctified Assembly will sue the estate of Richard Baxter for seventeen million dollars. Fortunately, Raymond didn't comment.

I have to tell Lovely. I spin around, sprint back up the steps, and hold down the doorbell until I hear footsteps.

She flings the door open. "Is everything OK?"

"Yeah. No. I just got this message from Raymond Baxter that—"

She touches my lips with her fingers, a mythical goddess striking me mute. "I absolutely will not discuss work. Tell me tomorrow night after sundown."

"You're right. It was rude of me. I just thought—"

Again, she brushes my lips with her fingertips to quiet me, and this time she doesn't lower her hand, but instead places it on my cheek and leans in to kiss me. And though I should put a stop to it, I kiss her back, quite certain that the velvety heat enveloping and uplifting my entire body is that divine embrace she described earlier.

She finally draws away, her smile almost leveling me. "Good night, Parker. And don't get hung up about me being your student. You're just an adjunct professor. Anyway, you're so crazy that the law school probably won't hire you again." Without waiting for a reply, she shuts the door.

CHAPTER 27

After an early morning run through the Marina and down the Venice Boardwalk, I spend Saturday at The Barrista waiting for the sun to go down. I speak with Raymond, who doesn't know anything more about the rumored lawsuit than I do. I'm sure the source is Christopher McCarthy, laying the groundwork for the Assembly's litigation PR campaign.

Late-morning, Manny Mason stops by with his three teenage sons. While the boys sit at their own table and gawk at the Goth girls and sorority sisters and hot young soccer moms, I tell Deanna and Manny about the call from the reporters and about meeting with Ed Diamond. After Manny and his sons leave, I scarf down a turkey sandwich for lunch and then take a walk through the streets of West Hollywood—up Melrose, past the design center they call the Blue Whale, and all the way to Barney's Beanery. Just when I think that the low clouds and incessant traffic will make the day permanently dreary, the sun breaks through, and LA's gaudy version of an urban village sparkles. When I get back to the coffee house, I work some more and sit and think of nothing and watch Deanna glad-hand the customers and manage her employees and take her turn behind the coffee bar. I wonder what our relationship might have been if upbringing or circumstance or a trick of genetics hadn't shaped us into people whose bodies meld together perfectly but whose hearts can't fully connect.

Mostly, I just bide my time until I can call Lovely.

An hour after sunset, I sequester myself in an empty corner of the coffee house, take out my cell phone, and punch in Lovely's number. When she answers, I tell her about the rumor that the Assembly is going to file suit. I would've thought she'd be full of ideas about the next steps in the defense, but she's doesn't say anything.

"Is something wrong?" I ask.

"What makes you think that something's wrong?"

"You seem so quiet. Distant. After last night, I thought—"

"I'm fine. You, my father, and I had a productive working session and a nice dinner. Is there anything else you want to talk about? I don't have a lot of time. I've got a lot of studying to do."

Over the past twenty-four hours, I've allowed myself to make assumptions. I usually don't make assumptions. Not about people. Not about love. I misunderstood last night. Or maybe she thinks it was a mistake. I haven't felt this callow since I was ten and had a crush on Erica Hatfield, the actress who played my mother in *Doheny Beach Holiday.* "I just thought we could talk a little about the Baxter defense," I say. "But you're right. Your schoolwork comes first."

She doesn't respond. Her silence feels impenetrable. I strain to hear breathing or background noise, but it's so quiet that for a moment I think she's dropped the call.

"Lovely?"

"Yeah. I'm . . ."

"Can you meet Monday afternoon at school to go over this? With Kathleen and Jonathan? Two o'clock?"

"If I don't have too much work."

I find that despite the frostiness, I want to keep hearing her voice, want to hold on to this ever more tenuous connection for just a little while longer. I struggle to think of something else to say, but I'm tapped out.

"Parker, there's . . ."

"What is it?"

"Nothing. I've got to go."

"Lovely, come on. You need to—"

"I said I've got to go."

"So I guess I'll see you Monday at school."

"If I don't have too much work."

The next day, over Sunday brunch at a cafe in Culver City, I meet with Raymond Baxter. He reaffirms his determination to fight a lawsuit, but I want him to know the risks. He'll have to pay the costs—emotional and financial—and there's little doubt that the Sanctified Assembly will churn the case to try to drain us of money and resolve. He asks about a retainer, and I tell him that I'll take the case pro bono. I'm not sure he can afford the fees, and I don't need the money, and for now, I'm a law professor, not a practicing attorney. He insists on paying me. I quote him an hourly rate that's half of what I charged when I was in practice with Harmon Cherry.

For the rest of the time, he talks about his son, telling stories about Rich as a toddler, Rich playing junior golf, Rich's broken collarbone, Rich's first fistfight, Rich skiing in Mammoth, Rich as a college fraternity pledge. Tedious, rambling stories that only a father would care about. Yet the old man's stories captivate me. I have no experience in the ways a father loves his son. I know nothing of how the boy's most trivial successes cause the parent to swell with pride; how each memory seems fully preserved with a three-dimensional clarity; how the instinct to protect is so powerful that it persists even after the boy has become a man—even after the son's life has ended.

CHAPTER 28

By two o'clock Monday, the Assembly still hasn't filed a lawsuit. Lovely doesn't show up for the strategy session at the law school. Dispirited by her absence, I summarize for Kathleen and Jonathan the status of our investigation and confirm again that they're willing to help out on the case as part of their classwork.

"We're on board with it, Professor," Jonathan says. "Right, Kath?"

She shrugs, which for Kathleen is the equivalent of a resounding *yes*.

"There's something the two of you could get started on right away," I say. "The Assembly holds weekly orientation meetings at its Grand Temple downtown. A way to recruit new members. I'd like the two of you to attend one. Let me know what the Assembly's preaching these days."

"How would that help the case?" Kathleen asks.

"It's important to know your enemy. If this goes right, we're going to put the Church of the Sanctified Assembly on trial."

"Gotcha," Jonathan says.

"Isn't it . . . is it dangerous?" Kathleen says. "I mean, these Assembly people—"

"I wouldn't worry. This is a public orientation meeting we're talking about. A sales pitch. They won't know who you are."

Kathleen glances at Jonathan and actually smiles. "Should we . . . should Jon and I act like a married couple or something?"

"So, I'm not really comfortable with that," he says. Kathleen twists sideways and hits him in the shoulder. She's smiling, but he winces. It seems that she's not so timid where their romance is concerned.

"I meant the lying," he says.

"Don't ever lie," I say. "That doesn't mean that you volunteer information or put your name on a mailing list. But always tell the truth."

"So we just walk in and listen?" Jonathan says.

"Not just walk in. Arrive separately and sit separately. Don't talk to anyone, especially the people putting on the program. Only one of you should take notes."

They leave. I linger in the classroom for a while and then go out into the plaza, stopping at the campus food truck to buy a roast beef sandwich and bottled water. I find an empty table and sit down. It's an overcast day, so gray that it feels as if the city is suffering from a kind of urban hangover. Before I can unwrap my sandwich, I see Lovely hurrying across the plaza. She doesn't see me, or if she does, she ignores me. She's dressed for work in one of her conservative business suits and a cotton blouse, in theory loose-fitting enough to hide her curves, but in practice an utter failure at that task. She's pulled her blonde hair back in a low chignon. Although it's only cold by LA standards—the temperature must be in the low sixties—she's wearing leather gloves and a bright carrot-orange scarf. I watch her disappear into the building.

Just as I force down the last of my sandwich, she comes out of the building. She stops and scans the grounds until she sees me. She primps the bun in her hair and walks over, her stride purposeful. Only when she reaches the table do I see how somber she is.

"I don't mean to interrupt your lunch," she says. "But we have to talk."

"Yeah. Sure. Take a chair."

"No. Not here. Can we go somewhere private?"

We walk in silence to the still-empty classroom. She removes the scarf and the gloves and stuffs them in her backpack. She sits down in a chair, and with that demure reflex that women have when they feel exposed, stretches the hem of her skirt over her knees.

I lean against the conference table and cross my arms. "Listen, let me save us both some embarrassment. What happened Friday night was—"

"Don't! Just listen to what I have to say."

"I'm listening."

She bows her head. A deep intake of air makes her chest heave. She lets her breath out slowly and says, "When Lou Frantz offered me a job as an associate at his firm, I accepted on the spot. I didn't consider interviewing with the big downtown firms or applying for a judicial clerkship or talking to any of the boutiques that recruited me. I said yes to Lou's offer because it's my dream job. I'm sure you know Lou's reputation. Great trial lawyer, huge ego, a real shark, borderline ethics. A *cut-you-off-at-the-knees* lawyer. All true. But he's been great to me. As a boss and mentor. After he saw that I was a good paralegal, that I loved trial work, he encouraged me to go to law school. He wrote letters of recommendation, and not just for St. Thomas More, but for a lot of schools, more prestigious, but I knew he wanted me to come here—he graduated from here—so when I got admitted, I accepted. Because of him."

She clearly feels about Frantz the way I felt about Harmon Cherry. She takes my hand. "Parker, the Assembly has hired Lou to represent them in their lawsuit against the Baxter estate. And . . . and they know that I've been helping you out on it. I found out Saturday night. Lou called me shortly before you did. I mean, I know coincidences happen, but this—"

I jerk my hand away. "You don't get it, do you? It wasn't a coincidence. The Assembly obviously found out about your father's little investigation and decided to become proactive where you're concerned. So they hire the top trial lawyer in the state and at the same time conflict you out from working with me."

"There's no way. Dad swore that—"

"What? That those people are untraceable? He actually believed his wise-guy friends are better connected than the Church of the Sanctified Assembly?"

"Those people are—"

"These aren't the 1950s. Your father's over-the-hill Mafia buddies are dwarfed by a machine like the Assembly. The Assembly has the aura of legitimacy and the power of its false gods and the protection of the First Amendment. Something Ed Diamond's so-called *friends* never had."

She averts her eyes.

"Their investigation has been thorough," I continue. "It always is. They must know how much I need your help."

I wait for her to meet my gaze, and when she doesn't, I understand why she's here, and the truth lacerates my gut. I struggle to speak in an even tone. "You and Frantz want Raymond Baxter to waive the conflict of interest so your law firm can represent the Assembly even though you've worked for our side. Have I got it right?"

She looks at me through vacant eyes. We stare at each other in silence until I notice her chin quiver ever so slightly.

"You know what?" I say. "You'll get your conflict waiver. I'll get Raymond to approve. But there's one thing I won't give you and Frantz. I will never agree to let you work for the Assembly against me on this case. That I will not do. And I trust you won't tell Frantz what you know."

"Why would you agree to any of it?"

"Because a scorpion like Frantz doesn't turn down a chance to represent a major client like the Assembly. Especially when he thinks he might recover a multimillion dollar contingency fee. It's not in his nature. So if it's a choice between you and the Assembly, he'll pick the Assembly, no matter how loyal or kind he's been to you in the past. Am I right?"

She gives a slight nod of her head.

"Well, I'm not going to let my lawsuit get you fired. I'm not going to be the one who destroys your dream. And in the long run, it doesn't matter who represents the Assembly, does it? Because I'm going to win the case and I'm going to get to the truth." I gesture toward her backpack. "I'm sure you and Frantz have already prepared the waiver letter. Let's get this over with. I'll get Baxter to sign it by the close of business hours."

She stands and rummages through her bag until she locates a piece of paper, which she pulls out of a file folder with trembling hands. Even from a few feet away, I can see the letterhead bearing the words *The Louis Frantz Law Office*, the overblown embossed lettering a testament to the extreme narcissism of her boss.

The persistent white noise of the heater has stopped for the moment. We stare at each other in absolute silence. I reach out to take the document from her, but instead of handing it to me she pulls it away and briefly shuts her eyes.

"Oh, fuck it," she says, and to my astonishment crumples the letter up with a deft motion of her fingers. The crinkling sound reverberates like percussive explosions.

I gape at her.

"I can use the extra free time to study for the bar." She tries to force a grin, but her raspy voice reveals her true emotions.

"I will not let you throw away your future. Not over a lawsuit."

"*You're* not letting me do anything. It's my decision. I'm not going to be Lou's pawn. I decided a long time ago that I won't be any man's pawn."

"But your income. In this economy you can't just—"

"My father—"

"Even so, you can't just quit your job. Not because of me."

"You know, I promised myself years ago I'd be independent, that I'm no kid and shouldn't be leeching off my father, but I guess . . . I guess quitting my job is another kind of independence. And as for the other, I can get hired as an associate anywhere. Somewhere just as good." She squeezes the wadded ball of paper hard and lets it drop. As soon as it hits the floor, her entire body slackens. She shrinks into herself like a forlorn child.

I take a step forward and embrace her. She encircles my waist with her arms, nestles her head in my shoulder, and starts sobbing. The palms of her hands press tightly against my back. She smells of orange blossoms and ginger, the scent so faint that it seems more like a memory of a fragrance. The only sound in the room is her crying, strangely melodious, a dirge for her newly buried plans.

The door latch disengages with a mechanical *click*. We both stiffen and jump back from each other just before Manny Mason walks into the room. Lovely turns her back on him for a moment and uses the heels of her hands to wipe away the tears. I lean back on the table, a bit of stage business designed to make me look casual.

He stands by the door glaring down at me from his considerable height. He's carrying a leather file folder under his arm.

"Hey, Manny. Do you need this room?"

"I've been looking for you. Jonathan Borzo said you might be in here. We've got a major problem."

Manny must have seen us hugging. I glance at her. She's glowering at him, daring him to mention the embrace.

He reaches into his folder and pulls out a section of a newspaper.

"Today's *Times*," he said. "Page one of the *Local* section."

Lovely moves in close to look over my shoulder. Her breasts brush against me, and even with Manny here, I feel a surge of heat. Then I see the headline:

Professor and Student at Catholic Law School Defend Child Pornographer.

The article was written by Brandon Placek of the *Times*. His story asks why a Catholic institution like St. Thomas More would let a teacher and student defend a child pornographer as part of a class assignment, especially in light of the ongoing revelations about Catholic priests abusing children. Placek goes out of his way to emphasize that one of Tyler's stories involves a sexually depraved priest and nun. The article uses the hot-button words—*graphic, torture, sexual abuse of young children.*

Manny spends the next twenty minutes interrogating us. During our law firm days, he never took a deposition, but now his questioning is masterful. It feels as if Lovely and I are the ones on trial. Manny doesn't like what he's hearing. When I describe Tyler's stories, he utters a rare expletive.

As distraught as Lovely was before Manny came in, she rallies when he questions our judgment in taking on Tyler's defense. She insists that she won't abandon Tyler to an implacable government that wants to trample on the First Amendment, even if it means expulsion from school. Lovely is one of those people for whom conflict provides an odd kind of solace.

"It sounds like a legitimate case," Manny says. "We'll see what the powers-that-be say. Meanwhile, if I were you, I'd get a First Amendment law firm involved."

Instead of thanking him, Lovely says, "I'm not giving this case up to another firm, Dean Mason. It took me forever to win Tyler's trust. She won't want anyone else. And she won't need anyone else. We're going to get this case dismissed."

Manny shrugs like Harmon Cherry used to when he disagreed with our judgment but had decided to let us sink or swim.

Lovely heads off to her afternoon class. Manny walks with me across the plaza. When we reach the parking lot, he says, "I'm going out on a limb for you, Stern. It's going to be hell dealing with my bosses. Don't let me down."

"I don't say it enough, but thank you. And not just for this."

He frowns. He's never been comfortable with displays of sentiment.

After we say goodbye, I get into my car and drive down Beverly Boulevard toward The Barrista. It's only early afternoon, but the traffic is gridlocked. It wasn't always that way. Ten years ago, I could have made it to West Hollywood in twenty minutes. As I wait at the intersection of Beverly and La Cienega, my Blackberry buzzes. Trying to keep one eye on the traffic signal, I open the message hoping that it's from Lovely.

It's from Manny. At first I think that someone has used his e-mail address to send me incomprehensible spam. Then I see that it's a warning:

From the St. Thomas More School of Law's Manual of Policies and Procedures, Section 4.2.1: The integrity of the relationship between student and teacher provides the bedrock of the law school's mission. The teacher serves as the student's evaluator and mentor. The unequal power inherent in this relationship makes the student vulnerable and heightens the potential for coercion. Whenever a teacher is responsible for academic supervision of a student, a personal relationship between them of a romantic or sexual nature, even if consensual, is inappropriate and therefore forbidden.

CHAPTER 29

The seventy-three-page complaint in *Church of the Sancti-fied Assembly v. Estate of Baxter* pleads causes of action for fraud, constructive fraud, breach of fiduciary duty, and conversion. The Assembly prays for compensatory damages in the sum of $17,000,634, for punitive damages in an amount to be determined at trial, and for such other relief as the court may deem just and proper. Lou Frantz's name appears on the last page, his signature executed in a bombastic flourish worthy of a superlawyer. Stripped of the formal language, the complaint charges that over several years, Rich Baxter stole more than seventeen million dollars from the Assembly and that his estate has to pay it back, along with millions more to punish him.

When I phone Raymond to discuss the case the first thing he says is, "I want you to sue them for malicious prosecution."

"We can only do that if we win."

"Then let's win. How long will it take?"

"LA Central's got a crowded docket. Usually two years minimum, more likely three."

"That's too long. I'm seventy-eight years old, and—"

"That's why I said *usually*. Since you're over seventy, you can get an early trial date if you can prove that the state of your health is such that you'll suffer prejudice without one."

He's quiet for a moment. There's a hoarse sound with every breath he takes. "By that legalese, you mean I only get to trial early if I'm so sick I'll probably die in the next two years?"

"That's about right."

He laughs bitterly. "I've got stage-three emphysema and a bad heart. Triple bypass surgery three years ago. An assortment of less severe though no less annoying ailments. And chronic back pain from spinal stenosis, though I supposed that doesn't count."

"It all counts. I'll file the petition for a preference today."

An hour after I submit the petition, Frantz's office files a response. I thought they'd oppose just to harass me, but to my surprise they've agreed with my position. Frantz isn't doing me a favor. Far from it. He obviously thinks that a quick trial works to his advantage because he has the better facts, that delay couldn't make his case any better than it already is.

Late in the afternoon, the court clerk calls. He tells me that the judge just settled a case, which opens up a slot for our trial at the end of May, only four months away. I hadn't expected this. My heartbeat speeds up, and I begin to sweat the way I do when I walk into a courtroom. Even expedited cases usually take more than a year to get to trial. Four months isn't nearly enough time to get ready. I'm the victim of what attorneys call a *rocket docket*. But there's nothing I can do about it—I was the one who asked for a quick trial, so how can I complain about getting it? I tell the clerk that the May trial date is fine.

Harmon Cherry used to insist that, despite what the general public and all too many lawyers think, the vast majority of judges and other court personnel are honest people who take their oaths of office seriously and remain impervious to outside pressures. But after my call with the clerk, I wonder. Did Frantz agree to an early trial date because he had inside information about the judge's schedule? Worse, did he actually influence the judge's decision? With his legal connections and the Assembly's raw power, it's a strong possibility.

During the day, The Barrista is packed with young professionals, would-be screenwriters, stay-at-home moms and their toddlers, and senior citizens stopping for coffee after their morning walks. The knotty pine beamed ceilings, wrought-iron fences, and redwood tables give the place a benign, welcoming feeling, especially when the sun is shining through the skylight. But at night, the place caters to neo-punks, Goths, and bikers, groups that don't always mesh. This diversity creates a tense, enticing ambience. Quarrels that escalate into fistfights aren't uncommon.

"They keep me entertained," Deanna once told me when I asked her about her nighttime clientele. "You know how I like to be entertained."

On this Tuesday night, the crowd is particularly rowdy. Deanna isn't here. She has a date, one of the baristas tells me. For the first time in years, I don't wonder with whom. I imagine how out of place I must look, the studious lawyer sitting in a corner drafting pleadings and reading legal opinions and jotting down notes while all around me young rebels and edgy misfits shout and laugh and curse.

I spend some time writing the answer to the Assembly's complaint, denying the allegations of wrongdoing. I next turn to the anonymous e-mails sent to Monica Baxter, who left copies with Deanna. The first reads:

Dearest Monica,

Rich was strangled by the demon who shot Harmon. You and your child are next—death by throat-slitting. Your Assembly can't protect you, not against the conjoined wrath of Satan and God, even less the wrath of man. You CANNOT trust. Disloyalty lingers on the tongue, acrid taste of scorched earth. Escape is your obligation, your commu-nion. Soon we'll all be awash in blood.

The other messages are just as gory and just as unenlightening. Rejected pages from a slasher film script, sparing neither mother nor child. By the time I finish, driblets of coffee speckle the papers, the product of trembling hands.

I put the e-mails aside and turn to the Tyler Daniels obscenity prosecution. I want to be prepared when Lovely finishes drafting the motion to dismiss the felony charges. I grew up in Hollywood of the 1980s, when censorship seemed a quaint vestige of the past. So I, like Lovely, had assumed at first that the government couldn't legally stop anyone from publishing words. I was wrong. During Tyler's arraignment, Neal Latham tried to tell Judge Harvey about a 1973 Supreme Court case called *Kaplan v. California*. The defendant, who owned an adult bookstore, had the bad luck to sell an undercover cop a book with the rather obvious title *Suite 69*. Warren Burger, the chief justice at the time, noted that the book contained a tenuous plot and descriptions of every conceivable variety of sexual contact, both gay and straight. He wrote that *Suite 69* was so explicit and offensive as to be "nauseous." The case is a major problem for us because, like Tyler's stories, *Suite 69* contained no photos or drawings or cartoons—just words. Yet the Supreme Court held that a jury could find the book obscene and therefore illegal. In the face of *Kaplan*, we'll have to convince Judge Harvey that times have changed, that words shouldn't be found illegal just because they might make a judge want to puke.

For the next few hours, I guzzle coffee and immerse myself in a series of law review articles about obscenity prosecutions against famous books—*Ulysses, Lady Chatterley's Lover, Tropic of Cancer*. Works by literary giants, part of the curriculum in university lit classes. Any mention of these historical injustices fuels Lovely's moral outrage at the government's prosecution of Tyler. "Persecution," Lovely calls it. She insists that as far as the First Amendment is concerned, Tyler Daniels stands on equal footing with James Joyce, D. H. Lawrence, and Henry Miller. She quotes Justice Oliver Wendell Holmes: "It would be a dangerous undertaking for persons trained only to the law to constitute themselves final judges of the worth of a work of art." But while Joyce, Lawrence, and Miller created art, Tyler Daniels littered the Internet with filth. It shouldn't take a PhD in literature to know that there's a difference between the two, so what's so bad about letting the law distinguish between the sublime and the obscene? Is it really true that judges and juries make bad critics?

I hear the jangling of keys in the background. I look up to find The Barrista employees closing up for the night. I check my watch. It's already five past midnight. I slide my laptop and my papers into my computer bag and sling the bag over my shoulder. I take a last sip of coffee and leave.

It was still warm when I arrived this evening, so I'm dressed in a light T-shirt. Now, a biting wind blows off the ocean. Even though The Barrista fronts on a major thoroughfare, the street is deserted. Los Angeles isn't like New York or San Francisco, where you can see large numbers of people walking on the streets long past midnight. LA is like some gawky adolescent who grew too fast and so hunches his shoulders in a futile attempt to hide his size.

I start walking to my car, which I parked two blocks north on a quiet residential street. It's my usual parking place, the closest street that doesn't have restricted parking.

Most of the houses are dark. The people in this neighborhood go to bed early, probably because they're mostly families with small children or seniors who've owned their homes for decades. The only light comes from the dim, outdated streetlamps, which do little more than cast shadows and attract moths. There are no sounds—no whirring of automobile engines, no music or voices coming from the houses, no birds chirping or dogs barking. And fortunately, no footsteps, not even mine, because I'm wearing sneakers.

The wind blasts through a large pepper tree, rattling the branches. Leaves rain down on the sidewalk in front of me. The dust swirls and blows into my eyes, abrading them when I blink.

Just before I reach the corner, I hear a loud metallic *click*. I'm not sure what it was or where it came from. Maybe it was the sound of a car radiator settling in the night air. I chide myself for being so skittish. I've gone down this street late at night a hundred times before.

I walk the next block quickly. As fast as I'm going, the cold has gotten the better of me, and my teeth begin to chatter. I stop where I think I parked my car. It's gone.

I turn and look back before hurrying down the street another quarter block, but there's no sign of my car. I retrace my steps a block back. Nothing. I rummage in my pocket for my security key. If I hit the panic button, the car alarm will go off, and I'll be able to locate the car—unless it's been stolen. Then it dawns on me that when I arrived at The Barrista, it was street-cleaning time on this side of the street. To avoid a ticket I made a U-turn and parked on the other side. When I look across the street and see my Lexus, I exhale in relief.

I start across the street, passing between two closely parked cars. I turn sideways so I can fit more easily in the space between the bumpers. That's when the hand grips the back of my neck and shoves me face-down onto the hood of the car in front of me.

I try to pull away, but he pins first one arm and then the other behind me. His sheer strength sends a sickening chill through me.

The beating starts immediately. He's not alone. They aim their fists at my back and side, their kidney and liver punches generating pain that turns in on itself, increasing by orders of magnitude with each succeeding blow. I cry out for help as loudly as I can, but I'm breathless, the pain like an iron straitjacket that compresses my chest, collapses my lungs, forces me to gasp for air in small gulps. I draw in so little of it that my frenzied shouts come out as thin, impotent grunts.

There could be as few as two and as many as four, all sheathed in black and wearing masks. I don't know if they're smiling or gritting their teeth or going about their business impassively, don't know which of them is punching me at this moment, or maybe they all are because I can't tell where one blow ends and another begins.

They're not taunting me, not cursing, not laughing. Their work-manlike silence is more ominous than if they were. This battering feels nothing like that sharp, stunning, heroic pain you feel when someone punches you in the head. This pain is dull and internal and primitive, the kind that makes you sure that when the beating ends—if it ever ends—you'll piss rivers of blood, you'll forever walk stooped over in chronic misery, you'll never go outside at night again, you'll always sleep with the light on, you'll die a lingering death. The maxim *kill the body and the head will die* rattles through my brain. And then they beat it out of me.

I struggle, don't stop struggling, but it's useless because someone is pinning my arms expertly in some sort of wrestling or martial arts hold.

And if he were to let go, I wouldn't have the strength to fight back, couldn't lift my arms or legs, much less counterattack. Yet I'm fully conscious, hyperaware, and I sense that that's exactly how they want me so I'll remember every second of this beating—some sort of brutal object lesson. They continue jackhammering their fists into my torso. Finally, I retch, spewing liquefying chunks of a half-digested turkey sandwich and five cups of coffee all over the hood of the car. One of my attackers grabs me by the hair and jerks my head back.

"I got a message for you and your loved ones," he says, his voice like coarse-grade sandpaper. He forces my face back down into the rancid bile and rubs my nose in it. "This thing with the Assembly? Back away. Back completely away."

CHAPTER 30

The emergency room physician, a young woman with the face of an earnest middle schooler and the attitude of a benevolent despot, is worried that my kidneys have shut down. She won't let me leave until I prove I can urinate. So I pee into a cup, and the tests for blood in the urinary tract come back negative. She won't let me drive home though I drove myself to the hospital. After a five-minute debate that I lose, I make the phone call. In years past I would have called Deanna, but now I call Lovely. It's three thirty in the morning. I don't know if her cell phone will be on. She answers in a voice that's all at once groggy, annoyed, and worried, but as soon as I tell her what happened, she promises to get here as soon as she can.

After my attackers left the scene, I slid off the hood of the car and crawled on the pavement until I found my car key. It took me four tries to pull myself to my feet. Every breath was unbearable. By the time I got across the street, I was light-headed. I had to measure my breathing so I didn't faint. I reeked of vomit. When I opened the car door and fell into my seat, I bellowed. I managed to start the car and drive myself to the hospital. Fortunately, it's only a mile away from Deanna's shop. I staggered into the ER and collapsed onto a bench before I could get to the reception desk.

The doctor said I was lucky. It seems that the assailants knew how to inflict maximum pain with minimum injury. Contusions, hematoma, a couple of cracked ribs that they can't treat but that will heal with time. No other broken bones. No apparent internal bleeding. But I have to watch for light-headedness, shortness of breath, blood in the urine, a precipitous drop in blood pressure. Don't take aspirin or other anti-inflammatory drugs no matter how much it hurts, because they can trigger bleeding.

After they examined me, I spent the rest of the time talking to the cops. I told them about my lawsuit against the Assembly and the attacker's parting words. The officer in charge took down all the information and said that he'd try to run down customers of the coffee house that night, but I could tell that the authorities wouldn't do much. How can they? I wasn't killed or maimed, and the most information I can provide is that the attackers really knew what they were doing. The police certainly won't learn anything from talking to Christopher McCarthy and his underlings.

Now, I watch the emergency patients trickle in. Health facts are supposed to be confidential, but all you have to do is listen. A morbidly obese middle-aged man was awoken by chest pains. An elderly woman fell while getting up to go to the bathroom; now she's arguing with her daughter, who chides her for continuing to live alone. An infant has a temperature of 104.6; the father spends more time comforting his distraught wife than he does attending to the baby. Secrets revealed under harsh fluorescent lights.

At about three thirty, Lovely walks into the emergency waiting room. I try to stand using the chair arms for leverage, but sit back down from the pain in my ribs.

She reaches out her hands. "Hold onto me."

"I can handle it."

"I'm sure you can." She takes my hands and helps me to my feet. She has a strong grip. When I'm upright, she latches onto my arm and pulls me close. "Lean on me."

I feel a flood of embarrassment and try to pull away. "I stink like a garbage heap. Worse."

She pulls me close again. "Don't be a jackass. Let's get you home. Tell me where you live." I'm too tired to argue, too tired to talk.

When we reach my building, I ask her to drop me off in the passenger-loading zone near the entrance to the complex.

"I'm coming in," she says.

"Pull into the next driveway. It leads to the garage. You can park in my space."

As soon as she parks the car, I open the door and pull myself out, unable to stifle a groan. We walk—actually, I shuffle—to the elevator and down the corridor to my condo.

"Thanks," I say. "You've been great."

"I'm not leaving you alone."

"You don't have to—"

"I'm staying."

I unlock the door and we go inside. I tell her that the sofa has a foldout bed and that I'll help her with the linen after I clean up. I shower, doing my best to ignore the pain that comes with each move I make. When I return to the living room, she isn't there. I assume that she changed her mind about staying. I limp to the bedroom and find her lying in my bed.

"I hate sleeping on fake beds," she says. She lifts the blanket and top sheet. She's fully clothed in her sweats. "Get in."

I maneuver myself next to her. She slides close and gingerly presses her body against mine. It's as though every inch of her is caressing me. With all that's happened to me in the last five hours, I couldn't have sex if I tried. But this isn't about that. It's about something else entirely.

I would've bet the deed to my condo plus ten years of SAG residuals that I wouldn't get a minute of sleep. I drift off right away and sleep until one in the afternoon. When I awake, she's gone.

CHAPTER 31

During the past week, Lovely has visited my apartment often, checking in on me and bringing me food. She says she has a bright future as a Jewish mother. She hasn't slept in my bed again.

The pain from the beating persists, and not only in body. My attackers might lurk around every street corner. I continually glance over my shoulder when I'm in my building's underground parking lot. Once out in public, I gravitate toward crowds. I leave The Barrista and the law school well before dark. I double- and triple-check the door latches before I go to bed. Most nights, I get no more than three hours of sleep. When I do sleep, I have nightmares, the narration of which features the terrifying, eerily familiar voice of my assailant. The police have made no progress. My attackers were too adept, and the cops are too uninterested in what they consider an act of random street violence that resulted only in minor injury.

I go to the kitchen, rummage through a cabinet below the sink, and find an old thermos that I haven't used in years. I rinse out the dust and gunk and fill it with black coffee from a pot that I brewed earlier. I didn't sleep last night, and I have a long drive ahead of me. I'm counting on the coffee and the pain to keep me alert.

I get on the 405 freeway south and weave in and out of the congested lanes, hoping that the highway patrol isn't lurking. Driving in the middle lane, I pass LAX, and at the last possible moment veer to the right and into the lane that feeds into the 105 freeway. I take the Inglewood exit, drive the side streets to Century, and get back on the 405, going north this time. I'm no expert at these things, but I must have lost anyone who might've been following me.

For the next ninety minutes, I fight the traffic snarls on Highway 101 west all the way to Oxnard, continually checking my rearview mirror. The traffic clears just past Ventura. The highway curves to the north along the coast, and I can see the ocean from my window for the next forty miles.

It takes me another half hour to reach Santa Barbara. I exit the freeway and turn onto the San Marcos Highway, drive through the city, and head up into Los Padres National Forest. The hillsides are blanketed with chaparral and oak woodlands interrupted by barren swaths of charred hillside, remnants of the deadly Gap Fire that raged through here a few years ago. I exit on Stagecoach Road and follow a narrow two-lane strip that about two miles up changes from bitumen to gravel. The three-mile drive up a steep grade taxes my car's transmission. I compulsively check my rearview mirror. There's no one behind me. The road levels off at the top, revealing an isolated ranch-style home that overlooks the vineyards and pastures of the Santa Ynez Valley. A ten-year-old maroon Ford Expedition is parked out front, two of its fenders dented. There's a grassy area in the front yard with a termite-ridden picnic table that looks like it hasn't been used in years.

I park my car on a patch of gravel and climb out gingerly. The long ride has made my body stiffen up. Walking on the uneven surface doesn't help. I hobble to the front door and ring the doorbell three times, but no one answers. I walk around to the back toward what looks like a small guest cottage. Through the mesh door I see a potter's wheel and floor-to-ceiling shelving filled with ceramics at various stages of completion. A woman sits hunched over a table near the back of the room. Wearing plastic goggles, she uses a Dremel tool to sand the glaze on a ceramic pot. I knock hard on the screen, making it rattle. I worry that I've startled her, but without looking up she says, "Hello, dear. Come inside and sit down," and it's my heart that pirouettes.

As soon as I step inside, the acrid odor of burning clay dust fills my nostrils. Avoiding stacks of tiles scattered on the floor, I cross the room, pull up a stool, and sit down at the table next to her. "How are you, Erica?"

She doesn't answer right away, just continues to work on her project as if I'm not there. After a long time, she shuts off the power tool and removes her goggles. "My name's Bette now."

"Of course. I know that."

"It's my real name. I hated it back then."

"I remember."

"I don't hate it anymore."

"I'm glad."

Erica Hatfield and I appeared in five movies together, the first when I was eight years old. Each time I was the star and she was a supporting player. The roles were beneath her. She should have resented me—so many of the adults resented me—but instead she looked after me better than my own mother did. She made sure that I didn't work more than the state-mandated maximum and that I saw my tutor and did my homework. She shielded me from Harriet's wild behavior. When our world exploded, we both became other people.

She turned fifty-five last January. I scrutinize her face for recognizable features. Her straight hair, once whatever color the script or the director or her whim dictated, is now a natural silver. She wears it short and pulled back behind her ears, unisexual—no, mannish. Her red potter's apron covers a blue long-sleeved man's shirt and jeans. Her face, without makeup, is scored with sharp wrinkles and stained with brown freckles. Her high cheekbones and pouty lower lip are the only remnants of her past beauty. She's no longer the woman I described when my students asked me about *Doheny Beach Holiday*.

"I'm sorry to trouble you," I say. "I won't stay long. I don't think I was followed, but—"

"They shouldn't see us together." She really looks at me for the first time. "You're hurt."

"How did you know? They didn't touch my face."

She reaches out and caresses my cheek, a palpable reminder of the boy I was, the boy I abandoned. Her skin is coarse from working with her hands for so many years. I'd have expected to flinch at the suddenness of the gesture, at the roughness of her fingers, but nothing could feel more natural. I reach up and press her hand to my cheek for a moment.

I survey the room. "Your work is wonderful. They say you're this generation's Beatrice Wood."

"Nonsense. This is just a way to keep busy. If people want to take the trouble and visit my studio, fine by me, but . . ."

"Anyway, they're beautiful." I place my hands on my knees to steady myself. "You know I'm a lawyer?"

"Of course. I've kept track of you." She stands up and uses her hands to smooth out the wrinkles in her apron. She's much smaller than I remember. Over the years, she's become hard and angular. She walks over to a shelf and straightens some unglazed plates that don't need straightening. She comes back and sits across from me. "I know why you're here. It's OK. You have to protect yourself."

I don't doubt her clairvoyant ability to divine why I'm here, but I have to say the words anyway. "I'm going to fight them. With the truth, if I have to. Unless you tell me not to. Because if the story comes out, you could . . . The statute of limitations hasn't run. It never will."

"You do whatever you have to do." She takes my hand, an intense look of concern in her eyes. "Listen to me, though. It's important. Make sure that the Assembly's really doing what you think they are. Not just for my sake, but for yours. You were always so impulsive, Parky."

"I was a kid. I'm a man now."

She studies me for a long time. "No. You haven't changed."

"I'll give that due consideration."

"Now I really know that you're a lawyer with that answer." She smiles, and for a moment, she's Erica again. I didn't think such a light moment possible.

"How has your life been, Bette? Because mine's been—"

Her smile fades. "You should go, Parker."

"But I came all this way, and I just got here." I sound like that kid, whiny and self-centered.

"We've survived all these years by staying apart."

"I only wanted . . ." I exhale. "You're right, of course."

"Do take care. And remember. Be sure you know the truth."

CHAPTER 32

I'm about to teach my first trial advocacy class in three weeks. Kathleen and Jonathan know only that I was mugged late at night. I see no reason to tell them that the Assembly was behind the beating. Why alarm them when they're in no danger? Lovely disagrees, but I've persuaded her to go along for now.

Meanwhile, the lawsuit has moved ahead rapidly, as it must with a May trial date. We've filed our answer and asked the other side for documents and scheduled depositions. During class, I use tomorrow's deposition of Christopher McCarthy as a teaching tool. We discuss technique and strategize about the best way to organize my questions. I divide up responsibility for reviewing the voluminous documents that the Frantz firm produced. I thought that Frantz would sandbag and hand over next to nothing—that's what most lawyers in Frantz's position would do—but he went the opposite route, inundating us with documents. It's a highly effective technique when facing a lawyer with scant resources—a lawyer like me. In the two million-plus pages of documents that the Assembly has burned onto a DVD, it's inevitable that very few, if any, will prove useful.

Toward the end of class, I say, "There's something we have to decide. I'd like to take all three of you to the deposition, but there's only room for one."

"I'm going," Lovely says.

"It's a bad idea, Ms. Diamond. Given your history with Frantz, I don't think—"

"That's bullshit. I'm going to be there. Even if Jonathan or Kathleen go, I'll fit myself in the room and stand in a corner for nine hours if that's what it takes. I deserve it after what I . . ." She looks at Kathleen and Jonathan. "Are you guys cool with my going?"

"That's not fair. Kathleen and Jonathan—"

"Lovely should be the one, Professor," Kathleen says. "I mean, she gave up her job for the case. And she's done depositions before. It should be Lovely."

I look at Jonathan.

"No problem," he says.

As a teacher, I wish one of them had at least insisted on a coin flip. But selfishly, I want Lovely there.

I'm about to end class when Jonathan says, "Kathleen and I were going to report on the Sanctified Assembly's orientation meeting that we went to last Saturday. Do we have time for that?"

"Of course."

"How do I put this," he says. "The Assembly hates you."

"Jon!" Kathleen says.

"Well, it's true."

"How could you possibly get that from a public orientation?" I ask.

"They had a question and answer session where someone asked about the Baxter case. So this woman from the Assembly starts talking about enemies of truth, lost souls who need to . . . how'd she put it . . . heed the words of the Fount. She said that the lawyer for the Baxter estate was one of those people. That he . . . you . . . lost your way. Said the same thing about Raymond Baxter."

"Did they actually use Professor Stern's name?" Lovely asks.

"No," he says. "All she said was that the lawyer was an enemy of truth who won't be sanctified in the celestial universe."

"That's good news," I say. "I was afraid I was going to have to spend forever in the afterlife with those freaks."

"That's not funny," Lovely says.

I look at Jonathan. "What did you think about the substance of the presentation?"

"Well . . . Kathleen and I don't agree on that."

Kathleen's already ruddy cheeks turn scarlet. "Jon, I told you not to."

"What do you think, Mr. Borzo?"

"I think those dudes are flat-out scary. Money-hungry. Reminds me of this pyramid scheme my big brother got himself into a few years back. My brother dragged me to a couple of meetings even though I was a teenager. This frenzied get-rich-quick scheme, where they said that all you had to do is work hard and you could be a millionaire. They had a clean-cut man and a sexy woman leading the sessions. Of course, my brother lost all his money like he always does. That's what the Assembly reminds me of. The fast-talking con artists with the bogus smiles who ran that pyramid scheme."

Kathleen stares down at the tabletop.

"You don't agree?" I say.

"Professor, I don't feel comfortable."

"This is what being a lawyer is all about, Ms. Williams. Especially in a trial advocacy class. Stating your position in front of people and persuading them to adopt your point of view. That's what a lawyer does, no matter what kind of law you end up practicing. We've been at this for four months. You should feel comfortable by now."

She closes her eyes for a moment. When she's agitated like this, she usually has this nervous laugh, but now she's serious. "It's just that . . . OK. You know what? It came as a surprise to me, but I found that the Assembly people had real interesting things to say. We've been totally negative about them in this class, and I'm not saying you're wrong because maybe that's how lawyers have to be, but the people talking at that orientation seemed sincere and dedicated. They weren't wild-eyed monsters or anything like that. They were like normal people. Nice. And even funny. And they . . . like, they do all this work on suicide prevention and they fight drug abuse and they have a low divorce rate and—"

"I don't believe those claims," I say. "As for suicide prevention, they shun the family of suicides. Innocent spouses and kids. Look what they're doing to Monica Baxter and her son. He's two years old. How is that anything but inhumane?"

"So what, if it lowers the number of suicides? I mean, it's not as black and white as you make it, Professor."

"I can't believe you're buying into that crap, Kathleen," Lovely says.

"If nothing else, you should dislike that group because of their sexism. They think women should stay at home and raise kids. And their position on abortion is disgusting. They'd force a twelve-year-old who's been raped by her father to—"

"It's not your turn to talk, Ms. Diamond," I say in a peremptory tone I've never used with her.

Her jaw drops, but she stops talking.

"Ms. Williams, you were at the Assembly's downtown headquarters, correct?" I ask.

She nods.

"And they took you on a guided tour of some of the facilities?" How easily I've taken to using the Socratic method I so despised in law school, when the teachers would ask questions instead of saying what they mean.

"We took the tour."

"How can you possibly justify the Assembly's spending their adherents' hard-earned money on that monstrosity?" The Assembly finished construction on the building nine years ago, during my time at Macklin & Cherry. They invited the entire law firm to the preopening of the facility. Everyone at the firm assumed that I'd boycott the event, but I went out of curiosity. There were slabs of Carrara marble on the main floor and a garish atrium and expensive stained glass windows and gilded main doors carved with images of the place where Bradley Kelly supposedly passed through the crease in the universe.

"For my college graduation present," Kathleen says, "my mom bought me a plane ticket to Europe. I went with a friend. And when we got to Rome, my friend wanted to go to the Vatican because her mother's Italian. Anyway, how can you get more lavish than the Vatican, right? But no one seems to complain about the Catholic Church wasting its members' money. And both places are beautiful. The Vatican and the Assembly's Grand Temple. Maybe there's something, I don't know, exhilarating about having a beautiful place as your center of worship.

I mean, the Grand Temple is a work of art, and art is like a gift from God, right?" She goes on to tell us why she finds the Assembly's religious doctrine fascinating, maintaining that it represents a brand new take on the source of mankind's ills and tragedies and triumphs. The last person I can remember sounding like her was Rich Baxter.

"Ms. Williams, if you're so enamored of the Assembly—"

"Geez, it's not like I joined or anything. I just said I found it interesting."

"If you're so enamored, you shouldn't be working on the Baxter case. You don't have to, you know."

She laughs, not that nervous giggle of hers this time, but a derisive laugh. "So much for it being OK to express my opinion, huh, Professor? You're saying that because I disagree with you I shouldn't work on the case? That's hilarious, you know? Lovely disagrees with you all the time about everything, and you've never once said anything like that to her."

I glance at Lovely, who seems as surprised at Kathleen's words as I am. Jonathan is staring out the window.

"I'm not going to debate this with you, Ms. Williams. I need your assurance that you're committed to working on this case. I'm fighting formidable opponents. Not only the Assembly, but Louis Frantz."

"Of course I'm committed. I'm . . . I'm going to be a lawyer, right? And like you just said, that's what lawyers do—advocate for clients. Even clients they don't agree with. I get it."

I study her face, trying to gauge her sincerity. Inconclusive. Kathleen Williams has given me yet another reason to look over my shoulder.

CHAPTER 33

Because I'll be asking the questions, I get to choose the location of McCarthy's deposition. When I notice it for a law school conference room, Lou Frantz accuses me of insulting McCarthy's religious beliefs by selecting a Catholic institution. It's petty gamesmanship. I'm sure McCarthy doesn't care one whit about where I take his deposition. But I don't push back. Instead, I reschedule the deposition for the Law Offices of Parker Stern. Frantz must think I don't have the stomach to fight, which is exactly what I want him to believe.

Lovely and I arrive early for the ten o'clock deposition. At a quarter of ten, the court reporter arrives, wheeling her laptop and stenography machine on a fold-up handcart. She's a distinguished woman who looks more like an English professor than someone who preserves a record of petty legal skirmishes and pitched discovery battles. The videographer, a burly man with a scraggly beard, follows her inside, toting two large black carrying cases.

The woman glances around with a bewildered expression. Her eyes fall on me. "My goodness, Mr. Stern. I thought I had the wrong address."

"You've come to the right place, Janine." When I worked at Macklin & Cherry, she was my favorite court reporter. She records testimony with deadly accuracy, and can make or break your deposition just by deciding whether or not to transcribe your verbal ticks and pauses and stammers. She sits down at the head of the table next to me. The videographer takes his place behind me and to my left so he can focus the camera lens only on McCarthy, who'll sit across from me.

We wait. Lovely warned me that Frantz would be intentionally late. It's one way he marks his territory. Early in my career, Harmon Cherry taught me how to handle attorneys who play this game—always give them forty-five minutes to show up before calling off the deposition. Ninety-five percent of the time, they'll show. If they do, keep them an hour longer at the back end, advantageous, because a tired witness is a poor witness. And be sure to blame the need to go late on their morning tardiness.

At ten thirty, the door creaks open. Lovely takes an audible breath. Christopher McCarthy walks in, followed by Nick Weir, Frantz's associate. The renowned Louis Frantz enters last. When they see the room, they hesitate, looking as if they're going to turn around and leave.

McCarthy is dressed in a dark silk suit and expensive monogrammed dress shirt. Good. I might have to play the video of this deposition in court someday, and I want our judge and jury to know that McCarthy is rolling in Assembly money. Although this room is especially dim, he doesn't take off his sunglasses. Also good. He'll look either ridiculous or sinister on video, and if I get lucky, both at the same time. The smell of his cologne drifts across the room—the sticky-sweet odor of decomposing roses. We don't shake hands, don't say hello, don't even exchange nods.

Weir is frat-boy handsome—tall, dark, and smug, clearly reveling in his role as one of Frantz's anointed. He has arrogant eyes, as if he's a powerful man like Frantz. He has no inkling that he radiates no light of his own, that he's merely an insignificant satellite that reflects the energy of his superstar boss. He looks right past me and stares at Lovely, a smirk on his lips.

Frantz is about six feet tall, with the fit, wiry body of a long distance runner, impressive for a man of seventy. His hair is thinning, and what remains of it is more white than gray. In contrast to the impeccable dress of his colleagues, his ill-fitting suit hangs off him. His slacks are wrinkled. His face is long and thin, a feature that along with his droopy eyelids gives him a hangdog look. His eyes are clear and remote. He's no one you'd identify as one of the most successful trial lawyers in the country; no one you'd think could captivate a jury better than anyone else. Until you hear his voice.

"You're Stern, right? I'm Lou Frantz." He sounds like the Lord God in one of those old Cecil B. DeMille spectaculars. He makes a show of acknowledging Janine and the videographer and then turns his whole body to face Lovely, an orator's affectation because he could just as easily have turned his head a few degrees. He starts to say something, but instead just smiles. Her shoulders dip slightly.

He and I shake hands. He has a strong grip.

"Nice of you and your client to drop by," I say.

"We got caught in traffic." He scans the room. "You've got to be kidding, pal. This is some kind of joke, right?"

Deanna uses this room for storage. Bare concrete floors, naked light bulbs, a single window set high up on the wall that abuts the back alley. If you listen hard, you can hear the voices chattering in the main room. Yesterday, we stacked cartons of coffee and supplies against the walls to create space, pushed a few wooden tables together, and brought in enough chairs to accommodate us. It's a tight fit.

"You objected to my noticing it at the law school," I say. "Something about disrespecting your client's religious beliefs? Well, The Barrista Coffee House West Hollywood is completely nonsectarian." I point to the carafes on a side table. "And I assure you, the coffee here will be by far the best you've ever had at a deposition."

Weir says to Lovely, "So this is what you trashed your future for?"

She doesn't answer, just stares at him with a hard expression. I'm about to snap back when Frantz gestures for Weir to keep quiet. So I let it go. Over the next eight hours we'll have plenty of skirmishes.

Frantz drapes his coat over the back of his chair and sits down. Because of the cramped quarters, Weir has trouble getting into his chair.

"Need some assistance, Nick?" I say.

He scowls at me. Frantz actually seems amused. All this time, McCarthy has remained stone-faced, staring at the video camera behind me.

I nod toward Janine. "When you're ready."

She administers the oath to McCarthy, who won't *swear* to tell the truth because false oaths violate his religious beliefs. So he *affirms* that he'll tell the truth. Janine leaves out the words "so help you God." Good enough, so long as he's testifying under penalty of perjury.

A deposition and an actual court trial have a lot in common. You question a deposition witness just as you would if you were cross-examining a witness at trial. But there's a big difference—at a deposition, there's no judge present to keep your opposing counsel in line. So a guy like Frantz can make repeated objections and just generally try to make your life miserable.

I inhale deeply and savor the aroma of coffee, which doesn't quite mask the smell of McCarthy's perfume. I haven't taken a deposition since Harmon Cherry died two years ago. In the six weeks before the law firm dissolved, I didn't have one scheduled, and after that I haven't practiced law. So I don't know whether I'll get stage fright like I do in a courtroom. I've felt confident all morning, but now there's a flutter below my diaphragm, and a thin layer of moisture covers my palms. If I can't handle a deposition, I'll be worthless as a lawyer.

CHAPTER 34

I ask McCarthy to state his full name for the record. Although it's the simplest of questions, my ability to utter the words means that I can function, at least for now. Not that I'm home free. When I follow up with a flurry of questions about his past experience as a witness, I speak so fast that for the first time since we've known each other, Janine asks me to slow down. A lot of lawyers talk too quickly under stress, but I'm a trained actor, so not me—until now. My hands start trembling and won't stop. I pray that my adversaries don't notice.

McCarthy testifies that he's had his deposition taken between forty and sixty times, mostly in copyright infringement and libel lawsuits against people—McCarthy calls them "apostates"—who have revealed the Assembly's secrets or spread injurious falsehoods. He summarizes his education and work history. He had an undistinguished academic career—two years of community college, a BA in communications at a second-rate state university, followed by a job in promotion at an FM rock and roll radio station in the Midwest and then a gig as a disk jockey. When he volunteers that he abused alcohol and drugs and cheated on his ex-wife, I know what's coming—a canned speech about how Bradley Kelly's autobiography literally saved his life. After his religious epiphany, he joined the Assembly. Since then, everything in life has been wondrous. He left his job as a popular radio personality to come to California and found the Technology Communications Organization in 1995. He's served as its chief executive officer and president ever since.

"What does the TCO do?" I ask.

"We provide public relations, community outreach, and reputation protection and enhancement for our clients. We also provide crisis management and litigation support."

"Doesn't your company provide damage control and propaganda services for the Church of the Sanctified Assembly?"

"Objection," Frantz says. "Argumentative. Also insulting."

"But you have to answer, Mr. McCarthy," I say. Because there's no judge present, McCarthy must answer even objectionable questions, so long as I don't try to invade his privacy or impinge upon the attorney-client privilege.

"We don't do propaganda or damage control," McCarthy says.

"Well, you used the phrase 'reputation enhancement'. Isn't that just another name for propaganda?"

"No."

"The Assembly is your only client, isn't it?"

"We have other clients."

"All affiliated with the Assembly?"

"Could be. We're a tight-knit community. We take care of each other, unlike most people in today's world."

"But the Assembly is by far your largest client?"

"Just like it was your law firm's largest client when you were practicing at Macklin & Cherry, counsel."

Frantz and Weir both grin. I glance at Lovely, who's frantically writing notes on her legal pad. It's unnecessary, because Janine can give us a rough digital copy of the transcript at the break. But the note-taking gives Lovely an excuse not to look at Frantz and Weir.

"Let's explore that answer," I say. "You were the Assembly's point person dealing with Macklin & Cherry, weren't you?"

"I guess you could say that."

"Who at the Assembly did you report to?"

"Objection," Frantz says. "The question violates his First Amendment freedom of religion. You know full well that my client considers that information sacred and confidential. On top of that, I object because the question is irrelevant to your so-called breach of contract claim. I instruct him not to answer."

"Highly relevant," I say. "I'm entitled to know the names of the decision-makers who stiffed my client. This is to give you notice that I

intend to bring a motion to compel your client to identify the people
in charge."

"Good luck to you on that," Frantz says.

Although the law is on my side, history isn't. So far, only one judge
in the country has had the courage to order the Assembly to identify
its leaders, whom the Assembly calls "elders." She died three weeks
later, falling from a ledge during a weekend hike in the hills behind her
home. There were no witnesses and no signs of foul play. The deceased
judge's successor rescinded the order a week after he inherited the case.

For the next forty minutes, I question McCarthy about his relationship with Rich Baxter, going back to when they first met at
Macklin & Cherry. McCarthy never volunteers information and takes
his time before answering so Frantz has time to object. He shuts his eyes
and ponders every question. He's elusive without seeming evasive—in
other words, a formidable witness.

We take a short break, during which Lovely and I caucus at an isolated table in the main room. Deanna comes over and asks about the
deposition.

"I hate to admit it, but McCarthy's good," I say. "Smarter than I
thought. Perceptive."

"Of course he is," she says. "I trained him."

Lovely perks up. "Really?"

"I defended him in ten, twelve depositions. Before I worked with
him, he was a shitty witness."

"Have you two talked about this?" Lovely says excitedly. "About
his weaknesses and—"

"We can't ask Deanna questions like that."

"You're right," Lovely says. "I'm sorry. Privileged information."

"Not really," Deanna says. "Parker's a tight-ass. I never represented
McCarthy individually, I represented the Assembly. I don't owe Chris
anything."

"It's not worth the risk," I say. "The Assembly will try to use it
against us if they find out. Besides, there's nothing that you can tell me
about that guy that I don't know already."

Deanna points to a large stack of papers on the table in front of Lovely. "What you got there?" I suspect she already knows. She was reading upside down.

"A bunch of documents I got off the Internet," Lovely says. "Disgruntled ex-Assembly members and critics speculating about the identity of the Assembly elders. McCarthy won't answer questions, but maybe if we get lucky, his demeanor will give it away, or—"

"I wouldn't waste your time," Deanna says.

"Why would we be wasting our time?" Lovely says. "I know it's not likely, but—"

"Because McCarthy's guys planted those names," Deanna says. "A diversion to keep the identity of the Assembly's leaders secret."

"You know this how?" I ask, though I should put an end to this discussion.

"A few years back, Manny and I got bored. We'd done all this legal work for the Assembly, and the highest-ranking person we'd met was Chris McCarthy. Most people who care about this shit actually believe he's the head of the Church, including a lot of people in the media. We checked some of our law firm files, and it was clear that McCarthy was reporting to someone. Anyway, we started doing some research. The names are bogus."

"How could you know that?" Lovely says.

"We had a paralegal try to run down the names of the critics. None of them are real."

"No more," I say, trying to keep my voice low.

"All I'm saying is that the Assembly protects the identities of its leaders. What did Bradley Kelly call it, the Commitment of Purity of the Sanctified? He was the charismatic leader, divine, so his name was publicized everywhere. But the names of the other top members are secret. Manny—you know how he gets—started showing me this stuff on how to identify members of the mafia and on structures of sleepers cells and even on game theory to figure out the structure of terrorist networks."

"That's how you guys spent your time when you were supposedly representing the Assembly?" I say. "I hope you didn't bill for it."

Her lips turn up slightly, and she unconsciously fingers one of the four titanium rings that pass through her right eyebrow, twisting her flesh so grotesquely that I cringe. "Then Rich found out what we were doing and freaked. He threatened to go to Harmon if we didn't stop. But you might as well forget about that Internet stuff. The face of the Assembly consists of McCarthy and the celebrity devotees, of course—they're the best proselytizers—and the pastors who interact with members. The Assembly elders could be anyone. Manny and I even speculated that Harmon was an elder."

"You can't be serious."

She bugs out her eyes and says in a cartoon-creepy voice, "Who knows? Maybe I'm one of them. Deanna the Elder of Universe Lesbia."

"We've got to get back inside," I say, not in the mood for jokes. "Stop sharing information. Frantz will jump at any excuse to bring a disqualification motion."

Ignoring me, she tilts her head toward the table where Frantz and the others are sitting and says to Lovely, "How're you doing with those guys?"

Lovely shrugs. Deanna gives her some consoling pats on the shoulder.

"Hey, Parker," Deanna says. "I think I'll pop into the depo and say hi to McCarthy for old time's sake."

Her devilish smile immediately dissolves my irritation. "Why not?" I say. "Maybe the tattoos and the piercings will freak him out so much that he'll answer some of my questions."

"Fuck you, too," she says.

We go back to the conference room. Deanna greets Janine, who finds it hard to believe that this tattooed Goth girl is the same woman who used to litigate complex business cases at Macklin & Cherry.

Frantz, Weir, and McCarthy return thirty seconds later. Deanna waves at McCarthy and says, "Waz up, Chris?"

He studies her for a long moment with no hint of recognition. Then the mist clears. "Deanna? Deanna Poulos from Harmon's firm?"

His shades obscure his eyes, but I imagine that they're filled with disgust.

She introduces herself to Frantz and Weir. "I worked with Chris when I was a lawyer representing the Assembly. But now I own this place. Your host for the day."

"That's fascinating, Ms. Poulos," Frantz says dismissively. "Now, shall we get going so Mr. McCarthy can get out of here?"

"You and I fought quite a few battles together, didn't we Chris?" Deanna says. "The Hathaway/TruthScour.com case was my all-time favorite. We definitely made some law on that one."

McCarthy grins and says to Frantz, "We stopped this apostate Montel Hathaway and a company called TruthScour from posting the Assembly's confidential teachings on the Internet. Deanna here found a theory to hold TruthScour liable. Before that, no one thought you could win against a service provider. She was superb."

"You're embarrassing me, Chris," Deanna says, grinning.

"Let's get started," I say. "Back on the record."

Frantz holds up his hand "Before you start asking questions, counsel, there's an ethical issue that we need to discuss. Nick?"

Deanna, who was about to leave, stops short.

Weir pulls his shoulders back and raises his chin. "Mr. Stern, we just want to make sure that you've complied with California Code of Professional Conduct Rule 3-320."

That rule says that if a lawyer's close relative, spouse, or significant other is representing the other side, the lawyer has to share that fact with his client. In other words, if I had a sister who was representing the Assembly, I would have to tell Raymond Baxter about it. We have nothing like that going on in our case.

"I have no idea what you're talking about," I say.

Weir leans forward and puts his elbows on the table. "The rule says you have to tell your client if someone on your side has an intimate personal relationship with any of the lawyers on our side. Ms. Diamond and I have such a relationship."

"That's not true!" Lovely says.

He leers her. "Are you denying the fact that we were . . . *intimate* . . . just four months ago?"

She glares at him, but says nothing.

"And for the record, I'm not the only one at the law firm to, how shall I put it, have the pleasure of Ms. Diamond's company," he says.

Strobe-like pulses of jealousy and anger make everything move in slow motion, leave me unable to form a coherent thought, much less counterattack as I should. Deanna's power of speech isn't similarly impaired, and like that day in court when Rich was killed, she comes to my rescue. "Hey, Lou . . . It is Lou, right?"

Frantz gapes at her as if she's deranged. "Just because you own this place doesn't give you the right to speak. You're not part of this deposition."

"I am now," she says. "Hey, Lou, did you know that I run a very trendy shop? Zagat rated. The upscale meets the underground, the review says. Part of the reason for my success is that I get to know my customers. Did you know that your wife, Ginny, is a regular?"

"You don't know my wife."

"Auburn hair as of last week. Honey blonde before that. And if I'm not mistaken, she's the only one other than your mother who's allowed to call you Louie."

Frantz flinches.

"I didn't think you knew that she comes in here. Usually at night when you're working late, which seems to be almost every night. She's, what, in her early forties? She looks younger, lucky you. Do people think she's your daughter?"

"Last warning, Ms. Poulos," Frantz says. "Stop talking and get out."

"Were you aware that your wife likes bikers," Deanna says. "You know the type—burly, primitive, dominant, and . . . *hirsute*, that's the word I'm looking for. Oh, and young. Definitely young. Just two nights ago she left my place with a guy who calls himself Renegade. Quite a hunk, if you like the type, which I do once in a while. Couldn't have been more than twenty-four, twenty-five years old. Of course, he was probably just being chivalrous, escorting a lady to her car, but . . ." She shrugs.

Weir squirms in his seat. McCarthy leans back in his chair and sets his lips, unsuccessfully trying to hide his admiration for Deanna's showmanship. The veins bulge out from Frantz's forehead. "Listen to me, madam," he says, making the word *madam* sound profane. "You obviously have no idea who you're dealing with. You have no idea of the depth and breadth and raw force of the misery you've just brought down upon yourself. I'm Louis Frantz. You can expect my wife and I to—"

"Oh, give me a break," Deanna says. "Chris can tell you that back in the day I was a hell of a libel lawyer. Representing the Church of the Sanctified Assembly, of course. You're not going to sue me. For one thing, truth is a defense. Go home and ask your wife if what I said is true. For another thing, if you sue me, you and your wife's reputation will be fair game, and rest assured that I'll use the discovery process to poke around in every nook and cranny of your personal lives. But the best thing is that whatever I say on the record in a lawsuit is absolutely privileged under section 47(b) of the California Civil Code. It doesn't matter if my words are true or false, I get a free pass. And you didn't ask to go off the record."

Frantz sputters, and then looks at Janine, who's staring downward, still entering keystrokes into her stenograph machine. He pretends to shuffle some papers. Weir leans over to whisper something to him.

"Not now!" he shouts.

Abashed, Weir slides his chair away.

"You've made your point, Deanna," McCarthy says. "Now may we get this farce going so I can get out of here?"

"Nice seeing you again, Chris," she says. She gestures toward Weir. "As for you, you're just a flaming asshole. Please put that on the record, too, Janine."

Janine's eyes blink rapidly, but her fingers keep moving on her steno machine. Deanna's words will indeed be on the record, not to mention captured on video.

I glance at Lovely, searching for a reaction, but she stares down at her legal pad, not blinking.

"Can we start?" McCarthy says.

"One moment, sir," I say, finding my voice much too late. "Mr. Frantz, your position regarding Ms. Diamond is legally untenable because she's not a lawyer. The rule you cited only applies to lawyers. What you've done today is dishonorable, vindictive. Now that you've exacted your pound of flesh, I expect that you and your firm won't repeat this kind of behavior."

Frantz's eyes burn with a lupine intensity. "A pound of flesh, you said? Not close. We're just getting started."

I study him for a moment. "You know, Lou, you're the perfect attorney for the Assembly. You pretend to take the high road when all the time you're wallowing in the gutter. Are you also on board with their extrajudicial methods? The beatings and the even more violent forms of physical intimidation?"

McCarthy scowls at me. I guess I should worry about antagonizing him further, about hastening the Assembly's decision to do more to me than dole out a bad thrashing, but I don't care about that now. I'll just have to stay off dark streets and make sure to lock my doors. I glance at Lovely. I'm not naïve. I don't for a moment discount Weir's statements about her. As tough as she is, she can't hide the crimson flush of humiliation on her cheeks. But my desire to protect her—to fight for her— trumps my jealousy. What right do I have to be jealous, anyway?

She taps me on the shoulder. I lean close to her, covering our mouths with a legal pad so no one can read our lips.

"It wasn't enough," she says.

"What wasn't?"

"What Deanna did. I need you to make McCarthy's life miserable. Because that's the only thing that'll truly make Frantz miserable. He cares more about his lawsuit than his wife. Can you do that?"

I nod. I'll do it simply because she's asked me to. No matter how high the cost.

CHAPTER 35

Over the next several hours, I ask McCarthy mundane questions that I hope will lull him into complacency. He claims not to know the names of Rich's friends and employees, a falsehood because the Assembly keeps tabs on the intimate details of all its members' lives. Despite Deanna's admonition, I do ask him about the alleged names of the elders that Lovely found on the Internet. He refuses to answer, of course, and just as Deanna predicted, the questions don't faze him. He perks up when I ask about the Assembly's religious doctrine. He loves talking about his religion. His answers are so rambling and long-winded that I often have to interrupt him just to move on to a different subject.

It's three thirty in the afternoon, the time when even the best deponents are apt to let their guard down because of fatigue or low blood sugar or just an understandable reaction to a particularly tedious brand of stress. Lovely hands me the financial documents retrieved from the hard drive of Rich Baxter's computer, the ones that her father analyzed for us. I show the documents to McCarthy and get him to confirm that Assembly money traveled a circuitous route until it was deposited into an offshore bank account in the name of The Emery Group.

I put a document in front of him. "I'll represent to you, Mr. McCarthy, that this is a record of bank transactions involving The Emery Group's bank account."

"If you say so."

"Don't you know? You were the signatory on that account."

"No I was not." He's lying, but I can't prove it. Not with Ed Diamond's third-hand information obtained from mobsters.

"Let's look at a transaction for The Emery Group's account that occurred on May second. There's a six million dollar deposit into the account. According to the FBI, that money was later transferred out to someone. Where did the six million go?"

"Richard Baxter stole it."

"What evidence do you have of that?"

McCarthy rests his arms on a box behind him and leans back like a man luxuriating in a Jacuzzi. "Hmm. Let me count the ways. There's the fact that he formed all of the Assembly's corporations and had unfettered access to Assembly financial information. There's the fact that the IRS traced unusual movement of money to accounts that he, and only he, controlled. There's the fact that he had a major drug problem and that he was sleeping with prostitutes. Expensive vices, in other words. There's the fact that he was found with a false passport and a large amount of money, indicating that he was going to skip the country, something that even you can't explain away, Mr. Stern." There's a slight tugging at the muscles in his cheeks, and then a full twitch, and a dot of spittle at the corner of his mouth.

"But neither the IRS nor the US Attorney, with all their resources and experience, could trace where that money went after it left The Emery Group, much less prove it was paid to Rich Baxter, am I right?"

"For once, it appears you're right."

"Didn't you agree to pay Mr. Baxter the six million as a fee for the legal work he did, but when the Assembly elders balked at the amount, you welshed on the deal and framed him?" I don't expect McCarthy to answer. I just want him to know that he's a target, too.

"Objection!" Frantz shouts.

McCarthy points a finger at me. "Stern, if you say what you just said outside of this deposition room, I'll sue you for slander."

My muscles have cramped from sitting so long on the unforgiving wooden chair, and my ribs throb with a dull pain—a stark reminder of the beating that the Assembly's thugs gave me. I glare at McCarthy, willing my vision to penetrate his tinted glasses so I can read his stare. Then I don't need to. I can *feel* the scorching rays of hatred.

"You and your so-called church will do anything to stifle your critics, won't you, McCarthy?" I say. "Well, you won't silence this one."

We glare at each other, fists clenched. There's a moment of combustible silence, during which either one of us could lunge over the table at the other.

I feel Lovely's hand on my wrist. "I think we need a break," she says.

"I certainly do," Janine says. Without waiting for permission, she gets up and leaves the room. The stunned videographer says, "We're off the record at 4:32 p.m.," and follows her out.

We all return from the break subdued, but the underlying hostility remains.

"Mr. McCarthy," I say, "in our discovery requests, we asked you to look for some notes that Harmon Cherry wrote shortly before his death in 2010. Did you look for such notes? Or a copy on a DVD?"

"We couldn't find anything like that."

Lovely hands me McCarthy's calendar for 2011. Many of the entries, probably for his meetings with Assembly hierarchy, have been redacted on the grounds of confidentiality. I direct his attention to the months of May and June. The three-week period ending June 18 has handwritten lines through it. "Why no entries for these dates?"

"I was on vacation."

"Have you produced a copy of your itinerary? Because we can't find one in the documents you provided to us."

"That's because they're not there," Frantz says. "Where he goes on vacation is his business, not yours. We're not going to let you invade his privacy."

"Did you leave the United States?"

"Objection," Frantz says. "Privacy. Instruct not to answer."

"What countries did you visit?"

"Objection," Frantz says.

"What cities did you visit?"

Frantz objects to this and my follow-up questions about the trip, but I ask them anyway just to waste McCarthy's time.

"All done, Mr. Stern?" McCarthy says when he realizes that I've exhausted this line. "Too bad. I was so enjoying this exercise." He uses the palm of his hand to brush back his hair.

I'm fed up with the preening bird's threats and lies and stone-walling. So I keep my promise to Lovely by asking, "Let's see how much you enjoy this next question. Is there now or has ever been an Assembly elder by the name of Quiana Gottschalk?"

Lovely and Weir flip through their respective document stacks, searching for a reference to this person. They won't find it.

McCarthy removes his sunglasses, and for the first time ever, I see his eyes. They're round and closely set, framed by deep hard lines etched in sun-damaged skin. Less predatory than I would have expected; small and round, almost porcine. His face registers a combination of confusion and fear. The right corner of his mouth ticks repeatedly.

"One moment," Frantz says. He huddles with McCarthy. Their frantic whispers reach me as angry, unintelligible hisses. But I get the gist—Frantz wants McCarthy to tell him about Quiana. McCarthy just keeps shaking his head.

"Instruct not to answer," Frantz finally says.

Lovely leans toward me. A strand of her hair tickles my cheek. "Who is this person?" she whispers.

I ignore her, keeping my eyes, my entire reserve of energy, directed toward the witness. "Mr. McCarthy, you've heard . . ." I fight to keep my voice clear and level. "You've heard the name Quiana Gottschalk, haven't you?"

McCarthy's body rolls up into itself like a pill bug under attack, while his face softens and bloats.

"Objection," Frantz says. "You just asked that. Confidential."

"You're wrong about that. Before, I asked the witness whether Quiana Gottschalk was an elder of the Assembly. Now I asked him if he's heard the name. That's not remotely confidential."

Frantz considers this. "You can answer that one."

"I will not answer that one," McCarthy says, making no effort to hide his displeasure with his lawyer.

Frantz unsuccessfully tries to mask his own irritation. No one talks to him that way, not even his most important clients. "Well, in light of my client's refusal to answer, I object."

"Mr. McCarthy, didn't you once tell me that belief in secrets is a superstition? Did you actually believe that you could keep Quiana Gottschalk a secret?"

His eyes cloud over in rage.

"Objection," Frantz says.

"Mr. McCarthy, who was the First Apostate?"

"I don't . . . I mean, I won't . . ."

"Does that mean that you don't know or that you won't respond?"

He doesn't answer.

"Move on to another question, counsel," Frantz says, nervously riffling the pages of his legal pad.

"You know, I think I'll do that, Mr. Frantz. Mr. McCarthy, do you . . . um, do you know . . . Strike that." I grip the edge of the table. "Mr. McCarthy, has the Sanctified Assembly ever practiced what's called Ascending Sodality?"

He goes slack-jawed. Frantz turns to Weir, who shakes his head in confusion.

"The First Apostate rejected the practice of Ascending Sodality, am I right?"

"Vile mythology!" Aware that he's said too much, he clamps his mouth shut. Frantz and Weir whisper to each other, evidently too befuddled to object.

"Answer the question," I say.

McCarthy glowers at me with molten rage, but also with a kind of awe. He starts buffing his sunglasses with his expensive silk tie, an action that lasts much longer than necessary and becomes ever more compulsive as the seconds pass. In the process, he looks up at the ceiling, his irises rolling up into the sockets. It's as if I'm looking at a cardboard cutout of a face and the artist didn't bother to draw in the eyes.

"I insist on an answer," I say.

"We're done!" he bellows, bolting up out of his chair. He spins toward the door, bumping hard into the crates behind him. He staggers past Frantz and Weir like a drunkard. The videographer tries to warn him, but he rips the microphone cord clipped to his tie clean out of the sound system and hurries out of the room. Weir belatedly follows.

"Let's pack up," I say to Lovely, who's having a hard time stifling a grin. "This deposition is over."

"He'll be back shortly and we'll finish this travesty," Frantz says.

"McCarthy's not coming back," I say.

Five minutes later Nick Weir returns, looking shaken and disheveled. I imagine him pursuing McCarthy all the way down Melrose, pleading with him to come back. The arrogant son of a bitch had no clue what he was getting into when his boss brought the Assembly in as a client.

Deanna comes into the room. "Are you guys done?"

"Absolutely," I say.

Frantz looks at Weir, who nods in confirmation.

She addresses Frantz. "Then pack up and get the hell out of my store." She points her finger at Weir. "And take *that* with you."

Weir starts to respond, but Frantz silences him with a wave of his hand. Without saying another word, they gather up their things and walk out.

"What happened?" Deanna says.

Lovely starts to answer, hours of pent-up adrenaline bursting out. "Parker asked McCarthy about—"

"I asked about the Assembly's religious beliefs. I guess I got a little too sarcastic. McCarthy got his nose out of joint and bailed."

Lovely gives me an odd look, but stays quiet.

"So you might have another go-round," Deanna says. "Although I doubt Frantz will agree to come back here. And I've lost his wife as a customer, for sure, though the look on his face was worth it. Priceless. I'll be out front if you need anything."

When she leaves, Lovely and I check our e-mails. We both have urgent messages from Jonathan Borzo asking us to call him right away. Lovely punches in his number. I can hear Jonathan over her speaker, talking fast, but I can't make out what he's saying.

She places her hand over the microphone. "They want us to come out to the Valley. Alan Markowitz refuses to meet with them. He'll only talk to you." Markowitz is the man whose identity Rich allegedly stole to forge a passport and rent the Silver Lake apartment. A few days ago, I assigned Jonathan and Kathleen the task of interviewing him, a way to make up for leaving them out of the McCarthy deposition. It obviously hasn't worked out.

"I'm whipped," I say. "Can't we go back another day?"

She shakes her head and mouths the word, *please*. Like a generous favored sibling, she always wants me to pay more attention to Kathleen and Jonathan.

"Fine. Tell them to wait and I'll be there as soon as I can."

When she ends the call, an unbearable awkwardness separates us, a malicious gift from Lou Frantz and Nick Weir. With a formality that might have made sense a few months ago but that now sounds absurd, I say, "I'm very grateful for your assistance today."

Meeting my contrived reserve with forced joviality, she says, "Hey, I'd love to hear what Markowitz has to say, so how about we ride out to the Valley together?" and without a second's hesitation I reply that we'll take my car.

CHAPTER 36

We travel the 405 at an LA crawl. Unasked questions and unspoken words hang in the air like invisible cosmic matter, cold and dark. My body aches. Not until we reach the Mulholland Drive exit does Lovely say in a quavering voice, "It's all true, you know. What . . . what Nick said about him and me and . . ."

"You don't owe me—"

"Parker, I want to owe you an explanation. I want to so much."

I don't speak, only remove my right hand from the steering wheel and take hers.

"You have to know something about me," she says. "I—"

"Please don't." It's not only that I don't want to know about her sexual history. It's that if someone shares their secrets with you, they expect you to reveal yours in return, and I won't do that. "Just tell me it's over between him and you."

"It really never was."

"Then let's not talk about it anymore."

We drive in silence for a while. Finally, she asks about *Keanu* Gottschalk and the First Apostate and Ascending Sodality. I don't tell her that the name is *Quiana*. I say that I heard the words whispered years ago when my mother joined the Assembly, but I don't know what they mean. I don't think she believes me, but for once she doesn't push back.

It takes a full hour to reach North Hollywood in the east San Fernando Valley. The area isn't geographically close to the real Hollywood, although it's only a few miles away from the Burbank-based studios—Disney, Warner Bros., and Universal. The neighborhood near the studios has become chic in recent years, but Alan Thomas Markowitz's used car dealership is on the border of a barrio.

I pull up to Lankershim Preowned Automobiles, an asphalt slab jammed with low-end used cars and a showroom/garage no bigger than a double storefront. Jonathan and Kathleen wait on the sidewalk near the entrance. She's carrying a briefcase and wearing a threadbare polyester black pantsuit and black blouse obviously intended to conceal her plumpness. Unfortunately, the outfit is more appropriate for a funeral than a witness interview. Jonathan is dressed in a plaid sport coat and tan slacks too large for his wiry frame. His necktie hangs almost to his crotch, and there are gaps in his red goatee where he over-trimmed it. No wonder Markowitz insists on speaking with a grownup.

"We're sorry we dragged you out here," Jonathan says. "Markowitz will only talk to a real lawyer. He's really suspicious."

"It's the lot of a young lawyer to be disrespected, Mr. Borzo."

"So, how did it go?" Kathleen asks.

"Weird," Lovely says. She gives them a recap of the deposition, leaving out Weir's slur against her.

We go inside the dealership, dark and gloomy despite the glass walls and the bright afternoon sun. The place smells of floral deodorizer and automotive grease. The room is bigger than it seemed from the outside, large enough to house a long front counter, desks for five or six salespeople, and a private office in the back. A door at the far end of the room leads into the garage, where the sounds of air ratchets and blowtorches contend with Led Zeppelin blaring over the speaker system.

A middle-aged woman with bleached hair and pasty skin greets Jonathan and Kathleen. "Welcome back, kids." She turns to me. "You must be the boss."

"I'm their law professor. Parker Stern. I understand that Mr. Markowitz would be willing to meet with me about a case we're handling."

"OK, Parker. I'll tell Alan you're here." She picks up the phone and identifies me as the young people's boss.

"Head on back," she says. "There's all kinds of crap lying around on the floor. Don't trip."

We navigate back to the private office like a ragtag platoon. I knock and open the door to a tiny room that can't possibly accommodate all four of us.

"Lovely and Jonathan, why don't you wait outside."

"Gotcha," Jonathan says. Lovely grins. To her credit, Kathleen acts like this decision was the logical one.

Markowitz sits at his desk typing on a computer keypad. I expected him to resemble a character out of a David Mamet play—profane, hard driving, a scavenger. Instead, his drooping eyes, jowly face, receding chin, and salt-and-pepper toupee make him seem mild. He's a sports fan—baseball memorabilia, trophies, and athletic photographs adorn his shelves and walls. We sit down in uncomfortable vinyl client chairs, and I tell him why we're here. He told the FBI that he doesn't know anything about Rich's alleged identity theft, and I don't expect him to say anything new or different now. Still, we have to find out what he knows just to button up our investigation.

"I'm not sure why I should help you," he says. "Your client stole my identity."

"Richard Baxter isn't my client," I say. "Richard Baxter is dead. My client is his father, an elderly man who's been unfairly sued by the Church of the Sanctified Assembly for millions of dollars."

"The Assembly consists of a bunch of anti-Semites. I abhor their pro-Palestinian propaganda. Ask me anything you want."

"We won't take up much of your time," I say.

"I have hours to kill. In this economy, you'd think the public would want to buy used vehicles, but business is the pits. So fire away."

"Did you know Richard Baxter?"

"I did not."

"Do you know how anyone could have gotten your name and social security number?"

"As I told the FBI, your guess is as good as mine." He shrugs and holds his arms out as he talks. "My wife rented a safe deposit box at a new bank. I opened up an online stock trading account. Someone dug through my garbage and found a document I should have shredded. An unscrupulous psychic read my mind."

There's a deafening burst of what sounds like artillery fire—a pneumatic drill. I flinch and Kathleen covers her ears. Markowitz acts as though he doesn't hear a thing.

"What about a former employee?" I shout over the din.

"The Feds asked me that, too. I gave them some names. But people come and go. Selling used cars on commission isn't easy, especially with the economy in the toilet the way it is. I've had so many sales people here over the past five years that . . ." His weary eyes sag a bit more. He looks as tired as I feel.

I ask a few more questions—or more accurately, pose the same question in several different ways—and get nowhere. "Is there anything you want to ask, Kathleen?" I say, expecting her to say no.

"I . . . I do have a question," she says. "I was wondering whether . . . you know, if you ever met this woman. I have a picture of her." She reaches into her briefcase and takes out a sheet of paper, which she hands to Markowitz. In my haste to finish up with Markowitz, I forgot to ask about the Outsider. Good catch, Kathleen.

"You won't be able to see her face," Kathleen says. "But there's this tattoo on her left ankle you might recognize, maybe."

I expect Markowitz to respond with the perfunctory "I don't know this woman" until he raises his brow so forcefully that it looks like his hairpiece might slip backward. He stands and turns his back on us. On tiptoes, he lifts a photograph off a metal hook and then comes around to our side of the desk and sets the photo down in front of us. "Our company team—the Seminoles. We were the East Valley slow-pitch softball champs two years ago. Sandy was our short fielder." He points to a woman sitting cross-legged in the front row wearing a green softball jersey with the yellow letters *Lankershim Pre-Owned* appliquéd across the front. "Sandra Casey. Worked for me until a little over a year ago."

I can't tell from this picture whether this woman has the Strength tattoo on her ankle or not. I study the face—lips curled downward even in the midst of a victory celebration; longish nose; eyes so dark that they seem to absorb all the light around them and emit nothing in return. I take the photograph and hold it up, unable to stop looking at that face. As tired as I was feeling, as stressful as this day has been, I'm now all at once hyperalert.

I do my best to concentrate on what Markowitz is saying. He tells us that he hired Sandra after she answered an ad on Craigslist. He remembers that she got a great reference from an ex-boss, a lawyer who said she was top tier in office management and accounting, although he doesn't recall the lawyer's name. She was only supposed to keep the books and do other clerical work, but it soon became clear that she was better than that. She eventually filled out finance contracts, dealt with credit companies, and interfaced with the Department of Motor Vehicles. He gave her access to the corporate tax returns, which is where she must have gotten his social security number and date of birth. About a year ago—just after New Year's 2011—she quit suddenly, leaving no forwarding information.

"I trusted her," he says. "And she was interesting. You rarely meet someone so smart in this line of work."

After he makes a copy of the photograph for us, we walk out front to find a bored Jonathan and a wilted Lovely sprawled out on a ratty synthetic sofa. We huddle on the sidewalk, and I summarize what Markowitz told us about Sandra Casey. I have to find her, but that won't be easy. She's intelligent and slippery and unpredictable—and dangerous. I strongly suspect she wrote those awful e-mails to Monica Baxter. One phrase in particular sticks with me—*soon we'll all be awash in blood.* Then I tell them something that I didn't want Markowitz to know— the woman who went by the name Sandra Casey is actually my ex-colleague, Grace Trimble.

CHAPTER 37

Lovely and I crawl through traffic on Highland Avenue. "Turn left," she commands. Although The Barrista lies in the opposite direction, I make the turn.

"I don't live far from here," she says. "We can have a glass of wine." A pointed pause. "Or something."

Except for Lovely giving sporadic driving directions, we make the rest of the trip in silence. My mind and body are anything but silent. She is still my student. I don't make light of that. I believe you should respect the rules, especially rules that protect those weaker than you. Then the bargaining starts. Am I really a law professor? I have three students and a one-year deal that's going to expire in a few months, and anyway Manny gave me the job as a sinecure just so I could feel useful again. And whose trust would I really be breaching? How much pleasure, how much human connection, must we forgo for abstract principle?

We pull up to a châteauesque six-story building. With its restored mansard roof and wrought-iron balconies, the apartment house is supposedly an example of how the neighborhood is gentrifying, but the refurbished façade and upgraded masonry can't quite mask a lingering decrepitude. We park behind the building and take a creaky elevator to the fourth floor. There's a faint fusty odor of decaying redwood. She unlatches the original lock and two security locks. When the door opens, she lightly places her fingers on a mezuzah affixed to the doorpost and says, "A gift from my mother." She recites the words, "May God protect my going out and coming in, now and forever."

She flips on an old electrolier in the entryway. The living room is decorated in Bohemian chic—light gray walls, a quatrefoil mirror over the mantle, a brown throw rug, a loveseat upholstered in a green and ivory floral pattern. Mix and match with a purpose.

She drops her knapsack on the floor, takes off her jacket, and faces me. I wrap my arms around her, and we kiss with aggression. She captures my lower lip between her teeth and bites, releasing it only when I thrust my tongue into her mouth. I put my hand under the hem of her skirt and run my fingers up her inner thigh, linger at the margin of wet heat, and then move beyond. She moans and says breathlessly, "Oh yeah, baby, right there." When her breathing becomes ragged, she jerks my hand away. Kneeling before me, she unfastens my slacks and takes me between her lips. There's a kind of anarchy to her touch—fervid, raunchy, disquieting, a flawless blue flame.

She stands up suddenly, places both hands on my chest, and shoves me away. She removes her jacket and camisole, lifts her right breast to her mouth, and slowly licks the nipple, all the while keeping her eyes glued to mine. I've seen this in porn, but I've never been with a woman who's done it, couldn't have imagined taking it seriously, and yet now I experience a fresh surge of arousal as if she touched me and not herself. Her eyes, steely gray in the dim light, signal challenge, hunger. I grab her shoulders and draw her to me. When my lips touch her breast, she arches her back and gasps.

We sink to the floor. No thought of the bedroom or even the couch. No thought of shedding the rest of our clothing. No thought of protection. No thought of pain from the beating. She's like no one I've ever been with, not the desperate groupies who pursued me as a teenager even as my fame dimmed, not Deanna before the sex became rote and aimless. She makes me feel as if she's been waiting all her life for us to find each other.

I return to my condo the next morning and spend hours scouring the Internet, trying to get some kind of lead on the whereabouts of Grace Trimble. Nothing. Late in the afternoon, my security bell rings. It's Lovely. After I buzz her into the building, she arrives at my door carrying several bags of groceries. She sets them down and kisses me.

"It's Friday," she says. "I brought dinner. I'll get it together."

I remember that inedible pasta she served me at her father's house. "Are you cooking?"

"Reheating. Some stuff from Gelson's."

Trying not to show my relief, I take her hand and lead her out to the balcony. The sun is setting in the northwest. Vast cirrus clouds glow scarlet on the horizon, their wispy tendrils curling downward as if to consecrate the sea.

"Awesome," she says. She rests her head on my shoulder.

We stand outside watching the ocean until the sky darkens and the first stars are visible above the horizon. We go inside, and she lights the Sabbath candles. While she warms the food, I mix boxcar martinis, something I learned to do my senior year in college when I worked as a bartender. We eat dinner, avoiding the subject of work, easy for her but almost impossible for me.

After we finish, she goes into my second bedroom, which I use as a combination office and storage room, and returns with a DVD jewel case still in its original shrink-wrap. It's a copy of *Fourth Grade G-Man*. The garish cover art depicts the clownish images of its stars— Parky Gerald and Lake Knolls, in the worst roles of their careers. I was eleven, almost twelve, trying to pass as a nine-year-old. Even the gullible kids among my audience didn't buy it, much less the critics. Dramatic actor Knolls insisted on trying comedy but didn't have a sense of humor. During his election campaign, his critics used his appearance in this film to mock him mercilessly.

"I want to watch this," she says.

"Be my guest. In fact, keep it. It's yours."

"I thought we could watch it together."

"I haven't seen any of my movies in twenty years, and I don't want to see one now."

As usual, the word *no* means *yes* to Lovely. She takes my arm and pulls me toward the living room. I turn awkwardly, wrenching my torso. I wince, a residue from the beating.

"Oh my God, I'm sorry. Are you all right?"

"I will be if you don't make me watch that bomb."

She shakes her head and leads me to the sofa. She powers on the television and the DVD player and loads the movie. I don't know why I'm going along with this. I don't want to see that kid.

I watch myself playing a fourth-grade genius who helps Knolls, a rogue FBI agent, fight two madcap underworld mobsters who're trying to fix the Little League World Series. In the movie, Erica Hatfield plays my teacher. I still find it hard to imagine that this beautiful young woman on the screen is the same person whom I visited in the mountains just a few weeks ago.

"How does this feel?" Lovely says.

"Like I'm being forced to watch a really bad kids' movie." I don't feel connected to anything unfolding on the screen. What I do remember are the grueling hours on the set—and the turmoil. This was the picture on which my mother got into a shouting match with the director, eventually hurling a prop stapler at his head. No matter that the director was a horse's ass—Harriet Stern was banned from the set and arrested for assault.

To my surprise, about halfway through the film, Bradley Kelly appears, playing Erica's boyfriend. He has a bit part, little more than a walk-on. Even so, I can't imagine how I could have forgotten. When I hear his voice, a hairline crack in my memory splits open. The images on the screen blur into meaningless flickers of light. Then the cotton mouth, the quivering hands, the constricted chest, the grubby beads of sweat, the nausea—the classic symptoms of stage fright. I grab Lovely's wrist. "I . . . I can't watch this. Please turn it off."

She starts to protest, but then sees my face. She picks up the remote control and powers off the television set. The symptoms subside almost immediately.

"Do you want to talk about it?"

"I can't."

"Parker, wasn't that Kelly?"

"I said I can't!"

"OK. It's OK." She takes my hands in hers.

As soon as I feel her touch, my fear turns to mortification. "Look. It's stupid, but I just couldn't watch that thing. Those days were . . ."

"I understand," she says, but she couldn't possibly.

We're quiet for a long time. Finally, she says, "It's time for your lesson in Judaica."

"Excuse me?"

She slides her body against mine and says, "Did you know that Jewish tradition encourages sex on the Sabbath?"

If her goal is to make me forget about my panic attack, she's succeeded. "I'd have thought it would be forbidden. I mean, you can't work, so I would think—"

"You can't work on the Sabbath, but you can play. You think fucking is work?"

"Definitely play."

"Actually, it's a double mitzvah to do it on Shabbat. According to the Kabbalists, the earthly joy of sex is worthy of celebration anytime, but on the Sabbath, you're also merging the divine male and female aspects of God. Of course, you're supposed to be married, but . . ." She lies back and pulls me on top of her. She spends the rest of the evening showing me several ways for an observant Jewish girl to honor the Sabbath.

CHAPTER 38

The next day, a Saturday, Lovely doesn't work, but I do. I arrive at The Barrista at ten o'clock. Manny Mason is there, sitting at a table with Deanna. I get my coffee and join them. I immediately pull out the photocopy of the Lankershim Preowned Seminoles coed softball team, set it on the table, and point to Grace Trimble. "She calls herself Sandra Casey."

"What the hell?" Deanna says. "She looks malnourished. What did that poor girl do to herself?"

Manny spends a long time examining the photo. "What's this about a Sandra Casey?"

I tell them what I learned from Markowitz.

"Have you told the authorities?" Manny asks.

"I'm going to call Neil Latham Monday." It's not true. I have to get to Grace before the authorities do or I'll never get to talk to her.

Manny takes a long drink of coffee and makes a face.

"Something wrong, dude?" Deanna says.

"Yeah. It's decaf. I can't stand decaf."

"Then why are you drinking it?"

"My doctor. Blood pressure's up." He frowns and narrows his eyes. "Faculty members giving me stress by flouting school regulations."

I laugh it off, but he seems to have some kind of psychic radar that's alerted him to what's happening between Lovely and me. "I need to find Grace," I say. "And I need to do it before the trial starts."

"You'll never find her," Deanna says. "She's got seventeen million dollars stashed in an offshore account. She's probably in Brazil or Costa Rica or wherever."

"I can't believe that she'd do something like that," I say.

"Come on, Parker," Deanna says. "I'm sure it's occurred to you that she turned on Rich and took the money herself. She's much smarter than he ever was, not to mention that she was far ahead of anyone technologically, so all she had to do was work her magic and make an electronic bank transfer into a shell account that she created for herself. Poor Rich wouldn't have had a clue. When the Assembly got wise to the scheme, she skipped out and let him take the blame. Something like that could have driven him to suicide once he figured it out, which he had plenty of time to do in that cell. He always had a thing for Grace, you know. What I'm saying doesn't fit your theory that the Assembly murdered him, but it makes a lot more sense."

I look at Manny.

"I hate to say it, but she's right," he says.

"I don't see it that way," I say. "There's the pathology report showing that Rich had a fractured hyoid. Grace certainly didn't sneak into the detention center and kill him. And whatever she is, she's not someone who could arrange a contract hit."

"Weirder things have happened," Deanna says.

"Not Grace. When I talked to Rich at the jail, he didn't say a word about her. If he thought she had anything to do with taking that money, he would have said so. He was protecting her. He might have been trusting, but he wasn't that naïve."

"Yes he was," Deanna says. "And seventeen million dollars will make your pet Labrador drop a dime on you and hop a jet to Brazil."

"My gut says otherwise," I say. "So stop the negativity and help me find her. She's now become my most important trial witness."

Deanna shrugs. "I'll ask around."

Manny points to the picture of Grace. "May I get a copy of this? If Grace really is on the run as you say, maybe some of my pro bono contacts can find some leads. It's remote, but . . ."

"Definitely a long shot," I say. "But I like it."

"I've also gotten to know one of her old law school professors at Penn," he says. "You should hear how highly she talks about Grace after all these years. A once-in-a-generation legal mind, she calls her. Sometimes Grace communicates with her. I'll e-mail and see if she's heard from her recently."

"Did you ask whether Grace was embellishing her law school grades?" Deanna asks.

Manny shakes his head sadly. "She truly did have the highest GPA ever up until that time."

"So one of those crazy stories was actually true," Deanna says. "Remember the time she told us how she flew off to Paris with Kevin Costner after meeting him at a party in Laurel Canyon?"

"The worst was telling people that she'd been kidnapped by pygmies in the Amazon rainforest," I say.

Manny piles on. "Worse than shooting heroin with Kurt Cobain?" We laugh at this oft-repeated gossip, the bracing cruelty of it drawing us together.

"The liar's curse." Deanna says. "She was such a bullshitter that she didn't get credit for a lot of what she did accomplish."

"Except for being the most creative lawyer any of us ever met," I say.

Deanna and Manny nod in agreement. We reminisce about how Grace's inspired work on a supreme court case resulted in victory even after every wonk had called our firm's position hopeless, and how she taught stubborn Andrew Macklin, a good negotiator but a horrible writer, to construct cogent sentences after thirty-plus years of writing gibberish.

"I saw Grace a few years ago in court," Manny says. "I told you about it, right?"

Deanna and I look each other and shake our heads.

"I was down on one of my pro bono cases, representing some Lazers accused of unlawfully assembling out in Pacoima. I was standing in the courtroom before the calendar call, and Grace came from out of nowhere and gave me this big, inappropriate hug. All the lawyers in court saw it. I knew right away she was manic. She asked about my case, and when I told her about it, she began shouting at me, saying that my clients were no better than terrorists and that the First Amendment should be repealed."

"She had to be messing with you," I say.

"She was serious. When she got up to argue her case, it turned out she was representing this guy suing Best Buy because a big screen TV allegedly fell off a shelf and crushed his foot. Can you imagine? Grace Trimble working a sleazy personal injury case? She could barely get an articulate sentence out. The judge slammed her. It was pathetic. It actually made me want to cry."

"I don't get it to this day," I say. "Editor of the Penn Law Review and clerk for a supreme court justice, and she wanted to be a music lawyer?"

"She was a shy girl overwhelmed by LA, but enraptured by it, too," Deanna says. "She wanted in."

We're silent for a moment, as if honoring the memory of an icon who died an early death.

"She should have been a law professor or a judge," Manny says. "She couldn't deal with anyone, much less difficult entertainment clients."

"Grace is like a feral cat," I say. "She wants you to get close, but if you try, she'll fight or flee. She couldn't even get along with the people who tried to be her friends."

"She and I got along fine," Manny says. "You and Deanna were the popular kids at the firm. Grace was intimidated by that."

"That's bullshit," I say. "Harmon treated us equally."

"Hardly. Grace and Rich and I were one rung down. I don't know, maybe it's because the two of you were litigators." He rests his elbows on the table and leans his long torso forward. "And then Rich lucked into heading up the Assembly's legal work, and he was a cool kid, too."

"Rich was never cool," I say.

Deanna is mindlessly drumming her fingers on the sides of her coffee cup. The muscles in her neck visibly tense. "I've never told you guys this, but I was responsible for getting Grace into all that crap."

"Oh come on," I say. "Grace was—"

"Grace was a fragile girl with no experience. She told me she'd never had a boyfriend. I took her to some rock concerts in Hollywood, introduced her to a bunch of predatory men. Out of pity or friendship or whatever. I was twenty-five years old with a law degree, and yet . . . Manny's right, hanging around nerdy Grace Trimble made me feel special, superior. The second time we went out, we got to go backstage and hang out with the band. I got her high on weed and ecstasy. She'd never even smoked before. She refused at first, but I was this brilliant advocate who could convince anyone of anything, so . . . Next thing you know, she's ingesting any drug handed to her and fucking every guy who claimed he could strum a power chord. I should've known from the start that she couldn't handle it."

"Grace was a grownup," I say.

She blinks her eyes. "It's been eating at me for years. I've always been able to tiptoe to the edge of a cliff and keep my balance. Grace couldn't. She tumbled right over. I had no right to lead her there."

"She was ill," Manny said. "You couldn't have known."

"Couldn't I? With all the lying and the hyperactivity and the absences from work, shouldn't we all have known?"

"It was Harmon who should've done something," Manny says, an edge of resentment in his voice.

"He did," I say. "After she self-destructed, he—"

"The key word is *after*," he says. "Harmon had to know about Grace's problems. He knew everything that went on at the firm. Everything. He . . . never mind. It doesn't matter."

"I want to hear it," I say.

"Grace was too valuable a commodity for Harmon to lose to therapy or a leave of absence. Once he made her give up the music lawyer fantasy and work on matters for the Sanctified Assembly, she was indispensible."

I lean back in my chair. "Harmon wasn't like that."

"The sicker Grace got, the more work he piled on her," Manny says. "And when she embarrassed the firm with that Knolls debacle, he got rid of her."

Harmon fired Grace after his client Lake Knolls had complained that she was stalking him, crashing campaign fundraisers and loitering outside his Nichols Canyon mansion at all hours of the night. One night, Knolls's security guard found her trying to scale a wall at the side of the house. When the police arrived and arrested her for trespassing, they found a gun in her car. Grace claimed she carried it for protection. Harmon managed to pull some strings and get the gun charges thrown out because Grace had a permit. He also convinced Knolls not to press charges in exchange for promising that Grace would get help.

"What other choice did he have but to fire her?" I say.

He purses his lips and gazes downward. "If that neighbor hadn't found her, she would've done just what Harmon and Rich . . ." Two weeks after Grace lost her job, she went into her garage, sealed all the doors and windows with duct tape, got behind the wheel of her car, and started the engine.

"Harmon and Rich were murdered," I say.

"Forgive me, my friend," Manny says. "But you've always had blinders on when it comes to Harmon. To this day, you can't accept the fact that he committed suicide. I'll be forever grateful to him for hiring me and teaching me how to be a good lawyer. But he was a flawed human being like the rest of us. He put his law firm above the people in it, above his own family even."

"How long have you felt this way, Manny?" I ask.

"Since the firm fell apart and I got some perspective on what the place was about. Since Grace went crazy. Since Deanna left the practice. Since you fell to pieces. Since Rich died. All byproducts of the Macklin & Cherry culture."

"You're wrong about him," I say. I look to Deanna for support, but she averts her eyes. "Deanna . . ."

"I got out of the legal profession for a reason, Parker."

"But Harmon got the firm to pay her psychiatrist bills. And the firm sued Grace's insurance company pro bono for refusing to cover her."

"To assuage his guilt," Deanna says.

"It wasn't that way," I say. "It wasn't that way at all."

—⁓—

Monica Baxter arrives at The Barrista two hours later. When I tell her that Grace Trimble is the person she calls the Outsider, she says something that I can't hear over the clatter of dishes and crescendo of the patrons' voices.

"Say again?"

She leans in close, her teeth clenched. "I said, *not that whore.*"

"I don't understand. Rich and Grace were friends, but—"

"You think they were just friends? They were engaged to be married once. In a sanctioned ceremony."

"A sanctioned . . . ?"

"You are a sightless man. Trimble was an Assembly convert. She brought Rich into the fold."

"But didn't you—?"

"You thought that *I* lured him in with my feminine wiles. He told me. No, Trimble joined the flock and he followed her."

I feel the blood pulsing in my cheeks. I stare down into my coffee cup. "I didn't know she was an Assembly member."

"If anyone could drive my poor husband to suicide, it was that Trimble woman. She lived to drag him down. And she'd like nothing better than to get back at the Assembly." She grabs her handbag and gets up to leave. "I have to tell Christopher McCarthy about this."

"Monica, wait." I reach out and grab her wrist.

She jerks her arm away in disgust. "Don't you dare put your hands on me again. Ever."

"OK. I'm sorry. But please listen. Before you tell anyone about Grace, give me a chance to find out what really happened. Rich was murdered. There's the botched autopsy report. There are other irregularities in the financials that prove that something else was going on. And now that I know that Grace was involved, I can get to her. She knows something. So give me some more time. Please."

She hesitates, and sits back down. "Trimble stole the money. And had Rich killed. I want you to prove that."

"I know . . . well, I knew Grace. She didn't care about money. She was desperately looking to connect with people, but she couldn't because of her illness. And you're right, she had feelings for Rich. That's why I don't believe that she'd hurt him."

"She's not ill. She's weak and selfish, desirous of empty self-gratification. And she certainly would hurt him. Revenge for his leaving her."

"I truly think that Grace was helping him sort out the facts," I repeat with as much conviction as I can muster. "The only way I can figure this whole thing out is to find her. If you tell the Assembly about Grace, that'll never happen, because if they're responsible—"

"They're *not* responsible."

"If they know about Grace's role in this, they certainly won't let me find her. They'll lay the blame on her to get this case over with, and Rich will forever be branded a defective."

She flinches at my use of the word. "What do you want from me?"

"Right now, just tell me all you know about Grace's relationship with Rich and the Assembly. Then keep this information to yourself so I can find her. And I promise you—if she did have something to do with Rich's murder, I'll get the evidence to prove it."

She takes a deep breath. "I got to know her when she first joined. She wanted to purge the impurities from her cells." The Assembly preaches that insanity and addiction result from contamination of the body's intercellular water and can be cured with faith and an intense exercise regimen. "She seemed like a true adherent, engaged in an earnest quest to heed the Fount. Sober and on her way to being crystalline." *Crystalline* is Assembly-speak for contaminant-free.

"When did Rich become a member?"

"She ushered him into the Assembly in 2005."

"My God, that was two years before he told us that . . ."

"Rich didn't tell you because he was afraid of what you and the others would think of him. Especially what you, his good friend Parker, would think. I'm proud to say I helped him find the courage not to be ashamed of his beliefs."

I glance down at my coffee for a moment, and then with difficulty meet her eyes.

"Grace's transformation didn't last long," she continues. "She started dressing in a way that flaunted her body, started telling these crazy stories about herself, pursuing male members of the congregation. Especially married men, like they were some kind of challenge. She even seduced a pastor. And all this time, she was supposed to have been engaged to Rich. Everyone in the community knew what she was but him." She shakes her head. "He was so trusting, so positive about his friends and partners, and they took advantage and destroyed him."

"And you think I was one of those people?"

"That's to be judged on a higher celestial level." She stares at me, expressionless. "We're a compassionate community. The hierarchy tried to help Grace, but intervention and reconditioning didn't work. When she corrupted one of the new members—they were caught in the back seat of her car like rutting teenagers—she was excommunicated. She wanted Rich to leave with her, but he didn't because I convinced him to stay. After that, she terrorized us with her constant phone calls and e-mails and threats and . . ." She stops to take a breath. "I don't care what you say, she's capable of great violence. I feared for our lives. She only left us alone after the hierarchal guard convinced her to stay away from us."

I'm sure that the guard was quite forceful.

"Rich promised me in the name of the Fount that he wouldn't see that woman again," she says. "Why would he go to her for help? Why not Deanna or Manny? Or you, like he did when he was arrested?"

"When I find her, we'll be able to answer that question."

"There's only one answer. He still had feelings for her."

"Monica, Rich loved you and Josh. When I saw him at the jail that was the one thing that he was absolutely clear about."

"No. That's why he rented the apartment. So they could . . ." She curls her lips. She's one of those rare women who looks prettier when she's about to cry. She picks up her purse and gets up to leave.

"Wait. Will you keep what I've told you to yourself?"

Without answering, she hurries away.

CHAPTER 39

"You're going to unravel your coat if you keep doing that," Lovely says.

I glance down at the sleeve of my navy blue suit and find myself tugging at a loose thread. We're in Judge Harvey's courtroom for the hearing on the motion to dismiss the indictment against Tyler Daniels. In deference to Judge Harvey's admonition at the end of the last court hearing, she's wearing a black woolen skirt that falls to midcalf.

When we sat down, I made sure to put my briefcase on the chair between us. I don't want anyone to suspect that she and I have anything more than a teacher–student relationship. In a courtroom, everyone—the judge, the spectators, the jury if impaneled—has extrasensory powers of observation. The attorneys are particularly exposed, maybe because the courtroom resembles a stage, with the lawyers in the leading roles.

Neil Latham is standing in the aisle, speaking to a group of news reporters. The Daniels case has become widely known to the media. The courtroom doors swing open, and Lou Frantz and Nick Weir walk in. They don't have a case on the docket, so they have no business being here. Then Christopher McCarthy comes through the door, followed by a phalanx of his minions, all with the imperious bearing of followers of the Church of the Sanctified Assembly. From my half-twisted position I count eight of them in addition to McCarthy, all dressed in well-tailored blue suits, the men wearing red power ties, the women attractive and wearing skirts much shorter than the one that Lovely wore at the hearing when Judge Harvey snapped at her. It will cost the Church a fortune in time and legal fees to have all these people watch a criminal case that should mean nothing to them.

Latham greets Frantz warmly. The Frantz law firm likes to hire former US Attorneys, so maybe Latham is angling for a high-paying job in private practice. Lovely, who's reviewing her notes, doesn't seem to notice Frantz and McCarthy. Even as a child actor, I was acutely aware of everything that was going on around me. I envy Lovely's ability to focus and detach, seemingly to shut out irrelevant stimuli. I wish I could do that, because maybe then I could stave off the stage fright.

Latham finally walks to the front of the courtroom, acknowledging me with a slight nod. I expect the Assembly crew at least to show enough restraint to take seats on the opposite side of the courtroom, but they all file into the two rows directly in back of us, with Weir behind me, Frantz behind Lovely, and McCarthy next to Frantz. Only then does Lovely turn around and see them. Her eyes narrow, but to her credit she goes back to studying her notes.

I feel a heavy hand on my shoulder.

"You know what, Stern?" Frantz says. "When she worked for me, she wanted my firm to take on this case pro bono. I wouldn't do it. There are some things you just don't do, and representing a pedophile is one of them."

"You should've followed your own advice before you decided to represent that cult," I say, making sure that McCarthy hears me. "It's nothing but racketeering enterprise masquerading as a religion."

"Truth be told," he says, "I advised her not to take your class. I'd never heard of you. I didn't want some inexperienced hack posing as a trial lawyer to lead her astray."

With her back still toward Frantz, Lovely raises her right hand to ear level and shows him her middle finger.

"That's your idea of courtroom decorum these days?" he says. "I guess I was right about your working with this guy."

At least for the moment, my disgust over Frantz's tactic trumps my gathering stage fright. "And you want us to believe that you've acted respectfully by showing up and sitting right behind us and needling us just before an argument? Not to mention that stunt you pulled at McCarthy's deposition. Under the circumstances, Ms. Diamond has shown remarkable restraint. And actually, I'm glad you're here, because it'll be good for you to see how someone young handles a case. You botched the McCarthy deposition. Time has passed you by."

"My recent press clippings prove otherwise."

I glance over at Lovely. Though she's still looking down at her documents, she's grinning.

I look around the courtroom. It's filled with spectators. McCarthy stares straight ahead. He bears no resemblance to the terrified man who fled his deposition. Farther back, the news reporters wait with laptops poised. I can pick out the lawyers here on other matters, because they're flipping through their own case files, oblivious to the gathering tension brimming up on all sides.

A man in the back row waves an arm. I have to stand up to recognize him as Jonathan Borzo. Dressed in a suit and clean-shaven, he finally looks like someone about to graduate law school rather than a high school sophomore interested in texting and videogames. Kathleen is sitting next to him. She's wearing an ill-fitting polyester dress that makes her look plumper than she really is. I tap Lovely on the shoulder and point them out. She glances up, but doesn't acknowledge them.

The *click* of the chambers door quiets the courtroom.

"All rise, this court is now in session, the Honorable Cyrus Harvey presiding, all those having business . . ." At the sound of the clerk's voice, my heart starts hammering my ribcage.

The judge takes the bench. Usually, there's a hint of detached glibness to Judge Harvey, as though he's signaling that while everyone else in the room must take the proceedings seriously, he doesn't have to. Today, he looks somber.

"Please be seated," the clerk says.

As soon as I sit back down, my stage fright disappears, the way a constant din abruptly stops and leaves your ears ringing with the memory of it. The interior wall of my gut has unclenched; the skin on the nape of my neck no longer crawls. I feel that elation that lifts you into a sublime weightlessness. By trying to intimidate me, Frantz and McCarthy have accomplished just the opposite: their blatant grandstanding has freed me from an affliction far more powerful than they. I want to pump my fist in triumph.

When the clerk calls our case, I make my way to the defense table, while Lovely takes a place behind the lectern just as I told her to do. This is her motion, and she has the right to go first. Latham sits at the prosecution table across from us.

"Counsel, please state your appearances," the clerk says.

"Neil Latham for the United States."

"Parker Stern for the defendant, Tyler Daniels." My voice sounds strong and clear, like it did the last time when I reflexively came to Lovely's aid. "Arguing today will be Lovely Diamond, third-year law student at St. Thomas More School of Law and certified to represent the defendant in this case."

"Oh, yes," the judge says, casting his murky eyes at Lovely. "Our law student. Now, where's your client?"

Lovely doesn't waver. "Your Honor, we filed a motion asking that she be excused from—"

The judge raises a hand. As Lovely and I expected, he's not pleased. He thinks for a few seconds before turning to Latham. "Any objection from the government?"

"None," Latham says.

"Why should I excuse her appearing this time, Miss Diamond?" the judge asks.

"Because this is a legal argument, Your Honor. Unlike an arraignment, there's no need for her participation. She'd play no part in these proceedings if she were here."

The judge blinks his eyes hard several times, and then writes something on a legal pad. "The defendant is excused this time. But only because this is, indeed, a legal argument. I'm not going to keep doing this."

"Thank you, Your Honor," Lovely says.

"You want me to dismiss this case," the judge says. "Tell me why I should."

She presses a couple of keys on her laptop, and the courtroom monitors flash on. There's an audible gasp from the gallery. The screens display a graphic drawing of two nude women lying on a bed, their bodies touching, their arms and legs intertwined—the cover art for de Sade's *Justine, Philosophy in the Bedroom, and Other Writings*. I interlace my fingers and squeeze hard. She didn't tell me about this because she knew I wouldn't approve.

The judge shakes his head. "Miss Diamond, I don't think—"

"Your Honor, this is the cover of a book I bought online from Amazon a few weeks ago. In one of the novels in this book—the one called "Philosophy in the Bedroom"—a fourteen-year-old girl is seduced by a woman and her brother and several other men, engages in group sex, and then willingly participates in the rape and mutilation of her own mother."

There's a shuffling in the courtroom, followed by murmurs of shock and discomfort.

"Kind of sounds like the stories on my client's Wild Cavalier website, doesn't it?" Lovely continues. "And believe me, Your Honor, this book isn't any less explicit than my client's stories. But you don't see the government prosecuting Amazon or the publisher of . . . ," she pauses for effect, "*Philosophy in the Bedroom* for obscenity. In fact, a lot of modern critics praise de Sade's book as an early example of modern existentialist philosophy. And it gets First Amendment protection, just like my client's Wild Cavalier website should."

I expect Judge Harvey to cut her off, but he leans forward, his chin resting on his hand. I thought that by taking this route, Lovely had destroyed the case. I was wrong—she's grabbed this unpredictable old man's attention.

She moves to her next slide. "This is the cover of a novel called *Under the Roofs of Paris*, by Henry Miller. He's universally acknowledged as a groundbreaking writer of modern literature. This book begins with the protagonist having sex with a child prostitute in the presence of her father-pimp and another prostitute. Again, graphic and explicit. And again, the government isn't prosecuting the publisher or Amazon for obscenity." She goes on to make similar points about acclaimed books like a *Clockwork Orange* by Anthony Burgess, *The End of Alice*, by A. M. Homes, and *The Night Listener* by Armistead Maupin. She switches to a slide with the heading *The Apprentice*. "Your Honor, this book, published in 1996—"

Before she can finish her sentence, indistinct grunts come from the back of the room, followed by a commotional clattering of metal and shuffling feet and a loud shriek. A woman stands and points at Lovely. "You're disgusting! Evil! You and your client are monsters. You'll both burn in hell." Others near her begin chanting the words "morality now" over and over.

"I'll have quiet in this courtroom," Judge Harvey says, his voice booming over the hubbub. The woman and her supporters keep shouting. He nods at a marshal and points at the instigator. "Escort that person and anyone else causing a disruption out of here."

Frantz sits with arms crossed, his lips curved up in an incipient grin. McCarthy and his colleagues stare straight ahead. Lovely glances at me, her chest heaving with each breath. I go to the lectern and place my hand over the microphone. "That outburst was McCarthy's and Frantz's handiwork."

"How do you know?"

"I just do. It means they're afraid of us. Just their being here proves that. Show them that their tactics won't work."

She shuts her eyes and nods. I return to my seat. When the marshal comes back, the judge tells Lovely to resume her argument.

"As I was saying, Your Honor, I've projected on the screen the cover of a novel called *The Apprentice*. Published in 1996. The author is a man named Lewis Libby, better known as *Scooter* Libby, once chief of staff to former Vice President Dick Cheney. Now, I won't go into great detail, but this book is full of scenes involving homoeroticism, incest, and . . . how shall I put this delicately? Let's say, descriptions of different kinds of intimate bodily fluids. One passage describes a madam putting a ten-year-old child in a cage with a bear trained to have sexual intercourse with young girls so that the girls will be frigid and not fall in love with their clients. Groups of men paid to watch this happen." She lets her words sink in. "And yet, your honor, Scooter Libby wasn't indicted. Well, at least not on obscenity charges."

The spectators who remember that Libby was convicted for obstructing justice laugh loudly, more to release the tension in the room, I think, than because of the quality of the joke.

"OK, OK," Judge Harvey says. "You've more than made your point. Please turn off the monitors now and move on to something else."

She powers down the computer and seamlessly transitions into the next part of her argument—that the difference in literary merit between the books she just mentioned and Tyler's stories not only doesn't matter in the eyes of the law, but is just one of degree. She cites the sworn statement of our expert, a dual humanities–psychology PhD, who opines that Tyler's stories have artistic, literary, and scientific merit because they explore *power dynamics in human relationships*— just like Shakespeare and Joyce Carol Oates do. From the way the judge is rocking back and forth in his chair with eyes focused on the ceiling, I'm guessing that he considers the expert's report a load of nonsense.

He stops rocking and leans forward, tapping his pen on the counter of his desk. "Your time is short, Miss Diamond. I want to hear why I shouldn't just follow *Kaplan v. California* and let this case go to a jury."

"Your Honor, the Supreme Court decided *Kaplan* in 1973. A single case decided in a bygone era shouldn't—"

"Careful," the judge says, his eyes sparkling. "It wasn't all that long ago."

There are titters in the courtroom. Lovely smiles. "I stand corrected, Your Honor. I'll put it this way. Since the early 1970s when *Kaplan* was decided, the world's changed because the Internet has changed it. Today, the ready availability of the books I just mentioned for immediate online purchase—books no less distasteful than my client's stories—proves that a democratic society *can* survive words about horrific behavior. And yes, even words glorifying the abuse of children." The fervor in her voice intensifies. "If you make Tyler Daniels go to trial, there will be a chilling effect on speech that could stifle the next Henry Miller or Anaïs Nin who would ordinarily post his or her stories on the Internet. To quote Justice William O. Douglas, 'Full and free discussion even of ideas we hate encourages the testing of our own prejudices and preconceptions. Full and free discussion keeps a society from becoming stagnant and unprepared for the stresses and strains that work to tear all civilizations apart.' The defendant respectfully requests that you dismiss the indictment. Thank you, Your Honor." She shuts her laptop cover and sits down. I stare straight ahead and nod slightly, hoping to convey that she did a masterful job. I allow myself to feel a flicker of hope that we can actually win this thing.

The judge sits with his hands steepled, considering her words. "Thank you, Miss Diamond. We'll hear from Mr. Latham, now."

Latham sidles up to the podium. He looks at the judge with a detached expression. When he speaks, his voice carries the utmost authority. "Section 1462 of the Criminal Code makes it a crime to distribute obscene matter by way of book, pamphlet, letter, writing, print, etc. So the statute itself contemplates that the pure written word can give rise to a criminal offense. As far as the issue of the statute's constitutionality, the last pronouncement on the issue is the Supreme Court's opinion in *Kaplan*, which holds that a purely written description *can* be held obscene. Your Honor, with all due respect, only the Supreme Court can overrule itself, which means that you're bound by *Kaplan* and should not dismiss the indictment. The question of obscenity is for the jury. Thank you." He sits down. His bare bones approach shows his vast experience. He's refused to play our game, instead simply reminding Cyrus Harvey that a district court judge can't countermand a ruling of the United States Supreme Court.

"Anything further from the defense?" the judge asks.

Lovely looks at me wide-eyed, unprepared for Latham's brevity. "Should . . . should I respond?" she whispers.

"You nailed your argument. There's nothing more to say."

She tells the judge that she has nothing further. Before she can sit down, the judge says, "Stay up at the podium a moment, Miss Diamond. I want to say I was hesitant to let a law student handle a case as important as this. But your argument was excellent."

Lovely smiles, but I cringe, because a compliment like that to a lawyer is usually a death sentence for her argument. Winners don't need praise.

"But I feel that I have to deny the motion," the judge continues. "I do believe that the defense has raised serious First Amendment issues worthy of consideration by a court. But not by this one. Mr. Latham is right. I simply cannot overrule a holding by the US Supreme Court."

"Very well, Your Honor," she says, her voice taut.

Even when a lawyer expects to lose a motion, the actual defeat inflicts a nearly intolerable sting. As I begin gathering up our files, I feel that sting intensely.

"Just a minute, counsel," the judge says. "Before you go, we have a housekeeping matter. Because this is a complicated legal case, I'll want ample time for everyone to prepare. Is there any objection to my entering an ends of justice continuance?" The judge has made an innocuous request. He doesn't want to rush to trial under the Speedy Trial Act before both sides are ready, so he's asking the parties to agree that the trial can be continued to a date later than the statute permits. Our side sure could use the extra time.

"No objection," Latham says.

Lovely turns to me in confusion. She doesn't know what the judge means. I stand, needing only to utter the words "no objection." As I lift myself from the chair, my throat constricts and my head begins to spin. I flail my arms, and then darkness.

CHAPTER 40

There's a buzzing noise in my head, like the kind that comes from a dying fluorescent light. I'm lying on the floor a few inches from a table leg. Lovely and the judge's courtroom deputy are kneeling beside me. So is Neal Latham. I realize what happened—I passed out from stage fright. I'm suddenly aware of that uneasy quiet that comes when a crowd of people witnesses a stranger's distress. Fighting the feeling of disorientation, I try to stand.

"Stay down, man," Latham says. "Take it easy." He puts his hand on my shoulder to restrain me.

"Listen to him, Parker," Lovely says, the color gone from her cheeks.

I shake Latham off and struggle to my feet. I look for the Assembly group. Everyone but Frantz is gone. No reason to stay once they've done their job. Frantz strokes his jaw with the tips of his thumb and fingers, as if he's watching a sickly tropical fish flounder in a waiting-room aquarium. He turns abruptly and leaves the courtroom.

"Tell the judge we stipulate to the ends of justice continuance," I whisper to Lovely.

"Parker, you—"

"Just do it."

She hesitates, but Latham turns and says, "Your Honor, Mr. Stern is OK and wants to go on the record as agreeing to the ends of justice continuance."

Once I realize that the hearing is truly over, my head clears. Out in the corridor, I tell Jonathan and Kathleen that I fainted because I haven't eaten all day. I refuse to go to the ER. When Lovely and I reach the parking lot, we decide to go to her apartment, which is only a few miles from the courthouse.

She won't let me drive. The day is still hot, even this late in the afternoon. I turn the air conditioner up full blast, the vents directed at my face. We drive down Sixth Street without speaking, the radio turned to some pop station that plays Lady Gaga and Pink. One thing I don't appreciate about Lovely is her choice of music. I glance over at her. Her jaw is set, and her hands are choking the steering wheel so hard that all the blood has pooled at the tips of her fingers. I know she wants an explanation. And maybe because she hasn't pressed me for one, I feel the need to fill up the silence with excuses.

"I've been working too hard," I say. "Not enough sleep. And like I said, I haven't eaten anything since—"

"Please spare me the horseshit. In case you don't remember, I was there when you freaked out while we were watching that old movie of yours a few days ago. Last time we were in court there were signs."

I reach over and shut off the radio. I feel as if I'm about to reveal a hidden deformity to her, one that will make her think of me as not only unmanly, but also grotesque. I take a deep breath and force out the words. "I . . . I suffer from something called glossophobia. It's fancy term for fear of public speaking."

She swerves hard to the right and parks at the curb, leaving the engine running. She waits for me to say more.

My first halting words unspool into a confession. I explain that unlike most people who suffer from the disorder, I panic only in the courtroom. I tell her how the stage fright started moments after I learned of Harmon's death, how I botched that important motion for Lake Knolls a week later because of the fear. I remind her how much Harmon meant to me, and not only as a boss. I describe the drugs and the therapy and the meditation and the biofeedback and all the other failed treatment.

"No," she says. "It can't just be about Harmon Cherry. You panicked when we were watching *Fourth Grade G-Man*."

Without replying, I flip the radio back on.

She closes her eyes for a moment and sighs. "We are all entitled to our secrets." She puts the car in drive and pulls out into traffic. We don't speak until we arrive at her apartment building. She finds a space on the street and parks at the curb. I reach for the door handle.

"Wait, Parker."

I sit back in my seat.

"Have you told Raymond Baxter about the stage fright?"

"There's no reason to."

She pounds the steering wheel with her palms. "You've got a trial starting in six weeks. How in the hell do you expect to try a case against Lou Frantz and not have to go to court?"

"It won't always be like today. You saw how I well I did last time we were here. And how we dominated McCarthy at his deposition. Frantz was the one who was on his ass."

"Even if that's true, you still have an ethical obligation to tell Raymond." She turns toward me and takes both of my hands. "You're courageous to take on the Assembly all alone. After the beating, most people would've quit. I admire you more now that you've told me how hard it is for you to . . . you know, to talk in court. It must be torture. So I hope that you'll do something else that takes courage. Call Raymond Baxter right away and tell him the truth."

"If I do that, he'll fire me. I'm the only person who—"

"Then he'll fire you. But I don't think that'll happen. No one else will take the case. Not so close to trial. Not at a discounted fee."

"Lovely, I—"

"You have to tell him." Her gray eyes, compassionate but unyielding, drill down into my conscience. I search my arsenal of argument for a reason not to tell Raymond the truth, but it's been depleted.

"OK. You're right."

She leans over and kisses me.

And then I realize how selfish I've been. "I haven't told you how terrific you were today. No one could have done a better job."

She frowns. "I lost. I was so sure that we'd win. What amazes me is that I'm not pissed off at the judge. Why aren't I pissed off?"

"Because he gave us a fair hearing. That's all you can ask."

"How will we ever get Tyler to come to trial?"

"Maybe if we both talk to her—"

"There's only one thing you can do for me. Tell Raymond the truth."

CHAPTER 41

Though I spend hours with Raymond Baxter preparing him for his deposition, I don't tell him about my stage fright. Lovely doesn't call me out on it, but at odd moments—while we work in my condo or watch a DVD or jog along the boardwalk—traces of her disappointment hover around us. I resolve to tell him as soon as we finish his deposition in a few days. I just hope that, after seeing me go toe-to-toe with Lou Frantz, he'll think twice about replacing me.

At nine o'clock on a hazy Tuesday morning in April, Raymond and I arrive at Frantz's law office. Raymond is dressed in an expensive light-gray suit, the kind he must have worn every day for forty-plus years. It's the wrong color choice, because if the judge and jury watch the video of the deposition, it'll be hard for them to tell where the suit ends and his ashen skin begins. I told him to wear navy blue or black. At least he's wearing a vibrant pink tie.

The ground floor of Frantz's building is surprisingly run down, so poorly vented that the lobby is filled with the odor of overcooked eggs and rancid bacon grease from the coffee shop. We pass a cursory security check and take the elevator to the twentieth floor. This will be my first confrontation with Frantz since I collapsed in court last week. My stomach rolls in rhythm to the elevator's shimmying. I try to convince myself that I'm experiencing the natural anxiety that precedes the start of a battle.

The elevator doors open and we exit into the lobby. We take two steps forward and stop in tandem. The sight before us is panoramic, dizzying—nothing that you'd expect after walking through the building's malodorous and nearly decrepit ground floor. I feel as though I've parked at one of those scenic viewpoints on a boring interstate highway and discovered a lush canyon. The office opens to a floor above and three floors below, each separated by a tier that overlooks a large atrium. The entire suite resembles a vast bullpen made of pink marble and glass and polished steel, with skylights and unusable empty space and offices enclosed by transparent glass. Louis Frantz had his office designed like a modern-day Panopticon, allowing him to keep tabs on his underlings by looking through the glass walls.

"This is one of Ariella Sam's buildings," Raymond says. "You can tell by the octagonal shape of the atrium." When I don't recognize the name, he tells me that she's a disciple of I. M. Pei and just as expensive.

The entire suite serves as a shrine to Lou Frantz. He doesn't share the firm name with anyone else. The walls are lined with photographs of him standing beside athletes, actors, judges, and politicians. There are several display cases filled with awards and plaques—three Trial Lawyer of the Year awards, past president of the College of Trial Lawyers of the USA, Man of the Year for his philanthropic work for numerous charities. Awards that I once aspired to. Modern art takes up the remaining wall space. I think I recognize a Kenneth Nolan and a Mark Rothko.

We check in with the receptionist and take a seat in the lobby. After a few minutes, Nick Weir comes out. Before acknowledging me, he smiles brightly and introduces himself to Raymond, as if we're here for a friendly confab rather than a contentious deposition. When the two men shake hands, Raymond's face remains grim.

Weir nods at me. "Hey, Parker. I hope you're feeling better."

"I'm feeling great."

Raymond wears a puzzled frown, but thankfully doesn't pursue the matter.

Weir leads us into a large conference room. There's a massive granite table, a Morris Louis painting hanging on the far wall, and a north-facing view of the foothills that makes you feel that you can reach out the window and touch the *H* in the Hollywood sign. The room could accommodate twenty-five people, but there will be just six of us. The court reporter and videographer, men I don't know, ask for my business card. I don't have one, of course, so I write my name on a scrap of paper.

"I'll get Lou," Weir says. "Give us a minute or two. Help yourself to some coffee or a soft drink." He motions to the credenza, on top of which are assorted carbonated drinks and an elegant silver coffee service.

Raymond reaches for a can of Squirt. "Haven't seen one of these in years. I used to love it when I was young. Didn't know they made it anymore." He sits down in his chair, pops the top, and takes a long drink. "Now, why did Weir ask after your health?"

I glance at the court reporter and videographer, ostensibly neutral, but undoubtedly Frantz partisans. "I just felt a little ill in court the other day. Nothing to worry about."

Raymond studies me for a moment. He doesn't look reassured.

Twenty minutes later, Frantz and Weir walk into the conference room. Frantz wears a white shirt and tie, but no jacket. The shirt hangs off of him and the tie falls maybe four inches below his belt, making him look like a senescent scarecrow. The man's a contradiction—his office design stands as a model of conspicuous wealth, but he dresses like a hayseed. The wardrobe must be calculated, his way of relating to jurors and other nonlawyers. He makes no pretense of cordiality, and neither do I.

"Let's get started," he barks, as though Raymond and I kept him waiting and not the other way around. "Swear the witness."

I expect Raymond to perform well. He has street smarts and years of business experience as a real estate developer. He's testified in court before. And besides, he doesn't know much that's relevant to our lawsuit. This case is all about what the Assembly knows.

Frantz starts with what in most depositions are innocuous background questions. But no question is harmless coming from him. He turns out to be a master of distortion. An explainable ambiguity in Raymond's educational background becomes an inflated credential. Two ancient lawsuits filed in the 1970s—legitimate business disputes—brand Raymond a slumlord. Raymond's every pause and stutter, understandable for a man in his late seventies under this kind of stress, become indicators of perjury. Legend has it that Frantz can make the most honest and articulate witness look like a liar. It turns out that the legend is true.

I do my best to protect my client. I object frequently and insist on breaks and raise my voice and make caustic comments about Frantz's abusive style of interrogation. I interrupt Raymond's answers so I can coach him, a tactic that crosses the line of propriety. It's all to no avail. The pummeling gets so bad that Raymond's normally ashen pallor gives way to scarlet patches on his face and neck, his forehead so red at one point that I become worried about his health. He hunches his shoulders, and his already sunken eye sockets deepen further. By mid-morning, he looks defeated. I call for a break, but when we resume, Frantz continues the battering without a scintilla of conscience. I truly believe that Frantz wants to give Raymond a stroke.

After several hours of what feels like a bloodbath, I take stock of the morning's events. As effective as Frantz has been, it's all been rhetoric and sleight-of-hand. Raymond hasn't uttered one word that will hurt us. So in the final analysis, he remains the grieving father who's outlived his child, automatically sympathetic to a judge or jury.

At one o'clock, I suggest that we break for lunch.

"I just have a couple more questions," Frantz says. "So, let me finish and we'll get you out of here."

I look at Raymond. He takes a deep breath and nods wearily.

"Please make it quick," I say. "My client deserves a break."

Frantz throws me a sidelong glance of displeasure and asks, "Mr. Baxter, in the last year, have you been in touch with someone named Grace Trimble?"

"I have not spoken to that woman," Raymond says.

Frantz glances at Weir for effect, folds his hands on the table, and leans in. "Have you had any communications at all—e-mail, letter, telephone, face-to-face—with a woman named Sandra Casey?"

Fighting to remain impassive, I bite the inside of my cheek so hard that I draw blood. I take a sip of water to rinse out the metallic taste.

"Never spoke with anyone by the name of Sandra Casey," Raymond says.

Raymond's answer makes no difference to Frantz. He's asked the question solely for my benefit. He wants to communicate that the Assembly knows that I'm looking for Grace. He waited until the end of the deposition so he could ambush me the way I ambushed McCarthy.

"No further questions," Frantz says tersely. Without a word of goodbye, he and Weir stand up and leave the room. They don't bother to collect their documents. Frantz has employees for that.

Frantz might not have any more questions, but I do. How does the Assembly know that I'm looking for Grace Trimble? Did they really uncover the same treasure trove of epiphanies that I did—Dale Garner's photos of Baxter's hookers, the discovery that there was only one woman, Markowitz's picture of the dealership softball team, the realization that Sandra and Grace are one in the same? Doubtful. We gave Frantz copies of Dale Garner's photos, but not the clearer ones that showed the tattoo. The enhancements are confidential attorney work product, created by Jonathan's client and our consultant, computer hacker Dmitri Samoiloff. I don't think the Assembly could enhance the photos the way Dmitri did. With all the Assembly's resources, when it comes to technology, I'll stake my money on a Ukrainian hacker.

Alan Markowitz couldn't have told the Assembly that Sandra Casey is Grace—I kept that information from him. Besides, he hates the Assembly because of their pro-Palestinian stance.

Monica Baxter? Unlikely. She knows that Grace is the Outsider, but I never said the name *Sandra Casey* to her. And as devoutly as she believes in the Assembly, her maternal instincts are stronger, and to protect her son she needs me to exonerate Rich and show that he was murdered.

This leaves one more possible source for the leak, one that I don't want to consider.

Raymond and I get our cars and drive over to the Lansing Bar and Grill, the restaurant where we had our first meeting shortly after Rich died. It's dark inside, and even though it's the height of the lunch hour, the place is only half full. When the waitress takes our drink orders, I ask for an Arnold Palmer. Raymond orders a Dewar's.

"I know it's early in the day for liquor, but I need to unwind," he says, his voice creaky with a combination of age and fatigue. "That Frantz is one mean son of a bitch." He pulls an old-fashioned cotton handkerchief out of his pocket and wipes his brow. "So, how did I do?"

"You did great." It's a fib that I hope he'll believe. "Frantz didn't get anything remotely useful."

The waitress brings us our drinks and takes our orders. I wait until he has a couple of sips of scotch. I try to sound matter-of-fact, but my voice is stilted. "There's something I need to discuss with you."

"Fire away."

I glance at his scotch, wishing I'd ordered one myself—a double. I launch into the history of my glossophobia, starting with Harmon Cherry's death and ending with my fainting in court last week. I talk about my attempts to cure the fear with medication and therapy and describe how well I did in my first appearance before Judge Harvey. I try to sound positive about the future.

His face has folded in on itself. His rheumy eyes swim with disappointment. "I don't understand. You gave as good as you got with Frantz today. And I read the McCarthy deposition transcript. You creamed him. I saw nothing that would—"

"It only happens in court. Nowhere else."

He swallows his scotch in one swig. A seasoned drinker, he doesn't flinch. His eyes, just moments ago murky with fatigue, now scrutinize me with incisive clarity. "I have one question and one question only."

I expect him to ask how I can possibly defend him at the trial next month when I can't even stay conscious in court. I'm prepared for that one, ready to talk about my drive and my past triumphs and my will to win. But he asks a different question.

"Before you agreed to go into court to represent my son last fall in the fight of his life, did you tell him about your . . . your so-called *condition*?" He enunciates this last word the way an Assembly devotee would say the phrase *mental illness*.

"When Rich hired me, I had no intention of—"

"No intention of what? Of seeing your representation of him

through once you satisfied your curiosity? And yet you still walked into that courtroom the very day they found him hanging from a pipe in that hellhole of a jail." He drinks from his glass even though it's empty, then holds it up and looks around for the waitress. When he can't catch her eye, he slams the glass down in disgust. "So, tell me, Stern. Were you scared when you went up in front of the judge the day they murdered my son?"

That afternoon remains vivid. The fear so paralyzed me that I couldn't say my name. "Yeah. I was scared."

He retrieves his handkerchief and swipes at his mouth hard with it several times. When he speaks, his voice is made powerful by spite. "You know your trouble? You're one of those people who think the world is one big boxing ring for you to fight your battles in. As far as you're concerned, this case hasn't been about Rich or me at all. You've always felt that *you* were the client and I was just a pawn in your match against the Assembly. In fact, I think that Richie's death was just an excuse for you to file."

"That's not fair, Raymond."

"Isn't it? I knew you had a hard-on for those Assembly people for some reason, which was fine. I thought that would make you a better advocate for my side. But you're not better, are you? You're scared shitless."

"If you just give me a chance to—"

He sets both fists on the seat of his chair and uses his arms as levers to hoist himself up, teetering at the top like older people do when they suffer from poor equilibrium. He turns and shuffles away.

"What're you going to do?" I call after him, but my words are drowned out by the suddenly loud volume of the patrons' voices and the clanking of dinnerware. I watch him walk out the door.

I sit at the table sipping my drink, one of those rare times when I don't try to formulate a strategy. A minute later, the waitress brings our food. The heavy smell of charred ground beef turns my stomach. Or maybe it's not the burgers at all. Maybe what's making me sick is my own shame.

CHAPTER 42

In the ensuing weeks, I take the depositions of FBI agents and accounting experts and the employees of the federal detention center who found Rich's body. I depose the medical examiner who performed Rich's autopsy, not asking him about the fractured hyoid bone. I'm saving that for trial. I haven't hired my own pathologist—I don't want Frantz to learn through a deposition that the ME made a mistake.

Two witnesses keep ducking me—Congressman Lake Knolls and his chief aide, Delwyn Bennett. They're in from Washington, DC this week, so a couple of days ago I called Knolls's secretary and told her that if I didn't get in to see them within forty-eight hours, I'd serve deposition subpoenas and take my case to the media. The secretary called back an hour later and set up a meeting for today.

I drive through a dense fog, the precursor of a smoggy afternoon. At ten o'clock, I arrive at the Westwood office building where Knolls maintains his headquarters. I take the elevator to the sixth floor, where the doors divide to reveal a drab waiting room and a bored receptionist. On the back wall hangs the Great Seal of the United States, under which the words *Representative Lake Knolls, 54th District* appear in bronze lettering. A marshal dressed in a blue blazer and khaki pants stands near the corridor with hands folded in front of him, a two-way headset in his left ear, a service revolver visible under his coat.

At a quarter past ten, the receptionist calls my name and leads me down a long corridor and into an office overlooking Bel-Air and the Santa Monica Mountains. Knolls sits behind a desk reading a document, or pretending to. He remains the leading man despite the wrinkles near his mouth and at the corners of his eyes. His hair is still dark brown, except for a few strategically placed gray streaks, the purpose of which is to fend off allegations of vanity. His high, almost bulging forehead gives an impression of intelligence that I'm not sure he really has. On screen, he seemed to have the ability to change the hue of his eyes, sometimes to a cobalt blue that conveyed raw power, other times almost to a turquoise that gave him a sense of masculine vulnerability. Now, they're cobalt blue.

Delwyn Bennett stands peering over Knolls's shoulder. He's tall and thin, with fair skin, a Roman nose, and long delicate fingers. Intelligent brown eyes. Both men are impeccably groomed and both wear expensive suits. The scene feels badly staged, kind of how I remember the first day of filming on that awful movie that Knolls and I starred in together.

Knolls glances up, stands, and smiling broadly walks around the desk to greet me. At five feet eleven, he's got only an inch on me, but his imperial posture makes him look taller. He reaches out and shakes my hand with a politician's pump, placing his left hand on my forearm. "Well, well. Parker Stern from Harmon's firm. Long time." His powerful voice resonates even in this acoustically challenged government office. He acts as if he's genuinely glad to see me, though I know he isn't. He's an excellent actor and politician, but an elusive human being. He doesn't bother to introduce me to Bennett.

He motions for me to have a seat and then sits back down behind his desk. In a tone that sounds as if he's reminiscing with a fraternity brother about their misspent college days, he says, "You know, Parker, you really hung me out to dry with that sorry performance of yours in the *Repulsion* lawsuit. After I replaced you, I ended up settling that case for several million more than I could have before you dragged me down with a loss in court. The new lawyers recommended I sue you and your firm for malpractice. If it hadn't been for my political campaign and my great affection for Harmon, I would have." He's still smiling. Harmon Cherry warned me years ago that Knolls has a unique ability to disarm and intimidate by coating serious accusations in sugary tones.

"You would've lost, Lake," I say in an equally flippant voice. "And if you paid that much to settle, it was your new lawyers who gave you bad advice, not me. We only lost the opening round. I don't quit after one round. If you would've stayed with the law firm, I would've taken the case to trial and won it for you in front of a jury."

"And now you want to talk to me about some lawsuit involving the Church of the Sanctified Assembly."

"I have reason to believe that the Assembly has paid you or your chief of staff half a million dollars. Unreported." I shouldn't let on that I know this, but I have no choice. It's the only way to convince Knolls that I have some real dirt on him.

"That's absurd, not to mention defamatory," Bennett says. His voice is tinny, like two empty soup cans clanking into each other. "The Assembly has poured millions into campaigns to defeat the congressman. I'm sure you know that. And we also believe you have a conflict of interest because you once were the congressman's attorney."

"I'm not here to talk to you," I say. "I'm here to talk to Lake." I turn to Knolls. "To set your mind at ease, there's no conflict because I never represented you on anything that had to do with my case against the Assembly. And there's no conflict because you and I aren't adversaries." I wait a beat. "We're not adversaries, are we, Lake? Because the news media would be very interested in hearing that you're taking the Assembly's side in my lawsuit. Especially with a highly publicized trial about to start in a couple of weeks."

My threat isn't lost on him. "No. We are not adversaries. How can I help you?"

"But I'm not so sure that Delwyn and I aren't adversaries." I glance at Bennett. "It's OK if I call you Delwyn, isn't it?"

"*Mr. Bennett* is my chief of staff and his interests are aligned with mine," Knolls says. "Now, tell me what you think this is about so I can ease your mind and move on to other things. Like passing the nation's laws."

"I represent the estate of Richard Baxter. You might remember him as a corporate lawyer at the law firm."

"I do remember him. I'm told that he was found hanging in a jail cell some months ago. Killed himself just like his mentor did, ironically."

"How Rich and Harmon died is open to question."

Knolls arches one brow, a signature mannerism in his movies.

"Rich represented the Assembly after the firm broke up," I say. "On May 2, 2011, after a series of money laundering transactions, six million dollars of Assembly money was paid out by a company called The Emery Group. No one knows who got the money. As I'm sure you know, the Assembly has sued Baxter's estate, accusing Rich of embezzling that money. But it's not true. I want to know where that money really went."

"And what does any of this have to do with me?" Knolls asks.

"On the same day and from the same bank account, The Emery Group paid your chief of staff here half a million dollars."

"There was no such payment," Knolls says.

"Christopher McCarthy of the Assembly's TCO wing was the signatory on the account out of which the money was transferred. You know him, don't you Delwyn?"

Bennett folds his arm across his chest. "I have no idea what you're talking about." His eyes are impassive, almost lifeless. I used to see Assembly types visiting my law firm, dressed in their Brooks Brothers suits, all with the same automatous expression on their faces.

"I'd like to speak to you privately, Lake," I say.

Knolls breathes from the diaphragm, an actor's technique of calming himself down. "That's not going to happen. I have a busy schedule, and I'm losing patience with your nonsense."

"I'm afraid I'll have to insist."

Knolls puffs out his chest. "You've overstepped your bounds. But you've done that before, haven't you? Now, get out before I have Del call the marshal."

"Hey, Lake, do you ever see Billy N. these days?"

Knolls sputters, but nothing comes out.

"Billy *Ness* was his full name, remember? Claimed to be a distant relative of Elliot Ness, the guy from *The Untouchables*?"

In the 1980s, William Ness sold coke, weed, Quaaludes, and more exotic drugs to half the people in Hollywood. He also furnished women, men, boys, girls, or all of the above, depending on kink or sexual preference. People called him The Tinsel Town Pusher. Although there was gossip at the margins during Knolls's election campaign about possible drug use and sexual peccadilloes, there were never any witnesses or specifics. I could be a witness; I could give specifics.

"Leave us alone, Del," Knolls says to Bennett, who was in the process of picking up the phone, but now freezes.

"But—"

"I said, get out!"

Bennett reacts as though his beloved parent has just slapped him in the face. But he sets his jaw and walks out with his nose in the air, his pomposity still intact.

Knolls leans forward, his forearms resting on the desk. There's fear in his eyes, the startled-animal kind, and that makes him dangerous. "Who the hell are you?"

"Billy N. supplied my mother with drugs, too. You might remember her. Harriet Stern? I believe the two of you got high and slept together when we were on location shooting *Fourth Grade G-Man*. A movie we'd both like to forget."

He looks at me as if he's seeing me for the first time. He slowly shakes that head. "You can't be that kid in that awful picture. You don't look anything like him."

"I was Parky Gerald."

"Why didn't you say anything when we met at the law firm?"

"I had no interest in that old life. I still don't. The only thing I'm interested in is finding out why the Assembly paid your chief of staff half a million dollars and where the other six million went."

He lowers his head and shuts one eye, as though lining me up in his gun sights. Every move he makes is expressive, wonderful to watch. "Billy Ness is dead, you know. Shot many years ago in some drug deal gone bad in a house up in Laurel Canyon. A messy, vindictive business. His murder was probably the best thing that ever happened to my political career. He'd have sold his soul to the tabloids."

"Are you threatening me, Lake?"

"Didn't you just threaten me?"

"I'm not interested in hurting your career. But I will subpoena you and question you under oath about your relationship with the Assembly."

"You do what you have to do. I'll resist the subpoena in court for as long as I can. And if I do have to testify eventually, you won't get what you want from me. You see, you only know about my past. The Assembly controls my future. I'm far more concerned about them than I am about you."

I fight not to squirm in my chair. A sitting member of Congress, a man who seems destined for even higher office, has just admitted that he's beholden to the Church of the Sanctified Assembly—or even worse, an Assembly member. "Stay cool even when they strike you squarely in the jaw," Harmon would say. "Then at least tell me whether Rich was involved."

He shakes his head. "We're done."

I read his expression. There's no chance of getting him to cooperate. I stand up to leave.

"Wait a moment, Parker." His tone has softened. "I was wondering . . . how's Harriet? I do remember her, of course. She was really quite something."

"Expect a subpoena," I say. "The trial begins in two weeks."

CHAPTER 43

I arrive at court at seven thirty in the morning, though trial won't start until nine. Unlike the more exalted federal court where the Tyler Daniels case is pending, this is LA Superior, where the more routine personal injury and landlord tenant and marital dissolution cases go forward. While the federal court retains some character and gravitas despite its age, this building reminds me of a dilapidated self-storage facility.

The courtroom doors usually stay locked until eight thirty, but yesterday I arranged with the judge's clerk to have them opened early. I use the time to try and soak up the dated atmosphere of the room. I want to get reacquainted with the tinny rattle of the ventilation system, with the stagnant air, with the uncomfortable wooden chairs set aside for the attorneys. I want to lay out my pens and legal pads, to arrange the black vinyl notebooks containing the trial exhibits, to plug in my laptop computer and watch it boot up, to rub my hand over the dark mahogany attorney table. I want to schmooze the clerk and the court reporter, stand behind the lectern, scout out the jury box. I try to focus on the events that lie ahead—the cattle call of prospective jurors; the judge's explanation of the case; *voir dire*, the prelude to jury selection; and the lawyers' opening statements.

Before I left my condo this morning, I popped a Xanax and a Valium without even checking for adverse interactions. But still, my mouth is dry, and I can feel the droplets of perspiration forming on my upper lip, which I keep wiping with a paper towel from the courthouse men's room. Despite these symptoms, I still hold out a faint hope that the pills will blunt enough of the fear for me to communicate. Right now, all they're doing is producing an ever-thickening glaze between me and reality. I have to make a conscious effort to accomplish the most reflexive tasks, like picking up a legal pad or turning the page of a document. Sometimes I have to remind myself to breathe.

At eight fifteen, the rest of the world starts trickling in. Lovely, Jonathan, and Kathleen escort a dour Raymond Baxter into the courtroom. Since I told him about my stage fright, he'll speak to me only when it's absolutely necessary to prepare our defense. He's made no secret of his desire to hire another attorney, but no one else is foolhardy enough to step into a hopeless case against the Assembly and Frantz on the eve of trial. During our phone conversation last night, I impressed upon Raymond how critical it is that the jurors not perceive the tension between us. Yet as soon as he sits down, he swivels his chair so that his back is toward me.

The students begin unpacking and organizing our trial exhibits. This is the last week of school, but they're all cutting classes. I urged them to work shifts so that they'll have enough time to study for finals and the bar exam, but they all insist on attending the whole trial.

"The luxury of being second-semester 3Ls," Kathleen said.

"We're taking a trial advocacy class, and this is a trial," Jonathan said. "Anyway, it's only for a week or two."

We don't have to work out courtroom logistics. Everyone assumes that Lovely will sit on the other side of Raymond at the defense table and that Kathleen and Jonathan will sit behind us on the bench reserved for younger lawyers and paralegals.

Lou Frantz enters the courtroom with his team—a swaggering Nick Weir; a younger female attorney whose name I don't know, undoubtedly responsible for legal research; and a case assistant, a young man appearing uncomfortable in his tight suit, who'll keep track of the exhibits and just generally carry his bosses' bags. The woman waves to Lovely, who nods in reply. They set up on their side of the room, moving like a precision drill team on its home turf.

Moments later, Christopher McCarthy arrives with his Assembly functionaries, their facial expressions as starched as their clothing.

With little time to spare, Deanna Poulos hurries inside. She's dressed in a white blouse and navy blue skirt and looking unhappy about it. She and I agreed last night that she'll sit in the gallery unless I need her help. If I manage to muddle through this first day, tomorrow she'll go back to running her coffee house.

Five minutes later, Manny Mason walks in. To my surprise, he's with Andrew Macklin. Standing beside Manny, the five foot five Macklin looks more like a cartoon gnome than ever.

In the final moments before a trial, everything is frenzied, and yet it feels as though the trial will never begin. But it does.

"All rise," the clerk says, and I flinch.

Judge Valerie Schadlow takes the bench. A petite woman in her early fifties, she has a sparrow's face and short straight hair, which she colors light brown. Her cream tortoiseshell glasses are too large for her face. She's attractive in a perennially cute sort of way, a look that must have hindered her when she started out, especially with older male lawyers and judges. Her ascent to this lofty position shows how tough and competent she is. She's a recent appointee, a former partner in the labor and employment department of a large downtown firm. Word is that she's smart but unsure of herself.

"The Church of the Sanctified Assembly versus the Estate of Baxter," Schadlow says. "Counsel, state your appearances." Her voice, too, is birdlike—not the expected voice of a judicial officer.

Frantz stands. "Louis Frantz for the Church of the Sanctified Assembly."

"The great Lou Frantz," the judge says, beaming. "When was the last time?"

The vast majority of lawyers want to impress judges. With Frantz, it's the other way around, even at the expense of propriety. Such is his power in the legal profession.

"We shared a table at that California Business Trial Lawyers Association soiree last December when they gave me their lawyer of the decade award," he says. "The Biltmore."

"Right, The Biltmore," Schadlow says.

Raymond clears his throat, and Lovely shuffles her feet under the desk.

When the judge looks at me, her smile is gone. I lift myself inches off my chair, only pretending to stand, because I don't dare test the stability of my legs. "Parker Stern for the defendant." My voice isn't much louder than a whisper, but at least I can say my name. The drugs have enabled me to do that much. I hear Lovely exhale. Raymond just stares straight ahead, his gnarled hands clasped on the table.

"Bailiff, bring the prospective jurors up," Judge Schadlow says.

The prospective jurors file in ten minutes later, sitting both in the jury box and the first three rows of the gallery, which have been kept empty for them. There are fifty people, twelve of whom will be chosen. Because this is a civil case, the verdict doesn't have to be unanimous. The side that can convince nine of twelve will win. Jurors draw conclusions the moment they walk into the courtroom, so in front of the jury pool, I become self-conscious of my every move—my posture, the way I hold my pen, the direction of my gaze. Stage business, props, and costumes are my concern. I'm an actor again.

Judge Schadlow tells the panel what the lawsuit is about. This is by far the largest trial she's had during her short tenure on the bench, and it shows—she reads too quickly and her voice quavers. The most important instruction she gives is that the Assembly, as the plaintiff, has the burden of proof by the preponderance of the evidence, meaning they win only if they prove their case by a fraction over fifty percent. It's not a hard burden to meet—nothing like the *beyond a reasonable doubt* standard in a criminal trial—but it's something.

During voir dire, the judge will first ask the prospective jurors basic questions and then Frantz and I will interrogate the jurors in more detail. The judge starts by asking whether anyone will suffer personal or financial hardship if they have to serve on the jury. Her voice is so high-pitched that, upon first hearing it, a few of the venire members titter. They soon learn that while her voice might seem weak, the judge isn't. Many of the prospective jurors claim hardship and ask to be excused. Schadlow tersely rebuffs them all.

She then inquires about the panelists' backgrounds, jobs, families, and hobbies to see if they have biases that require disqualification for cause. She asks each juror whether they're affiliated with the Church of the Sanctified Assembly. None of them are, or so they claim. If, like

Lou Frantz, I were still a high-powered lawyer with a wealthy client, I'd have hired a jury consultant and a private investigator to ensure that an Assembly mole doesn't get on the jury. But now I have only my gut reaction to go on. Most important to me is religious affiliation—though we can't ask about it directly, some jurors give hints when discussing their background. Foremost, I'm looking for jurors who are devout adherents of mainstream religions. People like that will probably mistrust the Assembly and dislike what it stands for. As a second choice, I want the exact opposite—jurors who distrust religion, who'll view the Assembly as a predatory cult. So I'm looking for zealots and atheists and trying to avoid the in-between. Other than that, I don't have a demographic preference—no juror, no matter what the age, race, or income, will sympathize with an alleged crooked lawyer, even a dead one.

Judge Schadlow excuses three jurors who say they've read unflattering things about the Assembly. One woman announces that she's sure the Assembly is a demonic cult bent on taking over the government. She won't be a juror, of course, but I'm grateful to her. If I were to say something like that, I'd land in jail for contempt.

Each time a panel member finishes answering one of the judge's questions, I check with Raymond. He never ventures an opinion on whether he approves of the person or not, but I don't care. My consulting with him is for show, to lead the prospective jurors to believe that he and I are working together in his defense.

When Schadlow runs out of questions, it's Frantz's turn. I brace myself. I wish we were in federal court, where the judges handle all the voir dire themselves. An artful lawyer like Frantz can frame questions that seem innocent but that can pollute the jury pool. And that's exactly what he does, asking the prospective jurors to raise their hands if they believe that freedom of religion is an important right guaranteed by the founding fathers, and getting them to agree that a large institution like the Assembly has the right to a fair trial even against an individual like Raymond Baxter. He gets several panel members to promise to put aside any reservations they might have about the Assembly's beliefs. I don't object to any of this, because I worry I won't sound articulate. But when he asks an elderly man if he agrees that a lawyer who steals from a client should be punished, my outrage trumps my fear.

"Objection, Your Honor. That's argument, not voir dire." I sound whiney, but to my relief, Schadlow sustains the objection. She goes out of her way to instruct the prospective jurors that they may not consider the lawyers' questions in deciding the case. She admonishes Frantz in a curt tone that he can't ask questions that go to the merits of the lawsuit. It turns out that she's not a pushover for Frantz after all.

When my turn to ask questions comes, for a moment I consider passing. I'm light-headed and drenched in sweat. But Raymond and Lovely are looking at me expectantly, and Frantz is smirking, daring me to get up and try to speak in court. I stand on wobbly legs and say, "Is there anyone here who doesn't understand the judge's instruction that the Church of the Sanctified Assembly has the burden of proof by the preponderance of the evidence?" My voice is weak and thin. I sound nothing like the lawyer I was two year ago. But I've discovered something important—my phobia doesn't stop me from asking questions. I think I know why. Courtroom argument, like acting, is about exposing yourself to an audience. But you can hide behind questions.

After a few hours, we've picked a jury of five men and seven women. There are two Asians, two African-Americans, three Latinos, and a newly naturalized citizen from Lebanon. There's a retired financial manager, a twice-divorced waitress, two college students, a nerdy website designer, a health care consultant, a construction manager, an ex-school teacher who's active in Catholic charities, a personal assistant at a talent agency, a legal secretary, a screenwriter, and a housewife. There are three alternates to whom I'll pay little attention unless and until one of the first twelve drops off the panel. I'm happy with the ex-school teacher because of her religious work, the health care consultant because she sings in her church choir, and the financial manager because he seems like a political liberal who'll recoil at the Assembly's beliefs. Though I shouldn't, I like the website designer because he reminds me of Jonathan Borzo. I'm leery of the waitress and the personal assistant, who are younger and edgier and might feel an affinity for the Assembly's mysticism, and the writer because he's the kind of person the Assembly most wants to attract. I don't know about the others.

—⁓—

After the lunch break, during which I order only a cup of coffee to wash down a Valium, we go back into the courtroom. The jury is already in the box. The judge takes the bench and tersely announces, "The attorneys will now give their opening statements. We'll hear from plaintiff's counsel first. Please remember that the attorneys' opening is an outline of the party's case and not evidence."

I breathe deeply, waiting for Frantz to start. Throughout his opening, I'll have to seem unfazed by any attack that he mounts against Rich Baxter. I'll make sure not to clasp my hands too tightly, or fiddle with the cap of my pen, or stretch my neck, or do anything that might show anxiety. I'll allow myself one nervous outlet—pressing my left big toe into the sole of my shoe. The jury can't see inside my shoe.

Frantz rises to full height, leaving his coat unbuttoned to keep that disheveled look he so enjoys cultivating. His brow is knit, his eyes solemn. Like the legendary trial lawyers, he doesn't use notes. Although I'm sure he knows his opening by memory, he sounds as if he's having a casual conversation with the jury. He's a storyteller, and now he recounts the story of how a greedy Richard Baxter, the Assembly's trusted counselor and supposed devotee, betrayed client and church by stealing millions of dollars, all to pay for prostitutes and crystal meth and a lavish secret life. Through a flashy PowerPoint presentation, he describes in meticulous detail the illegal bank transfers that supposedly all lead back to Rich. Somehow, he makes these opaque transactions seem both straightforward and undeniably illicit by first grossly over-simplifying them, and then using his misleadingly simplistic conclu-sions to prove that only Rich could have set this Byzantine scheme in motion. Next, he hammers away at the phony passport and the cash and the drugs found in the Silver Lake apartment.

Opening statements, they say, must only recount facts, not make argument. But all experienced trial lawyers know that this legalistic ideal is a fantasy. Every great lawyer strives to make his opening statement a riveting drama that will draw in even those jurors with the shortest attention spans. So far, Frantz has constructed a perfect narrative, and he's delivered it masterfully. What makes him brilliant is that he sounds like he believes every word he says.

He concludes, "Like most common thieves, Richard Baxter got caught. Instead of facing justice, what did he do? He took the coward's way out and hanged himself. He killed himself on the day of his arraignment, the very day he was going to answer for his crimes. Ladies and gentlemen, Richard Baxter's suicide is the single most important piece of evidence in this case. Innocent men don't kill themselves. Please remember that when you listen to the evidence, and later at the end of trial when I ask you to deliver a plaintiff's verdict in the sum of seventeen million dollars." He half bows and sits down.

I fight the urge to smile. Frantz has unwittingly made Rich's death the centerpiece of his case. I'll destroy his theory when I prove that the presence of a fractured hyoid bone means that Rich was murdered.

"Counsel for defendants will now give his opening statement," Judge Schadlow says.

I stand, ready to present the opening that I've worked on for weeks, the one that promises to tell the jury how Rich was framed. But I can't speak. As if my body is mocking me, my mouth and throat are parched, while the rest of me is drenched in flop sweat.

"Are you all right, Mr. Stern?" the judge asks.

"Your Honor, I . . ." The words come out as an adolescent crackle. There are titters in the courtroom. I'm sure everyone knows about my problem by now. I take two deep breaths and say, "Pursuant to section 607 of the Code of Civil Procedure, the defense will defer opening statement until after the plaintiff has produced its evidence."

Schadlow's eyes widen in disbelief. "Pardon me, counsel?"

"We'll defer opening."

She starts to say something else, but thinks better of it. At the plaintiff's table, Nick Weir snickers.

Lovely and Raymond both visibly stiffen. There's a shuffling behind me, and I turn to see a concerned Deanna making her way up the aisle. I hold up a trembling hand. She hesitates, half-shrugs, and goes back to her seat.

According to the Code of Civil Procedure, the defense can either give its opening statement immediately after the plaintiff does, or defer until after the plaintiff puts on its witnesses. In actual fact, though, no good defense lawyer ever defers, especially in a civil case, where the plaintiff's burden of proof is so low. The statistical surveys say that most cases are won or lost by the time opening statements are over, and that's when they occur back-to-back. By letting Frantz pile on the evidence before I utter a word in my clients' defense, I'm almost guaranteeing a loss—if you believe the statistical surveys. Harmon Cherry didn't. Anyway, I couldn't get through an opening no matter how hard I tried.

"Call your first witness, Mr. Frantz," Schadlow says.

Frantz stands and mugs for the jury. "Your Honor, we, as I think you did, anticipated that Mr. Stern would give his opening today and that we'd start with the witnesses tomorrow. We're not ready to proceed with testimony. I'd suggest a recess until tomorrow."

I'm sure he's lying. Pretrial, Schadlow ordered both parties to have their witnesses ready so there would be no lost trial time. But Frantz doesn't want to call a witness. He wants a recess so the jurors will go home with his powerful opening resounding in their memories, with his accusations against Rich Baxter standing unrebutted. I should object, should insist that he call a witness, but I can't.

"You should've been ready, counsel," Schadlow says impatiently. "It's only three thirty. But hearing no objection from Mr. Stern, we'll recess until nine o'clock tomorrow morning."

We all rise and remain standing until the judge and jurors exit the courtroom. Frantz and his entourage quickly pack up and leave, followed by a crowd of reporters anxious to speak with the legendary trial lawyer. After Lovely and I arrange to meet at my condo at five thirty to work on tomorrow's cross-examination, she joins Kathleen and Jonathan, who are packing up our documents.

Moments later, Andrew Macklin, followed by Deanna and Manny, approach me and usher me to a corner of the courtroom out of Raymond's hearing.

"Deanna and Manny told me what's going on with you," Macklin says.

When I look at them, they both avert their eyes. I feel my cheeks burn.

"Just listen to Andrew," Deanna says.

"You can't wait on the opening statement," Macklin says. "It'll destroy your case. You might as well default and get it over with."

"Manny and I have been talking," Deanna says. "Let me do the opening tomorrow morning. We'll work through the night and I'll get up to speed. Andrew's volunteered to help. You can ask to see the judge tomorrow and tell her about the phobia. I had a case against her about five years ago. I know it doesn't seem like it now, but she's reasonable, a decent person. She'll understand."

"I'd lose all credibility with the jury if you did the argument," I say. "You'd be lead counsel, not me. Besides, there's no way you can learn the facts in one night."

"Deanna and I will split the argument up if we have to," Manny says. "She can cover the basic facts and the medical issues and I'll handle the financial evidence. Under the circumstances, I'm sure the judge will let us split up the opening."

"Thank you all for your concern, but no. This is my case to try."

"Parker, please be reasonable," Macklin says. "You've got a client to protect. Do the prudent thing. The honorable thing." He puts his hand on my shoulder, trying to play a paternal role, something he was never good at.

I remove his hand from my shoulder. "The only way Raymond Baxter wins this case is if I try it. All of it. That's the honorable thing."

Macklin takes a step back. "You're still the same ungrateful, arrogant son of a bitch you always were. Except now, you can't back it up." He turns on his heels and walks out. Manny and Deanna look at each other and shake their heads.

"He was only trying to help," Manny says.

"I don't want his help. I'll get through this."

"I'll be at the shop if you change your mind," Deanna says.

"And I'll be at school or at home," Manny says. "I'll leave my cell phone on. Don't hesitate to call me no matter how late."

When Raymond and I are alone, I start to talk to him about the day's events, but he holds up his hand and leans in very close. His breathing is labored; his breath smells like sour coffee. "Rest assured, Stern, that if you botch this case, I will sue you for malpractice. I've talked to plenty of lawyers who'll take *that* case." Before I can reply, he turns and shuffles out of the courtroom.

CHAPTER 44

When I arrive home from court, there's a package on my doorstep. It has a neatly printed mailing label and a plain brown wrapper. I can't imagine how it got here—all deliveries are supposed to be left with the security guard.

I go inside and open the package. There's a DVD inside with the title *Raunchy Co-ed Orgies, Vol. 3*. The picture on the cover is an overhead shot of what at first looks like a serpentine cord of bare flesh, a kind of Photoshopped expressionism that doesn't have a recognizable shape or substance. Then I realize that the photo depicts a dozen or more people engaging in group sex on mats spread out on the floor of a warehouse. One of the performers has been circled with a blue marking pen. She's thrown her head back in ecstasy, which has caused her to look directly into the camera lens. She has her hand wrapped around an erect penis, while another penetrates her from behind.

Lovely Diamond. Much younger, but unmistakable.

I feel as if my brain's neurons have been riffled like a deck of cards. I flip the DVD over to the back cover, not to see more pictures, but to check the copyright date, as if that matters. And yet at the moment, it seems vitally important. I have to squint to make out the fine print. I pore through the legalese that in our world accompanies even prefab sexual fantasy—*FBI warning: unauthorized reproduction is prohibited.* And another legal disclosure—*All models are over eighteen.* Is that what she was—a model? In what sense? As some standard to be imitated? Hardly. As someone who poses for an artist? There's no art here. As a representative of something? Maybe so. The video was shot in 2001, when she was eighteen or nineteen. So this was her job in the entertainment industry before she entered college.

I take the DVD out of its package, load it into the player, and hit the play button. I don't take my eyes off the screen for the next hour and twenty-seven minutes, during which Lovely has sex with multiple partners, both male and female. At one point, she simultaneously engages in oral, vaginal, and anal sex with three men. At another, she and seven other women connect to form a writhing circle, each receiving oral sex from one person and performing it on another. Near the end of the video, several men in succession ejaculate into her mouth, after which she swallows their collected semen and smiles for the camera.

The dehumanization is calculated. Factory porn, with the performers merely robotic workers on an assembly line. Even the setting, a shabby warehouse with unpainted drywall and no furnishings except gray floor mats, is barren.

I sit on the edge of the sofa and stare at the wall. Lovely defiled herself, enjoyed defiling herself. She's slept with many men after that, and probably women, too. We've had unprotected sex since the first time. And I recognize in the video some of the same techniques that she uses when she and I are making love. I've mistaken prepackaged erotic choreography for love and passion.

I pick up the DVD box and walk out onto the balcony, hoping the air will be purer outside. A fulvous layer of smog hangs over the ocean, locked in place by a lid of hot, stagnant air. I stand at the ledge and stare out at the horizon.

Because Lovely's been spending a lot of time at my condo, I gave her a key. Around five thirty, I hear her putting it in the lock. I don't turn around when she comes inside. It takes only a moment for her to see me standing on the balcony. She comes out and joins me.

"Hey, you," she says. "I know today was tough, but—"

I turn around and hand her the DVD cover.

Her eyes narrow slightly when she recognizes it, but otherwise she doesn't react.

"I found this on the doorstep when I came home."

She opens the box and sees that it's empty. "You watched it?"

I nod.

She sets her jaw with an icy certitude. "I'm not sorry for any of it. I'm not embarrassed. I was an adult, and adults have the right to express themselves sexually with anyone they want and however they want, as long as no one gets hurt. And I never hurt anyone, including myself."

"This hurts *me*. It destroys us." I struggle for a breath. "Did that son of a bitch you have for a father—?"

"God, no!" she says in horror. "My father would never . . . I was *not* abused. He hated it. He didn't speak to me for two years." She shakes her head as if trying to banish the idea from her mind. "Don't you dare think that about him."

I believe her. At that Friday night dinner at Ed's house, he implied that there was a time when he and Lovely were estranged. The video is a perverse repudiation of him, the ultimate *fuck you* to a man who spent his career directing beautifully filmed movies that for all their explicitness depicted sex in a tender way.

"There are reasons why I did it and why I stopped," she says. "But I won't waste your time explaining unless you want me to."

"Don't bother."

She shuts her eyes for a moment, little more than a blink, but enough to reveal a tear. She starts to say something, but then raises her hand to her mouth and bites down on her knuckles hard, so hard that I fear she'll draw blood. I want to pull her hand away, to shout at her to stop, but I'm not brave enough.

She finally lowers her hand and looks at it curiously. No blood, but purplish indentations where her incisors bit into the skin. "I'm leaving," she says. "But the trial. You need my help. And I'm . . . I'm still going to need you to sponsor me on the Daniels case."

"I guess I don't have much choice on either of those things, do I? I wish I did."

When she passes by me, her shoulder brushes against my chest. Her touch is still electric, and the air stirs slightly in her wake, leaving a trace of that citrus-ginger scent that I'll always associate with her. I wait outside on the balcony until I hear her walk out the front door.

The moment I saw the cover of that DVD, I knew that the

Assembly had left it on my doorstep. That's how they operate—by doling out intimidation in stages, each escalation more painful than the one before it. If a physical beating doesn't work, they move on to more sophisticated methods. They want to destroy me, and at this moment they've succeeded.

CHAPTER 45

I walk into The Barrista at precisely six o'clock the next morning. Deanna repeats her offer to give the opening statement today, but I decline. She suggests that I ask the judge for a trial continuance for medical reasons, but I won't do that either. Then I tell her about Lovely.

"Let it go," she says.

"I can't do that."

"That girl is special. And more importantly, she's good for you. Nothing else should matter. That video happened a long time ago. She was—"

"Don't tell me she was just a kid. She wasn't a kid. And it doesn't matter anyway. Some stains can't be washed off. I can't help what I feel, and what I feel is disgust. Right here." I tap my stomach with my fist. "I couldn't touch her if I tried. I wish I weren't forced to work with her."

She tilts her head and studies me for a while, like a bemused art patron staring at a bizarre oil on canvas.

"What're you doing?" I say.

"It's just that I wish I knew why you're such a sanctimonious man."

"*Sanctimonious*," I say, bristling. "Such a ten-dollar word from a simple barista."

"Oh, don't get me wrong. It's never bothered me. It's what drives you, I'm sure. But this thing with Lovely—"

"Drop it, Deanna."

She shakes her head slowly. "Secrets can be so destructive."

"Hers sure is."

"I'm not talking about hers." She sighs. "It's getting crowded. I've got to get back to work. Good luck in court today. And call me if you need me." She starts to leave, but comes back and kisses me on the cheek.

At seven forty-five, I pack up, dose up on Valium and Xanax, and head downtown. I find myself fantasizing about a traffic jam so massive that I'll miss the entire session. How will I be able to sit in the courtroom next to Lovely Diamond for the eight hours? But the traffic is unusually clear.

When I get to court, I find my three students already setting up for the day.

"Hey, Professor Stern, how are you?" Lovely says in a syrupy voice. Is she mocking me? Covering up? Conveying that she's not ready to give up on us? Whatever. Those sleazy images on that DVD won't go away. I say a curt good morning to all of them and find an isolated place to work.

When Raymond arrives, he greets the law students warmly and takes his seat at the defense table. Kathleen and Jonathan exchange looks. They haven't asked what's wrong with me, haven't asked why Raymond will barely acknowledge me. They've just gone about the business of preparing for the trial sessions. I'm grateful.

Lovely sits down next to Raymond and whispers something that makes him smile for the first time since the trial started. At one point, she covers his hand with hers. I wait as long as I can before sitting beside them. As soon as I do, he turns away from me, not facing forward until the judge takes the bench and the jury files in.

"Call your first witness, Mr. Frantz," Schadlow says.

"The plaintiff calls Special Agent Stephanie Holcomb."

Holcomb is the FBI's forensic accountant who worked on the Baxter investigation. She got her bachelor's degree from Brown University and has an MBA from the UCLA Anderson School of Business. In her late thirties, she's an attractive brunette who looks professional and self-assured. Through her, Frantz will convey to the jury that the United States of America is his ally. She's a perfect opening witness.

After reciting her stellar credentials, Holcomb testifies that in the autumn of 2011, the IRS got an anonymous tip claiming that Richard Baxter had made some suspicious bank transfers from Assembly accounts. She says she contacted Christopher McCarthy, the Assembly's designated representative for all legal matters involving the church, who gave the FBI permission to track movements in and out of those accounts. She testifies that a subsequent FBI investigation revealed that earlier in the year, six million dollars of Assembly money had been diverted from the Assembly's accounts and deposited into an offshore account in the name of a shell company called The Emery Group. She says that, while she doesn't know where that money went, the FBI believes that Rich received it because he controlled the other Assembly accounts through which the money was laundered and because he engaged in other questionable banking activity shortly before his arrest.

"Agent Holcomb, how did the FBI reach the conclusion that Richard Baxter stole the Assembly's money?" Frantz asks. He nods at his young associate, and almost instantaneously a flashy Power-Point presentation appears on the five flat-screen monitors scattered throughout the courtroom.

With the judge's permission, Holcomb leaves the witness stand and goes to the screen facing the jury. She points to the first entry in a timeline and says, "In October 2011, the FBI observed some unusual activity in Assembly accounts that Richard Baxter controlled. Suspicious deposits and subsequent withdrawals, though none as large as the six million dollar Emery Group transfer earlier in the year."

She spends the next hour and a half methodically taking the jury through the many bank transactions that the Feds monitored. It's laborious testimony, but compelling because she's showing the jury that the Feds more than did their job. As tedious as the testimony is, the jurors all seem to be paying attention. She comes across as an engaging college professor. She often—but not so often as to be annoying—looks at the jurors when answering Frantz's questions. They clearly like her.

After she finishes her presentation, she goes back to the witness stand. Frantz waits a few moments and asks, "Agent Holcomb, can you summarize again why the FBI concluded that it had probable cause to arrest Richard Baxter?"

"Because he was the Assembly's lawyer, in a position of trust and confidence that gave him complete access to the Assembly's bank accounts.

Because he and only one other person, Mr. McCarthy, controlled these accounts, and Mr. McCarthy was fully cooperating with us. Based on that evidence, we obtained a warrant and arrested Mr. Baxter."

"And when he was arrested, did you find anything unusual in his apartment?"

"We certainly did. The arresting agents found a false passport, a large amount of cash, and a stash of methamphetamine—crystal meth—hidden in a gutted computer frame."

"In your professional opinion, what do you conclude from finding those items?"

"Objection," I say. "Calls for a legal conclusion without foundation. Speculation."

Judge Schadlow takes a long time to consider my objection. She's clearly a novice. She should sustain the objection, but she says, "Overruled. You may answer, Agent Holcomb."

Holcomb turns and speaks directly to the jury. "The presence of a false passport and a large amount of cash is compelling evidence that Baxter intended to flee. And intent to flee is strong evidence of guilt."

"And after conducting your forensic accounting analysis, what is the total amount of money that the FBI believes that Richard Baxter embezzled?"

"A minimum of seventeen million dollars. It may be substantially more."

I could object to the part about the amount being more than seventeen million as rank speculation, but I'd only underscore the vast amount of money that was stolen. So I keep quiet.

"Thank you, Special Agent Holcomb," Frantz says. "I have no further questions."

"Do you have any questions, Mr. Stern?" the judge asks in a solicitous tone. She's actually worried that I'll pass on the chance to cross-examine a key witness. I suspect that Raymond and my students and probably everyone else in the courtroom share the judge's concern. But I really *can* ask questions—unless the stage fright decides to encroach on that ability, too.

Just as I get up from my chair, the courtroom doors open behind me. I glance back to see Manny Mason walk in and take a seat in the last row. I'm glad he's here, but I wish he'd arrived earlier so he could have heard Holcomb's testimony on direct. With his expertise in business law, maybe he would have noticed a weakness in her testimony that I missed.

An effective cross-examination requires that the interrogating lawyer make declarative statements in the guise of asking leading questions—questions that call only for *yes* or *no* answers. So I'll keep my questions short, no more than fifteen words if possible. I'll make them sound like a statement by lowering the inflection in my voice instead of raising it the way you do with a real question. And I'll start with a topic that the jury won't forget.

"Agent Holcomb, didn't you testify that Richard Baxter wasn't the only signatory on the bank accounts in question?" My voice quavers, but it's loud enough to be heard.

"Yes."

"Christopher McCarthy of the TCO was also a signatory on those accounts?"

"That's correct."

"And Christopher McCarthy had the power and ability to make the fraudulent transfers that you attribute to Rich Baxter, did he not?" There's a rumbling behind me from the Assembly side of the gallery. I'm sure there must be at least ten devotees ready to jump over the railing to attack me.

"It was Baxter who—"

I raise both hands. It's an effective way to get a witness to stop talking, but now also a kind of victory sign, because my hands are steady, my palms dry. "Didn't you understand my question, Agent Holcomb?"

"I understood it."

"Then please answer it. Christopher McCarthy had the power and ability to make the fraudulent transfers that you attribute to Rich Baxter. Yes or no?"

"Objection, Your Honor," Frantz says. "Speculative. Argumentative."

"Overruled," Schadlow says.

"Yes, but McCarthy was cooperating fully with us," Holcomb says. "Embezzlers don't usually cooperate with the FBI in the investigation of their own crimes."

"Let's explore your answer. The Church of the Sanctified Assembly isn't your ordinary victim, is it?

"I'm not sure what you mean."

"They have a militaristic structure."

"I wouldn't know."

"Totalitarian, wouldn't you say? Fascistic?"

"Objection!" Frantz says.

"Isn't it a fact that the way the Assembly's structured, Christopher McCarthy could've embezzled the money by ordering his underlings to make the bank transfers? They wouldn't have questioned him for a second. He could even have ordered them to frame Rich Baxter and they would've obeyed, correct?"

Frantz springs out of his chair and shouts, "Objection! Argumentative! Speculative! Compound! Completely outside the bounds of appropriate courtroom decorum!"

"I'll withdraw the question," I say, because the jurors have gotten the point.

"Calm down, Mr. Frantz," the judge says. "The objection is sustained. The jury is instructed to disregard Mr. Stern's argument, because that's what it was, not evidence. Time to move on to another topic, counsel. And do not repeat this behavior." Despite her admonition, there's a hint of amusement in her eyes, maybe because it's the first time since the case started that I've shown some life.

"Very well, Your Honor," I say. "Agent Holcomb, in your investigation, did the name *Grace Trimble* come up as a possible suspect?"

She thinks for a moment. "That name never came up."

"So, you're not aware that Grace Trimble once worked for a used car dealer named Alan Markowitz?"

"No."

"Or that Ms. Trimble stole Markowitz's identity and created the false passport found in Mr. Baxter's possession?"

I'm sure everyone in the courtroom expects Frantz to object, but he doesn't, because he knows that what I've proposed is true. I doubt he expected me to offer Grace up as a suspect, though.

"I have no information about a Grace Trimble," Holcomb says.

"Have you ever heard that Grace Trimble used the alias *Sandra Casey*?"

"No."

"Christopher McCarthy never shared that information with you?"

"No, he didn't."

"And he never told you that Grace Trimble frequently visited Mr. Baxter's apartment disguised as a prostitute?"

"He didn't."

"And he never told you that Grace Trimble was Rich Baxter's former law partner and girlfriend?"

"No."

"And he never told you that Ms. Trimble was excommunicated by the Church of the Sanctified Assembly some years ago?"

"No."

"And I take it that means you don't know that Ms. Trimble is an expert in the law of corporate finance?"

She looks over at McCarthy and frowns. "No."

Of course, neither Frantz nor McCarthy told the FBI about Grace. Grace's involvement threatens their theory of the case, or at least makes it more complicated. I had a different reason for not talking to authorities—I think Grace is innocent, and so I wanted to get to her before the cops did so she could tell me what she knows. I don't like offering her up as a suspect now, but my obligation is to the client, not her.

I can't help glancing at McCarthy. I'm not sure, but I think he's trying to suppress his nervous twitch. I take a few steps away from the lectern and ask, "So, now, Agent Holcomb, we have two persons other than Mr. Baxter who might have been involved in the embezzlement scheme—Mr. McCarthy and Grace Trimble. Do you agree?"

"I don't agree with that, Mr. Stern. And your theories are inconsistent."

"I don't have to be consistent," I say. "My side doesn't have the burden of proof."

"Objection," Frantz barks. "Argumentative. Not a question."

"Sustained," Schadlow says. "No more, Mr. Stern." The frostiness in her tone means that I can't cross the line again today.

"As a law enforcement officer, Agent Holcomb, would you have liked to have known about Grace Trimble?"

"Yes, sir. I would."

I look over at the jurors. Most of them are leaning forward in their seats. I haven't come close to discrediting this witness, but I've gained a bit of ground back.

"One final question, Ms. Holcomb. You said that the cash and the false passport found in Mr. Baxter's apartment were evidence of guilt. Couldn't those items also be evidence that Mr. Baxter feared for his life and thought he would have to flee for his own safety?"

"No, sir. If he was innocent and wanted protection, he could have come to us."

"You think the Feds could have protected him?"

"Absolutely."

"If that's true, Agent Holcomb, then why was he found hanging by the neck in a federal jail? Why did he die on your watch?"

Manny joins us for lunch in the attorneys' lounge. After we finish eating—I force down a sandwich of canned tuna and dry multigrain bread—I swallow a tranquilizer and prepare for the afternoon session. Lovely keeps her distance.

Just as we're about to return to the courtroom, my cell phone vibrates. Caller ID says it's from Deanna. When she tells me why she's called, my body fills with a mixture of exultation and disbelief. I make her repeat the information twice more before I truly believe it.

"That was Deanna Poulos," I say. "She's found Grace Trimble. I'm meeting them both at The Barrista at midnight."

"Shut up!" Lovely says.

"For real?" Jonathan asks.

Raymond's eyes widen in surprise.

"What did Deanna tell you?" Lovely asks. "Will Trimble testify?"

"I don't know," I say. "Deanna didn't want to talk over the phone. She'd only say that Grace is paranoid and scared shitless."

"What else is new," Manny says.

"Yeah, but Deanna says that this time, she has every right to be."

CHAPTER 46

I can barely concentrate during the afternoon session. Fortunately, Frantz's witnesses are straightforward and uncontroversial. Nick Weir examines two bank officers and an Assembly bookkeeper, who merely authenticate the documents that reflect the bogus transfers of money that Agent Holcomb discussed in detail this morning. Weir, a ponderous questioner, puts the jury to sleep. Frantz then calls one of the FBI agents who arrested Rich, but he just repeats Holcomb's testimony. At four thirty, we adjourn for the day.

I return to my condo and do my best to prepare for tomorrow, but it's hopeless. At eleven thirty, I leave my apartment for the meeting with Grace. As soon as I pull out of the underground garage, a light drizzle coats the windshield—June gloom a week early. I turn on the wipers, which leave grimy smudges that obscure my vision. I expect the fog to lift when I get farther inland, but the droplets keep coming in a fine mist the entire trip.

Will Grace be lucid, or will she be delusional and strung out on drugs? Can she tell me what happened to the money? Did she hear that I implicated her in the embezzlement scheme? Will she come to trial?

The car radio is still tuned to one of Lovely's favorite stations. It's playing a Green Day song called "Good Riddance," about a man sending a message to a woman who just broke up with him. The song makes me long for a reconstructed world in which I could abide failings in others. If Lovely were with me, I wouldn't be so frightened.

I arrive at The Barrista and find a parking space directly across from the shop. When I get out of the car, I zip up my thin nylon windbreaker. Melrose is empty—just like that last time. Few things are as eerie as when a normally busy thoroughfare is deserted; I always think of the neutron bomb. The drizzle has created a moist sheen on the surface of the street, making it slippery even in my running shoes. The roadway lamps and traffic lights cast shimmering oblongs of red, green, and amber on the slick asphalt.

I jaywalk across the street, my hands stuffed into the pockets of my jacket, less from the cold than to prevent myself from running. Deanna told me to come around back to the storeroom door, but I want to avoid doing that if I can, so I go to the shop's front entrance. The blinds have been pulled down over the doors and windows. I cup my hand to my face and peer through a crack in the blinds. There doesn't appear to be a light on in the main room. Still, I try the front door handle. Locked. As a reflex, I rattle the door to see if it'll open. No luck.

I pull the collar of my jacket around my neck and head down the street. How could it be so cold in May? I reach the corner and stop short. The entrance to the alley is a hundred feet up the street where the beating took place. With my first step, my teeth start chattering. I force myself to walk. The buildings fronting Melrose Avenue border the alley on the right; an ivy-covered Cyclone fence separates the homes on the left, the ivy an excellent hiding place for vermin. The area often attracts the homeless, and I look to see if anyone's lurking or sleeping against a building, but it's pitch black, except for a bare incandescent bulb halfway down the alley over the back door to The Barrista. In the daytime, the shop never seemed this far from the side street, but now that light seems miles away. I take a deep breath and walk toward the light, gingerly navigating past the pots piled outside the ceramics studio next door to Deanna's shop. The asphalt is full of potholes and slick from the drizzle. I slip, stumble into a rut, and twist my ankle. Why aren't I one of those handy men who always have a Swiss Army knife strapped to their belts and a powerful mini-flashlight hooked to their key-chains? Luckily, when I test the ankle, I can walk. When I reach The Barrista, I start to knock, but stop myself and try the doorknob. The door opens. The overhead fluorescent lamps are off. The only light comes from the bulb over the alley door. I take a step inside. I don't see anyone. I'm about to call out when my left foot slides on something wet and tacky, and I think that maybe someone spilled a syrupy caramel concoction on the concrete floor and the clean-up crew missed it, and I lose my balance and almost do a split and fall hard on one knee, sending a jolt of pain up my femur. I'm about to curse when I realize that I've slipped on a pool of blood and am kneeling over the lifeless body of Deanna Poulos.

With quivering fingers, I search for her carotid artery, hoping to find a pulse. Nothing. Only the instinct for self-preservation prevents me from shrieking in horror and despair. I stand, warily make my way across room, and feel for the light switch. Is the assailant still here? No, because then I'd already be dead. I turn on the lights and look for Grace Trimble's body. Nothing. Just Deanna on the other side of the room. I lock the door separating the storeroom from the rest of the shop and call 911. Then I go back to her.

She's lying in a fetal position. She has multiple gunshot wounds to the chest. Her black T-shirt is heavy with blood. Her head is turned slightly upward in my direction. Her eyes are open, her mouth an oval void, the last vestige of surprise and pain. There's something else in her expression, or more accurately, the artifact of an expression—the look of someone who's been betrayed.

If I hadn't pursued the Assembly, Deanna would still be alive. In the cold language of the law, my actions are the *proximate cause* of her death. I know I shouldn't touch her again, but I reach out and stroke her hair.

"I'm so sorry," I whisper, tears flowing down my face.

After a lengthy interview with the cops—which, when they notice my blood-streaked jeans, becomes for a harrowing forty minutes an interrogation into whether I had a motive to kill Deanna—I somehow manage to drive home.

Sleep is out of the question. I go to the pantry and pull out a bottle of mastika she gave me one Christmas long ago, 90 proof. It's unopened because I promised her we'd drink it together when one of us had something big in life to celebrate. I uncork the bottle, pour myself a shot, chug it down, and then pour myself another. I find my one Metallica CD and put it in the player, not because I like the group, but because Deanna did. I keep replaying that night six months into our legal careers when she barged into my office and ordered me to draft jury instructions on a dog-shit case of hers. Who was this brash girl to tell me what to do? After we finished at two o'clock in the morning, we collapsed onto my office sofa (who seduced whom?) and made love for the first time. Though we later called it sport-fucking, it *was* making love, because sexual intimacy leaves an indelible mark no matter how vehemently one denies its meaning.

I down a third drink and for some reason think of my mother. When I was a toddler, she read Shakespeare to me at bedtime. Like everything else she did, the reading was calculated to advance my career as an actor. She wanted to instill in me a sense of the dramatic and a feel for the rhythms of speech. She favored Jaques's famous monologue from *As You Like It*, the one that begins with the line, "All the world's a stage, and all the men and women merely players." No wonder—Harriet Stern was the archetypal stage mother, so what could resonate more strongly for her than a speech equating life with acting? But life's not a play or a movie. It's a dark cybergame rife with ominous repetition and fragmentary success and taunting moments of self-delusion when you think you've conquered the world only to find that you've bumbled into a fatal trap. It's a place where you rescue a beautiful princess only to discover that she's something else entirely. It's a series of street battles with multidimensional ghouls that blend chameleonlike into a prefabricated landscape, all bent on destroying you for no discernible reason. And the worst thing is that when you die, you're not just an avatar whose pixels gently flicker out. You can't push the reset button and start over at Level One. No one beats the game.

CHAPTER 47

Thirty-six hours after I found Deanna's body, we're back in court. Judge Schadlow gave me all of one day to mourn Deanna's death. After saying how sorry she was, how terrific a lawyer Deanna was—Schadlow had worked with her on that case five years ago—she ruled that we've lost enough time already because I deferred my opening statement. It's not fair to the jury, she said.

Now, Manny Mason and I are in the courtroom an hour early, fighting a legal battle against Lou Frantz outside the jury's presence. Frantz seems to view Deanna's murder as nothing but a legal problem. He's brought a motion *in limine*—a motion *at the threshold*—to prevent me from using the murder as evidence that Rich Baxter was killed as well. Manny and I were up all night drafting the opposition papers. The legal issues are beyond Jonathan and Kathleen, and I refused Lovely's offer of help.

I intended to argue the motion, but I've been so distraught over Deanna's death that Manny insisted that he handle the hearing. This time, I agreed. Though he, too, is heartbroken over losing Deanna, he wasn't the one who found her body. And because the admissibility of this evidence is purely a legal question, he'll do a good job. These are the kinds of issues that law professors thrive on.

"I've read the motion and the opposition," Schadlow says. "And I'm inclined to agree with the plaintiff. The fact of Ms. Poulos's tragic death is irrelevant and inflammatory. And based on hearsay. It has nothing to do with Richard Baxter or this elusive Grace Trimble."

"Ms. Poulos's death couldn't be more relevant," Manny says, for once speaking with passion in his voice. "Richard Baxter always maintained that he was set up, that he was in danger. He's dead, and now

Deanna Poulos is dead because someone is gunning for Grace Trimble. Alternatively, Grace Trimble is behind the embezzlement scheme and murdered Deanna Poulos and framed Rich. Trimble is a highly unstable individual. Either way, Ms. Poulos death throws doubt on the plaintiff's entire theory."

"It does nothing of the sort," Frantz says. "We don't know if Grace Trimble actually intended to show up at the coffee house night before last. We don't even know that Grace Trimble really called Deanna Poulos. All we have is Mr. Stern's word that he got this phone call."

"I resent the implications of that statement," Manny says. "Mr. Stern will—"

"I'll submit a sworn declaration that I received the call from Ms. Poulos," I say in a shaky voice.

"Your Honor, the police believe that Ms. Poulos's death resulted from a burglary gone wrong," Frantz says. "There's been a rash of burglaries in the neighborhood."

"What Mr. Frantz says goes to the weight of the evidence, not its relevance," Manny says. "Deanna Poulos's death—"

The judge holds up her hand. "I've heard enough, Mr. Mason. The plaintiff's motion is granted. The defense will *not* refer to Ms. Poulos's death in front of the jury. I'll see you back here at nine o'clock." She leaves the bench.

Manny shakes his head. I glare at the judge's back. By forbidding me to utter Deanna's name in court, it's as if the judge has dishonored her memory, has expunged it from the record. As soon as Frantz walks out, Manny slams his notebook down on the table, the reverberation so loud that the clerk comes out to check on us.

I spend the next hour preparing for the upcoming cross-examination of Frantz's witnesses, praying that the antianxiety pills can do double duty by staving off both the stage fright and the unremitting grief. At a quarter of nine, Raymond Baxter arrives. "Damn shame about your friend," he says. "Seemed like a good person." He emits a raspy whistle that comes from deep in his throat, an unnerving geriatric harmonics.

"She was a wonderful person," I say. "She and Rich were great friends."

He clears his throat and says, "You were good the other day. Cross-examining that FBI agent, I mean."

I nod and go back to my examination outlines. I've been waiting for this—Frantz intends to call McCarthy and the county medical examiner who concluded that Rich committed suicide. Our entire defense hinges on my performance today.

—⁊⁊—

The Christopher McCarthy I've come to know isn't on the witness stand, isn't anywhere near the courthouse. There's none of the "sorry I won't see you in the hereafter, sinner" condescension that has always defined him. There are no opaque sunglasses. Now, he's a successful CEO with a warm smile and a sparkle in his eye. He's the former radio personality who could captivate his listeners with nothing more than the rich timbre of his voice. He's the pious devotee who responds to Rich's apostasy with the wounded look of a man whose closest friend has betrayed him.

In response to Frantz's softball questioning, he describes how Rich, while a partner at Macklin & Cherry, earned the trust of the Assembly. He testifies that Rich eventually left the firm to live his life in the service of the celestial host, gaining unprecedented access to the Assembly's bank accounts. Apparently on the verge of tears, he describes how shocked he was to learn that Rich betrayed the Assembly to pursue illicit pleasures.

"During the examination of Special Agent Holcomb, counsel for defendants mentioned that you also were a signatory to Assembly accounts," Frantz says. "Do you remember that?"

"Oh yes."

"Mr. McCarthy, were you in any way involved with diverting Assembly funds?"

"Absolutely not. In fact, we subjected our financial records to the scrutiny of the US government. That's an extraordinary thing for us to do, considering the religious oppression that we've suffered at the hands of that very government. But we wanted to get to the truth, wanted to see justice done."

"How do you respond to Mr. Stern's suggestion that a woman named Grace Trimble was involved in stealing Assembly money?"

"Oh, it's likely that Mr. Stern is right about that. Grace Trimble is a troubled individual who dislikes the Assembly because she was excommunicated for behavior that violated our tenets. She holds a grudge. She's also a brilliant lawyer. But that doesn't mean Rich Baxter wasn't involved. Just the opposite. I think it's likely that Baxter and Trimble were in this together. They were former law colleagues and carried on a longtime romantic relationship." It's a well-rehearsed answer that obliterates my earlier attempt to exonerate Rich by blaming Grace.

"And where is Grace Trimble now, to your knowledge?"

"She's disappeared. Wanted by the police."

"No further questions," Franz says.

I stand up to cross-examine, my options now limited. I hoped that McCarthy's arrogance would hang him, but it didn't happen. I can't probe into the Assembly's secrets like I did at the deposition, because they're irrelevant to whether Rich embezzled. I can't ask him if he was a signatory to The Emery Group's account or question him about the payment to Delwyn Bennett, because he'd deny everything, and there would be no way to expose his perjury—the evidence that Ed Diamond got from his shady source was not only illegally obtained, it's rank hearsay. So I decide to test Judge Schadlow's patience.

"Mr. McCarthy, you mentioned on direct that Grace Trimble has disappeared. Is that because a woman named Deanna Poulos was found—?"

"Objection!" McCarthy says. "Violates the court's order on the motion *in limine*."

"May we have a sidebar?" I say.

Schadlow motions us over to the side of the bench out of the jury's hearing. She's glaring at me. When the court reporter joins us, she says, "How dare you, Mr. Stern? Tell me why I shouldn't sanction you?"

"I'm aware of your order, Your Honor, but Mr. Frantz opened the subject up on direct by asking the witness about Grace Trimble's current whereabouts."

She blinks for a moment. This obviously hadn't occurred to her. "My order stands. You shall not mention Deanna Poulos's murder. It's irrelevant and unduly prejudicial. If you try this again, I'll sanction you."

I stare at her. She knows I'm right, but she's stubborn, another common weakness in new judges.

"Step back, counsel," she says.

After her ruling, all I can do is ask McCarthy a few more innocuous questions in a tone that signals moral outrage. When he leaves the witness stand, he smirks at me, making sure that the jury can't see it.

During our ten-minute recess, Manny, Kathleen, and Jonathan wait with me out in the hall, doing a piss-poor job of trying not to act glum. Lovely stays in the courtroom organizing exhibits for the next witness.

After the jurors file in and the judge retakes the bench, Frantz says, "The plaintiff calls Dr. Arun Vakil."

Vakil is a handsome, athletically built man in his early thirties. Frantz immediately gets him to testify to his background. His family emigrated from India when he was ten years old. He got his Bachelor of Science degree in biology and chemistry from the University of Michigan and his medical degree from Baylor University in Texas, after which he served a four-year residency in pathology at the UC Irvine Medical Center. He's a board-certified pathologist in anatomic, clinical, and forensic pathology. As an assistant medical examiner for the county since 2005, he's performed hundreds of autopsies.

"What is your opinion as to the cause of Richard Baxter's death?" Frantz asks.

"It's my opinion that Richard Baxter committed suicide."

"Please tell us why you came to that conclusion, Dr. Vakil."

Vakil's testimony parrots his autopsy report. Rich was found hanging in a holding cell. A ligature, fashioned from a silk necktie, was wrapped around his neck. He was partially suspended from a low hanging sprinkler pipe attached to the ceiling—*partially* suspended, because his toes were touching the ground. The cause of death resulted from Rich's body weight tightening the ligature around the jugular vein and carotid artery and cutting off the blood flow to the brain. The body was found facing away from the door. There was no evidence of a struggle, no defensive wounds. And there was no ligature furrow.

Raymond Baxter's breathing becomes audible, more labored than ever. Lovely leans over and asks if he needs a break, but he shakes his head.

"What's a ligature furrow?" Frantz asks.

"It's a mark left by the ligature—the cloth or cord or rope that causes strangulation."

"What was the significance of the absence of a ligature furrow on Richard Baxter's neck?"

"It leads me to believe he committed suicide. It's common in cases of suicide that a soft ligature—like the silk tie used here—won't leave a mark. In a homicide case involving strangulation, the victim usually struggles. When that happens, the force needed to subdue the victim creates a ligature furrow in the large majority of cases."

"Now, Dr. Vakil, isn't it possible that someone forced Rich Baxter in the noose and up onto that pipe?"

"Murder by hanging is highly unusual. You have to be exceptionally powerful to lift an adult male up into a noose, especially if the victim struggles. In this case, the decedent died in a crowded jail. There wouldn't be much time to accomplish murder by hanging without being seen."

"Your report says that Mr. Baxter had evidence of hemorrhaging at the back at the skull. Why was that?"

"I believe that the cell door hit the back of his head when the marshals came in. As I said, the decedent's body was facing away from the door, with the back of the head closer to the door than the rest of the body. There was a tilt of the body because the decedent's feet were touching the ground. It was as if the body was reclining."

"Were there any other factors that you considered in reaching your opinion?"

"Yes, his life circumstances and mental state. He'd been a very successful, very financially secure man. Now he was facing many years in prison. He was disgraced in his community. And he was found in the possession of methamphetamine—crystal meth—a drug that can cause depression and suicidal thoughts."

"No further questions," Frantz says.

I pour myself a glass of water, slipping slowly from the glass to mask my elation. Neither Frantz nor Vakil have realized that the report failed to consider Rich's fractured hyoid bone. I glance at Lovely. She, too, is trying not to smile.

I go to the lectern and say, "Dr. Vakil, would you agree that there are a lot of physically powerful men incarcerated in the Metropolitan Detention Center?"

"I don't know for a fact, but I assume so. It's a crowded jail."

"Richard Baxter was just a bit under five feet eight inches in height and, at the time of his death, weighed one hundred and thirty-three pounds?"

He refers to his report. "That's correct."

"So it's possible that one of these powerful inmates of the Metropolitan Detention Center could lift a man the size of Richard Baxter into a noose?"

"Anything's possible."

"You also mentioned that you noticed a wound on the back of Richard Baxter's skull?"

"Yes."

"You think it came from the cell door?"

"I do."

"But that wound was also consistent with someone sneaking up on him and hitting him in the head with a blunt object, wasn't it?"

"Yes, although I don't think that's what happened."

"You don't think, but you don't really know, do you?"

"No. I can only give my opinion."

"If the wound occurred while Mr. Baxter was still alive, was the blow to the head severe enough to have knocked him unconscious?"

He hesitates and then checks his report, flipping through pages.

"You won't find the answer in your report," I say.

He shrugs. "I guess I don't know the answer to your question, then."

"Wouldn't that have been relevant to your opinion?"

"Not really."

I glance at the jury. While during direct they clearly liked him, now they don't seem so sure. He's much too blasé about death, even for a pathologist.

"Well, if someone snuck up behind Richard Baxter and hit him in the head and knocked him unconscious, it would have been much easier for one of those powerful inmates to hang him from a noose, wouldn't it?"

"If that had happened, you're correct."

"There are ways to strangle a man without leaving a ligature furrow, correct Dr. Vakil?"

"I think . . . possibly."

"Certain martial arts holds and military holds?"

"I believe so. I've . . . I've never encountered a case like that."

For dramatic effect, I return to the defense table and pretend to consult with Lovely. Then I ask, "Richard Baxter had a fractured hyoid bone, didn't he?"

"He did."

"And the hyoid bone is a small bone in the neck."

"Yes."

"And how old was he?"

"Thirty-eight years old."

"Dr. Vakil, isn't it Pathology 101 that when a decedent under the age of forty has a fractured hyoid, the default cause of death is homicide unless there's strong proof to the contrary?"

"That's generally true, but not in this case."

Stunned by the answer, I forget the cardinal rule of cross-examination and ask a question I don't know the answer to. "Why not?"

Only after the words are out of my mouth do I understand that Frantz has ambushed me and that Dr. Arun Vakil is his spring gun.

Vakil addresses the jury, not me—just as Frantz undoubtedly coached him to do. "It's true that the hyoid bone is not usually fractured in a partial suspension suicide in younger people, people under forty. But Richard Baxter was found in the possession of methamphetamine, as I testified to earlier. Meth use causes severe weakening of bone structure. That's why you see those horrible pictures of meth users with rotten teeth. In any case, Baxter's meth use would make hyoid fracture likely, especially in a man of thirty-eight. That's not that far away from forty, you know."

I glance back at Lovely. She's buried her face in her hands. She can't do that. We have to act confident, even though our case has just disintegrated. I check my notes and wrack my brain for a face-saving question. I can't think of one. Then Manny, holding a legal pad, leaves his seat in the gallery and comes to the podium.

"May I confer with Dean Mason, Your Honor?" I ask.

"You may, Mr. Stern. But be brief."

Manny scribbles furiously on his legal pad. Then he tears out two pages and hands them to me. They're follow-up areas for Vakil, just random ideas, conceived in less than five minutes. I'll have to do my best to translate them into leading questions on the fly and hope that Vakil doesn't burn me with an answer. This is one of those times where I'll have to ignore the basic rules of cross and hope to get lucky.

"Nowhere in your report did you mention that Mr. Baxter's hyoid was fractured because of drug use, did you?" I ask.

"No. I did not."

"You didn't consider the issue of the broken hyoid until Mr. Frantz, the Assembly's counsel, told you there was a problem, correct?" I have no idea if this is true, but I have to take a shot.

"I don't . . . I don't know if it was Mr. Frantz or Nicholas Weir. But it was someone from his office."

"Did the Assembly's lawyers also tell you that meth use weakens bone?"

He crosses his arms and his legs at the same time. "They didn't have to tell me that."

"But they did tell you that, didn't they?"

"I don't recall, sir."

"Nowhere in your autopsy report do you conclude that Mr. Baxter was using drugs, do you?"

"That's correct, sir."

"And that's because the tox screens came back negative for drugs in Mr. Baxter's system."

"Yes, but—"

"You've answered the question."

"I object," Frantz says. "He interrupted the witness' testimony. Dr. Vakil has the right to finish his answer."

"Was there something you wanted to add, Dr. Vakil?" the judge asks.

"Yes, Your Honor. Just because the toxicology screens were negative doesn't mean anything. The decedent was in jail long enough for any methamphetamine to have passed from his body. And as Mr. Stern pointed out, he was very thin. His medical records showed that the decedent was a bit overweight for most of his adult life. That's further evidence of methamphetamine use."

My next question isn't on Manny's list. "Couldn't Mr. Baxter also have lost weight because he knew his life was in danger? Because he was thrown in jail for a crime he didn't commit? Wouldn't that cause a rational, healthy human being to lose weight?"

Frantz gets up to object, but before he does, the judge says, "That's argumentative, counsel. I'm going to sustain my own objection. The witness will not answer that and the jury will disregard Mr. Stern's questions. Now move on."

"I'm finished with this guy," I say, for effect tossing my notes on the table in disgust.

Schadlow peers at me from over her glasses, undoubtedly debating whether to admonish me for my rude conduct. She lets it go and turns toward the jury. "Ladies and gentlemen, since this is Friday, we'll adjourn early so you can have the afternoon off. We'll reconvene Monday at nine o'clock."

I have to bite the side of my cheek hard not to remind the judge that she wouldn't give me more than a day to grieve over Deanna, but now she's sending us home three hours early. It's just as well. I need all the time I can get to find a way to recover from today's debacle, though I doubt it's possible.

As soon as we exit the courtroom, Raymond heads toward the elevator without acknowledging me.

"Thanks for the lifeline," I say to Manny. "At least we were able to ask a few questions that made him look bad."

He shakes his head in disgust. "That witness killed us. I have to get to school." What's left unsaid is that he warned me months ago—I shouldn't have relied on a law student for a forensic analysis. He turns and hurries down the corridor.

When we're alone, Lovely says, "I'm so sorry, Parker. When I talked to my pathologist friend, I didn't mention the drugs. The report never . . . I should've told him about the drugs."

"There's nothing to be sorry about. This was my fault. I didn't hire my own expert because I wanted to surprise Frantz at trial. I took a risk and it backfired. I should've known better. You're going to be a great lawyer. I just wish you'd had a better teacher."

An awkward moment passes between us, but before either of us can speak, Brandon Placek, the *Times* reporter, walks up. I'm about to say "no comment" when I realize that it's not me he's interested in.

"Ms. Diamond, we're doing a story about you. You're Shane Edmonds's daughter, right? And you were a porn star yourself? Would you comment on how your background in adult films impacts on your defense of Tyler Daniels in her child pornography prosecution?"

I take a step toward Placek. "Listen, asshole—"

"Here's my comment," Lovely says. "First, I'm defending Tyler Daniels because she's being oppressed by an overzealous prosecutor who wants to deprive her of her basic First Amendment right of free speech. And that's the only reason I'm defending her. Second, I'm not ashamed of my past. But I'm not going to talk about it. All I'm focusing on is passing the bar exam and practicing as an attorney so I can fight against the type of injustice that Tyler is facing."

He starts to ask another question, but I get between him and Lovely. "Who's your source for this information?"

He holds up his hands. "You know I can't—"

I crowd him, pushing him up against the wall. I dig my finger into his chest several times as I say, "Cut the First Amendment bullshit and tell me who gave you that information. Was it Frantz? McCarthy?"

Lovely grabs my arm. "Parker, please don't."

I hesitate, but step back when her grip tightens. Placek scurries away like the little weasel he is.

"Thank you," she whispers. "For trying to protect me."

"I have to go."

"Can't we just—?"

"No. We can't."

—◊◊◊—

When I get home, I immediately open the pantry and pour myself a shot of mastika, drink it down, and pour myself another. I go out onto the balcony and gaze out at the expanse of ocean. How long, I wonder, do drowning victims struggle to hold on, even as the body rebels and consumes the precious molecules of oxygen in the lungs? Do people fight to the end, or does there come a time of resignation, even acceptance, when they willingly succumb to the inevitable temptation to exhale that last breath of hope and actually welcome the flood of lethal seawater into their bodies? Are those who struggle until the bitter end the brave ones, or merely fools who trade a last chance at tranquility for futile self-torture?

I go back inside and grab my keys, get in my car, and drive over to the TCO building in Santa Monica. I check in at the front desk and ask to see Christopher McCarthy, not knowing whether he's even coming in after court. The security guard tells me to wait. I take a seat on a hard marble bench off in a corner. A few minutes later, McCarthy hurtles out of an elevator and comes toward me.

"You really are insane," he says. He sniffs the air. "And drunk. Get out or I'll have you arrested for trespassing. And I'm definitely going to have Lou Frantz report you to the state bar for trying to communicate with me without his consent."

I stand up and look into his eyes, or more accurately, in the direction of his eyes, because all I can see is my own reflection in his sunglasses. "Do what you have to do. But I want you to arrange a meeting for me with Quiana."

He jerks his head back. "What did you say?"

"I said I want to meet with Quiana Gottschalk. Immediately. And don't tell me she doesn't exist. We're way beyond that."

He lifts his arm and massages the back of his neck with his hand, a movement that causes his coat to fly open. Patches of sweat have stained his custom-made silk shirt. "You're more warped than I thought. What in heaven's name makes you think that she'd ever meet with you?"

"Because," I say, "she's my mother."

CHAPTER 48

Two hours later, McCarthy calls and confirms that the meeting with Quiana is on for tomorrow morning. He tries to sound curt and businesslike, but his tone contains an undercurrent of respect, as though he's discovered that the lowliest peon has royal blood. I feel neither excitement nor fear, only the heady self-satisfaction lawyers feel when they one-up an adversary.

The next morning, I drive to a seedy shopping center in Mar Vista, a few miles from my condo. I park my car and lean against the hood, waiting. After fifteen minutes, a blue Mercedes drives up. Bradley Kelly insisted that Assembly staff drive only blue cars because blue is the color of the celestial angels' wings. There are two men inside. The one in the passenger seat gets out. He's dressed in the obligatory dark suit and red power tie. In that polite, emotionless voice typical of the Assembly functionary, he orders me into the back seat and then slides in next to me. He reaches into his jacket pocket and pulls something out. The driver, from my vantage point just broad shoulders, brown hair, and sunglasses, gazes out the window without acknowledging me.

"You're to wear this," my handler says. He shows me a black cloth. A blindfold.

"You're joking, right?"

He stares at me with vacant eyes.

"That wasn't part of my agreement with McCarthy. Besides, I already know where we're going. The compound in the hills above Trancas Beach."

"You're to wear this," he repeats.

I want this meeting, and it won't happen unless I agree to their demands. I nod, and he wraps the blindfold tightly around me. I wait for him to bind my hands, but he doesn't. I guess I'm on the honor system.

The driver starts the engine and pulls away. For the next twenty minutes, the car weaves in and out of traffic and stops and starts and makes sharp city turns. Then the ride gets smoother. We must have reached the coast highway.

I sit in darkness, listening to the hum of the tires on the asphalt. I begin to welcome the variety of the *click-rumble* of the car going over the Botts' dots when changing lanes. The men don't speak, to me or to each other.

"How about putting something on the stereo?" I say.

No response.

"How about some smooth jazz? Your church founder liked smooth jazz."

The man next to me takes three deep breaths, forced and evenly spaced, as though he's trying to control his temper. I wait for a minute. There's no music. I sniff the air for a hint of the ocean, but the air conditioner has filtered out any hint of an odor. With nothing to see or hear or smell, I have no choice but to remember.

For most of my childhood, only one part of my mother's life was stable—her involvement in my acting career. She effectively kept the agents and the lawyers and the directors under her thumb, making sure that my financial and creative interests were served. She would flatter and cajole and reason with such people, and if that didn't work, she would terrorize them.

To this day, I don't know how she did it, because the rest of her life was a shambles. Over the years, Hollywood pusher Billy Ness sold her everything from marijuana to magic mushrooms. With her wavy light brown hair, roundish face, slightly crooked nose, and boyish figure, she could have been viewed as plain, especially compared to the curvaceous, classically gorgeous actresses on the set. But her flower-child eyes exuded, I've come to realize, an invitation to chaos that men found irresistible. When she wasn't shouting or in hysterics, she had the melodic voice of a mythic Siren. And I'd often overhear guys on the set singing the praises of her lips in words unsuitable for my childish ears.

She hopped from one man's bed to another, falling desperately in love with the hunk actor or the brilliant director or the powerful producer. If she couldn't hook up with one of them, she'd choose someone from the crew. Her romances had one thing in common—they all expired at the completion of principal photography, leaving her as astonished and broken-hearted as a lovelorn teenager.

How could a child know this? Because on so many mornings-after, my still high or hungover mother would come into my trailer and tearfully spew out the mistakes that she'd made the night before, often in terms too graphic for me to understand. Her behavior frightened and confused me. Once, in the early eighties during the height of the AIDS epidemic, she shared with me—that's what she called it, *sharing*—that she'd had unprotected sex with strangers and that she was worried about getting sick. I was a child, so I was sure she was going to die. Even after she told me that she'd tested negative, I still had nightmares in which she was infected. For months afterward, I would obsessively monitor her for symptoms of the disease.

Harriet hooked up with Bradley Kelly in 1986, when he and I were both cast in *Doheny Beach Holiday* along with Erica. Kelly was one of those dark-haired, square-jawed men with perfect teeth who managed to keep working because he fit a particular character type. Never the star, he played the put-upon father, or the comic lothario who served as a foil to the leading man, or the top cop's partner. I assumed that he'd be history by the end of shooting, just like all the others. I was wrong.

In front of the camera, he was a mediocre actor. Off the set, though, he was a master performer, a storyteller whose stories featured his own exploits—his heroism under-fire in Vietnam; his court martial for protesting the war when he recognized its evils; his life as an itinerant musician, waiter, avant-garde photographer, street performer, actor, drunkard, junkie, time traveler, and quantum explorer able to straddle universes. In the early years, he feigned reluctance to talk about the spiritual transformation that he experienced in 1978 when he passed through a crease in the universe and communed with the Celestial Fountain of All That Is. It seemed as if his listeners had to pry the precious secret out of him with a verbal crow bar.

His other stories masqueraded as self-deprecating anecdotes about his personal history. But they weren't self-deprecating at all, because they always ended with an epiphany about some mystical truth that only he knew, imparted to him through his encounters with the Fount. It was insidious and highly effective proselytizing. Though all of his stories were fiction, what was true was that he held the deepest conviction that he was God's divine messenger on earth. Most people ended up rolling their eyes and recoiling from him. But he didn't care. Convince just one in fifty and soon there will be millions of adherents, he preached. He had a magical ability to make certain people believe in him—wounded souls desperate to find God or sobriety or earthly success or spiritual awareness or love or immortality. My mother yearned for all of those things, and she was willing to give Kelly everything she had to get them. She was even willing to deliver up her only child.

By anointing Harriet Stern *Quiana Gottschalk*—an absurd bastardization of Hawaiian and German meaning *celestial servant of God*—Bradley Kelly saved her life. In the months after they got together, she soaked up his pop-religious doctrine. She came to believe that he truly purged her cells of contaminants—drugs, pride, depression, lust. The trade-off: she provided not only the business acumen that he sorely needed to build his nascent church, but also the obscene millions that the studios paid me to star in their movies. Together, they were crafty enough to evade the Coogan Act, which was supposed to protect my money. They found a loophole that let them get a court order to invest money in my future. They diverted that money to Kelly's embryonic Assembly. He rewarded her by appointing her an Assembly elder, which allowed her to realize her life-long dream of becoming someone important. He needed her organizational and business skills. Once a wild social butterfly, she withdrew into the Assembly's cocoon, a kind of reverse metamorphosis. Even the upper echelon of the Assembly rarely saw her. She became a divine shadow, which gave her a powerful mystique.

The car makes a sharp turn and lurches to a stop. I hear muffled voices and then the metallic scrape of an electronic gate opening. We're at a security checkpoint. I still remember the barrier after more than twenty years—an imposing wrought-iron fence topped with razor wire that destroyed any illusion of stateliness. I reach for the blindfold. The man sitting next to me grabs my arm. I lower my hand.

The car creeps forward, the tires making a crunching sound on what I remember is a graveled private road. We drive another few minutes up a steep hill. I hear the car door open. The man next to me takes my arm.

"Come with me," he says. "Watch your head." He puts his hand on the crown of my head as though I'm an arrestee exiting a police car and guides me under the doorframe.

"Walk slowly," he says, keeping hold of my arm. "Don't stumble."

I stop for a moment and stretch my body. I smell eucalyptus trees and salt air, beautiful fragrances individually, but in combination enough to send a chill through my body.

"I know where we are," I say, in a show of false bravado. "We're at Bradley Kelly's compound up above the Pacific Coast Highway. Near the Ventura County line. I told you this blindfold's a joke."

"We have to go up some stairs," he says.

We ascend seven steps. A door opens. My minder guides me inside the house. But instead of leading me forward to where I remember the staircase, he takes my shoulders and spins me a quarter turn to the right, and suddenly I feel disoriented. The illusion that I have even a modicum of control evaporates, and my legs begin to quiver. I strain to remember—am I facing a wall or a closet or the entrance to another room? There's a loud rumble, and without warning the man gives me a half-shove forward, and my toe catches on something, and I stagger, but before I go to the ground, he grabs me and holds me up, wrenching my shoulder in the process.

"My apologies, sir," he says. But I'm sure the push was payback for taunting him with my knowledge of Kelly, knowledge that a Philistine like me shouldn't have.

He's taken me into an elevator that didn't exist twenty years ago. The doors close. We ascend so slowly that it doesn't feel like we're moving at all. At last, the doors slide open. He leads me out of the elevator and down what I take to be a hallway. We make a right turn and walk another ten steps. He pulls off my blindfold.

"Wait here," he says, and leaves before I can turn and look at him.

It takes a while for my eyes to adjust to the light. When they do, my heart ripples. They blindfolded me not to hide the location of the residence, but to make sure that the first thing I saw was this room.

CHAPTER 49

They've converted the space into an elegant library with a parquet floor and red-oak paneled walls. They've installed modern recessed lights in the high ceiling. The curtained windows have an unobstructed view of the ocean. The walls are divided into alcoves that house bookshelves. There are two dark-stained double doors at the far end and a smaller door behind me. There's a long leather sofa on one side of the room and a walnut desk on the other. In the middle of the wall across from me is a massive oil painting in a gold frame. Kelly is shown on one knee with his arms outstretched. His luminous face is bathed in the radiance of the Fount. His alternate universe has elm trees and babbling brooks and maidenhair ferns and palisades and blue-winged angels.

I expect them to let me stew for a while, but the door swings open almost immediately. She strides into the room, swinging her arms purposefully—in the old days, her signature grand entrance. Over the past two days, I've tried to imagine my mother at fifty-seven. I've pictured a wrinkled grandmother, a surgically altered Barbie doll, a hideous crone scarred by wickedness, a fleshy earth mother, and any number of other permutations of Harriet Stern twenty-three years after I last saw her. She looks nothing like I imagined, precisely because she's unmistakably the same woman. The aging process hasn't passed her by, of course. She's dressed in a cream silk blouse and dark pants, stylish and tasteful. She never dressed tastefully when I was a kid. Though she's still slender, the lines of her body are softer, fleshier. She appears shorter than I remember, but that makes sense because I grew three inches after I left. She still has light brown hair—out of a bottle now—which she wears pulled back in a tight bun. She's plucked her eyebrows and filled them in with pencil or maybe tattoos. Her face has become more angular, verging on severe, which accentuates her curved nose, but also gives her a reserved, almost regal bearing unimaginable in the mother I used to know.

She comes over and stands a foot away from me, as if we're a normal mother and son greeting each other at the start of our weekly visit. I reflexively step back. I don't feel a twinge of filial affection or guilt or regret. I spent my reserves of those emotions when I visited Erica Hatfield. She turns and walks over to the leather sofa and sits, then pats the space next to her. Is this an act, an attempt to disarm or unsettle me? I pull up a chair from the desk and sit across from her.

"Tell me, Parky," she says in her still familiar fluty voice. "What is this mess?"

"The Assembly has hurt people very close to me. But I'm sure you know all about that."

"True adherents do not harm anyone. The Fount promotes peace and tolerance for all people. You were taught that when you were a child. You're here because of our lawsuit."

"I'm here because Harmon Cherry, Richard Baxter, and Deanna Poulos. All dead because someone inside your church killed them."

"Would you like something to drink, Parky? Some tea? Or water?" Her composure astonishes me. She waits a moment for my reply, but I can only gape at her. She shrugs daintily. "I think I'll have some tea." She goes over to the desk, pulls open a drawer filled with bags of exotic teas, drops one into her cup, and pours steaming water from a ceramic kettle. She sits back down, balancing the cup and saucer on her knees. "Harmon Cherry was a friend of the Assembly. His suicide was a tragedy. We could have helped him."

"Rich Baxter told me that Harmon was murdered."

"Rich Baxter was a thief and a drug addict. He took millions of dollars destined for good works and killed himself when he was found out. I don't know anything about this third person . . . Diana?"

"*Deanna*. Shot to death. Am I next on the list?"

She sighs. "Do you know why we hired Harmon?"

I, too, can play the game of answering a question with a question. "Who's this *we* you're talking about, Harriet? Who's this clandestine hierarchy who leads your church? Back at the firm, there was just McCarthy and the faceless drones who worked for him. Now I know there's still you. Who are the others?"

"In accordance with the words of the Celestial Fount, we're everywhere and nowhere. We're material and incorporeal, of the flesh and of the spirit, woven into the fabric of society with invisible thread. We'll show ourselves only on that glorious vernal night when the Sanctified Founder translates back from the Sixth Level Universe, when the word of the Fount burns with heavenly fire across the starry sky, turning night into day. McCarthy and the others are but earthly clarions trumpeting the Fount's word. You were taught this, Parky."

When I see her fervent expression, I feel a familiar heaviness in my limbs. After so many years, I somehow forgot that it isn't an act, that she really believes this stuff. "In answer to your question, you hired Harmon Cherry as your lawyer because there was no one better."

"It's true the Harmon was the best. But we sent . . . I had McCarthy send the business to Macklin & Cherry because you were there."

"I don't believe you."

"You couldn't have thought it a coincidence."

It never occurred to me that it was anything but.

She smiles indulgently. "Oh, Parky. You *did* think it was a coincidence. How incredibly naïve of you. And yet at the same time strangely narcissistic, as though the twin lights of fate and destiny shine only on you. No, we hired Macklin & Cherry because you were there. I wanted you to work on our matters. If you'd advocated for us, truly understood our beliefs, maybe we wouldn't have seemed so bad to you after all. Maybe you would've finally seen the light. Maybe you'd have returned to the fold someday."

"I would've quit the firm before I touched any of that work."

"You were a rising star at the law firm. You've always been a star. Then you strayed, and you lost it all. You've shut your eyes like a frightened four-year-old who believes that if he doesn't see the truth, the truth no longer exists."

A sickening thought occurs to me. "Did Harmon know I'm your son?"

"Of course not. He didn't know that I existed. No one knows that I exist except a select few in the Assembly." She smiles. "I've become a mythical character, you know."

My smile mocks hers. "So have I. The First Apostate. You should've seen McCarthy's face when I used those words at his deposition. Traces of the truth have survived no matter how hard you've tried to suppress it, right Harriet?"

Her expression hardens, and her eyes blaze with threat.

I shake my head in disgust. "How were Rich and Harmon killed? Who killed Deanna?"

"Harmon and Rich killed themselves. I have no idea what happened to your other friend."

"Prove it to me, Harriet."

She takes a sip of tea. "I'd prefer it if you called me—"

"You know I won't call you Quiana. And I can't believe you'd ask me to call you *Mom*."

If I didn't know better, I'd swear there was a tinge of hurt in her eyes. I couldn't care less.

"What is it that you want?"

"Three things. First, I want a copy of Harmon Cherry's notes."

She shakes her head as though she doesn't understand.

"Rich found some notes that Harmon prepared just before he died. They have something to do with the embezzlement scheme. Lou Frantz claims they don't exist, but I think they do and that you're hiding them."

"We have no such notes."

"Come on, Harriet. Rich said—"

"He was a liar. If something like that existed don't you think we'd want to know about it? They do not exist."

As a child, I developed an uncanny ability to detect her lies. It was a matter of self-preservation. Now, she seems to be telling the truth. Have the years dulled my ability to gauge her credibility?

"What are your other requests?" she asks.

"Let's be accurate. They're demands, not requests. I want you to tell me why the Assembly paid Lake Knolls's chief of staff half a million dollars last year. And I want you to spread the word that Rich Baxter was murdered so your members won't shun Monica Baxter and her son."

The muscles of her neck tighten, in years past the sign of an impending explosion. She puts her cup and saucer down so hard that they nearly shatter. "Why would I share information with you, our sworn enemy? Someone who even as we speak is our antagonist in a court trial? Why would I ignore the truth and my own religious convictions by exposing the flock to contamination from the family of a suicide?"

"Because if you don't, I'll go public."

She studies my face for a moment. Her chin drops when she realizes what I mean. She bolts up from the sofa and goes to the window, standing with her back turned. Then she spins around and walks back, coming within inches of my face. "You know what happens when you detonate a nuclear device? You not only destroy your target, you destroy everything, even the things that you hold dear. You destroy yourself. You've never been prepared to do that."

"Things have changed. Namely, Deanna Poulos. Richard Baxter. Harmon Cherry. There's also the hatchet job that McCarthy did on my law student, Lovely Diamond."

"Your law student? You mean your girlfriend, don't you? She's quite the little whore."

"*You* think *she's* a whore? Talk about the pot calling the kettle—"

She slaps my face hard. I revel in the sting. She's afraid of me.

CHAPTER 50

When I was a child, this room wasn't a library. The windows weren't bright and airy like now, but closed off by blackout curtains and iron security bars. The soundproof walls were covered with crimson drapes. There was a powerful stereo system with ceiling and wall speakers constantly pumping out the smooth jazz that Kelly liked. The lights were on dimmers, and during the "celebrations," as Kelly called them, they would be turned down low. One of the attendants would light candles and burn incense. All these years later, I still can't stand the smell of patchouli. In the middle of the room was a vast bed, far bigger than a king, at least eleven feet wide and fifteen feet long. Kelly bragged about how he'd imported it from England. He called it a super-Caesar bed, fitting because he fancied himself to be more powerful than a Roman emperor. The emperors couldn't flit between universes.

I started participating in the sacrament called Ascending Sodality when I was thirteen, according to the original tenets of the Assembly, set forth in the secret Chronicles of the Celestial Fountain: *When a young person reaches his or her fourteenth year, the parents shall deliver that young person up to the Elders, willingly and with love, the male to the female Elder, the female to the male Elder. And the youthful initiates shall cleave to the Elders, who shall teach them connubial love, and they shall be married to the Elders and the Elders shall be married to them in the eyes of the Assembly.*

The Assembly was becoming a new, hip underground religion, one that appealed to the wealthy because it didn't make them feel selfish and callous. Wealth was a sign of purity and heavenly grace. The most fervent believers, a group of twenty-two trusted insiders and their families, came to the compound to engage in Ascending Sodality.

Maybe the events of that evening happened because that morning, the increasingly volatile Kelly had engaged in a screaming match with my mother over some trivial decision she'd made without consulting him. Maybe they occurred because I was a fifteen-year-old who'd spent my entire life being the center of attention, who'd been a big star while Kelly struggled to land supporting roles. Probably he did it because he thought he could.

I hadn't been scheduled to participate in a celestial celebration that night, so I was surprised that they summoned me to the room. As usual, I simultaneously felt arousal, apprehension, and disgust. Despite Kelly's brainwashing, I knew innately that what I was doing—what *they* were doing to *me*—was twisted. Afterward, I'd feel a malaise, like the first vague symptom of a festering illness.

I knocked and went inside. The incense in the air felt heavier than usual. I took several breaths through my mouth so I could avoid the smell, but the smoke singed my lungs. Kelly stood in the middle of the room, fully clothed. Lying on the bed naked was a woman I knew as Greta, a wealthy downtown art dealer who had a son about my age. Greta was more attractive than most of the women—a brunette with a broad Slavic face, full sensuous lips, and aggressive, stony eyes, the darkest brown I'd ever seen. Most of the other women who practiced Ascending Sodality couldn't hide their embarrassment or trepidation, no matter how often they'd had sex with children. Greta had no such inhibitions. She truly enjoyed young boys.

Kelly always watched these sessions, but never participated. He called himself a steward of celestial love. After a while, I got used to his presence. You can get used to almost anything when it means you get to feel good.

Kelly ordered me to undress. When I finished, Greta stood up, took my hand, and led me to the bed.

"It's a great honor," Greta whispered. Her face was glowing with rapture, like that of a true believer who's just recognized the image of the Blessed Virgin in a water stain.

"I don't know what you mean."

"He's bestowing a great honor upon you. He's the celestial messenger. I offered him my son, but he picked you."

I still didn't get it, but before I could ask her what she meant she batted her eyelashes, a gesture so melodramatic I expected a director to yell "cut." She leaned over and took me into her mouth. She sucked on me for a while and then pulled away.

"Fuck me now," she said. The rawness of her tone startled me. In the past, spoken words had to stay romantic and tender—exalted, Kelly would say. Ascending Sodality wasn't supposed to be dirty or profane. I expected Kelly to chastise her for the language, but he didn't. I hesitated.

"Put your cock inside me," she said insistently.

Another aberration—no foreplay. We boys had been taught gentleness, kisses, caresses. I hesitated and then reached for the basket of condoms that were kept on the nightstand. It was the height of the AIDS epidemic, and Kelly made safe sex a sacrament.

"Never mind that," Kelly said from somewhere behind me.

"But—"

"Never mind that!"

I wanted to refuse, but I obeyed because I was afraid of what he'd do if I didn't. I entered her carefully, just as I'd been taught.

"Do it hard," Kelly ordered. "Hard and fast."

Greta looked up at me with her half-open eyes and nodded. I began pistoning inside her. She matched my thrusts, and soon I felt as if we were nothing more than complementary machine parts. As always during these so-called celebrations, my mind became numb, incapable of feeling any emotion, much less transcendent love—unless crude physical pleasure counts as an emotion.

"Don't stop until I tell you," Kelly said.

It wasn't difficult. One thing that we boys had learned from practicing Ascending Sodality with older women was self-control.

I felt something tickling the back of my neck, like the legs of a large insect. I flinched. It took a moment to register that I was feeling Kelly's hand, and I heard him say, *The time has come*, and I looked back and saw that he was naked from the waist down, his penis erect, and I felt Greta hump back harder in excitement, and I started to pull out and let him take my place inside her, but when I felt him press his chest against my back and wrap his arms around my waist, I realized that it wasn't her body he wanted, but mine. I screamed.

Even sodomy involving a male and female violated Assembly edict, and Kelly preached that homosexuality was a cardinal sin. In his public statements he made no apologies for his homophobia. He had this theory—AIDS was caused not by a virus, but by the mutation of T-cells resulting from the unclean act of anal intercourse itself.

"Relax, baby boy," Greta whispered. "If you relax, it won't hurt so much."

I discovered then that I was no longer a child, that I could fight if I had to. I'd grown strong in the last year, and the sheer terror made me stronger. I flailed my limbs and elbowed Kelly in the sternum with all my might. Greta shrieked, as if I had struck God. Kelly backed away. I used the brief window of his surprise to roll off the bed and onto the floor. I got to my feet, but when I tried to run I tripped over the raised edge of the carpet and fell to one knee. Kelly reached for me, but I scrambled away from him, managed to stand, and ran out the door and down the corridor, stark naked. I made it back to my room, not knowing whether anyone saw me, not knowing whether Kelly was following me, certain that in short order he'd send his crew of Assembly goons after me. I'd not only disobeyed the wishes of the Assembly leader, I'd struck him. I would be punished for my heresy. I had to get out of there. But first I went into the bathroom and vomited.

CHAPTER 51

arriet and I stand face to face, glaring at each other. I point to one of the bookshelves. "Kelly used to keep the writings of John Humphrey Noyes right there for inspiration. Stirpiculture, complex marriage. Nineteenth-century cult euphemisms for eugenics and pedophilia. Is the book still on the shelf?"

"I get daily reports about your courtroom performance. Frantz demolished you yesterday. You have no credibility left after that pathologist's testimony. The media won't dare print a word you say because they'll know it's just a desperate attempt to salvage your lawsuit."

"Oh, someone will believe me. You've given me the perfect platform—the lawsuit. Starting Monday, I intend to use the legal system as my own personal PR machine. We live in a new world, Harriet. All I have to do is convince one blogger. He or she can be anywhere—Sweden, Panama, Moscow. And once it's out on the Internet, the story will go viral. They'll want nothing more than to believe that Bradley Kelly was a pedophile and that his perversion infects the Assembly to this day. Your group still isn't very popular with the general public, in case you haven't noticed. And then more will come forward. Who knows how many children Kelly and the others abused? At the compound alone, there were, what, at least two dozen of us kids who went through it? It only takes one to speak out, and then others will. They can't all still be Assembly devotees."

She takes a step forward as if she's going to slap me again. Then she backs away and crosses her arms.

"I'm sure you've followed the Catholic Church's molestation scandal closely," I continue. "The Vatican has paid billions in compensation and legal fees, not to mention suffered severe damage to its reputation. And the Catholic Church has existed for two thousand years. What do you think would happen to a so-called religion that's only been around for twenty-five?"

"Brad has been dead seventeen years. The Assembly's bigger than him."

"That's like saying that the Christian church is bigger than Jesus. And it's not just about Kelly, it's about Ascending Sodality as a core tenet." I pause. "And the child abuse is about you personally. You and everyone else who participated are criminals. Sex offenders."

Her eyes bloat in horror. "I never did that and you know it. Never. I stopped it when I found out what he did to you."

"That's what you've always maintained. Whatever. You didn't protect me or the other children from those predators. You're still just as guilty as every adult who touched a child. So is the Assembly as a legal entity. The statute of limitations hasn't expired, you know."

"Don't threaten us, Parker."

"You've had plenty of opportunities to kill me. You'll have plenty more. Why haven't you done it?"

"Oh, Parky. How did you get so lost? My poor child."

"I'm not your child."

Although not one hair is out of place, she brushes an invisible strand off her forehead. "No. You aren't, are you? You haven't been my son since you left that night. So think about why you've kept silent all these years. Because Erica Hatfield or whatever she calls herself these days will be exposed, too, and she's defective. She won't survive it."

Like my mother, Erica was a follower of Bradley Kelly. Unlike my mother, she did have sex with underage boys. But never with me.

"She saved me when you wouldn't," I say.

"You never gave me the chance."

"You had hundreds of chances. When I was a kid, you lived your entire life through me, but when you joined the Assembly I became an afterthought. Did you really believe Ascending Sodality would teach me celestial love? Or did you just not think about it at all?"

"She's the one who hurt children. Yet you forgave her and despise me."

"She rescued me."

"She stole you from me!"

After I ran from Kelly that night, I went to Erica's room. When I told her what had happened, she spirited me outside and hid me in the trunk of her car. I heard her tell the security guard that she was late to a movie premier. But Kelly had ordered a lockdown, so he wouldn't let her out. She pled and argued and cajoled, to no avail. Only when she promised to give him a blowjob when she got back did he open the gates.

Later, when we were free of the place for good, she begged me to go to the cops. I refused—she'd had sex with numerous boys between the ages of thirteen and sixteen. If I'd have pressed charges, she would have gone to prison along with the others. I hired a lawyer, whom I told about the Assembly's theft of my savings but not about Ascending Sodality. The Assembly repaid the money in exchange for my silence. A court granted my petition for emancipation from Harriet. I moved out of Erica's house after eight months, the only way either of us could start fresh. I got an apartment and used my real name and let my hair grow out to its natural color and went to a public high school in the Valley where no one suspected that I'd been an actor. The tabloids made some desultory efforts to find me, but I quickly became old news. Parky Gerald no longer existed.

Now, after so many years, I stare into my mother's eyes and feel the one undeniable genetic bond between us—a stubborn combativeness so ingrained that we could both destroy ourselves just for the sake of not giving in.

"You know what I want," I say. "Harmon's notes, an explanation of the payment to Knolls, and peace for Monica Baxter and her son. You have twenty-four hours. Except on the Monica Baxter point. That begins as soon as I leave."

"We won't give in to your threats." She turns around and storms out.

They leave me in that room for another half hour. At last, one of the men who drove me to the compound comes in, blindfolds me, and

ushers me out to the car. This time, he takes the blindfold off as soon
as we pass through the gates of the compound. I guess they wanted to
make sure I didn't see any of the elders walking around the grounds.

Unlike the bizarre trip to the Assembly compound earlier today,
the ride home passes quickly. Now, I welcome the silence. I hold out
scant hope that my mother will give in to my demands. In twenty-four
hours, I'll go to the media, starting with Brandon Placek at the *Times*.
At least, I'll get his attention. If he won't write the story, I'll contact the
other major media outlets. If they don't believe me, I'll work my way
down, until someone has the courage to publish the truth. I just need
one person to publish the truth.

We arrive at the shopping center where I left my car. My handler
parks in an isolated area of the lot, leaving the engine running. Before I
can open the door, he reaches back and hands me an envelope. As soon
as I exit the car, he speeds away.

With trembling hands, I open the envelope and pull out a stack
of papers, which I recognize immediately: McCarthy's itinerary for his
May 2011 trip and a wire transfer receipt memorializing The Emery
Group's $500,000 payment to Delwyn Bennett. My mother has given
me what Lou Frantz wouldn't.

CHAPTER 52

Jonathan and Kathleen arrive in the law school classroom together, followed by Lovely five minutes later. She's dressed in a leopard-print sports bra and matching skintight shorts, exposing a bare midriff. Wisps of hair have escaped from the band around her ponytail. She's been working out at the school gym, and her skin glistens with sweat. She looks terrific. I presume that the stories about her porn career have already hit the Internet. Her choice of wardrobe reflects her usual in-your-face attitude.

"Sorry to impose on your Saturday evening," I say. "I hope you didn't have plans."

"A girl like me always has plans," she says in a steamy voice.

Jonathan chortles. Kathleen slaps his arm. Lovely must be the talk of the law school. I wish I could protect her from all that. Thankfully, the semester will end in a couple of weeks and she can get away from here.

"We had a bad day in court yesterday," I say. "But I have something important to show you that might turn that around." I project a PowerPoint slide on the classroom monitor. "This is a document reflecting a five hundred thousand dollar wire transfer on May 2, 2011, from The Emery Group to a man named Delwyn Bennett. He happens to be Representative Lake Knolls's chief of staff."

Lovely's jaw drops. This document confirms the information that Ed Diamond got from his underworld sources about the payment to Bennett. When Jonathan and Kathleen start peppering me with questions, Lovely and I act as if we only learned about this payment today.

"Where did you get this document?" Jonathan asks. "Did Frantz finally—?"

"I didn't get this from Frantz. But let's just see if we can figure out what this payment was for." I project the next slide. "This is Christopher McCarthy's itinerary for his vacation in May and June of last year. I think the trip is related to The Emery Group's payment to Bennett."

"How do you know that?" Kathleen asks.

"I just do," I say, annoyed at her perfectly appropriate question. "Now, let's focus on the merits."

The slide reads: *Sunday May 22, 2011—Bratislava; Wednesday May 25, 2011—Sofia; Friday May 27, 2011—Chisinau; Saturday May 28, 2011—Helsinki; Tuesday May 31, 2011—Paris*; and then a flight back to Los Angeles on June 15.

"Any ideas about what to make of this?" I ask. "Because I don't."

"He likes Paris better than those other cities?" Jonathan says. "I know I would."

I glare at him. I'm in no mood for class clowning.

There's a long lull while we stare at the screen. Finally, Lovely says, "Aren't they all the capitals of their respective countries?"

Jonathan does a Google search and after a minute says, "You're right. They are all national capitals. I wasn't sure about Chisinau, but yeah, it's the capital of Moldova."

"I've never heard of that country," Kathleen says.

"It's next to Romania on the Black Sea," Jonathan says.

"McCarthy lied when he testified he was on vacation," I say. "It was some kind of business trip."

"Or politics," Jonathan says. "Where there are capitals, there are politicians, right?"

"Yeah," I say. "More likely politics. Anything else?"

We fall silent again. I stare at the slide, but I'm so tired from the day's drama that I can't form a coherent thought. "This is frustrating," I say. "We're so close to nailing those motherfuckers."

Kathleen's face flushes scarlet. "Professor Stern—"

"Sorry about the language Ms. Williams, but I—"

"Let me finish. This stuff doesn't prove that the Assembly did anything wrong. So what if McCarthy met with politicians. He's a lobbyist, right? Isn't it his job to meet with people in politics? And his trip doesn't necessarily have anything to do with that payment to that Bennett guy." Though she says all of this in a calm tone, her anger is palpable.

I strain to keep my own voice steady. "Ms. Williams, The Emery Group made the payment to Delwyn Bennett only a few weeks before McCarthy took this trip. McCarthy controlled The Emery Group's account. He went to great lengths not to produce this itinerary in discovery. There has to be a connection between the trip and the payment."

"No there does not," she insists. "It doesn't have to mean anything like that. You're always so quick to condemn the Assembly. And you've been so majorly wrong. Look at the debacle yesterday with Rich Baxter's broken . . . what's it called, hyoid bone. Check out the Internet. The media is laughing at us."

My anger wells up, the caustic kind that that's all too easy to direct at gentle people like Kathleen. "Ms. Williams, are you familiar with these words from Bradley Kelly? 'The Sanctified must turn their backs on profane temptations from whomever they come and abjure petty loyalties and banish those whose souls are defective and immerse themselves in the cleansing waters of the Fount.'"

"I've read that."

"*Abjure petty loyalties*, Ms. Williams. Your loyalties obviously lie elsewhere. I want the truth. Did you tell the Assembly that I was looking for Grace Trimble? That Grace used the alias Sandra Casey?"

"Parker!" Lovely says.

Jonathan's body goes rigid. "You got to be joking, dude."

"You're asking me if I . . . ?" Kathleen's voice cracks. Her jaw keeps moving, but no words come out. She blinks a few times and gathers herself. "You're seriously accusing me of giving confidential information to the opposition? Of being some kind of spy? I've been killing myself on your trial, and—"

"He didn't mean it that way, Kathleen," Lovely says. "He's just—"

"That's exactly what I meant."

Kathleen slumps down in her seat and turns away so I can see only the side of her face. She fans her eyes with her hand in a futile attempt to stave off tears.

Jonathan stands. "Fuck this, man. You've lost it. Kathleen wouldn't do anything like that." He takes her hand. "Come on, Kath."

"Mr. Borzo, I suggest you—"

"I don't give a damn what you suggest. This isn't a class, it's a circus. And we're done with your trial. Optional, right? You've fucked it up anyway. You aren't qualified to teach us anything."

I watch as he helps her gather up her things. All the while, Lovely has this disappointed yet detached look of a lab worker who's just witnessed a botched experiment. Jonathan leads Kathleen out of the classroom, making sure to slam the door hard behind him. Shaken, I lean back against the wall.

Lovely rests her chin in her hands and closes her eyes as if I've exhausted her. "I absolutely don't believe that Kathleen did what you accused her of. Do you know how hard she and Jonathan have been working? And she's right, you know. This stuff about McCarthy is definitely intriguing, but it doesn't prove anything."

I bow my head and use my thumbs to rub my temples in what I know will be a futile attempt to stave off a raging headache. "OK. You're right. Kathleen was right. All of you are a thousand percent right. I'm an asshole." I look at her, really look at her, for the first time since I watched that video. With her hair pulled back in that high ponytail, she looks, not sexy or brazen, but young and fresh, like one of the ingénues in the G-rated movies I acted in as a kid. "Why didn't you leave with Kathleen and Jonathan?"

She removes the scrunchie holding her ponytail and lets her hair down, which she pulls back to make a tighter ponytail. "You know, I probably *should* leave. But my father taught me never to abandon the people you love."

CHAPTER 53

Though Deanna's dayshift manager, Romulo, is trying to keep the place open, I won't set foot in there until Deanna's memorial service. Her parents won't schedule one until they get the final autopsy results, and that could take weeks. So I spend this Sunday morning sequestered in my condo, rereading the documents that Harriet gave me and trying to think of a way to use them in court. Kathleen's right—McCarthy's itinerary and the payment to Bennett don't prove anything conclusive. I don't even have admissible evidence that McCarthy was the signatory on the account from which the payment was made. Yet, the documents are all I have, so I'll use them and see if I can blow enough smoke to raise doubt in the jury's mind about Rich's guilt.

I grope around for a fresh approach, something that might lead some of the jurors to question Frantz's pat version of the case. My only chance is to convince at least four of them to hang the jury, which at this point would be a victory. I leave the condo and take a run down Venice beach, passing the skate park and the street vendors and the tattoo emporiums and the pot shops, dodging the rollerblading daredevils and the slow-moving cyclists. I find myself focusing, not on the trial, but on the loved ones I've lost. Soon, I'm running past a throng of people with tears streaming down my face.

When I get back home, I go to the computer and locate a document that I haven't thought about in months—an electronic version of disgraced private investigator Ray Guglielmi's report arguing that Harmon Cherry was murdered. After I met with her last October, Layla Cherry e-mailed me a copy even though I'd refused to take her case against the insurance company. Maybe there's something in the report I can use to raise questions in the jury's mind.

Reading the document closely for the first time, I'm struck by how specific Guglielmi is in describing his theory about Harmon's death. He believes that the killer had a second gun, which he or she used to subdue Harmon. The killer then took Harmon's Glock out of the desk drawer, forced Harmon to hold it, covered Harmon's hand with his or her own, and pulled the trigger. Or maybe the shooter fired and then put the gun in Harmon's hand and fired a second shot out through the open French doors toward the deserted beach. This would have left the gunshot residue found on Harmon's hand and would also explain the two sets of illegible latent prints, which the killer only somewhat successfully tried to wipe away. Guglielmi believes that Harmon had his back to the desk when he was killed—a position that would give the murderer more room to maneuver—and that after the shooting, the killer swiveled Harmon's chair to face the desk. This would account for the shell casing being found to the right of Harmon's body, even though the gun was found to the left. In a rare example of objectivity, Guglielmi admits that the blood spatter evidence is inconclusive on Harmon's position when he was shot. Guglielmi next hypothesizes that Harmon's eyeglasses were found behind a planter some distance away because at some point he struggled with his assailant.

I should have studied this report earlier, should have given Guglielmi more credit, no matter how unsavory he is. I could have taken his deposition. It's impossible to get him to come to trial—he's locked up in federal prison.

I read on, stopping at a description of the Malibu beach house at the time of Harmon's death. I actually smile when I read what Guglielmi says about the office—a panoramic view of the Pacific Ocean, obscured by file cabinets and cartons of documents.

Then my fingers go slack, so slack that I can't hold the mouse. I should've seen it months ago.

When I met with Layla Cherry last October, she told me that there weren't any law firm files in her house. But I didn't ask her about the beach house. I should've asked about the beach house.

She answers on the third ring, and I tell her why I'm calling. It's a long shot, probably worse odds than that—she might have finally sold the place or just decided to clean out Harmon's things. I hold out a sliver of hope only because he rarely threw a document away. When she says that she still hasn't sold the beach house, I try not to sound too pleased at her misfortune.

A half hour later, I meet her at her house in Hancock Park. She hands me a set of keys and a piece of paper containing the security codes for the access gate and house alarm, and I set out for Malibu.

It's usually overcast near the ocean in May, but today the sky is an azure color. I fantasize about walking into Harmon's beach house, pulling open a file cabinet, and finding the elusive notes. Isn't that our nature, to believe that that the pain will stop, that the disease will be cured, that justice will be done, that it'll all work out in the end, even though logic and probability say it won't? When I reach Malibu, I turn left on a narrow access road and drive towards the ocean. The road widens into a two-lane street divided by a median of Kikuyu grass and queen palms. Just before the beach, the road makes a sharp right and runs parallel to the coastline. I stop at a locked security gate and punch in the code that Layla Cherry gave me. The gate swings open, and I drive another two blocks to Harmon's beachfront house.

I recognize the Mediterranean-style house by its adobe tile roof and garish tomato-soup red stucco exterior. It's actually one of the more modest homes in the neighborhood. Layla told me that she and her broker have reduced the asking price to $6,650,000. That Harmon owned a huge house in Hancock Park is impressive, but not unusual for a successful lawyer. Few attorneys, however, can afford beachfront property in Malibu. Harmon inherited some money from his father, but not enough to live in this neighborhood. I have a sickening thought—what if Harmon himself ripped off clients?

I grab a pen and a legal pad from my backseat and cross the courtyard to the front door. I unlock the door, go inside, and disarm the security system. I take a deep breath and switch on the light. When I enter the office, I shudder—this was the room where Harmon was shot, the room where he last took a breath. His curly maple/mapa burl desk is still there. So is his ergonomic leather chair. The walls are lined floor-to-ceiling with storage boxes bearing our firm name, Macklin & Cherry. Looking through these boxes for Harmon's notes could take days. I knew that Harmon compulsively hung on to documents, but I had no idea he was a hoarder.

Seized with the irrational hope that I'll find the notes right away, I pull a box down from the nearest stack and remove the lid. Or maybe the documents inside will at least all be irrelevant and easy to exclude. Neither of those things happens. Documents concerning the Church of the Sanctified Assembly are interspersed with files from unrelated matters. I have no choice but to sit down on the couch and start reading. The house is so close to the shoreline that I can hear the crash of the waves on the sand.

Harmon scribbled notes on legal pads and in the margins of documents, his leaky pen bleeding ink over the pages. At the firm, I worked out a way of deciphering his handwriting, but in the two years that have elapsed since the firm folded, I've lost that ability. As I'm struggling to interpret some marginalia, the door creaks open. Standing there is a gaunt woman with long stringy hair. Her ill-fitting green cotton dress is so wrinkled that she must have slept in it. She has a tattoo on her ankle, a goddess petting a lion. She looks like she's doing a bad impression of Jack Nicholson in *The Shining*, but instead of laughing I say, "My God, Grace, put that knife down and tell me what's going on."

CHAPTER 54

Grace Trimble draws the carving knife farther back behind her ear, though I'm at least twelve feet away. Her hand is shaking so violently it's a wonder that she can hold on to the thing at all.

"Stay back." Her voice is tremulous, feeble.

I hold my hands up in front of me. "I don't have any intention of coming close to you, Grace."

I already know one thing just from seeing her sunken cheeks and gray-tinged teeth. She was using the crystal meth that the feds found in Rich's apartment, and since then she's been using a lot more. She looks nothing like the fake call girl in the photos that Rich's landlord took. Neither does she resemble the erratic genius with whom I once practiced law.

"You killed Deanna," she says, slurring the words.

"Where did you come up with that bullshit?"

She lowers the knife and shakes her head vigorously, like a little girl on the verge of a tantrum. "You were coming to the shop. You—"

"I found her body lying there. I didn't kill her."

"You—"

"I, nothing. Tell me what happened that night."

She brandishes the knife again. "It was you, Parker."

"Cut the crazy act, Grace." It's a cruel thing to say. Also dangerous, because she's tweaking.

She blinks her eyes as if trying to ward off the effects of a punch.

"You're the one who has to explain," I say. "The cops are looking for you, you know. I wasn't with Deanna when she died, but you were. I had no reason to kill her, but you did. I know you sent Monica Baxter threatening e-mails. I cooperated with the police, but you ran. You had access to Rich's computer, which means you could have hacked into the Assembly's bank accounts and stolen that money. Did you do that, Grace?"

She blinks her eyes rapidly again, then shakes her head back and forth for a long time, not blinking at all. "I didn't do any of that. I . . . I loved Rich. Deanna was my best friend."

"What happened the night Deanna was killed?"

She touches her forehead with her free hand, revealing a large perspiration stain on her dress. She comes toward me. As she approaches, I avoid looking at the knife by keeping my gaze fixed on her. When she gets close, I detect a sour oniony odor. She hasn't bathed in days.

"Deanna was so awesome," she says. "A goddess like the one she was named for, the goddess of the hunt. Truthfully, you know how she found me? She found me through my tattoo artist. Yeah, she was able to find him because she was a hunter, she could hunt for people with tattoos. A couple of her friends own ink shops themselves, you know." She coughs in my face. For a split second, I think it's intentional, but then the cough persists, dry and hacking. When it finally stops, she wipes her mouth with the back of her hand.

"Are you all right?" I say.

"I feel wonderful. How do you feel?"

"Tell me what happened that night."

"I guess Deanna asked around until she found the guy who remembered drawing an ankle tattoo that looks like mine." She half lifts her leg and gestures toward the drawing. "It stands for strength. It's unique. I'm unique, you know." She giggles weakly. "Truthfully, Deanna told me that she knew that once I got the first tattoo, I'd get more. She was right. She was *so* right. The tattoo guy I went to had my cell phone number." She does a childish pirouette, grabs the hem of her dress, and lifts it to her waist. She's wearing thong panties, a hideous lime green color probably intended to match her awful dress. The small triangular patch of cloth is badly frayed. On her scrawny right buttock is a cartoonish tattoo of a hooded woman with antlers growing out of her head. "Look. Isn't she beautiful?"

I avert my eyes. "Cover up, Grace."

She thrusts out her lower lip, then lets her dress fall back to her knees and smoothes it down roughly. "What the fuck, Parker. I just wanted to show you my Beiwe. She's the Sami goddess of sanity. She's on my ass, and I just wanted you to . . ." Her voice falters. She lowers her eyes, then tugs at her hair. She jumps forward, and with a roundhouse motion swipes at my chest with the knife. I twist sideways and lean back, but the point of the blade rips my shirt and slashes my arm. I grab for her, but she takes a step back, more agile than I anticipated. I should run or throw a punch, but I do neither. I still need to hear what she knows about Rich and Deanna.

We stare each other down. Finally, she lowers her eyes and gapes at her hand in wonderment, as if it belongs to someone else. Her fingers unclench, and the knife falls to the floor with a harmless clatter. Without taking my eyes off her, I reach down and snatch it up. I don't really know what to do with it, except that I want to keep it close to me and far away from her. I slide it into the back waistband of my jeans, hoping I'll remember not to bend or twist the wrong way and stab myself.

"Jesus, Grace."

She gapes at me. Her jaw starts quivering. "Omigod, Parker. Omigod. Omigod." She covers her face with her hands. After a while, she lowers her hands and shrugs helplessly. "I'm so sorry," she mumbles. "Please forgive me. It's just that I'm so frightened. I didn't really mean to . . . Please forgive me." She points to my upper arm. "Omigod, you're hurt. Please forgive me."

The blood has soaked into my shirt. I roll up my sleeve and look at my arm. Luckily, it's more of a scratch than a cut. "You want me to believe that you didn't mean to hurt me? Tell me what happened the night Deanna was killed. Tell me what you know about the embezzlement scheme."

"OK. OK. Yeah. I can do that." She takes a deep breath, then another. "OK. I didn't want to meet with you that night. I don't . . . I didn't trust you. But Deanna told me I should. She swore you'd help me." She stifles another cough.

"I would've helped you. I'll still help you if I can."

"I wasn't going to go into her store until I was sure, until I could sample your vibrations to see if they were crystalline."

She's using Assembly-speak, despite her excommunication. I wonder what she thinks of my vibrations at this moment.

"I hid behind the dumpster in the alley," she continues. "I waited. Deanna said you would come through the back. I was supposed to follow. When I heard the shots, I ran away. I thought you killed her."

"I didn't get there until after she died. I would never hurt Deanna. You know how close Deanna and I were."

"Yeah. The two of you had sex together sometimes, right?"

"Did you see anyone else go into The Barrista that night? Before Deanna was killed?"

"I didn't see anyone come through the back."

"What were you and Rich looking for?"

"Someone was embezzling the Assembly's money. Millions had been funneled out of their accounts. I didn't care. They kicked me out of their church. But Rich cared, and so I agreed to help him even though we both knew it was dangerous. I loved him, you know."

"I know."

"But he wouldn't sleep with me like you and Deanna did together. He loved *her*."

"Monica."

She sneers at the mention of the name. "That woman. She stole him away from me."

"Rich told me that he found some notes that Harmon wrote. Do you know anything about them?"

"Rich found them on a DVD. But someone got into the apartment and took it. You already know that. Anyway, they sabotaged Rich's computer and framed him to make it look like he stole that money."

"Someone from the Assembly? Christopher McCarthy, maybe?"

Her laugh sounds more like a shriek. "I don't think that guy knows how to power a computer on."

"Then who had access? That landlord? What was his name, Dale Garner?"

"That creep. Always trying to take photos up my skirt. But no, not him."

"I came here to find Harmon's notes." I gesture at the boxes around the room. "Can you help me look through all this crap?"

"There's no point."

"How do you know?"

"Because I've already found them."

CHAPTER 55

"Call your next witness, counsel."

Frantz rises and mugs for the jury before saying, "Your Honor, having met its burden of proof, the plaintiff rests."

This is gamesmanship. He could have said the same thing when we adjourned on Friday, but he wanted me to think he had more witnesses so I wouldn't prepare my case-in-chief for this morning. Since I found Grace yesterday, I've done nothing else.

Judge Schadlow invites me to make my opening statement. I nod at Raymond. Lovely isn't in court—she's with Grace. We're afraid if we leave her alone, she'll run. Jonathan and Kathleen aren't here. I'm sure they're finished with me.

I walk to the lectern. Like Frantz, I work without notes. This is the first time since the trial started that I'm not on antianxiety medication. I'm not afraid, don't even have butterflies. My clear-headedness is oddly disorienting, like breathing pure oxygen.

"Your Honor. Counsel. Members of the jury. You've just heard Mr. Frantz announce in open court that the Plaintiff has met its burden of proof. It's not true. In our legal system, the plaintiff gets to go first. So far, you've only heard their side of the story. You, as jurors, can't come to a fair and just decision until you've heard both sides. That's not only the law, it's what we teach our kids from the day they can reason—you always have to hear both sides of the story before you can make a fair decision. And when you hear our side, you'll understand that the evidence doesn't show what Mr. Frantz says it does. It shows the exact opposite."

The jurors are attentive, even rapt, probably because I have some passion in my voice. I must have underestimated how much the Xanax–Valium cocktail suppressed my affect. Until now, I've probably sounded like I've been talking in my sleep.

I start by telling the jury who Rich Baxter was—a loving son, husband, and father, an amiable work colleague, a loyal friend. I talk about his representation of the Assembly, how he became the Assembly's lawyer and devoted his career and then his entire existence to the Church. When I launch into a description of the Assembly's peculiar beliefs, Frantz objects.

"Overruled," Schadlow says. "Let's hear the actual evidence, and we'll decide its relevancy then." Last week she would have sustained the objection. My resurrected courtroom abilities seem to have influenced her interpretation of the rules of evidence.

I go on to describe the Assembly's belief in alternate universes, its view on suicide, its aggressive conversion techniques, its quest for political power not only in America, but worldwide. I tell the jury that this evidence will prove critical to exonerating Rich Baxter.

"In conclusion," I say, "I'd like you to remember the testimony of Special Agent Holcomb, the FBI's forensic accountant. She told you that the Assembly's money went into a bank account in the name of a shell company called The Emery Group. But she didn't tell you where that money went after that. It was paid out to someone, but she didn't know to whom. Members of the jury, when we're done with our case, you'll know exactly where that money went. And it wasn't paid to Rich Baxter. Rich wasn't a criminal, he was the one trying to *stop* the crime. He was loyal to his client and his church, and in the end his loyalty cost him his life."

———

Raymond Baxter is my first witness. On the stand, he looks tired and frail, a bereaved father forced to defend his child's good name. He describes Rich's childhood, college years, and legal career up until the religious conversion. By the time we're done, he's breathless. The jurors seem uncomfortable, but also sympathetic. When I pass the witness, I brace myself—Frantz tore Raymond apart in deposition.

As it turns out, Frantz can't push Raymond without looking like a street thug. This isn't a conference room where the only observers are the videographer and court reporter. The jury won't like a lawyer who bullies a grieving father. So Frantz asks just three questions.

"Mr. Baxter, you lost touch with your son after he joined the Sanctified Assembly, did you not?"

"Correct. According to the Assembly, his late mother and I were contaminated because we were nonbelievers. So he had to . . . *disengage* is what those people call it. I didn't have contact with him after that until he called me from the jail two days before he was . . . before he died."

"Would you say that your son changed after he joined the Assembly?"

"Yes."

"Changed so much that you didn't know him anymore?"

"Absolutely. Those Assembly people . . ." Raymond realizes his error, but too late. He's just proved Frantz's point—once Rich joined the Assembly the son that Raymond knew ceased to exist. The new Rich could have been a thief.

"No further questions," Frantz says.

When Raymond sits down, I say, "The defense calls Christopher McCarthy."

McCarthy strides confidently to the witness stand. In theory, he's my witness, which makes this *direct* examination. On direct, it's usually the witness who does most of the talking because his lawyer can only ask open-ended questions. Leading questions—those requiring a *yes* or *no* answer—are the purview of *cross*-examination. But the rules make an exception for an adverse witness, and McCarthy is downright hostile. So I'll be able to cross-examine him with yes or no questions, and if all goes well, lead him where I want him to go.

"The Church of the Sanctified Assembly is your client, is it not?"

"As I testified to earlier in the trial, that's right."

"And you promote the Assembly's interests worldwide?"

"That would be accurate."

"And like any other consulting firm, if you don't succeed, your client has the right to fire you?"

"I suppose so, but the TCO is the only consultant the Assembly has ever had."

"You work hard to keep the Assembly happy, don't you?"

"I devote most of my waking hours to the Assembly, sir."

Having established that his major goal in life is to advance the Assembly's cause, I switch topics, getting him to confirm what I told the jury during my opening about the Assembly's belief system. True to form, he views my questions as a chance to proselytize. By posing questions in a respectful, yet mildly incredulous tone, I do an effective job of exposing him for the religious fanatic that he is.

"Let's move on to something else," I say. "You were on vacation from May 22, 2011, to June 15, 2011, weren't you?"

He blinks his eyes several times, waiting for Frantz to object. But as obstructionist as Frantz was at McCarthy's deposition on this subject, he can't now object to this seemingly innocuous question without suggesting that McCarthy has something to hide.

"I don't remember the exact dates, but that sounds about right."

"You traveled to Europe, didn't you?"

McCarthy glances at Frantz, a big mistake because a trial witness should never look to his lawyer for help. I just hope some of the jurors notice.

"I was in Europe," McCarthy says.

"What cities did you visit?"

"Objection," Frantz says. "Irrelevant. I don't see how—"

"It's an obvious foundational question," Judge Schadlow says. "Overruled."

"It also invades his privacy," Frantz says.

Schadlow takes off her reading glasses and tosses them on the bench. "Are you serious, Mr. Frantz? Where he spent his vacation a year ago hardly invades his privacy. I assume he was in public much of the time. Flew on a commercial jet? Landed in a public airport? Overruled."

"What cities did you visit on your vacation?" I ask.

He grimaces, trying to control his nervous tick. He looks up at the ceiling. "Paris, Helsinki. Some other cities. I saw the sights."

"Let me try and refresh your recollection about those other cities." I move to the podium and use the laptop to project one of the documents that Harriet gave me. "Is this a copy of your itinerary for your 2011 European trip?"

"Where did you get that?"

"I get to ask the questions, sir, not you. Please answer mine."

McCarthy again looks over at Frantz, his appeal for help now blatant.

Frantz pretends not to see McCarthy looking at him, but Nick Weir pops up. "Your Honor, for the record, Mr. Stern never produced a copy of this document to us, so we object to its use with this witness."

"If I understand Mr. Weir correctly," I say, "he's complaining that I didn't give him a copy of his own client's trip itinerary. I would have thought that if Mr. Weir wanted a copy of this document so badly, he could have asked Mr. McCarthy for it. The real question is why Mr. Weir and Mr. Frantz withheld the itinerary from me after I repeatedly asked for it in discovery."

"May we have a sidebar?" Frantz says. "I'd like to explain to the Court—"

"Did you refuse to produce the itinerary to Mr. Stern?" the judge says.

"We objected to its production and he never moved to compel," Frantz says. "So he can't now—"

"Stop talking, counsel. I haven't been on the bench all that long, but one thing I've made clear is that I don't tolerate lawyers who play discovery games. Your objection is overruled." She turns to McCarthy. "You'll answer all questions about your trip. Do you understand?"

"Yes, Your Honor," he mumbles.

"Is this a copy of your itinerary, sir?" I ask.

"Yeah."

"Prepared under your direction?"

"Yeah."

"On Sunday, May 22, 2011, you traveled to Bratislava, Slovakia?"

He looks at the judge. "For the record, I want to state that this question invades my personal privacy."

"Answer the question, Mr. McCarthy," the judge says. "Did you or did you not travel to Bratislava on May 22, 2011?"

"I did."

"On Wednesday, May 25, you were in Sofia, Bulgaria?" I ask.

"Yeah."

"On Friday, May 27, you arrived in Chisinau, the capital of Moldova?"

"It's an invasion of privacy. But the answer is yes."

Through further questioning, I get him to admit that he arrived in Helsinki, Finland, and Paris, France, on the dates indicated. Ordinarily, it would be a monotonous examination, but the jurors now know that something is up. When I finish with the list, I ask, "When you took this trip in 2011, did you conduct any business for the Church of the Sanctified Assembly?"

"I'm constantly carrying out the Assembly's mission, just as I do for all my clients."

"But were you in Europe specifically on Assembly business? And I want you to be very sure of your answer."

"No. That's why I told you it was a vacation, not a business trip."

It's just the answer I wanted.

CHAPTER 56

Frantz does his best to rehabilitate McCarthy, but the duplicative testimony about how he helped the FBI catch Rich falls flat. We take a recess, after which I sit alone at the defense table, waiting for the judge to retake the bench. When she does, I say, "The defense calls Grace Trimble."

No one gasps. That rarely happens in a real courtroom. But the significance of my calling Grace to the stand isn't lost on those in the room. There's the *click-clacking* of the journalists' keyboards, the murmurs from the less-restrained spectators, the rustling of jurors' notepads. Frantz stands to object, but thinks better of it. Grace is on our witness list. He doesn't want to incur Schadlow's wrath a second time in thirty minutes.

On cue, Lovely walks in, followed by Grace, wearing one of Lovely's gray business suits and a white blouse that we bought for her at Macy's. The jacket hangs off her shoulders, and the skirt falls to mid-calf. But she looks presentable.

Since I found her yesterday, she's become ever more depressed. She's also going through drug withdrawal. Over my strenuous objection, Lovely insisted on spending last night at my condo, sleeping in the living room not far from the door so she could make sure Grace didn't bolt—or, as Lovely put it, try to kill me again. Lovely basically had Grace trapped in my spare bedroom.

When Grace raises her right hand to take the oath, her arm quivers. As soon as she sits down, I ask, "Ms. Trimble, what do you do for a living?"

"I'm an attorney. Currently unemployed." She shifts her knees from side to side. Her forehead is already glistening with perspiration.

"Could you please speak up, Ms. Trimble?" the judge says.

"Yes. I said I'm a lawyer." Her voice isn't much louder than before.

I start with questions about her stellar credentials. She's always enjoyed boasting about her accomplishments. But after describing her Supreme Court clerkship and her successful cases at the law firm, she says wistfully, "But that was a long time ago."

"What's your area of expertise?"

"Constitutional law. Corporate finance. Business law. I tried to be a music lawyer early in my career, but that didn't work out so well." She reaches over for the pitcher of water on the judge's bench next to her. When she pours, her hands are so shaky that some of the water misses the cup. She doesn't seem to notice that she's spilled on her skirt. She gulps the water down.

"Why did you stop practicing law?" I ask.

"I suffer from bipolar disorder. I cycle through different mood swings, ranging from mania to depression. Throughout my adult life, I've also suffered from drug addiction and alcoholism. Right now, I'm having a problem with methamphetamine. Crystal meth."

"When was the last time you used crystal meth?"

In all innocence, Grace says, "What day is this?"

There's laughter in the courtroom. The only one who doesn't smile is Grace. I tell her it's Monday.

"Saturday night," she says. "I've been drug free for about thirty-six hours. I'm suffering withdrawal symptoms right now."

"Will you describe those symptoms?"

"I'm anxious. I crave the drug. I'm cycling into a depression. I'm hot and sweaty. Excuse me." She reaches over and pours herself another glass of water.

"Is there some reason that you wanted us to know about your illness and your drug problem, Ms. Trimble?"

"Yes. I don't want any misconceptions about who I am. I'm here to tell the truth—all of it."

I next elicit testimony about her personal and professional relationship with Rich Baxter and her excommunication from the Assembly. She describes how she and Rich kept in touch even though Assembly tenets prohibited him from having contact with her. She talks about how her fear of the Assembly caused her to use the alias Sandra Casey. She testifies that the only person she told about the name change was Rich.

"At some point in the summer or fall of 2011, did Mr. Baxter contact you?"

"Yes. He said that he'd discovered some fishy transactions involving Assembly money. He told me he'd stumbled on a DVD containing some notes that Harmon Cherry wrote. According to Rich, the notes reflected some kind of wrongdoing involving Assembly accounts. He said he thought maybe Harmon hadn't committed suicide after all, that Harmon was murdered. He asked for my help. I didn't want to at first, but he pleaded with me, so I agreed." Beads of sweat run down her forehead. She's perspiring so badly that the clerk gets up and hands her a box of Kleenex. Grace takes a tissue out and uses it to dab at her face and neck.

"Do you know why Mr. Baxter turned to you for help?"

"Because he trusted me. Because I'm good at that kind of analytical thinking and he isn't . . . wasn't."

"Before we talk about that, Ms. Trimble, let's get something out of the way. Did you know that when Rich Baxter was arrested at the apartment in Silver Lake, he was found with a false passport and a quantity of crystal meth?"

"Yes."

"Who acquired the false passport?"

"I did." She goes on to describe how she stole Markowitz's identity and obtained the false passport without Rich's knowledge, and how she convinced Rich to use the false name to rent the Silver Lake apartment. She describes how she became so frightened of the embezzler that she disguised herself as three different women, intentionally dressing provocatively to divert attention from her real purpose. She admits that the drugs found in the apartment were hers and that Rich wanted her to go into rehab, preferably at an Assembly decontamination center, but even at a mainstream facility. She says that the cash found in the apartment belonged to Rich, but it was for her in case she decided to run. All the while, she squirms in her chair and compulsively wipes her face and neck with the Kleenex. I begin to fear that the jurors will focus not on her words, but on her fidgeting.

"Did you ever see Rich Baxter using drugs?" I ask.

"He never took drugs."

"Then why was he losing weight?"

"He was working days at his law office and nights at Silver Lake trying to find out who was diverting Assembly money. He was also trying to spend time with his family. He was afraid that what happened to Harmon would happen to him. That's why he rented the Silver Lake place, to protect his family. So he wasn't sleeping and he wasn't eating."

"You mentioned some notes that Harmon Cherry prepared. What happened to them?"

"Someone stole the DVD containing them from the Silver Lake apartment. But I later found the original notes at Harmon's beach house, where I've been hiding out for a while." She gulps down the rest of the water in her cup and pours herself some more.

"With the court's permission, I'd like to have Harmon Cherry's notes projected on the courtroom monitors."

"Objection," Frantz says. "We've never seen this document before."

"I only got a copy of it yesterday," I say. "And I e-mailed it to both Mr. Frantz and Mr. Weir yesterday afternoon at four forty-five."

"Your Honor, I never got—" Frantz stops talking when Weir touches his arm and whispers something, and I know what. Lovely told me that every Sunday afternoon at three thirty, Frantz's IT department shuts down its computer system for maintenance. Any e-mail sent during that time resides in a central server and doesn't get distributed until Monday morning. It's an antiquated system that the younger lawyers at the firm have complained about for years. But that's Frantz's problem, not mine. We served the document properly—even though we waited until after three thirty to do it.

When Frantz withdraws his objection, Lovely projects the relevant portion of Harmon's notes on the courtroom monitor:

For 4-27-10 mtg—

CSA→*TCO*→film fin→ laundry Bnk of Buttonwillow→
EU bnk→offshore→disb

CL, EC, PY, VE, BG, FI, FR, MD, SK

CPA

"Are these the notes that you were referring to, Ms. Trimble?"

"There are also several other pages of financial calculations. But these are the important lines."

"Can you tell us what this means?"

Frantz objects on hearsay grounds, but we're ready to counter that with a short legal brief that Lovely put together last night. We're offering the notes, not for the truth of what Harmon said—that would be hearsay—but to show what Rich Baxter's state of mind was when he began his investigation, and also to prove that Rich was telling the truth when he said that he'd found the notes. The judge skims through Lovely's legal memo and lets me proceed with my questioning.

"First of all, Ms. Trimble, Mr. Cherry's notes are dated April 27, 2010. What does that mean to you?"

"It was the day Harmon died. So the notes were prepared for a meeting he was going to have on the very day he was shot."

"What, to your knowledge, do the next lines mean?"

"*CSA* was Harmon's abbreviation for Church of the Sanctified Assembly. *TCO* is an acronym for the Technology Communications Organization. That's Christopher McCarthy's company. *Film fin* means film financing."

"When you and Rich Baxter saw these notes for the first time, how did you interpret this reference to film financing?"

"Rich and I concluded that Assembly money was being laundered through McCarthy's company via a film financing deal."

"Objection," Frantz says. "Improper opinion. Calls for speculation."

"I'll allow it," Schadlow says. "It goes to Richard Baxter's motive, which you've put in issue, Mr. Frantz."

"Continue, Ms. Trimble," I say.

"The money was moved through the Bank of Buttonwillow to one or more banks in the EU, and then offshore somewhere. Then Harmon wrote *disb*, which means disbursed. He was noting that the money was disbursed to various places."

"The line that reads *CL, EC, PY, VE*, etc. . . . What does that mean?"

"This is where Rich and I hit a dead end. We thought they were people's initials. But they're not."

"What are they?"

"Country postal codes. The first four are South American countries—Chile, Ecuador, Paraguay, and Venezuela. The rest are European countries—*BG* is Bulgaria, *FI* is Finland, *FR* is France, *MD* is Moldova, and *SK* is Slovakia."

I glance at the jury. The retired financial manager and the housewife are nodding. They have an inkling of what's coming.

I look over at Lovely, who moves on to our next slide.

"We've projected on the monitors Christopher McCarthy's itinerary," I say. "Do you see that he traveled to Sofia, Bulgaria; Helsinki, Finland; Paris, France; Chisinau, Moldova; and Bratislava, Slovakia?"

"Yes. Mr. McCarthy traveled to the capital of each and every European country that Harmon listed in his notes."

The courtroom falls silent, except for the tapping of the media's keyboards. The implication of Grace's testimony is clear. Harmon discovered that someone was diverting Assembly funds. The scheme involved the countries of Bulgaria, Finland, France, Slovakia, and Moldavia, along with several countries in South America. McCarthy traveled to each of those European countries in May of 2011. Ergo, McCarthy's 2011 trip had something to do with the ongoing scheme that Harmon had uncovered a year earlier, just before he died.

In his seat behind Frantz, McCarthy—the man with the perpetual tan—sits frozen, his cheeks blanched. He's glowering at Grace with virulent eyes. No wonder she and Rich feared him.

I move away from the lectern. "Last night, Ms. Trimble, did you research whether the Church of the Sanctified Assembly has a particular political interest in those countries identified in Harmon Cherry's notes?"

"Yes. In each of these countries, both in Europe and South America, the Assembly is waging a major political fight to be legally recognized as a legitimate religion for tax and other purposes."

"Let's explore that. What's the Assembly's legal status in France?"

"They're seeking to be legally categorized as an established religion. Against strong opposition."

"Finland?"

"Categorized as a cult without legal status."

"Bulgaria?"

"Seeking recognition as a religious organization."

"Moldova and Slovakia?"

"Seeking religious organization status. Very close to getting it in Moldova. Not so close in Slovakia."

"The countries in South America?"

She goes on to confirm that the Assembly is fighting a pitched battle for legal recognition in every country that Harmon identified in his notes.

"Let's go back to Harmon Cherry's notes, Ms. Trimble. On the last line of the slide, the letters *CPA* appear. What did you understand that to mean?"

"Rich and I thought it meant Certified Public Accountant, that Harmon wanted to hire an accountant to investigate the scheme or something. That also threw us off."

"What do you think the letters mean now?"

"Now I realize the letters mean Corrupt Practices Act."

"What's that?"

"Objection," Frantz says. "The witness hasn't been qualified as an expert."

"Oh, but I am an expert on that," Grace says. "I've litigated several Foreign Corrupt Practice Act matters that required extensive analysis, and when I was a Supreme Court clerk I wrote the draft of the opinion in *Creel Industries v. USA*, one of the seminal cases in the area."

"The objection is overruled," Judge Schadlow says, grinning slightly. "Continue, Ms. Trimble."

"The Foreign Corrupt Practices Act is a federal law that makes it illegal for companies to bribe officials of foreign governments to get business in that country. By writing the letters *CPA*, Harmon Cherry clearly believed that someone was diverting Assembly money and using it to bribe foreign officials. That would be a federal crime."

"To be clear, you believe that this bribery scheme included the countries that Christopher McCarthy visited just last year?"

Frantz objects to the question as leading and argumentative. He's right, and the judge sustains the objection. But I don't care. Now the jury knows that McCarthy orchestrated the bribery scheme, a serious federal crime. Which means he had a motive to cover up the scheme by murdering Harmon and Rich.

"No further questions," I say.

On cross-examination, Frantz attacks Grace mercilessly, questioning her about her drug addiction, her illness, her history of aberrant behavior, her hatred of the Assembly, her stalking of Lake Knolls, and her obsessive love for Rich. He accuses her of lying, of misreading Harmon's notes, of speculating just to please me, her former work colleague. At one point, I think he's going to ask her whether she murdered Deanna, but he doesn't want to open that topic up for me. I don't know if it's depression or resolve, but Grace parries all his questions calmly. Throughout the cross, she continuously fans herself with a piece of paper that someone left on the witness stand. I just hope it isn't a trial exhibit.

Frantz confers with McCarthy and then asks, "Ms. Trimble, when you were in that apartment with Rich Baxter playing dress-up, he gave you computer access to the Assembly bank accounts, didn't he?"

"He had to so I could analyze the transactions."

"You're an expert at using technology, are you not?"

"I was an early adopter of new technology."

"Far more adept at using computers than Rich Baxter?"

"Yes. That wasn't one of Rich's strengths."

"Weren't you in contact with Mr. Baxter far earlier than you say, Ms. Trimble?"

"No."

"You and he spent years together siphoning off millions in Assembly funds by laundering it through numerous shell companies that you and Richard Baxter set up, didn't you?"

"Absolutely not."

"Are you aware that a couple of days ago, in open court, Mr. Stern suggested that *you* might have stolen the Assembly money?"

She looks over at me in surprise, but then says, "I didn't know that. But if I were in his shoes, I would've done the same thing."

"Didn't you betray your partner in crime, Mr. Baxter, and turn him into the FBI because you wanted to keep all the money for yourself?"

She laughs out loud, a slasher-film cackle made all the more chilling because her voice has been without affect for her entire testimony. I fear she's about to have a manic episode that will in five seconds destroy all the credibility that she's built up.

"Do you find something funny, Ms. Trimble?" Frantz asks, and now he's the one who's violated the first rule of cross-examination by asking an open-ended question.

"I find what you said hilarious, Mr. Frantz. Because, if I'd stolen seventeen million dollars, I wouldn't have been living on the street for the past months or hiding in Harmon Cherry's deserted beach house because I'm afraid the Assembly is trying to kill me. If I'd taken that money, I would be far, far away from here. No, your Mr. McCarthy took that seventeen million, laundered it through these shell companies, and used it to bribe foreign officials in violation of federal law. He probably kept a lot of it for himself, to pay for his expensive suits and whatever. And when Harmon Cherry caught him, he . . ." She crosses her arms and glares at Frantz with a faint look of self-satisfaction. She sensed that Frantz would let his guard down, and she set him up perfectly.

Frantz doesn't even blink. "Ms. Trimble, you had the technological ability and the financial expertise and the opportunity to steal that money and blame Richard Baxter for it, didn't you?"

"That might be true. But it didn't happen that way."

CHAPTER 57

I served trial subpoenas on Lake Knolls and Delwyn Bennett two weeks ago. Knolls is in Washington, but I'm going to call him anyway because I want the judge, jury, and news media to know that a legislator sworn to support and defend the Constitution of the United States is ducking a valid subpoena. I hold out a scintilla of hope that Bennett will show only because he doesn't have his boss's clout. We made several calls to his office last week reminding him of his obligation to appear, but they all went unreturned.

Lovely and I spend the lunch break preparing a motion that asks Judge Schadlow to institute contempt proceedings against Knolls and against Bennett if he's a no-show. Grace is physically present in the attorneys' lounge, but not with us. She doesn't acknowledge me when I praise her performance on the witness stand. She barely shakes her head when Lovely asks her if she wants lunch. While Lovely and I work, she just sits on a hard plastic seat, gazing at the wall. When it's time for the trial to resume, she stays behind.

We get to the courtroom three minutes late. The judge and jury are already in their places. Lovely nudges me—to my amazement, Delwyn Bennett is sitting in the fourth row. If he knew that I had a document memorializing the half-million-dollar wire transfer to him, he'd be in DC with his boss.

"You're late, Mr. Stern," the judge says, her voice even more squeaky than usual. "Do you have a witness?"

"The defense calls Lake Knolls."

This time there are loud gasps from the gallery, followed by stage whispers that quickly crescendo into full-blown conversations. The jurors remain impassive. The judge has to call for order twice before the courtroom settles down.

"Is Mr. Knolls present?" the judge asks.

"No, Your Honor, he's in Washington, DC. But he was served with a valid subpoena. We'd ask the Court to issue an order to show cause why he shouldn't be held in contempt."

"We'll discuss that later when the jury's not present. Next witness?"

"The defense calls Delwyn Bennett."

Bennett remains in his seat, but the woman sitting next to him stands up and walks to the podium. Her business suit and militaristic gait brand her as his lawyer.

"Your Honor, my name is Myrna Burowski. I'm here on behalf of Delwyn Bennett to seek a protective order quashing this burdensome, oppressive, and illegal subpoena directed toward him."

Bennett understands the political consequences of not showing up, both for his boss and himself. He wants to look legitimate while at the same time avoiding the witness stand. He should have brought the motion days ago, but judges give third parties leeway that they don't give the litigants. By waiting until trial to object to my subpoena, he's trying to ambush me so I don't have a chance to counter his arguments.

"I'll consider your motion, Ms. Burowski," the judge says. This will test Schadlow's mettle—it won't be easy for her to force the aide of a sitting member of Congress to testify; it's even more difficult because his boss is a famous movie star.

We wait for the jury to file out. The jurors aren't allowed to hear the lawyers' legal arguments. As Judge Schadlow has constantly reminded them, argument isn't evidence. Burowski hands the court clerk her papers and then gives Frantz and me copies. As I read, Lovely looks over my shoulder. Occasionally, she'll whisper in my ear to point out a flaw in Burowski's reasoning. When I finish reading, I glance over at Frantz's table. Weir is frantically flipping through the document, but Frantz is sitting with hands folded and eyes closed, as if meditating. He's rooting for Burowski to be sure, but this motion presents a rare instance where one of the parties to a lawsuit doesn't get to take a position—this fight is solely between Burowski and me.

The judge finishes reading through Burowski's papers and

announces that she's ready to hear oral argument. Burowski goes to the podium and launches into a loud diatribe about how my subpoenas to Knolls and Bennett are part of a publicity stunt designed to divert attention from the real issues in the case. She argues that even if Bennett's testimony were relevant, Knolls has legislative immunity that extends to his employees.

Schadlow nods in my direction. I can't tell whether she's buying Burowski's argument. I glance through the notes that Lovely and I prepared at lunch and go to the podium. "Your Honor, under the Supreme Court's opinion in *Hutchinson v. Proxmire*, Mr. Bennett is only immune from a subpoena if we want to question him about Mr. Knolls's conduct as a legislator. We're not calling Delwyn Bennett as a witness because of any legislative action. We're calling him about something else entirely."

"And what would that be?" the judge asks.

"Through Mr. Bennett, we'll prove that what Grace Trimble testified to this morning is accurate."

I'm prepared to argue for another twenty minutes, but the judge says, "One moment, counsel." She spends what seems like forever writing something on a legal pad. When a judge does this during an oral argument, it usually means she's made up her mind and she's drafting an order on the fly. I just don't know what she's decided. At last, she stops writing and looks up at us. "Mr. Bennett's motion to quash is denied."

Burowski moves over to the podium. "Your Honor, we'd request a stay of your order so we can appeal your ruling."

"I'm not going to grant a stay," the judge says. "You can go across the street to the court of appeal and see if they disagree with me if you want. In the meantime, I order Mr. Bennett to testify. If he doesn't, he'll be held in contempt."

"Your Honor, the subpoena—"

"Enough, Ms. Burowski. No more argument. Bailiff, please go get the jury. Mr. Bennett, you're to remain in the courtroom."

Burowski confers with Bennett and sits down. It looks like they've decided not to appeal. As soon as the jury is seated, he takes the stand.

Before I can ask my first question, I feel a slight tremor in my fingers. The shaking quickly gets so bad that I can't turn the pages of my notes. My chest tightens and my legs wobble. The courtroom walls oscillate in nauseating sine waves. I grip the lectern with both hands so I won't fall. I'm incapable of forming the words to ask the judge for a break, to tell her I'm ill. Never again will I let myself believe that I'm cured of this. I look down at my notes, hoping to hide my terror from the jurors.

I feel a hand on my shoulder. Raymond Baxter is standing by my side, his body strategically placed between the jury and me.

"No matter what happens from now on, we've won," he says in a hoarse whisper. "Everybody knows that my son wasn't a thief or a drug addict. And the most important thing is that *his* son will know the truth. Thank you." He pats my shoulder and sits down. And in that moment, I remember why I love being a lawyer.

I gather myself and slowly pry my fingers from the sides of the podium. Lovely pours me a glass of water. I take a long drink and manage to say. "Mr. Bennett, what do you do for a living?"

He lifts his chin and points his long nose in the air. "I'm chief of staff for Lake Knolls, member of the US House of Representatives." Once I'm into the questioning, the residual stage fright gradually subsides. I go on to establish that he has a degree in communications from Harvard and a law degree from the University of Chicago and that he worked for a downtown LA law firm before going into politics full time. He served as an aide to a US senator and managed Knolls's first congressional campaign. As chief of staff, he oversees every aspect of Knolls's congressional life. I lay this foundation so the jury will understand that the man is powerful and intelligent, not someone easily duped.

"Mr. Bennett, are you familiar with Lake Knolls's signature?"

"Of course I am."

I hand him a document that Grace and I found at Harmon's beach house, a 2003 contract for a production financing deal for a movie called *The Gaunt Girl*. I tell him to turn to the last page. "Is that Lake Knolls's signature?"

"It appears so."

"Is this contract what's called a 'film financing agreement'?"

Frantz stands to object, but sits down when Bennett says, "I have no idea. I've never worked in the movie industry." But my point isn't lost on the jury. Harmon's notes said that Assembly money was being laundered through a film financing deal. This is a film financing deal.

"Let me direct your attention to page nineteen, paragraph twelve," I say. "Do you see language about allocating the movie's gross revenues among the investors?"

"It seems so. But I don't know for sure. As I told you, I don't know anything about the film business."

"It doesn't matter for my purposes if you do or you don't, sir. I'd just like you to look at this film financing contract and tell me the name of the eighth investor listed in paragraph twelve."

He pauses to read the paragraph. "It's something called the Bank of Buttonwillow." His tone is matter-of-fact because he doesn't understand the significance of his words. He's just tied his boss's production company to the money-laundering scheme. The Assembly hid the flow of money by running it through Knolls's company and calling it film revenue and then laundering it through the Bank of Buttonwillow, one of the entities referred to in Harmon's notes. From the rustling in the gallery, I'm sure that many of those in the courtroom get it.

"Would you also read aloud the names of the companies identified on page twenty-one, paragraph fifteen?" I ask.

"Octagon, LLC; Pentagon Investments, LLC; Hexagon, Inc.; Rhombus and Heptagon, both LLCs."

Lovely calls them the Geometrics—the shell companies through which the laundered Assembly money flowed before it ended up in The Emery Group's account. More evidence of Knolls's complicity.

I glance over at my adversaries, who are furiously flipping through the production contract trying to catch up with me. Only now do I realize that Christopher McCarthy isn't in the room, hasn't been since the lunch break. Before this, he hadn't missed a moment of trial. The jury will surely notice his absence.

"Let's move on to another subject," I say. "Do you travel with Mr. Knolls on legislative business?"

"Yes, sir, that's part of my job."

"Did you travel abroad with Mr. Knolls in the summer of 2009?"

"If you're referring to the trip to South America, of course I did."

Again, fraught silence in the courtroom. Judge Schadlow leans forward in her chair. I sense that Frantz wants to object but can't think of a reason.

Confused, Bennett says, "Congressman Knolls is on the House foreign relations committee. It's part of his job to visit other countries."

"I'm sure it is," I say. "What countries did you visit in South America?"

We visited . . . I'm not sure of all of them. It's been several years."

"Let's see if this helps." I show him a printout from the Lexis-Nexis research service showing that in July 2009, Knolls went on a so-called "fact-finding" tour of Argentina, Brazil, Chile, Ecuador, Paraguay, Peru, and Venezuela. Of the seven countries Knolls and Bennett visited, four were identified in Harmon Cherry's notes as part of the bribery schemes. An unsuspecting Bennett confirms that he accompanied Knolls to those countries.

"And then in May 2011, you traveled with Lake Knolls to Central and Eastern Europe?" I ask.

"That's correct. Another mission to serve the interests of the United States of America."

"Really?" I say. "Let's explore that." I mark as an exhibit another LexisNexis printout, this time Knolls's itinerary for the trip to Europe in 2011. Then Lovely displays McCarthy's vacation itinerary on the courtroom monitors. When Bennett understands what he's seeing, the color drains from his face.

"Let's look at Mr. Knolls's European itinerary. Start with the entry for May 22, 2011. Were you aware that you and Lake Knolls and Christopher McCarthy were all in the city of Bratislava on the very same day?"

"I . . . I don't know anything about that. Coincidences happen."

"You're aware you're under oath?"

"Yes."

"Were you and Mr. Knolls and Mr. McCarthy in Sofia the same day, as a comparison of the LexisNexis printout and the McCarthy itinerary indicates?"

"I don't know."

"If you were, was it just a coincidence?"

"I . . ."

"You what, sir?"

"I don't know," he says almost in a whisper.

"Could you speak up Mr. Bennett?"

"I said, *I don't know*." This time, his voice is much too loud.

"And if you and Knolls and McCarthy were in the same cities on the same days in the countries of Moldova, Finland, and France, as a comparison of the documents indicates, would those be coincidences, too?"

He stares at me, his eyes rimmed red. I don't press for an answer. His silence tells the jury all I need it to—McCarthy and Knolls were in on the bribery scheme together, simultaneously traveling to countries where the Assembly sought legal recognition.

"Mr. Bennett, on May 2, 2011, did you receive a half-million dollar payment from a company called The Emery Group?"

"I did not, sir," he says indignantly.

"You're quite sure of that?"

"Absolutely."

I hand the clerk, Frantz, and Bennett a copy of the other document that Harriet gave me, the wire transfer memo showing that the enigmatic Emery Group paid him five hundred thousand dollars a few weeks before the trip to Europe.

"Do you recognize this bank receipt, Mr. Bennett?"

Frantz bolts out of his chair. "I object to use of this document. This has never been produced to us."

The judge looks at me. "That's true, Your Honor. I'll withdraw it. May I have the exhibit back, Mr. Bennett?"

I approach the witness stand. It doesn't matter that I can't use the document, because Bennett has already read it, exactly as I hoped. He's fair skinned to begin with, and now his cheeks are almost translucent, like onionskin. His hand trembles so uncontrollably that he can barely hand the piece of paper back to me. This receipt proves that he personally received the laundered money and that soon after, he and Knolls and McCarthy together visited foreign countries where the Assembly is fighting for recognition. It implicates him and his boss—and McCarthy—in bank fraud, violations of the Foreign Corrupt Practices Act, and possibly murder. I might not be able to get the document admitted at this trial, but it will be compelling evidence in his criminal trial.

He turns toward Judge Schadlow. "May I confer with my attorney?"

"I think that would be very wise, Mr. Bennett."

He steps down from the stand and huddles with Burowski. As he whispers in her ear, her eyes narrow and her frown deepens. She speaks to him, and he nods. After several minutes, he returns to the witness stand.

"My question, Mr. Bennett, is did you receive a payment of five hundred thousand dollars from the Emery group in May 2011?"

"I refuse to answer on the grounds that any answer I give may tend to incriminate me."

He looks not at me, but at the clock on the back wall. He's clasping his hands tightly together as if to stop them from shaking. His upper lip glistens with sweat.

"Do you know what The Emery Group is?"

"I refuse to answer on the grounds that any answer I give may tend to incriminate me."

He goes on to plead the Fifth in response to my next ten questions. Although I could keep him twisting on the stand for another fifteen minutes if I wanted, I tell the judge I have no further questions. Bennett's cheeks have turned a sickly scarlet, and I fear that if I don't stop, some of the jurors might start feeling sorry for him.

Frantz asks for a recess, which Schadlow gives him. His haphazard style of dress has finally gotten the better of him—somehow during my examination of Bennett, his shirttail escaped from his slacks and is now hanging below the back of his jacket.

As soon as Bennett leaves the stand, the reporters race toward him. Burowski shoos them away and confers with Bennett in the corner. I'll leave it to the news outlets and the Internet bloggers to decide whether Knolls is an Assembly fellow traveler or a blackmail victim. I'm betting that McCarthy dug up dirt about Knolls's relationship with Billy Ness, The Tinsel Town Pusher. Knolls was certainly the perfect person to make contact with the foreign officials and dole out the Assembly's cash—what foreign politician wouldn't give access to a former movie star turned US Congressman?

Five minutes before the trial is to resume, Frantz and Weir walk into the courtroom. Instead of returning to his table, Frantz comes over and says, "Talk to you in private for a few minutes, Parker? The lounge?"

I nod.

"Nick will tell the judge we're conferring."

I look over at Lovely. "Come on. You're part of this, too."

"Are you sure, Parker?"

"Lead counsel only," Frantz says.

"You'll talk to both of us or neither of us," I say.

He frowns, but motions for us to follow him. We go to our conference room in the attorneys' lounge. I expect Grace to be there, but she's gone. Frantz gestures for us to sit down at the table, but Lovely and I remain standing.

"You know, the jury's going to get the case in a day or two," he says in an unctuous tone that he's never used with me. "We think we've met our burden of proof, but anything can happen. So I've been talking to my client, and they want me to explore settlement before that possibility is foreclosed."

"This is a waste of time," I say. "We're not paying the Assembly anything."

"My client was thinking of a nonmonetary settlement. Mutual releases and a walk away."

Lovely and I glance at each other. Frantz just offered to dismiss the case, and all Raymond Baxter has to do is give up his right to sue the Assembly for malicious prosecution. It's sounds like total victory.

"No deal," I say.

"You've got to be joking. I just offered—"

"I know what you offered. It's not enough."

Lovely grabs my arm. "Don't you think we should at least—?"

"When this case started, Raymond made it clear that if we won, he wanted to sue for malicious prosecution. Well, we're going to win. And we have a strong malicious prosecution claim, because McCarthy verified the complaint all the while knowing that he himself manipulated the accounts so he could pay those illegal bribes."

"That's bullshit, and you know it," Frantz says. "It's almost impossible to prove malice in a mal pro case."

"Not when your client has killed three people to cover up his crimes. By the time we go to trial in the malicious prosecution case, the cops will have arrested McCarthy for murder. The punitive damages in our case against the Assembly will be astronomical."

Frantz and I glare at each other.

"What do you propose?" he says.

"I'll recommend to Raymond that he release the Assembly from the malicious prosecution claim if the Assembly pays his legal fees. He won't be happy, but I think I can convince him that he shouldn't tax his health any further by involving himself in more litigation. And one more thing. No confidentiality clause. Our side can tell the press or whoever we want that the Assembly paid Raymond to get rid of the case."

Frantz thinks it over and says, "Let me go outside and call the client."

"He's going to accept it," Lovely says when we're alone.

"We'll see."

"No. I know him. He'll get them to agree. You've won."

"*We* have."

She smiles. And then we wait in silence.

Frantz comes back five minutes later. "We're close," he says. "Very close. The Assembly wants a cap on fees."

"How much?"

"Five hundred thousand dollars."

"That won't be a problem," I say. And it won't—I've only billed Raymond half that amount.

After that, events move at top speed. I confer with Raymond, who agrees to the deal immediately. The judge announces the settlement in open court and discharges the jury. Frantz and his team pack up as quickly as they can and flee. The losing team never stays in the court-room very long.

I ask Lovely to go out in the hall and speak with the media, to tell them in no uncertain terms that our side won. When she leaves, I find myself alone in the now deserted courtroom. I look around at the deserted jury box, at the suddenly spotless plaintiff's table, at the empty gallery. I wander over to the podium. The record of The Emery Group's wire transfer to Delwyn Bennett is still on the lectern. I stare at it for a long time, puzzled. Why did Harriet hand over evidence that let me destroy not only the Assembly's court case, but also Christopher McCarthy and his plan to insinuate the Assembly into every country in Europe? Was it really because I threatened to go public about Ascending Sodality? Maybe. But she's never been one to give into threats.

Who are you, Mother?

CHAPTER 58

G race Trimble and I sit in the elegant dining room of Manny and Elena Mason's Moraga Canyon home. The dinner is supposed to celebrate our court victory four days ago, but as far as I'm concerned, there's nothing to celebrate. I'm mourning the loss of our friends.

As always, the Masons are solicitous hosts. At the start of the meal, Manny lifts his glass of Chateau Montelena chardonnay—he makes sure to tell us the winery won the famous 1976 Paris tasting that put the Napa Valley on the map—and toasts our victory over the Church of the Sanctified Assembly. He's a bit intoxicated, but I think it's more from his love of wine than from the alcohol. He grew up in the vineyards, after all. Throughout dinner, he and Elena are constantly serving and clearing, refusing to let me help. Grace doesn't offer.

I'm poor company tonight, indifferent to my surroundings, capable of speaking but unwilling to—the opposite of stage fright, in other words. But I don't think the Masons notice, because Grace gets ever more manic as the evening progresses and can't stop talking. She tells long and exaggerated stories about her days as a music lawyer, recounting events that have no interest to anyone but her. She's binging on food—now it's a third slice of Elena's flourless chocolate cake. A little while ago, she gesticulated so wildly that she spilled a glass of St. Emilion Grand Cru all over her green dress—the same tattered dress that she was wearing when I found her at Harmon's beach house. I'll have to get her to leave when I do or the Masons will be stuck with her until tomorrow morning.

It's hard to believe she's even here. After she disappeared from the courthouse Monday afternoon, I didn't think I'd hear from her again.

Then, on Wednesday, she called my cell phone from a blocked number saying she wanted to talk about the lawsuit. At the end of the conversation, I told her that Manny had invited us for Friday-night dinner. I was sure she'd say no, but she accepted. When I asked for her phone number, she hung up on me.

Now, she and Manny and Elena are talking about the trial. It's funny how everyone but the trial lawyers wants to discuss a case that's ended, as if it was nothing more than an exciting sporting event. While the others talk, I sip my wine, pick at my dessert, and gaze at a Grant Wood print of a farm couple and a collie that hangs on the opposite wall. I catch only a smattering of the conversation, paying the minimum amount of attention necessary to answer coherently if someone speaks directly to me.

In response to a question from Elena, Grace says, "Rich truly did believe that all those companies he set up were being used to fund thrift stores and organic bakeries and whatever. He truly thought they were carrying out the Assembly's good works. I know he sounds naïve, but he didn't understand what was going on because he assumed the best in people."

"I've been following the news reports," Elena says. "They still haven't traced the money, right? They don't know if all of it went for bribes or if McCarthy kept some of it for himself."

"I'd guess it all went for bribes," Manny says. "When you think about it, seventeen million in eighteen months isn't really that much money to spend worldwide. There are what, a hundred ninety–plus countries in the world? The Assembly wants to have a presence in all of them. Accomplishing that takes way more than a paltry seventeen million. What do you think, Parker?"

I shrug.

"I disagree, Manny, I disagree." Grace says. She gulps down what's left of her wine and sets her glass down so hard it rattles the tableware. "Truthfully, it's like I said at the trial, I think McCarthy pocketed a lot of it, I think he skimmed money from the Buttonwillow Bank account and used the Geometrics as a conduit to The Emery Group."

"The Geometrics?" Elena asks.

"That's what we called the companies that were named after geometric shapes," Grace says. "Parker's *law student*"—and here she gives a Groucho Marx leer—"thought of that."

"It's silly, but the names of those companies fascinate me," Elena says. "Maybe it's because my father has started so many businesses in his life, and choosing the right name is always very important to him. Even if those companies just existed on paper, how could you keep track of one from the other?"

"That was the whole point," Grace says, an edge of hostility creeping into her voice.

Elena considers this and nods.

"Hey, Elena, can you name all those Geometrics?" Grace says.

"I'm sure I can't."

"Oh, come on, try." It's a command, not a request. I've seen Grace like this before, demanding that everyone play her irrational games. Now she's invented a perverse variation of Name the Seven Dwarfs. It's a sure sign that she's on the brink of a meltdown.

I say, "Grace, I don't think Elena wants to—"

"You can't play, Parker! That would be cheating."

"It's OK," Elena says in a soft voice. "Let me try." She's doesn't realize that humoring Grace will only make things worse.

Elena bites her lip. "There's Triangle, Pentagon, Hexagon, Octagon. Wasn't . . . wasn't one of the companies called Trapezius or something?"

"Close, but no cigar," Grace says. "I'll give you a do over."

Manny puts his hand on Elena's shoulder. "Trapezoid, honey. Though I think Trapezius would've been a much better name. The others were Isosceles, Heptagon, Nonagon, and Rhombus."

"That's cheating, too, Manny," Grace says with real irritation in her voice. "This was between Elena and me."

"Are you all right, Grace?" Elena says. It's absolutely the wrong thing to say.

"Oh, I couldn't be more wonderful. Awesome." Now her tone is completely hostile. "How about you, Elena? Are you all right?"

I reach over and touch Grace's elbow. "We're all fine, Grace. We're having a quiet dinner."

She gazes past me for a moment and then looks away.

"But I wanted to ask you something, Grace," I say in a soft voice. "Was it Harmon who liked to name companies that way? You know, with those generic names?" It's a blatant attempt to draw her attention away from Elena, but it works. Her body relaxes a bit.

"Not Harmon," she says. "Andrew Macklin. He once named a trio of his clients' companies A-One, Acme, and Apex."

"Why?"

"He had this ridiculous idea that a company was less likely to get sued if it had a nondescript name," she says, sounding calmer. "You know, like don't buy a red car because owners of red cars get stopped by the cops more often? I think Rich really bought into the program when Andrew started doing Assembly work."

Suddenly, something's puzzling me, something I never considered. I forget about Grace's behavior for the moment. "Manny, how deeply was Macklin involved with Assembly matters?"

"Full-time at the end. He had nothing else to do, so—"

"If he was willing to do their work, could he have been one of them? It never occurred to me before, but—"

"I don't think Andrew—"

"You guys!" Grace shrieks. She looks at us with a warped grin. "Remember that time when Deanna was dating that bass player from, what was that band called, Steel Angst? She'd do drugs and fuck until two thirty in the morning and be in court or meeting with a client. I never understood how she could manage that. When I did that, I was on my ass for a week."

Manny closes his eyes for a moment. Elena grimaces in disgust. She's religious and socially conservative, a straight-laced wife and mother who has no tolerance for swear words, much less a graphic discussion about Deanna's sex life and drug use. Worse, her three teenage sons are in the den just down the hall.

"Grace," I whisper. "There are kids in this house."

"Oh, yeah, sorry." Her glazed eyes emit hypomanic sparks.

As if on cue, Manny's youngest, the thirteen-year-old, walks in. He's tall for his age, not a surprise because he has tall parents. "Dad, do I really have to miss my game tomorrow? Papi won't—"

"This isn't the time, Kevin," Manny says. "We'll talk about it later."

Grace giggles, hiccups, puts her hand to her mouth, and giggles again.

"We've already talked about it," Elena says. "He's coming with us to the lunch." She looks at me as if she owes me an explanation. "It's my dad's birthday. Kevin can miss one basketball game for an important family event." She glares at Manny. "Even though I think his father would rather watch him play basketball."

Manny, expressionless, says nothing.

"You two remind me of my parents," Grace says. "They were strict, too." She pauses. "And look how fucked up I turned out to be." She shrieks at her own joke, but she's the only one laughing. Kevin bows his head and walks away.

"Where's the bathroom, again?" Grace says. "Shit, straight As in college and law school and I have no fucking sense of direction."

Elena directs her to the bathroom down the hall.

"I know it's very sad," Elena says when Grace is out of earshot. "But I won't tolerate this behavior in my house."

"I'll try to get her to leave with me now," I say. "I wish she'd let me help her. She won't even give me her phone number."

"No one has ever been able to help her," Manny says.

It's quiet, awkward. Then Kevin comes back into the room and tries again to negotiate a reprieve from his grandfather's birthday party. After ten minutes, Grace isn't back from the bathroom.

"I'll check on her," I say. I go down the hall to the bathroom and knock. There's no answer.

"Grace?"

Still no answer. I turn the handle. It's unlocked. I open the door slowly. The bathroom is empty. I walk down the hall to the family room, where Manny's sons are playing videogames.

"Have you guys seen Grace? The woman in the green dress?"

"The crazy lady," the eldest boy says without taking his eyes off the monitor. "She left."

"She . . . ?"

"She was, like, sneaking out the front door or something."

I hurry outside and look in the driveway. Her beat-up Honda is gone.

I go back inside and tell the Masons. We all assume that she overheard Elena say that she wouldn't tolerate Grace's behavior.

Elena is on the verge of tears. "I remember the days when she just seemed eccentric, you know? Or does it just seem worse because we've gotten older?"

I drive down the mountain road much too fast, hoping that somehow I'll catch up to Grace. But the only way I'll overtake her is if she's crashed. That's not an improbable scenario—she's had several auto accidents while manic.

Once I'm down the hill, I take Sunset Boulevard to the freeway. During the fifteen-minute trip to the Marina, I ponder the tragedy that is Grace Trimble. How did this happen to her? How will she end up? I'm afraid of the answer.

And then I think about Andrew Macklin again. What was his relationship with the Assembly? Why didn't I look into his role while the case was still going on, when I could have used the discovery process? What if he had access to the Assembly's bank documents?

Only when I pull up to my condo do I see it with absolute clarity. The truth is simply there, as if I've known it all along. I *should* have known it all along.

Now, it's too late.

A car speeds under the security gate just as it's about to close. I shift into reverse and try to back up, but the car pulls up behind me, blocking my escape route. The driver gets out, moving quickly but methodically.

I lock the doors from the inside and fumble for my cell phone, trying to dial 911. Before the call goes through, he's at my window, arm raised, handgun pointed at my head.

"End the phone call and get out of the car," Manny says. His normally smooth voice has a raspy quality that doesn't sound human. His lips are twisted upward in what could be a cruel smile or an expression of regret.

Grace is a much quicker study than I am, always has been. When Ed Diamond told me months ago that he learned from an underworld source that The Emery Group had paid six million dollars to a company called Nonagon, LLC, he swore me to secrecy. Only he, Lovely, and I knew the name of that company. I broke my promise to Ed only once—when I told Grace Trimble about Nonagon the Sunday before she testified at trial. I thought I owed her the whole truth.

During dinner, Manny identified Nonagon as one of the Geometrics. There's only one way he could have known that.

"Let's talk about this," I say after I get out of the car.

"Not a word." He gestures with the gun. "Let's go."

We climb the stairs. My legs feel heavy, useless. The fear I feel in court is nothing like this. This terror is like liquid nitrogen, so chilling that I'll shatter if I so much as twitch. And yet, I keep walking.

When we get to my front door, he orders me to open it fast. My hands are shaking, but I manage to get the key in the lock. When we're inside, he directs me into the bedroom.

"Put on your running clothes."

"I don't—"

"Put them on. You're going for a late night jog."

I undress slowly, trying to buy time. Is this how Harmon felt? The calculation, the mental bargaining, the ghoulish unreality of it all?

"Hurry up."

As I'm dressing he takes out his cell phone and punches in a number with one hand, never lowering the gun or taking his eyes off of me. "Victor, I need your help with something. I'll be in Venice. Dell Street. Linnie Canal Bridge, north side."

I live in the Marina. He's taking me to Venice Beach, less than a mile away. The area has gentrified in recent years, but there's a rough gang neighborhood just a few blocks north. And there's a homeless community living on the beach not too far away.

"Victor Galdamez. Your ex-gang member turned potential law student, right? But he's not an *ex*-member, is he?"

"Shut up."

"He was the leader of those goons who beat me up that night I left The Barrista. I see that now. His was the voice of my assailant in those nightmares."

"I tried to get you to stop. I really did." He waves the gun. "Now put your shoes on."

I go to the closet and get my running shoes. It would've been a good place to hide a weapon of my own, but I've never believed in them, never thought the Second Amendment was so important. Maybe if I can get him talking, then . . . what?

"It was you who tipped off the Assembly that Raymond Baxter hired me," I say. "And you told them that Ed Diamond looked at the financials and that Grace was posing as Sandra Casey. And . . . and about the stage fright. What, more anonymous e-mails?"

His shrug is almost apologetic.

"You know, I blamed Kathleen Williams."

He smirks. "I'd wager that Frantz believed it was Lovely Diamond still being loyal to him.

"The trial. You were helping me. But it was really a cover-up, a way to end all of this without further risk. I prove that McCarthy was using Assembly money to pay bribes and the cops would think he killed Harmon, Rich, and Deanna. And that's exactly what's happened, except you drank too much wine tonight and—"

"Finish tying those shoes, goddammit," he says through clenched teeth. "Do you imagine I don't know you're stalling?"

When I finish tying my shoes, he says, "Get your house key and wallet. Leave the cell phone."

We go outside and head back to the parking garage. Maybe someone will be down there. Or maybe a neighbor has reported to security that a strange car is double-parked. It's a clear night, only ten thirty. This place should be teeming with people.

As it turns out, the common areas are deserted. So is the garage. I consider shouting or making a run for it, but I remember what Deanna looked like when I found her.

He forces me into the passenger seat of his car. With one hand on the gun and one on the steering wheel, he backs out of the garage, drives out onto the street, and heads west down Washington Boulevard toward the beach. I have five minutes—ten at the most.

"Did Rich know about the bribery scheme?" I ask.

"You know why you're asking me these things, my friend?"

"Tell me."

"Because you don't know when to give up. You think you can talk me out of it. The silver-tongued orator who argued his way out of a death sentence. It's a shame, really. It makes it harder on you. It's easier just to accept it. Harmon accepted it. I could see it in his eyes."

"Did Rich know about the bribery scheme?" I repeat.

"The only thing Rich knew how to do was blow smoke up the asses of McCarthy and his stooges."

"That's why all this happened? Because you were jealous of Rich making more money than you?" My cheeks flush; anger and disgust cloud my judgment. "No. I don't buy that. There's got to be more to it. A woman? Gambling? Your wine collection? Or were you trying to show Elena that you could pay your own way without having her wealthy father finance your—"

He lunges toward me and hits me in the nose with the butt of the gun. The car swerves into the adjacent lane, providing a perfect opportunity to grab for the gun, but I'm dazed. Blood gushes from both nostrils. I put my right thumb and forefinger to my nose and pinch. Then I drop my arm and wipe some of the blood on the seat. I bend over, pretending that I'm trying to staunch the flow, and let several droplets fall onto the floor mat. The least I can do is leave some of my DNA behind in his car. Maybe a crime scene investigator will find it someday.

I should keep my mouth shut, but I just can't manage it. "Here's what

I think happened. McCarthy asked Rich to set up these shell companies, and as always, Rich came to you for help. Like you said, he was too dumb to realize that McCarthy was setting up a money-laundering scheme. But you're not dumb, Manny. You saw what was going on and took advantage of the opportunity to give yourself access to the Assembly bank accounts. There was so much illegal money passing through those accounts that no one would notice your skimming. And even if they did, how could a thief like McCarthy complain that someone was stealing from him? But you miscalculated. Harmon found you out."

He scowls at me, and his fingers tighten around the handle of the gun.

"There's one thing I don't understand," I say. "When Rich left the firm, how did you manage to keep your hand in the till?" As I talk, I scan the road for an avenue of escape. What if I were to open my door and jump out? No chance. He'll shoot me as soon as I reach for the handle.

"I'll answer that one," he says. "In a few minutes you'll have no memory, anyway. Rich kept asking me for help even after we weren't partners anymore, even after I took the job at the law school. The son of a bitch never once offered to pay me for my time. He thought I owed him free work because I was his friend."

"And then he found Harmon's notes."

"You know what's ironic? He actually asked me to help him find out who was diverting the money. I refused at first, told him I was frightened. So he promised not to tell a soul about my involvement no matter what. Not even Grace. He swore on it with one of his sacred Assembly oaths. And ever-loyal Rich Baxter kept his promise."

Rich was loyal, all right, but also a fool. If he'd told me that Manny and Grace were helping him in his investigation, everything would have been different.

"So that's how you were able to snatch the DVD from the Silver Lake apartment," I say. "After that, all it took was a few bogus transactions in his name and a call to the IRS, and Rich was behind bars."

We stop at a red light. There's a patrol car across the street, but it's going in the opposite direction. When it passes, I shudder.

"Are you cold, my friend? Should I turn down the air conditioning?"

We make a right turn on Dell Avenue, a narrow street that runs over the canals and past homes that sell for two million dollars and up. Bridges and walkways crisscross the system of canals that a man named Abbott Kinney built in the early twentieth century to mimic Venice, Italy. It never quite worked out. At this hour, the neighborhood is deserted.

"Why kill Rich?" I ask. "He was in jail. About to take the fall for your crimes."

"Because of you."

At first I don't understand, but then it comes to me—Rich would never have figured out what was going on, even with a smart lawyer. But I knew too much about the firm, about the Assembly. Sooner or later, Rich and I together would have discovered the truth. Manny couldn't wait around for that to happen.

"Galdamez arranged the hit?"

"There are always Lazers in the MDC. A fistfight for a diversion and it was done. You were right. The guy's a martial arts expert. Rich didn't feel a thing."

The car rollercoasters up and down an arched bridge. I'm already nauseated from the terror and the blood I've swallowed. My nose is throbbing. "I think I'm going to be sick, Manny."

"Hold on, my friend. We're almost there."

I take several deep breaths. It doesn't help. And yet, even now I'm driven to ask questions—a lawyer to the end. "Was Harmon killed the way the Guglielmi report says?"

"No more."

"And I assume Deanna just got in the way. Grace is still out there, Manny. You have millions stashed away. Drop me off in the desert and get on a plane to somewhere far away before I get back to civilization."

"Don't you wish. As for Grace, she won't be out there much longer. You saw her tonight. She's so far gone she'll probably take care of my problem herself."

"What about me? Why did you wait until now?"

"I'm offended, Parker. It's because you're my friend."

He's enough of a psychopath to believe it. More likely, killing me would've raised too many questions. I was Rich's lawyer. Now, he has no choice.

He parks the car just as we cross the bridge over Linnie Canal. When he starts to get out, I decide to run, but when I try the handle the door doesn't budge. He's set the child lock or something. Only when he gets to the passenger side window does he disarm the lock.

Dressed in running shorts and a tank top, I shiver in the cold ocean air. When I stumble over the curb, he grasps my arm to steady me. He orders me to walk down the bridge to the pathway that runs along the canal. I know what he's planning—the cops will think I was jogging down the pathway and was assaulted by a gang member or a transient. They'll find my wallet, but no money. Galdamez will be here soon to make sure that the scene looks legit.

"On your knees!" Manny says.

I want to plead for my life, to reason with him lawyer to lawyer, friend to friend, but nothing comes out. I want to tell Lovely she's perfect, that nothing she's ever done or will do could make me believe otherwise. I want to apologize to Kathleen Williams. Before Manny can move behind me, I go for the gun, grab hold of his wrist, and throw a punch with my free hand, but the blow glances off his cheek. He jerks his arm away and aims the gun at my chest, and I hear the shots and the sickening moan. There's a high-pitched whine in my ears, or is it the sound of my own voice shrieking in terror? I fall to my knees. I don't feel anything. Why don't I feel anything?

Manny crumples to the ground. I look behind him toward the canal. Just rippling moonlight on the black surface of the water. I look up at the bridge and see a swatch of green, stationary against the night sky. And then the swatch streaks across the bridge and down the walkway. She's holding the gun with two hands, aiming at Manny's body even as she glances at me. Her eyes are clear, cold, rational.

"Grace?"

"I always knew it was either him or you. Until tonight, I just didn't know which."

I struggle to my feet. "We have to go. They're coming for us."

CHAPTER 59

Lovely and I sit at my usual table in the back of The Barrista. Deanna bequeathed the shop to those employees who'd been with her from the start, though I hear her estranged family intends to contest the will. I've volunteered to represent the employees pro bono if they need a lawyer. Meanwhile, Romulo's done a good job of keeping the place afloat.

It's been three days since Grace Trimble shot Manny Mason to death. I've spent them undergoing treatment for my broken nose, talking to the cops and the FBI, and just trying to deal with the terror of that night. This is the first time I've had a chance to spend some time talking with Lovely.

Though she knows the basic outline, I now recount in detail the events of last Friday night—the abduction in the garage, the drive to Venice, the shooting on the canal. I describe how after Manny mentioned Nonagon, Grace had left the house and parked her car up the canyon, waiting. She was sure that Manny would immediately recognize his mistake and come after us. When he drove after me, she followed. When I asked her why she didn't just call the police, she said she hadn't carried a cell phone since the night Deanna was shot, that she feared the killer would use the phone to track her location. Besides, she doesn't trust the cops. Grace Trimble logic. She made a point of telling me that she shot Manny with the same gun she was carrying when she was arrested for trespassing on Lake Knolls's property. "See, it really was for protection," she said in a self-satisfied voice.

I take a drink of my macchiato and say, "You know, when I joined Macklin & Cherry it was the first time in my life that I didn't feel alone. It was only a law firm, but I fooled myself into believing it was my family.

So long as Harmon Cherry made me feel like his favorite son—and he certainly did that while my court victories were piling up—I closed my eyes to the firm's sinister side. I stayed at the firm when he agreed to represent the Assembly. I should've quit. I refused to see that he'd dumped so much work on an unstable Grace that she shattered, or that Rich got to take the lead on the Assembly because he was glib and charming and malleable, competence be damned. And when Harmon treated Manny as nothing more than a journeyman lawyer who—"

"Mason was a psychopath," Lovely says. "A sane person doesn't lie and cheat and steal and kill because he's upset about his compensation level."

"But the Assembly's very existence as a firm client brought out the worst in us. As for me, because of my dislike for the Assembly and my love for the firm, I viewed Manny as above suspicion and didn't save my friends."

"No one could've known he was a killer. So if you're blaming yourself—"

"The evidence was there all the time. In that house in Malibu and in the financial documents. If I'd been more careful, maybe Rich would still be alive. Deanna *would* be alive. The day she was killed I announced that I was going to meet Grace at The Barrista. Manny was observing the trial that day. He was with us in the conference room. If only I'd kept my mouth shut, she . . ." I take a couple of quick breaths. "I slandered poor Kathleen Williams. I spent all my energy proving that some blurry figures in the Assembly killed Rich, that maybe my own m—" My voice mercifully breaks before I blurt out the rest.

We sip our coffee in silence. Then Lovely says, "Have you turned in your grades for the trial advocacy class?"

"You're not seriously worried about that now."

"Absolutely. I have the reputation of being a grade grubber, you know." She tilts her head. "I'll tell you what. How about you give me an *A* and in return I'll sleep with you. Deal, Professor?"

"You're not funny."

"I so *am* funny."

I take her hands in mine. I won't be the first to let go.

"There's something I have to ask you," she says. "How did you get a copy of Christopher McCarthy's itinerary? And The Emery Group wire transfer to Bennett?"

"Lovely, I just can't."

She pulls her hands away and looks past me toward the back wall. Then she reaches down, picks up her knapsack, and gets up to leave.

"Wait. Please sit down."

She sits.

I shut my eyes, take a deep breath, and heft for the last time the agglomerated burden of my secret. "Let me tell you the story of the First Apostate."

EPILOGUE
JUNE 11, 2013

I pull the door handle so hard that the clatter echoes down the hall and flushes a grizzled US Marshal out of hiding.

"Is everything OK, sir?" he says in a gruff cop voice.

"I have a trial starting in Judge Harvey's courtroom at ten. I haven't been in a courtroom for a while. I just wanted to get reacquainted with the feel of it." It's been about a year since the Baxter trial ended.

"It's only nine o'clock. They don't open the doors for another forty-five minutes." He gestures down the corridor. "There's an attorneys' lounge across from—"

"Thanks. I know where it is."

I head toward the lounge but stop at the elevators. I consider going upstairs and watching some of the hearing in *United States v. The Church of the Sanctified Assembly*, but then I think, why bother? Once Manny was exposed as the murderer and thief, the media stopped believing that McCarthy acted alone when he arranged for the bribes to foreign officials. Now, everyone thinks he was just following orders when he carried out the bribery scheme. I'm sure they're right. But he's taking the fall on the Foreign Corrupt Practices violations so he can protect his church. Lake Knolls has avoided indictment altogether by blaming his underling Delwyn Bennett. Maybe Knolls's fellow representatives will punish him, but I doubt it. His party needs his vote.

Victor Galdamez was arrested for his role in the murder of Rich Baxter. So were two former inmates of the Metropolitan Detention Center, both members of the Etiwanda Lazers. It's a tough case to prove. Manny's cell phone records are the best evidence against them.

I walk down the hall to the attorneys' lounge and find an empty conference room, which smells of Lysol and dust. Ten minutes later, the door opens and Grace Trimble walks in, dressed in a dark suit and white blouse and looking like the powerhouse lawyer she was when she first started at Macklin & Cherry. She's followed by a frightened Tyler Daniels. After weeks of pleading and negotiation, Grace agreed to replace Lovely Diamond on Tyler's defense team. She only said yes after I convinced her that I couldn't handle the case alone despite my success in *Baxter*. She still won't give me her address or phone number. I can only contact her through a Gmail address.

Grace accomplished what neither Lovely nor I could—she persuaded Tyler to attend the trial. When I asked how she'd managed it, she would only say that she understands how Tyler's mind works.

"Hello, Mr. Stern," Tyler says in her southwestern drawl. "Oh God, I don't think I can do this." Her complexion is pallid and rosy at the same time, depending on which cheek you look at. She appears on the verge of collapse. She reaches out and holds onto a chair back.

Grace takes her arm. "Sit down, Tyler. Everything will be OK. Truly, it will."

Tyler falls heavily into the chair. "No it won't, Grace. No it won't." She begins to cry, a harsh wailing sound from deep in her chest.

I don't feel sympathy for Tyler. I don't like her, and I despise her odious short stories. In her case, I care little about the principle that representing an abhorrent client serves justice. Let someone else be Tyler Daniels's Defender of the Damned. I'm here only because of my promise to Lovely.

"Give us a minute," Grace says to me.

I leave the room. Through the glass partition, I watch Grace kneel down beside Tyler, hand her a stack of tissues, and whisper in her ear like a compassionate school nurse comforting a distressed child. Tyler soon stops crying.

After a few minutes, Grace beckons me back in. "Everything's cool," she says.

For the first time since Tyler arrived, I take a good look at her. She's wearing a cheap, ill-fitting silver pantsuit that she must have bought third-hand on eBay. The drab color makes her persimmon red hair appear more ridiculous than usual. The jury will know she's creepy just by looking at that hair.

"I'm very frightened, Mr. Stern," she says. "The trip took so long I thought I'd never get out of that car. And then the traffic jams and this huge building and all these people, why . . . I miss my home." She sits down and folds her hands on the table. "Oh, I wish Lovely was trying this case. She knew all the facts and the law and understood why I wrote my stories. And she's so smart and well-spoken. No offense, sir."

Grace speaks to her in a calm voice. "We've talked about this, Tyler. You're in great hands."

"Will Lovely be here?" Tyler asks.

"She's second-chairing a trial on the second floor," I say. "Prosecuting a bank robbery case. She promises she'll try to sneak in during breaks and sit on our side of the courtroom, no matter what her boss thinks."

This makes Tyler smile.

After Lovely finished the bar exam, she looked for a job. None of the top firms would grant an interview to an ex–porn actress. And she wouldn't settle for less than a job with a top firm. Then Neal Latham, who knew about her past, asked her to interview with his office. It was an almost unprecedented opportunity for someone fresh out of law school. Yet she refused, saying she didn't want to work for the man who was persecuting Tyler Daniels. After several days of arguing and cajoling, I finally convinced her that the two best ways to prepare for trial work are to train as an actor and to work at the US Attorney's office. But when she was offered the job, she had an immediate conflict of interest: her new employer is trying to convict Tyler of the crime of distribution of obscene materials. She said that she'd accept Latham's offer only if I agreed to defend Tyler in her stead.

Over the next half hour, I remind Tyler yet again that Latham will try to shred her into confetti on the witness stand, branding her a monstrous pedophile; that he'll read her stories out loud and project them on high-def monitors in large letters; that her own words will horrify the jury. I urge her for maybe the fifth time in the last month to plead guilty in exchange for a token fine and no jail time, a deal I know I can get from Latham.

"I've told you over and over," she says. "I did not do anything wrong. I will not plead guilty. Do not bring this up again, sir."

I shrug. "You're the client. As long as you know the risk, it's your call."

Grace jumps out of her chair. "Oh shit, Parker, we're five minutes late."

"Run ahead and tell Judge Harvey we're on our way."

She hurries out of the conference room. I gather up our papers, and Tyler and I walk down the now-deserted corridor. When we get to the door, she hesitates.

"I'm so scared," she says.

"Don't worry. Grace and I will get you through this."

She studies my face for a moment. "You look a bit peakish yourself."

"It's just the adrenaline. It happens before every court appearance. I'd be worried if it didn't." I take a deep breath and open the heavy door to the courtroom.

ACKNOWLEDGMENTS

Thank you: Christine Cuddy, Les Edgerton, Sue Grafton, Steve Kasdin, Lisa Lucas, Carmela Rotstein, Ethel Rotstein, Jimmy Rotstein, Samantha Rotstein, Matt Sharpe, and Les Standiford; Lisa Doctor's Tuesday night group colleagues Terri Cheney, Linzi Glass, Cynthia Greening, Terry Hoffman, Jeremy Iacone, Karen Karl, Helena Kriel, Leigh Leveen, John Whelpley, and Robert Wolff; Jill Marr, Sandra Dijkstra, Elisabeth James, and Elise Capron of The Sandra Dijkstra Agency; and Dan Mayer of Seventh Street Books.

ABOUT THE AUTHOR

Robert Rotstein is an entertainment attorney with over thirty years' experience in the industry. He's represented all of the major motion picture studios and many well-known writers, producers, directors, and musicians. He lives with his family in Los Angeles, California, where he is at work on the next Parker Stern novel.